FROM STARS TO SEAS

RECORDS OF REALMS, BOOK TWO

EMILEE NK ROBBINS

BR BOOKS

Content Notes

Language: Mild

Sex/Nudity: One explicit sex scene

Violence: Discussion of warfare, Near Death Experiences

Other: Anxiety, Mention of Sexual Assault (not described on page)

∽

Copyright © 2026 by Emilee NK Robbins

ISBN 979-8-9993436-1-1

All rights reserved.

No portion of this book may be reproduced in any form without written permission from the publisher or author, except as permitted by U.S. copyright law.

Without in any way limiting the author's exclusive rights under copyright, any use of this publication to "train" generative artificial intelligence (AI) technologies to generate text is expressly prohibited. The author reserves all rights to license uses of this work for generative AI training and development of machine learning language models.

Illustrations by Grace Morris

Editor: Molly Spain

❦ Formatted with Vellum

*To those who want to be loved
not for who they were,
or who they will be,
but for who they truly are.*

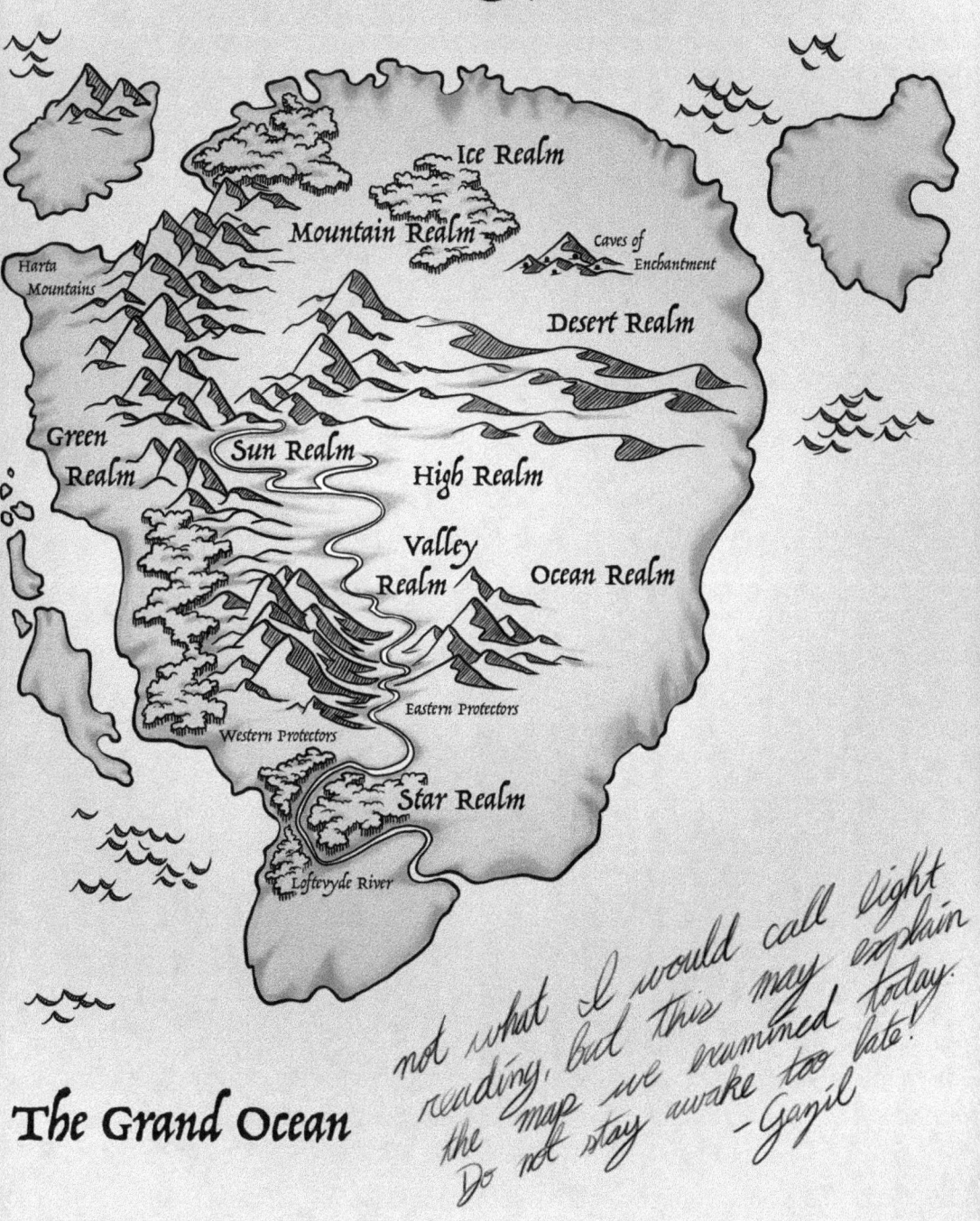

A WORD TO THE READER

Treat these hallowed pages with reverence as surviving relics of

The Records of Realms

penned by the Kingdom's first Keeper of Records.

May her words strike the hearts of all those who read.

May her stories uncover the beauty of our past.

May her legacy live on through all who relish in reliving ages of long ago.

1

Sol

Sol cradled a book in her hands as she sat cross-legged on the bundle of blankets collected in the corner of her tent. Sliding her hands over the leather binding, she attempted to center herself.

In one sense, the world had truly fallen into place the past few weeks. The Star Realm was her safe haven; her brother and his warrior band of Night Flyers made sure of it. That did little to stop the terrors of sleep. She woke many nights soaked in sweat, bits of her past spilling into her present. Exhaustion and pain followed Sol like a specter, trained to keep her from truly feeling at home here.

She should feel thankful, appreciative, satisfied. Instead, she often wondered if she deserved such a life, a world, a group of people so supportive and welcoming. Or if she deserved the nightmares more.

Sighing, Sol refocused on the pages: a story about a warrior princess who falls for her captor. Her closest friend Asha insisted she read the tale, claiming the romance held a literary trance over her besotted soul. Sol smirked at the hyperbole, her friend's passion for the romantic so endearing.

The tale was enchanting, the Sun Realm setting a vast contrast to the realm of the stars. Though, Sol wished these characters of fiction compelled her to ignore the issues she faced, the responsibilities she carried. Unfortunately, the warrior princess did not hold enough power to pull Sol from her troubles.

After trudging through the first chapter, Sol set the book's spine on her lap, allowing the pages to splay to the sides as she looked around the warm tent. The pale blue glow of the lights that lined the various paths in the city of Celestra filtered in through the glimmering golden fabrics settled atop a rectangular copper frame. Brightly colored carpets overlapped upon the rich brown soil. While her daily clothes hung on a metal rack, the rest were folded and tucked into a wicker trunk lining the wall. Beside it, a trunk of leather, protected with a golden lock, held more precious items—notebooks, her pair of onyx knives, a small locket with her mother's face inside, and a curious emerald ring. She rarely enjoyed often her free time upon returning as *Sol: sister to the king*. Yet, when she did, she often sifted through these precious trinkets. Palms still grasping the leather book, she looked toward the leather trunk, compelled to twirl the emerald ring between her fingers or examine the sharp jaw of her beautiful mother, hoping the glimpses into her past would provide her peace.

Instead, she turned the page. She typically enjoyed getting lost in another story. One where the woman found her way in the complicated world of Nourels or another fantastical, faraway place. One where relationships flourished wonderfully with little complication. One where battles and betrayals and death were plot points rather than a painful reality. It was absolutely marvelous to escape the stressors of the realm, the war, the lack of remembering, the social events and fundraising and royal meetings. It all wore on Sol and she welcomed even a momentary escape.

However, today the story was perhaps not as engaging as Asha claimed. She turned the next page with the ink-stained fingers of her right hand, her left sprawled comfortably behind her in the fluff of blankets. She stared at the open book in her lap. The words paled on the pages, offering no source of escapism great enough to pull Sol from her worries. Her thoughts flitted to anything else. To her brother. To her mother. To her memories.

When she lifted the book in a final attempt to focus, a familiar face popped through the entrance of the tent, snapping Sol from her overthinking.

"I believe supper is soon; are you intending to join?" Asha's brown skin glimmered delightfully in the perpetual starlight of the realm, the blue casting a pale gleam against her blonde hair. "I understand you are waiting for some sort of news. Now, what was it..." She tapped her index finger on her chin sarcastically as Sol hid behind the book.

"Quit teasing." Sol said in jest, shutting the book and lifting herself to stand.

Of course, both women knew what would likely be discussed over supper, and both women knew they were likely preparing for a long journey back to the freezing cold of the Ice Realm.

Rushing to ready herself for the evening ahead, Sol reached for a bit of bright pink kohl to line the inner lids of her eyes. She recalled the intricate designs her former Keeper created in numerous shades when Sol was a prisoner. Though she dreaded remembering her time in Endoneth, the swirls of colorful flowers that decorated her plump cheeks were images worth holding onto. While some memories...

Sol peered into the small mirror as she finished adding the color, then gently pressed a cold hand to the red scar on her cheek. No, some memories were too dreadful indeed.

Grabbing a thin silver cloak, Sol swung the fabric delicately over the traditional uniform of the Night Flyers—a long navy tunic that brushed just above her knees, black leather pants, and a pair of brown, sturdy boots. Satisfied, she followed Asha into the bustle of the city. The embroidered moth, the symbol of their realm, glowed a bright silver in the dim lights placed along the city's pathways. The tents lining the paths glowed from the lanterns hidden inside. The entire city, comprised of such simple structures, brought Sol a sense of comfort, as if the fabrics of each tent moving in the breeze reminded her to breathe deeply. To move slowly. To relish in the nightly glow.

Although the sky remained dark, lit only by the stars and beaming crescent moon, people filled the streets, many just leaving their daily posts to prepare for their own suppers. Asha held Sol's hand with friendly assurance as they weaved through the crowds, her smile shining brighter than the moon.

"Shall I tell a story as we stroll?" Asha suggested, hoping to stir something within Sol's mind.

Sol shook her head. "Not this night."

Grinning, Asha insisted, "I did recall this afternoon of a tale from our training days in the High Realm. It was year one, nearly a decade ago. We were all gathered with Master Zelan who declared you to be his most graceful yet vicious student in all his years of instruction." She laughed at the thought, "you were a gem in his eyes. Flawless."

A few painful seconds passed with no recollection to relay. Just looming frustration whirring in Sol's empty mind. She wished she could remember why the lines of tents in the city steadied her heartbeat or why the dim glow of blue lanterns settled her nerves. Yet such things evaded her. Whenever she pressed into the recesses of her mind, Sol found only blurs of what once was, mere swirling senses and feelings. Never concrete. Never tangible. Never enough.

Asha shifted the conversation with ease. "Then tell me of your latest interview instead. Something utterly fantastic."

Sol could not help her grin. "You mean, salacious."

"Well..." Asha beamed, a stunning sight.

"There was a romantic tryst between a plant tender and a carpet maker." Sol offered, Asha's wide eyes affirmation enough to continue.

As she divulged the details, Sol was reminded again of why she adored her position. As the Keeper of Records, she spent her days interviewing those living in the Star Realm: The Night Flyers; The tent builders; The bread makers; The artists. Each story was beautifully complex. Each person filled with years of relationships and events and places that forged their individual identity. At the end of each day, she spent hours poring over page upon page with her words, attempting to capture what Celestra felt like, what the people valued, what traditions flourished, and which were tucked away. It was a role she cherished. It made her feel tied to this place, even as she struggled to remember for herself what traditions she practiced or places she frequented.

"...and the two decided to marry on that very day!" Sol finished the story in a flourish of dramatics.

Asha cackled with delight. "You are perhaps too proficient at this post. How did Piré describe it once?"

"The last remnants of a time before time," Sol clarified, "where Keepers were more revered for their service, less ostracized, less deferential. You know, Gazil would often say..."

The thought of her fallen friend choked the words in her throat. Asha squeezed her hand earnestly.

"He seemed to be the best of them." She whispered, pulling Sol close as they pushed past a large group of school-aged children. "He held the last piece of that former world. A world when people of the Ice Realm saw the term *Keeper* as...as..."

She struggled to find the proper term before Sol finished for her,

"...beautiful."

The sounds of the street filled the sudden silence. Night

markets opened their stalls as cafes pulled their tents closed. Women hummed as they lifted laundry onto lines as children played in a small patch of unused soil. As the women followed the rounded paths, Asha cleared her throat.

"Does it frighten you? It has only been nine weeks since..." Asha's words trailed off, her grin wavering slightly.

Since Sol's capture by the Ice Lord. Since the loss of her memories. Since the death and pain and grief she caused.

Sol was frightened indeed. "Prisoners do not usually return to their prisons."

Asha squeezed her hand once more. "And this is truly the only way?"

The question sounded more like a plea. "I believe so." Sol responded as they strode through the city.

Her friend offered a nod and a supportive smirk before looking ahead at the rows of tents, the paths growing smaller and smaller as they neared the center of the city of blue.

Though Sol poured every ounce of herself into her written descriptions night after night, nothing could perfectly capture the way the lantern light rippled along the tent fabrics or how the sounds of crickets hiding in the shadows mingled beautifully with the constant commotion that hummed through the Celestran streets. The city smelled of jasmine and soil, like a forest after a summer rain, though rain never fell from the clouds above. The pebbled paths that ran in circular patterns throughout the large city connected the various tents. Each tent was structured similarly, although one's status was subtly seen in the materials. Some homes used wooden dowels rather than the flashier and sturdier metal seen in tents closer to the center of the city. Fabrics, too, could be of varying values. The golden sheets that lined Sol's tent were some of the finest, marking her as one of importance.

Despite these slight differentiations between the ladies or lords and those living on the outskirts of Celestra, it was nothing like the classifications she witnessed in Endoneth. Here there were no clothing markers nor ostentatious shows of wealth in one's home. The occasional splurging on tent fabrics and copper frames still made Sol uncomfortable.

She often wondered how Piré was faring in the city. The former Keeper helped successfully find and save Gallen and Asha and, in doing so, escaped her northern home to establish a new life here. The young woman claimed she was adjusting well, spending most of her time painting or baking breads. However, Sol sometimes witnessed Piré in moments of deep contemplation, even sorrow, when she believed no one could see. Piré never mentioned it. Not with words.

"How are you enjoying the latest tale?" Asha interrupted Sol's internal musings. "I believe this female character holds a bit more substance than the last, do you not agree?"

Sol nodded. "I have only finished the first chapter, yet I feel more connected to her than previous characters."

The two women spent the last two weeks exchanging books back and forth. The major book tender in Celestra eagerly awaited their visits every few days, offering stories both old and new.

"Young women such as yourselves often enjoy these outlandish stories," the middle-aged, husky man would say. Asha and Sol would merely giggle to themselves, usually because he was correct.

Asha was often quite opinionated and this trip through the pebbled paths to Alcor's tent only underscored her literary expertise.

Asha squeezed Sol's hand. "Trust me, friend. The author of this particular book understands how to weave a character into being. Using words like delicate threads to forge a tapestry that evokes such intense emotion. I cried at least five times."

"And crying is a positive reaction, correct?" Sol teased, twirling her hair in her hands. The shade had become so dark since arriving there, the brown almost purple in the dim light of the blue lanterns.

Asha rolled her eyes, the shades of gold glimmering amidst the bright orange color. "You should understand more than others, Sol. An author wishes her audience to *feel* something. And often, grief is the most difficult emotion to elicit." She nodded her head for emphasis as the two neared the very center of the city, where the Lord of Celestra's tent stood.

Only one path led to Alcor's tent, allowing the Night Flyers standing guard a chance to prevent any unwanted visitors from entering. Sol and Asha nodded toward the two Flyers, Malinar and Tress, sitting near the tent's entrance. The latter responded with an emphatic wave while Malinar remained stoic, staring past the approaching women in strained silence. Her straight hair barely reached the tip of her sharp jawline, which only accentuated the harshness of her features. Her coldness reflected the continued conflict with Sol.

"She will surely forgive you in time," Asha whispered as they passed, "Ranor's death is not on your hands."

Sol snickered, unconvinced, "I, too, would hate the person who caused the death of the one I cared for most."

"He volunteered to serve Alcor, to rescue you. We all did." Asha insisted.

Sol could not begrudge Malinar. Not in the slightest. However, she continued trying to ingratiate herself to the younger Flyer regardless. The cold reception told her that she would need to keep trying.

Despite the pit that now sat heavily in her stomach, Sol breathed in the excitement just within the fabric flap of Alcor's tent as she and Asha walked in. The tent looked like Sol's but much larger and with more papers and trinkets strewn about the carpeted floor. The sight of such disarray caused a bit of anxious energy to flutter briefly in Sol's heart, mingling curiously with both the shame of Ranor and excitement of the people gathering for nightly supper. Alcor sat on a sunken pillow at the head of the short table to the far side of the tent. He was joined by Zeffra, Luminor, Piré, Ott, and—

"Gallen!" Asha's voice did nothing to hide her mischief. "It is good to see you back from such a *long trip* to the Ocean Realm." She flashed a smile and cut her eyes to Sol as she continued, "we *all* missed you so *dearly*, you know."

Her implications were not lost on Gallen. Or Sol. Or anyone in the tent.

As Alcor sat, the dark green fabrics folded artistically over beams of silver frames, he ran a thoughtful hand over the top of his close-cut hair, the shade of deep black almost purple in the dim light in a way that made his olive skin look drastically tanner than it was in the brightness of the sun. He lifted his icy-blue eyes to Sol as she approached the table, ignoring Asha's not-so-subtle attempts to shepherd her toward Gallen's place to the right of the king.

A slight blush flushed his pale blue cheeks as Gallen replied, "The visit to my family was quite successful, Asha. Thank you for your inquiry." He deftly avoided the notion of who missed him so *dearly*, as Asha put it.

"In fact, Gallen has ensured another corps of Ocean warriors for the cause," Alcor's hearty voice boomed through the tent, nearly consuming Gallen's baritone words. "Hopefully this will provide our army with the advantage over the Northern retinues." He looked to Zeffra as he spoke, seeking her confirmation as his first-in-command over military affairs.

She provided just that, grinning a bit as she folded her auburn hair behind the nape of her neck. "In fact, we predict this additional assistance may place us in a position to end this war completely. We need the concession of the lords of the Desert and Mountain Realms. Perhaps not those within Rostair's inner circle, but those who might be amenable to change."

Sol winced at the name yet said nothing. The war was a complicated and unfortunate topic that she often avoided. She preferred reading and writing rather than wielding her blades against their enemies. However, the unfortunate reality of her position meant knowing such details.

Gallen chimed in, "I have heard confirmations of those loyal to the Ice Lord: Lord Kengal of the Desert Realm, Lord Elesiam of the Green Realm, and Lady Yneri of the Mountain Realm."

Zeffra scribbled the names on a wayward sheet of paper and nodded, "No need to attempt an alliance in those regions."

"Why ever not?" Alcor boomed. The room quieted in response, "our purpose is to unite *all* realms. Not those we deem worthy of us."

"Of course," Zeffra began quickly, stumbling over her words to justify her comment, "I…I only meant in this… strategic instance."

Gallen attempted to save her further embarrassment. "There is nothing we could offer those in Desert, Green, or Mountain that could compare to what he claims. To them, we are a threat to their status, their livelihood, their past and future."

"More importantly, they know what he is willing to do to those who oppose him." Asha said solemnly.

Eyes flitted momentarily to Sol before Alcor spoke again. "Together we are far more powerful than Rostair and his devious abuses of magic." He scratched his chin and continued, "we will ensure the protection of those who were left marginalized and voiceless in *all* realms. To eliminate injustices, or at the very least regulate the power of those in authority."

"We have those in the Valley and High Realms behind us. And my meetings with those in the Ocean Realm hold promise." Gallen stated, offering his friend advice. "Change will take time, we all know this. And the notion of a king, even one with regulations and representatives, it will disrupt every position and traditional power structure of Nourels."

"This, my friend, is true." Alcor nodded, "and such change will require commitment from each realm. Let us push forward."

Sol understood that her brother's efforts were of the utmost importance. The lives of so many stood in the balance. While she witnessed the plight of the fairies and the Keepers in the Ice Realm, she heard of others: the enslaved in the Desert Realm, the ogres in the Mountain Realm, the merpeople of the Ocean Realm. There was so much pain, so much hate, in Nourels, and her brother shouldered much of this reality. He took to heart the role he needed to play in the grander scheme of those who wished to right the many wrongs in the Nine Realms.

"Sister," he acknowledged her gently, "did you visit the edges of Celestra this morning? I heard a group of schoolchildren received an exciting visit from a warrior of great renown."

His pride was unmistakable. Sol nodded with a grin as she settled onto a pillow across from Gallen. Zeffra flinched slightly as she sat.

"The children were wonderful. Full of innocent versions of their favorite folklore," Sol said as she reached a hand toward a bowl of freshly baked bread sitting at the center of the table. "I am contemplating creating a record of the thoughts and experiences of the youth in the realm, how their recollections and understanding of our customs differ from adults."

Gallen reached for his own piece of bread. "That sounds like a marvelous endeavor!"

Asha shot Sol a devilish grin as she took a seat near Ott, the elderly Night Flyer with a sharp tongue and the heart of a gossip. The two together were insufferable but in a comforting way. Their nagging was like that of close family.

In a way, Asha's insistence upon Sol and Gallen reigniting what she called *A Love for the Ages* almost eased the tension between the two. Sol could not deny that she often contemplated what their former relationship was like. What they did during the moonlit days in Celestra. If they ever visited the Ocean Realm together to see Gallen's favorite boyhood places. Where they stayed together at night. What they *did* together at night...

A thick haze still surrounded the visions of such moments, as if she were peering through a thin, white sheet. The light presented her with shadows of people, muffled sounds, yet nothing concrete. Since returning to Celestra, Sol avoided conversations with Gallen, frustrated by the remaining holes in her memory and ashamed of the part of herself that missed the familiarity she had before.

"Sol, do you believe the records of our journey home from the Ice Realm will be complete before the end of the week?" Alcor asked.

While he clearly valued Sol's former experience wielding weapons, her brother threw his entire support behind her role as Keeper of Records. He checked in every few days to ensure she had enough materials to write or if she needed an introduction to another interviewee. It was genuine and sweet, a support that Sol did not realize she needed at first. And, with his doting and continued inquiries, she accomplished much in the months she'd been writing.

Though, the recollections of her time in Endoneth were left unfinished as she busied herself with stories of the city. No matter how much she focused, no matter how often she hunched over her parchment, she could not find it within herself to complete the words. To track the context and detail the losses. But she knew she needed to. If anything, she needed to close that chapter of her life and move forward

"I should finish the record soon. Perhaps by the end of the month?" She offered.

Alcor nodded, tapping his broad hand on the table. "Could you promise to finish the record by the time you return?" His nose crinkled with barely hidden glee as he asked.

Sol's eyes, blazing with the same icy-blue hue, turned to Alcor. "You are letting me venture to the Ice Realm? When? How long do you think the journey will take? Do you think my absence will cause another pause in the greater military plans?" She turned her head slightly to Zeffra in deference. "Because I would not want to do so…again."

Sol's final question hung tensely in the air for a moment before Zeffra offered a backhanded olive branch. "No need to worry about the war. There is nothing you could do now that would be quite as destructive as your last stunt."

Her comment garnered mixed reactions from the group: Ott gasped dramatically, Asha rolled her eyes as she crossed her arms across her chest, Piré awkwardly walked toward the other end of the tent to gather a platter of food for supper, and Gallen tightened his fists on the table.

"Zeffra, we have discussed this—" Gallen began, teeth clenched.

She scoffed, her brown hands slapping the table with a harsh thud. "She oft forgets her place, your lover."

Now it was Gallen who scoffed. "She is not my lover. Nothing of the sort."

Zeffra scowled. "She is also no longer Alcor's first. We do not need her here."

The words flung over the table hit Sol in the gut. She pulled apart the baguette into tiny pieces, wishing the had a ring or bracelet to busy her restless fingers.

Alcor simply sighed. "What Zeffra intends to say is that we will have a few weeks of regrouping and will not need your presence until our next big movement." He shot Zeffra a warning look before returning his attention to Sol. "Gallen and Malinar will accompany you. The journey to the caverns as you described them should only take two weeks to find if it is only the three of you and you ride the winged stallions instead of walking. You will depart tomorrow."

The piece of bread tumbled from Sol's hand. "I thought Asha might accompany me?"

"She is needed here, to help train the troops. Gallen must oversee important progress on the army encampments. Additionally, with all due respect, Asha is more adept at teaching." Sol silently cursed their former training as her brother continued, "Malinar is one of our youngest Flyers. She requires the experience before she serves in the army itself. Especially in these times."

This was an impossible scenario: her once-greatest ally alongside her newest enemy. Her former lover and the woman whose lover Sol was at fault for killing. The thought of traveling together, for two weeks, was daunting. Overwhelmed, Sol could only nod. She snatched a bunch of ripe grapes as Piré placed a fresh platter of fruit before her.

"Perhaps if the pools do not assist you in your memory," Alcor continued, "Gallen's company may be of assistance."

Alcor wanted a fallback plan. Though she initiated this argument many times over, her brother remained unconvinced that becoming reacquainted with her former partner would stir her former memories. Well-intentioned as it was, Sol was unsure if she would be able to handle such a journey.

Alone. With Gallen. And Malinar.

But if Alcor said it, it would be so.

2

Sol

"Perhaps the close quarters will allow you and Malinar to get to know one another. To come to a better... understanding?" Piré did not sound convinced by her own words as she and Sol strolled along one of the popular Night Streets.

Though the sun never appeared to light the skies in the Star Realm, the stars provided insight into the time of day. It took Sol a few days to learn the tells: The largest star in the North twinkled brightest at midnight while the constellation of Serrium—the stars arranged in a dazzling "S" shape—was brightest at midday. And, although darkness painted the sky all year, people of Celestra treated night with the respect it deserved, reserving revelry and merriment for the late hours.

Thus, while the dim days appeared calm as workers labored, night brought music and laughter throughout the city. In the Night Streets most of all. While Alcor encouraged the Night Flyers to use wisdom, he also understood that such activities were an important part of life. A time to release tension. A time to socialize and bond. A time to lose oneself in dancing and substance, temporarily silencing negativity or uncertainty.

Younger Flyers engaged in such activities nightly. But, approaching her thirtieth year, Sol could hardly keep up such a routine. She balanced the late nights of alcohol and dancing with twice as many spent sipping tea with Luminor, her middle-aged friend with no desire for such revelry.

When Sol did wander into the streets of sin, she typically stayed near Asha and Piré. Though they inevitably found Gallen, Tress, and Malinar, along with a few other warriors, Yetsm, Harl, and Parem. Sol wanted them all to know her as Sol the writer, not Sol the warrior. She felt less and less of a warrior the more time she surrounded herself by those who fit the description more fully.

Piré understood, the sweet soul certainly did not have it within her to cause harm, let alone wield a weapon. As she shuffled along the street, her lace dress swishing delicately along her legs, the brightness in her faint voice underscored her innocence. And, as she often did, she insisted upon finding the silver lining to Sol's difficult journey ahead.

Sol shook her head, unsure if any sort of positive could be gleaned from her position. "I merely hope the three of us can coexist long enough to reach the caverns."

"I wish I could join you." Piré ran a thin hand through her blonde curls. "King Alcor requested I stay. He says there is a famed chef visiting the city and wants to extend an introduction."

The crowds of people milling about could not drown out Sol's squeal of joy. "Piré! That is wonderful news!" She shook her friend's arm in emphasis. "Why am I only hearing of this now?"

Piré chuckled a bit, her soft voice not nearly as loud. "I wanted to save the news for a time when you needed a boost."

"Perfect timing, then." Sol squeezed her friend's shoulder just as Asha approached with a trio of drinks.

"Who would like to try the street's newest concoction?" Asha offered the drinks to Piré and Sol. The liquid swirling in the glasses glistened with specks of gold swimming in a sea of black. The drink tenders of each drinking tent on the Night Street attempted to create the most mouth-watering mixtures for their patrons to enjoy. With so many working in such a small space in the city, competition bred even greater creativity.

Sol reached for one of the glasses, taking a generous sip in light of the discussion earlier that evening. The drink tasted bitter at first before a tang of sweetness settled on her tongue. The golden flecks exploded with a fizzing sensation as they burst in her mouth, taking the edge off of the strong liquor while slightly numbing her inner cheeks. "Interesting," she noted aloud.

"Woah," Asha seemed to agree as she enjoyed her own cup. "The gold is certainly better than the sparking ice of last night's find."

The previous night's drink was a brewed drink that smelled like salt and spices. The tender who created the drink used special ice cubes that sparked as they touched your lips. An interesting concept in theory yet not as comfortable in reality.

Coughing after a small sip, Piré's eyes watered a bit before she shook her head. "I prefer my usual drink."

Asha and Sol grinned at each other. Piré's preferences were so steady and predictable. Each night they ventured out to the Night Streets, the young woman always ordered the same drink: a red wine with a touch of brandy. Sol could not comprehend the combination, yet Piré swore it surpassed all others. As if predicting this incident, Gallen arrived with her usual drink in hand.

"I thought you might need something to mask the taste of…" he gestured his head toward the black liquid in the three glasses, "whatever that is."

Piré grasped the red wine eagerly, passing the drink of the night to Asha before taking a long sip of her preferred beverage. Malinar and Tress, recently relieved of their guard duty, arrived behind Gallen with their own drinks. Tress was discussing her newest obsession with all things metal.

"Did you know that there are metals native to each realm that can only be smelt using fire from that realm? For example, the incandescent silver of the Mountain Realm can only be melted and molded into weapons if the smith uses wood from the forests within that realm. Fascinating stuff, I would say." Tress brought a bubbly drink to her lips briefly before delving back into the world of metallurgy.

A sudden flash of terror pained Gallen's features. Sol could imagine the mention of such metals brought back horrific memories - Endoneth, tortured, kissed by death. Sol did not know all that Rostair did to Gallen and Asha, though she knew they still suffered, even if only mentally.

Malinar only nodded absently to Tress's discussion, drinking a large pint of ale while she held her arm across her stomach. The young warrior often appeared this way—uncomfortable, unbothered, empty. It seemed the aftermath of her loss still affected her deeply. Sol assumed so, at least. The other Flyers attempted to provide support, Tress and Asha more than most. However, Malinar was a strong-headed woman, one who did not wish to talk of grief. She preferred spending her days focused on training and her evenings drinking pints of ale and taking any substance that would help her forget. As Malinar sipped, Sol noticed lids of her purple eyes droop unnaturally, her vacant gaze remained glued to the bubbles popping in Tress's drink.

"Please watch her closely as you journey forth," Asha whispered into Sol's ear, her voice low enough to ensure only she could hear.

Nodding slightly in response, Sol took another hesitant sip of the black and gold drink. Her face scrunched in concern. "Asha, please take this drink from me. I wish to feel my cheeks once more."

Gallen and Piré joined Asha in a hearty laugh as the music swelled around them. The pale blue light from the lanterns was just enough for Sol to see her friends' joyous expressions. After placing the drinks upon a nearby wooden table, Asha skipped back to the group, moving her hips in a manner that suggested now was the time of night she would try to make the rest of them dance. This, like the unique drink, was also a Night Streets tradition. And, like every other night, Gallen was the first to join Asha, twirling through the crowds to meet her on the pathway.

Soon, the entire group moved together, swishing and skipping around the pebbled ground. All save Malinar, who remained on the edge of the path, nursing a fresh pint and wearing a sinister gleam in her eyes. Hours passed like this. The group enjoyed the night as they swayed. The musicians strummed their various instruments to create an air of absolute magic. In the pale blue light surrounding them, the faces of Sol's companions shone almost miraculously, heavenly, otherworldly. Without them, the past three weeks would have been unbearable. Whether dancing like fools or sipping tea with Luminor, each night the group gathered together, she thanked the gods for their provision.

Sol turned to survey Malinar as the night wore on. The serious Flyer kept the group of friends at a distance, hatred practically seeping from her pale skin. Sol tried to ignore her glare, holding Asha's hand as her friend twirled under her arm. But the weight of Malinar's negative energy impacted her more deeply than usual.

Is this what Sol could expect for the next two weeks? Glares of malice and disconnections from reality? Instead of seeking the answers to her own questions, Sol sauntered away from the dancing crowd and toward a drinking tent to retrieve another glass. As she sipped on the cup of white wine, a hand slipped onto her back, pressing the cotton tunic against her skin.

"Should we address Malinar before we leave?" Gallen's voice was concern yet impressively steady, barely impacted by the alcohol in his system nor the vigorous dancing. "The journey will be difficult enough, the snow returns to the Northern realms soon. I know it will be challenging enough for us to be together," his voice faltered with this admission before he finished, "and all I wish is for you to arrive at the cavern unscathed."

Unscathed. An interesting word, one that stuck with Sol as she leaned away from Gallen's hand. Gallen sighed as he reached for another drink of his own. "We cannot ignore *us* forever. I will give you as much time as you need, but I also would like my friend back."

Internally, Sol echoed his sentiments but could not see a way to verbalize the conflict that still waged within her. Of course, she wanted to be friends with Gallen, perhaps even more than friends. But he fell in love with who she was, not who stood before him now. And the intimacy she shared with Rostair during her time in Endoneth, while coerced, still felt like a betrayal. One that Sol had yet to share with Gallen. Complications abounded.

Gallen's potential rejection was not worth the risk, especially when Sol believed she may have a solution in two-weeks' time. If she could remember, it would solve so much.

Sol turned on her heel to face him, ignoring his attempts to consider their friendship. "I do think we should ensure Malinar does not carry along substances that could harm her on the journey, or us in the process."

Rather than wait for his response, Sol marched outside. Her friends' smiling faces eased the soreness in her chest. She could feel Gallen's eyes boring into her as she walked back, but she refused to turn and meet his gaze. She could not face him, not like this, with her mind buzzing and tongue loose. And though the drink worked its way into her mind, blurring her thoughts like a delightful anesthetic, the soreness in her chest remained.

SOL HELD her heavy head in her hands, hoping to stave off a piercing headache. The perpetual darkness was another reason visitors to the Star Realm enjoyed the nightly entertainment—the pains of overindulging were never intensified by bright sunlight of the following day. The lanterns outside Sol's tent burned a bit brighter to indicate morning's arrival and the sound of people waking to greet the day slowly grew as she carefully lifted herself from her bedding.

To say she overdid it would be an understatement. To keep up with the nocturnal drinkers of this realm, Sol usually knew to pace herself. She sadly ignored her intuition the previous night. Perhaps it was the stress of the journey ahead or the fear of failure or the annoying glare of Malinar's purple eyes. Whatever the case, Sol was paying dearly for the last few pints of ale.

Sol squinted toward her clothing rack, dedicating her sights to her destination. The world slightly shifted for a moment, her legs abnormally off-kilter as she shuffled hopelessly forward. She held her arms out and shut her eyes. The thin silk fabric of last night's shift rustled against her bare thighs.

Pushing down the surge of nausea gathering in the pit of her stomach, Sol opened her eyes into small slits, just enough to reach the clothing that hung nearby. The feel of a clean cotton Night Flyers tunic gave her a sense of accomplishment. Though she only shuffled a few feet from her sleeping blankets, the success of dressing for the day provided her with newfound motivation. She knew she needed to gather what little belongings she had before the journey, but she surely had time to reset before the departure. Sol decided on a walk to clear her mind and steady her steps.

As soon as she lifted the silver fabrics, she heard the hiss of Luminor's snarky commentary: "Long night, eh Sol?"

Sol grimaced at the words, the pounding in her head nearly unbearable. With a grumble, she sulked past him toward the circling paths. In stark contrast to Sol's tired demeanor and weary strides, Luminor appeared well-rested and spry, his dark hair cleanly slicked back and pale eyes excited to meet the day. "You do know, Sol," he continued as he joined her slow steps, "the tenders of the Night Streets often encourage overindulgence. More drinks means more gossip." The lanky man's Desert Realm accent accentuated every "S" and brightly emphasized his vowels.

Sol barely nodded in response. This was not the first time she heard this conspiracy from the older Flyer. While the others in her close circle recklessly joined in the revelry of nightlife in the city, Luminor revealed himself to be most conservative in comparison. Even Alcor and Zeffra joined after supper every once in a while.

Luminor preferred a warm pot of tea and a cheery book. He often offered the experience to the rest of the group as a studious alternative. To his credit, the group did spend a few nights a week together sitting in one of the communal tents, chatting about plots and romance rather than imbibing in the tenders' latest drinks of choice. Sol almost wished she opted for Luminor's tea rather than endure the aching in her skull.

When Sol overconsumed at night, which had only happened twice before, she knew Luminor would be at her tent in the morning, eager to confirm that all was well. As she continued her labored stroll through streets of colored tents, she wondered if Luminor did so at Alcor's command or due to some sense of brotherly duty. Luminor was like a brother to her, an older and wiser version of herself in many ways. Either way, she appreciated his care.

"I assume you heard of the events of last night?" Sol's voice was more of a whisper, each syllable shooting daggers into her brain. She pressed her palms to her temples to relieve some of the internal pressure, to no avail.

Luminor noticed her discomfort and responded in a similar, quiet tone. "You mean the events of last night *and* early this morning?" The emphasis on the length of her nighttime activities only made Sol cringe further, her shoulders hunched and eyes still squinting.

In all honesty, Sol could not remember much from the night before. She knew her friends brought her dancing, and they walked down the many drinking tents and tasted drinks from each establishment. There was a faint recollection of discussing something with Gallen, then Asha. Or perhaps it was Asha and then Gallen. She shook her head and immediately groaned, her forehead beading with sweat.

Noting her increased discomfort, Luminor led her to a nearby bench, the metal cool on her hands as she settled. "I wanted to ensure you felt well enough to prepare for the beginning of a very long journey." He wiped her forehead with a crisp handkerchief. "I am certain Alcor would postpone…"

Sol's eyes opened wide. "Absolutely not. We will leave tonight!"

Again, her words caused more pain than her head could endure. To alleviate some of the pounding, she slid to the side, lying her cheek on the bench's arm, the feel of the metal numbing a bit of the pain.

Luminor rested a careful hand on her shoulder. "I hope this pain will finally convince you to join me in my nightly pursuits of knowledge. See? Tea would never betray you as wine."

Although Sol's face remained pinned to the metal, she heard the smirk on his face and managed to chuckle a bit in response, "You always know exactly what to say."

"Oh, I know," he responded delightedly, "would you like to continue your stroll of procrastination or shall we remain here for a while?"

Sol's silence voiced her opinion clearly. And so they sat as bakers and shopkeepers and instructors and all other Celestrans walked back and forth along the busy path, continuing their morning routines despite the pitiful display of their king's sister laying her head pathetically on a city bench, waiting for her hangover to dissipate so she could begin planning for a busy day.

It took almost an hour for the pain in her head to subside. Luminor, a dedicated friend, sat with her the entire time, carefully rubbing her back while describing the intricate plot of his latest book. "And I left the book just as the warrior learned of his true fate!" He turned his pale eyes to Sol to gauge her reaction.

"That is a complex circumstance," she said, unsure of the details yet still invested in Luminor's happiness at sharing the tale.

Admittedly, Sol spent most of the hour focusing less on Luminor's ramblings and more on the night before. She crunched the ends of her tunic in her hands, clenched as she continued thinking and thinking and thinking. Yet, with even the most intense concentration, she recalled nothing more than the dancing and the drinks and the knowledge of a conversation or two, the details and actual words of which eluding her.

Luminor helped lift her from the bench and walked her back to her tent.

"If you need a listening ear, please do not hesitate to find me. I should be taking a guard shift for Alcor's tent soon." He lifted the flap of fabric to the silver tent. "I know you will miss these unexpected walks whilst you are away." He winked, a sarcastic grin easing Sol slightly.

When the flap to her tent closed, Sol was alone once more, facing the two trunks and the blankets and the rack of hanging clothing. Emitting a heavy sigh, Sol stepped toward a stack of papers that sat hidden behind the leather trunk. Sifting through the draft of Alcor's requested record detailing the journey from the Ice Realm back home, she pulled a few pages to reference while they rested at night. One described the twenty or so Night Flyers chosen by Alcor to assist in the rescue; another detailed the campsite in the green clearing. In the final page of her latest draft, Sol wrote about the leaders of the group—Zeffra and Alcor—about their tension and power dynamics. Notably missing was their experience at Endoneth. Months as a prisoner who was oblivious to her own imprisonment. The strange dreams of Gallen and Alcor before she knew who they were. The night of the Greentime Ball and the sudden violence between hidden guards and the

Flyers. The moments they spent running through the Keeper's passages with kidnapped fairies and the study used as a prison. And the tortured Flyers chained to the tiled floor. The dried blood. The smell of torture.

She stuffed the papers into a leather bag, bigger than her personal satchel yet light enough to carry while flying on the pegasus. Along with the papers she packed ink and quills, blank pages, another uniform, and one of her silk night shifts. She opened the leather trunk to retrieve her knives, the strong steel glimmering grimly. When she placed those in the bag, she turned back to the open trunk where the locket and ring sat expectantly.

The locket lay with the silver chain folded sweetly, looking picturesque, as if intentionally positioned to highlight the delicate details of the spiraling silver. The frame that lined the hinged jewel included hand-carved swirls of filigree surrounding a singular flower. A flower Sol was quite familiar with.

The primrose on the locket's front, tinged a deep black, almost spoke to her as she reached into the trunk. Desperate to feel the metal on her fingertips, still stained with black ink from rummaging through her pages of records, she slammed her hand on the bottom of the trunk, creating a loud thud that rang through the small space. She held the necklace close to her face, using both hands to spread the chain wide enough for the piece of jewelry to hang naturally in the air, as if nestled on the neck of a ghost. The locket twirled enchantingly, before looking at Sol, centered on the expensive chain. The rose gold almost sang to her and it took only moments for Sol to succumb to the jewel's command. Her hands fumbled for the lock before fastening it safely around her collar. The chain's length allowed the locket to sit just between her breasts, the likeness of her mother hidden inside settled close to her heart.

Next, she set her sights upon the other piece. The emerald ring sat pleasantly, patiently, for her attention. Sol sighed as she saw it. The stonework was remarkable even when partially hidden by shadows. Sol twirled the emerald ring in her hand, the square-cut stone catching the light of her lantern and casting a glow throughout the tent. The stone itself was modest yet surrounded by nearly a dozen pale pink diamonds, creating a pattern that evoked a sense of royalty and significance. Her heart beat faster as she clutched the ring in her palms, carefully holding it captive as she considered whether it was wise to take it on the journey.

She slid the ring onto her index finger. A perfect fit.

To Sol's relief, the remainder of the day passed uneventfully. She spent some time writing thank-you notes to those she interviewed the past week, refolding her clothes to fit more neatly in the satchel, and sipping on a bowl of soup Piré so kindly delivered midday. The silence brought with it a sense of healing, freedom for her mind to stray from its typical worries and focus on one task at a time. Though she wished to spend time with her friends before her departure, she admittedly needed the renewal if she were to venture forth on this grand adventure.

The packing nearly complete, Sol walked the length of her tent, eyeing every carpet and blanket to be sure she did not forget any item of importance. Satisfied, she sighed once more, her head clearer than it had been all day.

She heard Asha's hearty laugh before her friend requested entrance to her tent. "I brought you an item of great importance!" The giggle that followed gave Sol pause; however, she could not deny her friend any pleasure.

"Oh, do come in, Asha."

The slender arms reached through the fabrics before her frame came fully into view. The freckles lining her cheeks practically twinkled like the stars above them as she smiled broadly toward Sol. She swiped the stray blonde strands from her face. "And here it is! In case you become terribly bored on your journey."

She reached into her leather satchel hanging heavily by her side and revealed a lovely book, bound with a fine fabric of deep maroon. The edges looked almost painted with golden accents and the title, *An Age of Longing,* shone in a golden hue.

"I have yet to complete our last book." Sol pointed disappointedly to the book lying near her bed blankets.

Asha shook her head. "No matter! You may continue that when you return. This book is special. Just look inside." Her smile widened, her teeth impossibly white and perfect.

Sol looked curiously at the book in her hands. Opening the front cover, she flipped casually through the pages, looking for what could possibly differentiate this novel from any other they read before. Then, she noticed another color amidst the typical black text.

"Have you…written in the margins?" Sol looked more closely at the words scrawled in pink and purple and bright green.

I do wonder how a character such as this falls for a complete imbecile. GROW A BACKBONE. Sol read the words gleefully before turning her blue eyes to her friend still standing by the tent's entrance.

"It will be as if I am there with you as you read. Just like our discussions now." She wrung her thin hands together awkwardly. "Do not feel compelled to do the same. I know at times one wishes to immerse themselves in the story and writing your thoughts could take that joyous aspect of reading away—"

"It is a beautiful gesture, my friend." Sol reached out to pull Asha into a warm embrace. "And I will miss you." The final words were muffled in the shoulders of Asha's tunic.

"I shall miss you too. Please, this time, promise you will return as planned. No heroic improvisations. Promise."

The words were a command. A desperate plea from a person formerly pained by loss and deception. Damp tears wet her shoulder as Asha attempted to stifle her small whimpers, her shoulders shuttering a bit as her body shook with emotion.

The scene pulled at Sol's heart. Her friend, taller and certainly stronger, leaned down, squeezing tight enough that Sol almost forgot to breathe. They remained that way for longer than a moment, until Asha's tears dried and shoulders stilled, though her face was flushed in pink.

"I promise." Sol lifted her hands in supplication, emphasizing the truth of her words.

Asha appeared slightly convinced, though her eyes still conveyed a deep sadness that chipped away at Sol's self-confidence. "Have you spoken with Gallen since last night?"

Sol tilted her head to the side at the question. "What do you mean?"

This response deepened Asha's look of concern. "Can you not remember? Last night—"

Before Asha could finish her thought, the fabric of the tent opened slightly. "Sol? Are you packed for the journey ahead?"

Alcor burst into the tent, interrupting the two women as they stood in the center. Unaware of his intrusion, Alcor and his broad shoulders filled the space; he wore a giddy smile. For the many ways Alcor represented the ideal king—strong, empathetic, wise—he often misinterpreted obvious social cues. And, as Asha walked to the water basin positioned in the corner, Alcor continued smirking with innocent glee, excited for his sister to begin the adventure she had longed for since arriving in Celestra.

"I believe I am ready." Sol's sounded a bit shaken, yet she stood tall.

The slight waver in her voice shook Alcor from his delightful demeanor, surveying the small tent to ascertain what he must have missed. "Are you quite well, sister? Asha?" His head turned from Sol to Asha with growing speed.

Asha turned to face the king, her face freshly washed, a few droplets still hugging her delicate skin. "Alcor, we were just saying sorrowful goodbyes. You understand."

A sense of relief visibly flowed through him. Releasing a sigh he said, "I apologize. I will leave you both if you would like more time."

Asha lifted a slender hand to pause him. "It is quite alright. Sol needs to prepare, and I have training responsibilities to attend to."

Alcor nodded. "Please, be kind to the newest warriors. They will not be as quick to learn as you and Sol."

She flashed him a clever smile, the freckles that sparkled on her golden-brown skin practically dancing at the compliment. "Dear King, I would never be harsh to those who wish to learn."

He rolled his eyes a bit, though his lips turned into a tight grin. He nodded and reached a hand to his bravest warrior. Asha grasped the inside of his arm as they exchanged the gesture of Night Flyers, Alcor's copper hand meeting her inner arm as well, the two revealing their strength.

Sol relished the interaction between her brother and her closest friend. Their relationship clearly born out of mutual respect.

She cleared her throat softly, "I will be ready soon, brother. Shall I meet you at your tent?"

He released Asha's inner arm and turned to his sister. "We have readied the winged horses at the edge of the city. Within the hour, yes?"

Sol nodded, though her brother already moved for the entrance, surely dealing with nearly a dozen more responsibilities for the day. In seconds, Alcor lifted the silver fabric and rushed out of the tent, closely followed by Asha who gave Sol one last smile before leaving her alone once again.

THE FINAL WALK through the winding paths of Celestra was sobering. Celestra was magic. The city illuminated a sense of wonder within its blue glow. The stars spoke stories to her, twinkling as she passed tent after tent. Her silver cloak swept past her calves as she walked, her pace intentionally slowing as she soaked in the sounds of the people striding past. Sol knew she would miss this feeling as she flew away from her home. Into an unknown future. Into the den of the enemy.

But, in Celestra, there was always a welcoming hand or a word of encouragement. Even the stars themselves spoke to its people. Alcor told her once that their city was blessed with the gift of night, just one of the complex categories of magic in Nourels. There were natural enchantments, like that of their home, but also oracles of the oceans and the learned magic of incantations and potions. Sol followed the curve of the path as she recalled the conversation:

> *"Magic protects Star Realm cities from the harshness of sunshine and the stars themselves requested their permanent residence. So the story goes,"* he once said, sipping a goblet of wine, *"that is what Mother would say."*
>
> *"How would she know?"* Sol asked.
>
> Alcor scratched his scalp, *"She claimed she had an allegiance with the stars. They spoke to her."* He took another sip, *"I only hope my studies of the skies can bring me closer to her."*

Sol reflexively pulled at the locket on her neck as she recalled the conversation. Her mother was an elusive figure in Sol's recollections. Even her emotional attachment to her parents was startlingly stagnant. She once loved them, to be sure. But it was not as tangible as her love for Alcor or Asha or Gallen.

As she ventured farther, the edge of the city rose into view. The lines of tents dissipated and the pebbled paths faded into smooth blades of grass. From the city's boundary Sol could see a group of Night Flyers gathered in a clearing. Her brown boots crushed the pebbles on the ground as she shifted her weight between her feet, memorizing the sound.

She took one step forward, grass crumpling solemnly beneath her.

She looked back at the fabric-covered tents, her eye catching a lone primrose sprouting near the edge of the path before looking ahead once more.

Still grasping the locket in her hand, she took another step.

3

Gallen

*G*allen had hardly slept, and it was obvious. He rubbed the soft side of his palm over his clenched eyelids, cursing himself for allowing one person to affect him so severely. Yet, that was not wholly honest. Sol was no mere person; she could never be.

The first week or so since returning from the Ice Realm, Gallen tried to keep his distance. He did not want to confuse her or misunderstand her intentions. While she lost her memories, *he* still very much remembered. The long chats. The laughter. The late nights and early mornings.

He groaned as he peered into the compact mirror settled on his sleeping blankets. He needed to find a way to mask his frustration.

"Put on a brave face," he could hear his mother saying. "People only know what they see."

He reached for a small paintbrush before haphazardly spreading blue kohl along his lids. The color needed several swipes to show vibrantly on his pale blue skin, though he was determined to use the remainder of the shade before purchasing a different color. Gallen groaned again, clicking the compact closed, the pearl design etched into the lid of glittered in the muted morning lamplight. Rising from his position on the blankets, Gallen sulked to pack.

He slowly pulled the cool linen of his Night Flyer tunic over his head, relishing in the comfort of the emblem of his loyalty.

Though it was Sol who pulled him into this rebellion, Gallen was one of Alcor's initial Night Flyers. The Southern leader and future king chose the name, thinking the notion of flying in the night an ominous and threatening one. Did the warriors fly? Well, only recently. The name itself spoke more to their dexterity, their ability to pass from city to city with deft and speed, and their impressive influence in gaining support for Alcor and his cause.

In just a matter of months, Gallen, alongside their first warriors, developed a robust following. People from throughout the realms whispered their shared words of solidarity, the words that drove the revolution: "For King and Sol."

Some reputations take time, require history and tradition. Not Alcor's Flyers. They were well-known in Nourels, this army of less than a decade. Could six years of training and bonding and fighting create an impenetrable force? Gallen believed so.

His mother, Mist bless her, required some convincing. Though Gallen assured her over and over of the importance of such an alliance, she needed far more convincing when Alcor declared his intentions of becoming king. However, picky and incessant as his mother was, she was no fool. Quite the opposite, in fact. She was likely the wisest lady in the Nine Realms and conducted herself as if she were fully aware of this fact.

As Gallen pulled the leather pants over his feet, a smile pushed his soft cheeks upward, thinking of his mother. While she perturbed him with her constant nagging, he respected her more than anyone.

Kattegat, the Lady of Coral as they called her, had good reason to hesitate. The Ocean Realm, whilst quite isolated, was known to possess mystical power. While not quite the natural magic known to fairies or nymphs, their people knew more tangible forms of power—gifts from the goddesses of the seas. Leaders of the Ocean Realm did not trust those in the "above world" to understand the importance of these gifts, believing the power-hungry would push to use them for their own advantage. Centuries passed, and the Ocean Realm grew. And the people of the ocean, those in towns and cities alike, remained detached from the rest of Nourels. The past decade knew a bit more inclusion, an attempt by some lords and ladies to open the realm to those from outside. Yet, most wanted to keep the Ocean Realm as it had always been. The past mistreatment of merfolk at the hands of other realms did little to quell fears of ending their isolation. Gallen sighed as he considered the impact of his departure yet again. His burden of action.

Gallen turned his thoughts toward the journey ahead. He walked slowly to the other edge of his tent. The soil beneath his bare feet glowed a slight green as the lantern light filtered through layers of green fabric that sat atop the metal. He itemized the necessities in his mind, considering what provisions he, Malinar, and Sol might need. He, Malinar, and…

Sol.

Her drunken slurs of last night immediately flooded his mind, leaving any reasonable notions of planning or preparation for the following weeks long behind.

Gallen did not want to admit it, but her words pierced his heart in a way he did not anticipate. What possessed her to say such things? And in front of Asha no less?

As redness stained the blue tips of his ears, he breathed in and out slowly. While Gallen knew she was not his partner anymore, not even really the same person he once knew, the comment still burned. He reached for the needle threaded through his latest design, wishing he had more time to work before leaving. Embroidery offered his hands a way to busy themselves and allow his mind to rest. Of late, his creations reflected all he had lost. A bit dramatic, perhaps. But Gallen required at least one outlet of irrationality to keep the rest of him sane.

He grasped the hilts of his sparkling knives before placing them carefully in the holsters sewn into the back of the navy Night Flyers tunic. During his years living in the Star Realm, he'd grown rather attached to these weapons. While not as imposing as the water spears of his native land, a pair of sharpened blades offered several options in battle that Gallen enjoyed. Holding his personal knives made him feel a part of something, a member of this world of night, one of few who owned a pair for themselves. At times when he glimpsed at the translucent hilts, Gallen remembered Sol's look of pride when the dagger ceremony ended. When her hand slipped from his. When he became a Flyer.

Looking down at the silver moth embroidered across his chest, Gallen felt at home. Even if he and Sol would never be the same, he loved her for bringing him into the fold. For finding him a place to belong. A brother in Alcor. A purpose in this idle world.

Turning on his heel, Gallen walked toward the entrance of his tent, gingerly reaching down for his brown, leather boots. He wiped the bottom of one foot against the opposite leg before pulling the shoe on and repeated the process on the other. He took one final look at his uniform, pressing his hands down his tunic with a grin.

A true Night Flyer of the Star Realm.

ALCOR MET his friend at the front of his large tent, broad shoulders mirroring the broad smile lining his tanned face. "Well, good morning, Gallen."

"Morning people are never to be trusted. My mother taught me that." Gallen stretched his arms above his head and yawned to emphasize his point.

Alcor merely swung his arm over Gallen's shoulders. "Each morning is a new beginning." He led the two through the main flap and into the large tent. "Everyone deserves a new beginning, eh?"

Gallen settled comfortably in the chair nearest a blazing fire pit at the center of Alcor's tent. While Celestrans at times chose to hold their own fires in their homes, not many did. Whether the fear of a fire spreading from tent to tent or the lack of sufficient space, Gallen did not know. But he did enjoy this luxury of his soon-to-be king.

The two needed to solidify the details of the journey before Gallen departing for the fields outside of the city. Yet, like many of their meandering meetings, the two friends discussed their personal concerns.

"Zeffra's temper flares during these heightened moments of stress," Alcor complained, scratching his close-cut hair somberly, "and, with the influx of new recruits, she's quite sensitive."

"I've seen her leave the temple most mornings, I'm certain that helps slightly?" Gallen offered.

Alcor nodded grimly. "Mornings and nights. It does much to quell her impatience."

Though the words seemed positive enough, Gallen saw the reservations written on the lines of his friend's face. "I sense your reservation. Temple is a positive influence, I'm certain."

"In moderation," Alcor crossed his broad arms as he stood close to Gallen, "at any rate, meditation can only heal so much."

Gallen watched the fire lick the cool air. "I refuse to judge how others choose to heal."

"Wise words, dear brother." Alcor's hand landed on Gallen's shoulder with a thud, "I require patience and humility and—"

"Let us discuss the details of this quest." Gallen interrupted, knowing how long the apology could last. At the mention of the quest, Alcor pulled away, walking away from his friend as Gallen continued.

"I believe we can reach the edge of the realm in two days' time. We have our contact in the Valley Realm who is more than willing to house us for at least a night, then I am hoping Sol's past with those in the High Realm is enough for a warm welcome." He pulled his hands behind his head as he stretched his legs out toward the flames.

As Gallen considered safe places of respite, Alcor began pacing across the rugs, rubbing a hand over his close-shaven hair. After years together, Gallen knew his friend's ticks, and this was not good.

"Is the plan unsatisfactory?" Gallen stared wide-eyed toward the sulking king.

He shook his head in response. "Not at all. As always, quite prepared."

The words were affirming yet slightly hollow. *Not good.*

"Dear friend, is something troubling you? If you wish to finish discussing Zeffra, certainly we shall." Gallen rose from the chair.

"No, it is..." Alcor turned his blue eyes toward him. "Is there something amiss? Something you have left unsaid?"

Gallen avoided the icy blue, staring toward the floor. Of course, he knew there were topics he could not address, not when the journey was at stake. Sol's journey. Her chance to return to who she was. Perhaps return to who he wanted her to be.

Thoughts swarming his mind mingled with a bit of guilt at his deceit. Gallen shook his head. "No. Those in the Ocean Realm know nothing of Sol's condition and I reported all that my mother informed me."

He tried to meet his friend's gaze, convince him of the truth of his words. The reality, though, was Gallen had never been a gifted liar. And, just as Gallen knew Alcor's ticks, Alcor knew Gallen's tells.

A deep, bellowing sigh filled the room as Alcor pressed his

fingertips against his eyes. "Whatever it is," he paused, looking toward Gallen in emphasis, "do not harm my sister. We need this to work. This cause, our kingdom, the people of Nourels. They need a warrior to galvanize them."

"She has not chosen the warrior's path." The words left him sounding harsher than intended. Yet, Gallen could not help the disappointment that billowed in his chest. Not because he believed records to be beneath her, but because it was yet another part of her he did not recognize anymore.

Alcor shook his head and scoffed. "Warriors are not just those of steel. There are warriors of words." He spoke definitively. "Yet, her memories could be important to this cause, to her wellbeing, to all we have sacrificed for. You must see to it that she is safe. She is the best of me. Of us."

Gallen saw the slight glistening of tears lining his lids as he spoke, the emotion of all he could lose rising to the surface.

"Promise me, Gallen."

Gallen shifted from one foot to the other, unsure of how much he should promise, how much he *could* promise. And, of course, he wanted to keep Sol safe. But he also did not understand this Sol the way he once did. He could not anticipate her movements, her choices, her feelings. He felt helpless and blind and foolish.

"I promise." Gallen's final word held in the air a long while before Alcor turned toward the empty dining table.

"Now, tell me again of the details. I should note them to keep track of my Night Flyer trio." Alcor's jolly tone returned as the two continued preparing for the flight.

Nearly an hour later, Zeffra frantically entered the tent murmuring something about uniforms and fresh sets of training targets. Gallen slipped out just as the military leader began listing further requests for ways to communicate between realms.

Zeffra came across as severe to most, religiously zealous and fiercely regimented, though Gallen understood her to be far more than just a temple dweller. She was far more intelligent than

Gallen or Alcor, throwing her talents into ways to improve their position in the war effort. The concept of better communication was her next big project. She claimed that ease of communication would further solidify their alliances while increasing opportunities to gain support.

Gallen considered her solutions as he walked through the blue-lit pathways. Gaining the assistance of birds was an option, many used for common letters over reasonable distances. However, the Ice Realm was known to also use such tactics and likely held far more sway amongst the beasts of the air than they even imagined. Gallen once suggested beasts of the water, yet that option was far slower, the waterways inconvenient for such a task. Zeffra's newest idea included some sort of sky lightning, creating coded messages that could be seen miles away. The concept held promise, though Alcor feared the potential of enemies decoding their intel. In the end, Gallen would leave the innovations to Zeffra and, instead, lean on what he knew.

As he walked slowly through the streets of Celestra, Gallen breathed in the smells of the city. The brewed morning teas and coffees. The freshly baked sweet morning breads. The crisp, earthy soil lining the paths and tents. He always missed such mornings when he was forced to leave.

Rounding a corner, he heard his name nearby. "Gallen! Oh, Gallen, dear!"

A short, slender, elderly woman stepped into the street with a napkin in hand. She walked briskly toward Gallen, her short, silvery hair swept backward as her wide smile accentuated the many wrinkles that lined her cheeks.

"Oh dear! I am elated to see you on this auspicious day!" The woman stopped directly in front of him, the napkin clearly folded around a round object.

Gallen could not help but return her smile. "Gramma Ishpa," he gently offered a nod of his head in respect, "elated to see you before my journey begins once more. My deepest apologies for the late hour, I required an audience with King Alcor."

She waved his apology away. "No need, no need. I am simply happy to see you off!"

Ishpa, one of the oldest and most sincere bakers in the city, grew attached to Gallen almost immediately when he arrived in Celestra. He appeared a bit sheepish in his unfamiliar surroundings and she was anything but. In those first weeks, Gallen visited her bakery every day, eager to try her rotation of pastries. Soon, the casual greetings each morning developed into a meaningful connection, and he had spent his mornings there ever since. Though, near midday, this was a late visit for him.

When Gallen left for quests, Ishpa claimed she would count down the days for his return, wanting to see her "favorite grandson" come home in one piece. He appreciated her care, knowing he had a motherly figure to turn to when he desperately missed his own mother.

Ishpa held the napkin out toward Gallen, a bit of worry shading her soft, green eyes. "A slice of bread. Imbued with my good luck, as always."

Gallen immediately smelled a delectable mixture of cinnamon and pear.

"What is this good luck you always mention? You must tell me one of these days."

The words barely left his mouth before he took a large bite. Ishpa always mentioned her special gift for luck. She alluded to something spiritual, or perhaps supernatural, yet Gallen attributed most of her morning ramblings to her old age and hyperactive imagination.

Though, to her credit, he did eat her bread before every quest, and he always returned.

"There are secrets even the strongest and bravest of men must not know." She beamed, the white streaks in her hair catching the blue light of the lanterns outside of her baking tent.

Gallen sighed. "And still left wondering."

He took another bite, then finished his slice with a third.

"I must leave you with something to lure you back, my grandson." Ishpa turned to leave, though paused for a moment, as if her mind were suddenly pulled away in an instant.

After she remained standing still for a few moments, Gallen took a step toward her. She shook her head and smiled once more, though the joy did not meet her eyes.

"Young one, be open to all. There may be much to fear; however," she took a step to him, grasping his sleeves in her shaking hands, "you are capable of more than you know."

With Ishpa, Gallen was accustomed to cryptic goodbyes. However, this was a bit extreme.

"I will return, Gramma Ishpa, as I always do."

He pulled the old woman into a hug, her arms barely moving to return the sentiment. When Gallen stepped back, her eyes appeared glazed, as if somewhere else.

"Goodbye, young one."

She turned with a vacant look and entered her tent. Worry pricked Gallen's mind. He considered entering after her, to assure himself the strange farewell was another quirk of this loving woman rather than an omen of a deeper threat. However, the time to depart was quickly approaching and there was still much to do.

As he walked past tent after tent, Ishpa's sweet voice echoed in his mind. He decided to focus on the positive element of her message.

"You are capable of more than you know," Gallen whispered to himself.

With what he knew lay ahead, the sentiment was a lifeline. For there was much to fear. And it was a threat he was unsure if he was ready to face.

4

Sol

The winged horses stolen from the Ice Realm were kept outside of Celestra. It was the only place large enough for the strong bodies of the pegasi. Stable hands from a rural town gladly volunteered to convert a former storage tent into a makeshift barn. Keeping the large horses outside of the crowded city provided them with fields to graze and trot and thrive. Alcor was initially worried the beasts would fly away, perhaps attempt to return to the Ice Realm and revisit the kin they left behind. But Sol refused to tie the beasts down.

"We would be no better than *him* if we kept these magnificent beasts against their will," she said to Alcor the day they reached Celestra.

Alcor agreed, although a bit begrudgingly. "Perhaps they could be of use in battle," he had said.

Regardless, it became clear in the first few days that the pegasi would remain. Those living in Celestra took great interest in them, many visiting to feed them, pet them, wash them. The winged beasts were living in luxury. And who would want to leave luxury?

Sol approached the grey, speckled pegasus with her bag slung across her back. She offered the creature a small apple before reaching her arms over his neck. The pegasus leaned into her touch, whinnying pleasantly as Sol's heart filled with delight, a reassuring tranquility replacing a bit of her anxieties. While she cared for each of the winged horses as much as the rest of Celestrans, he was her favorite, the horse who led her away from Endoneth and toward her new home.

"Hello, Kinsle. Are you prepared for a new adventure?" She whispered into his mane.

Kinsle neighed splendidly in response, shaking his braided tail gleefully. The horse shared the same love for Sol, she was sure. Her visits, which occurred whenever she had time to sneak away from her numerous responsibilities, always brought him trotting to her palm, eager to spend whatever time he could by her side. Sol often took a satchel filled with paper and ink to work on her records while Kinsle ran circles in the green grass of the field. With the shopkeepers' old storage tent far from the city, and the field even further, the blue glow of the lantern lights barely reached Sol as she watched Kinsle rush through the wisps of faded blue light.

Sol typically took a lantern with her on these visits and asked Alcor on a few occasions to invest in permanent lights to illuminate the field. It was admittedly low on the list of important matters to consider, but she requested it all the same.

Today, the field was a bit brighter as Sol stood close to her stallion. The other Night Flyers who helped the trio ready themselves each brought lanterns which, together, provided a blue haze to light up the field and the tent and the horses as if daylight were truly in the Star Realm. Dim, blue daylight. Gallen spoke with Zeffra as Malinar placed her pack on Storm's back, the startling white pegasus with feathery, white wings. Sol avoided looking directly in Storm's direction; the beautiful beast brought back memories she would rather forget. Storm, clearly the strongest of the fleet, was the Lord Rostair's favorite; the horse they rode together when they flew to the caverns the first time. A sick feeling pressed against Sol's stomach as she realized how ironic it was. Storm, of all pegasi, would help bring her to the pools of magic.

"Do not fret, Zeffra. I will remain uninjured and ready to do my part when I return." Gallen spoke matter-of-factly as Zeffra fretted over the next two weeks, insistent that Gallen's presence may be necessary if the Ocean Realm decided to change course.

Her worries were not unwarranted. The lords and ladies of the oceans and beaches wavered in their loyalties. A few months previously, they spoke against the need for a unified Nourels, utterly indifferent to Alcor's rise. However, the relationship between Gallen and the leaders proved an important resource for allies of the Southern realms. His latest mission produced an important connection, an ambassador of great intelligence with a foot in both realms: his mother.

Zeffra smiled grimly at Gallen before looking out to the field. "I wish for your safe return." Perhaps genuine, yet Sol sensed a note of underlying stress, of something still left unsaid.

She needed him. As Alcor's First, Zeffra constantly contemplated various scenarios of strategy. The actions of their tenuous allies. The sudden changes that often accompanied warfare. Sol did not envy such a position. She could see Gallen's annoyance as he internalized Zeffra's motivations for her concern—less so for his safety and more for his utility.

Alcor moved between the two. "Gallen, let us review the supplies one last time."

Sol noticed a slight glare Alcor sent toward Zeffra, his disapproval as visible as the blue glow. She sank toward Malinar in response while a few other Night Flyers provided helping hands to ready the three-winged horses.

Kinsle belonged to Sol, Malinar flew on Storm, and Gallen's pegasus, one of the younger horses, was called Cotton. The children in the city loved to walk by the field in the mornings, taking a longer path to their school to catch a glimpse of the pale-yellow steed. Her wings were unlike the other two, shining with a metallic sheen in numerous pastel colors. The rainbow looked most magnificent when she spread her wings as wide as she could, creating a wall of wonderful color. When the young horse galloped in the field, a blur of yellow preceded a trail of sparkling light, as if the soil itself turned into fantastic bursts of glitter.

As Sol walked past the group, she heard Zeffra complaining to Malinar about the issues such a brightly colored pegasus created. "I do hope you are not detected. Those wings will likely expose your position to anyone standing on land. I suppose never mind notions of stealth…"

Sol strode away from the conversation, focusing instead on the path they would take toward the caverns. She had grown accustomed to Zeffra's negativity, assuming it was more a manifestation of her anxieties rather than a reflection of her true countenance. Such comments bothered Gallen, who pet the pale blue, pink, and purple hair of Cotton's mane.

"Do not take her to heart, little one." His motions were tender, as if soothing a friend. "She could never understand your speed and strength."

Zeffra and Malinar chatted back and forth as Gallen pet Cotton, whispering reassurances of her value. As Sol witnessed both interactions, the reality of the trip suddenly clicked into place: The three of them—Sol, Gallen, and Malinar—would be forced to interact with just each other for at least a month with no beings other than their animal companions to ease the tension until they reached their allies beyond the realm. Then who would she speak to? She could not discuss her struggles or the intent of their quest to any other than the Flyers. Alcor insisted her memory loss remain a secret as long as possible. Though he was an amazing leader, their allies joined the cause for King *and* Sol. Without her former memories, her former self, what would people think?

Alcor's figure ripped Sol from her thoughts. "You will make it there and back." His words were desperate yet calm. "This will work. I believe, truly I do."

He appeared to Sol as the kind of man who often achieved what he set out to do. She witnessed such determination with her own eyes once before, and she hoped she would see it again.

"I do hope you are right." She smiled at her brother as he began walking past her, gesturing for the others to come together at the center of the field.

"All is well, Gallen?" Alcor's voice boomed with more authority now, abandoning the gentle tone he reserved for his sister.

Gallen nodded. "Indeed. All is accounted for." He continued running his hand over the neck of the yellow pegasus, and Cotton nuzzled his shoulder affectionately.

Zeffra whispered something to Alcor who waved a hand in response. She darted her eyes low. Sol selfishly wished she could hear the details of the spat, yet her brother continued bidding the trio goodbye, focused on one task before moving to another.

"My three Flyers!" Alcor threw his arms up emphatically. "The journey will be smooth: It is straightforward and will yield amazing success. Of this, I have no doubt!" He encouraged the trio so they could leave on a positive note.

Gallen folded his arms across his chest and Malinar huffed in a show of exasperation.

"Now, Malinar." He lowered his voice to address the young Flyer as Gallen and Sol held on to their horses. "I understand the journey may conjure former emotions, remembrances of our last quest." He touched her shoulder, his support exuding from the gesture. "Please, do speak to your fellow Flyers if you need a listening ear. If you believe it to be too much too soon-" He touched a finger to his jaw.

"I will do my duty," Malinar said gruffly, a sense of pride lifting her chest and chin.

Alcor nodded as she took Storm and pushed forward. He

turned to Sol and whispered, "Please be gentle with Malinar. Keep your eyes open. It is an emotional journey, the first after such a loss." He shook his head, his blue eyes filled with grief. "Loss occurs more often than not for a warrior. Though that makes it no less difficult."

Taking Kinsle's mane in her hands, the grey hair silky smooth in her fingers, Sol let out a deep sigh. "I will care for her, of course."

While Sol understood the privilege of being a Night Flyer, she was still learning the importance of each award, each post, each quest. Alcor was the sort of leader to hold high expectations for his best and only offered a quest such as this if he understood a Flyer to be prepared for the challenge. Malinar would certainly do her best to make a positive impression on the future king.

Alcor wrapped his muscular arms around Sol's thick body, a tender show of his love and dedication. "Come back, Sol."

A tear trickled down her cheek. "I will."

Gallen grabbed Alcor's arm in his own, shaking heartily before moving Cotton to meet Malinar and Storm. Sol followed behind, breathing in deeply as she walked with heavy steps over the crisp grass.

"Wait!"

The high-pitched voice pierced through the empty air as Piré's petite frame emerged into the blue light of the field. She gasped loudly, clutching her ribs as she attempted to address the group.

"Sol...do not...leave...without...hug."

Her pale face was flushed a red that looked even darker in the lantern light. She tumbled into Sol, both women falling to the ground in a heap by Kinsle's hooves.

"Piré!" Sol sounded pained but immensely amused.

Piré jumped up, pulling Sol alongside her while both voiced profuse apologies.

"I am sorry I did not see you before leaving!" Sol reassured her friend, stroking her wavy blonde hair while they shared a caring embrace.

"I-I did not want to miss you." Piré placed her delicate hands on Sol's cheeks. "It may have been slightly dramatic. I have just...we have never been apart since..."

Since Endoneth.

Sol shook her head. "Absolutely not. I am so glad you made it here before I left." She pulled Piré into another strong hug. "Enjoy your time here. Paint, bake, read, dance. I will return before you realize I have left."

Sniffling slightly, Piré nodded into Sol's shoulder. "I hope so. Stay safe."

Smiling sadly, Sol released her, then reached to grasp Kinsle's mane and slowly turned to join Malinar and Gallen.

"A good friend, is she not?" Gallen noted.

"Let us begin our quest," Malinar sighed deeply, "the quicker we venture forth, the quicker we may return."

Sol nodded slightly, emotionally spent from a day filled with tearful goodbyes.

The words from Piré began a spiral in Sol's mind, a chaotic thread of thought that stayed with her as the three pairs of wings flapped majestically toward the sky. The thoughts swirled as the wind kissed her cheeks. She had yet to separate from her friends since the night of the rescue so long ago. She spent every night with someone. Piré or Asha or Alcor or Luminor. Never once did she fear being alone. Yet, as she rode with Gallen on one side and Malinar on the other, she wondered what the weeks ahead would bring. How she would decompress after a stressful day or to whom she would turn to dispel her anxieties.

She remembered Asha's book, tucked safely in the leather bag that hung tightly across her back. The thought alone soothed her slightly.

As the three horses continued forward, heading north, Sol heard Kinsle neigh softly. He turned his head to make eye contact with his rider. She noticed her thighs tensing on his back, tightening his sides uncomfortably, and attempted to breath deeply and relaxing her body.

"Sorry, my friend." She reached a hand down to pat his neck. "I did not realize my remaining fear of flight."

She saw his mane shift from side to side, an assurance of his protection. The action relieved her greatly; a familiar comfortability settled deeply in her gut, anchoring her as they continued to keep pace.

She smiled, reaching an arm out to the clouds and the stars and the richly black sky before returning her hand to Kinsle's strong neck.

Hugging him, she whispered, "we can do this. We can go back together."

While on the surface, her words were meant to assure Kinsle, she needed the words to calm her own nerves.

The entire day consisted of moments of realization: The reality of leaving friends behind. The reality of an arduous journey. The reality of returning to a realm of ice.

Of all the realizations, it was the last that forced her heart to pound heavily in her chest and sweat to pool on her forehead.

She took a deep breath and returned to a thought that always brought her solace. Always reminded her of what she overcame. Always encouraged her to move forward:

You are brave. You are bold.

Her brother's poetry flowed like a mantra in her mind. They continued to fly until the stars twinkled in a slightly different pattern and the trees below shifted to a different shade of green. Both an indication of a frightening truth: They had left Celestra.

You are brave. You are bold.

The first day's flight passed with little to note. Sol whispered every now and again to Kinsle and the pegasus always provided a gentle nod or swish of his tail. Gallen hovered nearby, consistently floating in the periphery. Malinar and Storm approached the flight differently, speeding up and slowing down sporadically as though still unaccustomed to one another. Though Sol could not help but smirk, she sympathized with Malinar's plight. Gallen and Sol knew their horses, cared for them, recognized the cadence of their breathing and the subtle ways they communicated. Malinar hardly visited the pegasi, certainly not often enough to know Storm so intimately.

When Gallen waved his hand to stop for the night, Sol was exhausted. She allowed Kinsle to gently carry her below the clouds, his wings softly brushing against her legs as he descended.

The three Night Flyers landed unceremoniously near a large lake, where the ground was a mixture of pebbles and straw. Malinar sighed heavily as Gallen pulled the materials for their tents from a large satchel.

"We should find flat land to use for the night." He gathered a few wooden dowels from the satchel and began piecing together the elements of his tent.

Kinsle ducked his head low, guiding Sol toward the ground as she dismounted. From the corner of her vision, Malinar fumbled to the ground, landing on her leather boots with a painful thunk. Rather than draw attention to the younger Flyer, Sol walked to Gallen, gathering the materials for her own tent. Sitting in a pile of brown straw, she tinkered with the wood and tried to place their location. Brown sticks of straw covered a beach of pebbles, while trees swayed slightly in the breeze that drifted over the lake. To the north, the pebbles formed a path. The path that led from the Star Realm through the Valley and High Realms, into the Mountain Realm before reaching the Ice Realm.

Two sleeps until we enter the boundaries of the Valley Realm, she thought, *where the subtle hills and sprawling trees of the Star Realm taper off, replaced by wide-open spaces.*

The petals of nearby primroses moved with the wind as Sol tinkered with the tent materials, almost as if offering its own form of encouragement. As she sat near the water's edge, she squinted to see the other end of the lake, the faraway trees seeming so small from her place in the straw. The water looked still despite the occasional breeze, only as small fish kissed the surface did the water ripple. Though, the reflection of the sky still glimmered despite the occasional interruption, the moon like a blurry crescent amongst a flurry of stars.

Malinar grunted with effort as she pushed the dowels into the earth. Gallen, long finished putting his own tent upright, approached the edge of the water.

"We should rest. Tomorrow will be a full day of flight." Gallen bent over and lifted a flat pebble in his hand. "We can eat provisions in our tents tonight."

The surface of the lake erupted as the pebble skid across the sky's reflection. Sol traced the remaining ripples with her eyes contemplatively, thinking of a way she could address Gallen, to apologize for whatever she said or did the night before.

Just as she summoned the courage to speak, he was already walking back toward his tent.

Sol remained near the water a long while, staring at the mirror image of the stars and moon and clouds. She hugged her black leggings to her chest, resting her chin on her knees. Her clothes smelled of adventure. Of soil and sweat and grime. A bath in the serene lake would be welcome, though she was admittedly too tired to truly consider such. The presence of Gallen and Malinar nearby also encouraged her to remain on dry land.

Kinsle's rough tongue grazed her cheek, his fuzzy nose nuzzling her lovingly. Sol lifted her hand to rub his nose, the coolness easing some of the tension that she did not realize still clouded her mind. If she could only speak to Gallen, perhaps learn something about their discussion.

Letting such conversations sit in the air, uncomfortably stagnant, filled Sol with anxiety; yet the thought of sitting through such a discussion, the familiar feeling of wrestling with what she did not know, what she did not remember…It was too overwhelming to consider.

The breeze picked up once more, stirring the grass and pleasantly whipping the wisps of hair from the corners of her face, as if nature itself were coaxing her to relax and think of such stressors another day.

She took the wind's advice, peering up into the starry night to see the moon beam comforting light through the tiny tree line across the lake. The moon held her place atop the trees, her powerful rays casting shadows across the distant leaves and branches. Sol had learned to revere her. To look to her for guidance. While the sun burned, the moon soothed. And while the sun heated, the moon offered respite. In a way, she would miss her as they journeyed from the magic of the Star Realm to those of the day.

In that moment, she chose to relish in the touch of the moon, ignoring what happened last night and what would happen tomorrow. She buried the nervousness about Gallen and repressed her fear of failure, of completing their task with still no recollection of her past. And instead, she invited a sort of ignorant peace that afforded her time to rest.

She breathed in the moon's glow, and feigned content.

5

Malinar

Campsite tents never felt comfortable to Malinar. Perhaps it was the natural fear of danger that accompanied a quest. Perhaps it was her longing for her cozy blankets and brightly colored rugs at home. Or perhaps it was the circumstances of this journey that forced her to both face her distaste of Sol and her admiration of Gallen. Whether homesickness or anxiety or nerves, Malinar tossed and turned for hours before conceding defeat.

After a day full of flying, sleep should have pulled her into its grasp immediately. She was certainly tired, both body and brain. Hours in the sky meant hours of nothing but thinking and whistling and worrying. Worrying more than all else. Flying was not a part of her traditional warrior training, unaccustomed to the constant shifts in speed and elevation. She hated to imagine what Gallen thought of her, shivering in the sky like a child. Malinar needed to impress the best friend of the king. She needed to prove she was more than the girl form the countryside. This frustrating fact often popped into her mind when her heart raced, when her traitorous body shook at the notion of falling to her demise.

Yet, the comfort of having others with her, even if one *was* Sol, surprised her. It was as if her body constantly searched for an anchor and the sight of Sol's silver cloak or the tunic hanging off of Gallen's strong shoulders provided a sense of safety in the sky.

Not knowing which direction to turn was another unfamiliar feeling. When on land, she never got lost. In the air, however, her sense of space was completely distorted. Malinar always had an uncanny instinct for landscapes and locations. When she was younger, she could wander for miles and miles away from her small Star Realm village and always managed to find her way home. This talent was essential for a large family, one where her parents often lost track of their young children before Malinar was called upon to find them.

Now bundled in a traveling throw, she looked around the small tent, searching for anything to either ease her mind or force her to sleep. She reached for the leather satchel nestled near the blanket, trying to remember what she packed only a day ago. Her hand flipped the opening flap over to reveal the contents of the bag. Relief swept over her as she eyed a book stuffed between a leather glove and a woven scarf. Tucking her dark hair behind her ear, she pulled the book from the satchel and glided her hand over the embossed cloth: *The Stories of the Seven*.

Malinar opened the familiar pages, worn with time and attention. The story of the seven powerful women of the Star Realm's past constantly provided her with confidence and a renewed spirit. The book, a token of love from her mother, included details of the women's lives, their hopes and dreams, and their successes. Women with both courage and fear. Women who loved and lost and still loved again.

She turned the pages halfheartedly, instinctually. The words were written in numerous colors and sizes. Sketches lined the edges of each page. Years of notes and scribbles and stains. A book more than appreciated, it was cherished.

The image of the seven came into view as she flipped toward the front of the work. They looked delightful and inspirational. Each woman a different stature, size, and shape. Their various colors formed a rainbow of unity. The glow of starlight created a halo behind them as they stood shoulder to shoulder. Emotion brimmed in Malinar's chest at just a glance at the illustration.

Closing the book, she pulled it tight against her chest, squinting her eyes to avoid beginning another fit of tears. Since Ranor's death, any emotional indulgence led to hours of sobbing. And Malinar loathed sobbing.

It had been nearly three months since his passing, and Malinar could swear she felt his phantom touch when she awakened in the morning. Yet another reason to evade sleep.

But the grief itself was strange. It was not the loss of young love or even a potential future. She cared for Ranor, truly. Yet their coupling was new. Fresh. And unfairly one-sided. Which made the emotional loss even deeper, in some way. As if Malinar was most upset at letting Ranor die believing she loved him too. She hated herself for it. Hated that she did not love Ranor. Hated that she could see a life without him. Hated her interest in others' affections so soon after his passing. And rather than hold the full weight of that hatred, she placed it on another. And so, her malice toward Sol blossomed.

The disdain only grew as Sol continued to be so unnervingly *nice*. She was like the old Sol in some ways—confident, outspoken, driven. Though, the Sol Malinar watched from the shadows of the Night Streets all those months ago was harsher, colder, more driven by her version of truth. Even more infuriating was the lengths to which other Flyers embraced this new Sol despite her past. Despite what she had done.

"She cannot remember who she once was," Tress would say, "you cannot expect a person to suffer the consequences of a person she does not remember." The concept was perhaps accurate, though it did anger Malinar even more deeply.

It was not that Sol was an angry person. She did not mistreat others or commit bouts of cruelty. Rather, it was as if Sol hid any sense of warmth from the other Flyers, save Alcor, Asha, and Gallen. She had focused only upon goals, upon victory, upon avenging her fallen parents. Malinar often wondered if this motivation was what drove Sol to leave the group that fateful night in the Ice Realm—the night where everything changed for them all.

Malinar brushed aside the blanket and allowed her bare legs to cool. Rather than continue down a path of remembering her past, she stood. She set her beloved book upon the crumpled blanket, pulled her boots onto her feet, and stepped into the night.

Alone, Malinar closed her eyes, the empty air still as her companions slept in their respective tents. She quietly stepped across the many stones toward the nearby lake. The moon held her position high in the sky, her light almost muting the stars around her. Malinar carefully sat on the pebbles near the lake's edge, tucking the long tunic underneath her bare skin. She removed her boots, setting them by her side before placing her feet in the water.

The lake was surprisingly warm, pleasantly so. Small fish flitted around her toes as she settled them into the sand. The water was so clear and blue that Malinar could note even the smallest details beneath the surface, each grain of sand, smooth pebble, and jagged rock. How wonderful would it be to swim beneath the surface and see what lay in its depths. In that, she envied Gallen. His Ocean Realm roots provided him with the skills necessary to navigate waters both salt and fresh. His birthright afforded him the ability to consume water like air. Breathing in water and seeing through it—she could only imagine such a world.

Malinar often considered asking about his adventures, yet the thought of doing so was intimidating.

She tilted her head back, leaning against her arms and placing her hands on the smooth rocks behind her. The moon kissed her cheeks as the wind breezed through her dark hair.

"The water is a source of calm during a night of unrest, don't you agree?"

Malinar opened her eyes, Gallen's face hovering above her own. She immediately stared forward, her hands reaching for her legs, her tunic barely reaching her thighs.

"I did not realize anyone would be awake at this hour." Her voice caught a bit as she spoke.

While both Malinar and Gallen were Night Flyers, their positions could not be more different. Gallen was the former lover of the infamous Sol and King Alcor's personal friend. He had worked for years for his influence, building trust with the people of the realm and earning his place. Even though he was the son of a wealthy lady in a powerful realm, he refused to rely on the nepotism that sat so tantalizingly close and began his training like every other Star Realm warrior, from the lowest rank.

On the other end, Malinar was a young Flyer, newly chosen to be a member of the elite group. While many warriors enjoyed extensive training in their youth, Malinar only read of warfare in stories. While her peers sparred with their siblings as youths, Malinar spent years monetarily supporting hers. Gallen was particularly experienced. He had traversed hundreds of quests, traveled throughout the realms, and gained the trust of essential allies. She looked up to him as a warrior and a friend—both at which he excelled.

Gallen stepped to her side. "Do you mind if I sit?"

He tilted his head toward the ground between them. Malinar nodded slightly, attempting to remain calm as Gallen settled near the lake's edge.

"Sleep has not been my friend as of late." He placed his head in his hands, his shoulders easing a bit, begging for rest.

Malinar fidgeted with the hem of the tunic, self-conscious about the bareness of her upper thighs.

"How do you find peace?" she queried, looking at the moon's reflection rather than face Gallen to her right.

He put his feet into the water. "Most nights I think of my home. The sun shines in distorted rays, broken by waves of water. In the right light, you can see rainbows."

Malinar thought about the ocean light, of the sun filtering through waves and tides and marine life.

Gallen continued. "Picturing the calm movement of the water settles me. The way that the fish pass by, happily flipping in organized yet organic schools. There are so many wonders beneath the water. And the estates themselves, housed in air. They are magic."

As he described his home, Malinar watched his feet sift through the sand on the lake's shore.

"Does it ever work?" Her words were a whisper.

She stared up at the moon, but she could sense his golden eyes turn to look her way. Through the curtain of straight black hair that blocked her peripheral vision, she could feel him staring, attempting to understand her, this woman near the water.

"You know, there is no cure for it." His words were gentle, like an embrace Malinar desperately needed.

Every word sounded like wisps in the growing wind. "A cure?"

"For loss," he said slowly, "loss—it needs time to heal. There is no other option, no swift solution."

In that moment, she was frozen. Her hands still clinging to the fabric of her tunic. Her feet buried in piles of sand. Her heart burrowed deep in her chest, desperately seeking sanctuary. Her blood turned ice cold, the creeping kind that begins in the center of your stomach and oozes throughout your veins. All she could hear were whooshing sounds followed by thuds of her own heart beating.

Then, suddenly, her hand warmed. As if doused in a beautiful ray of sunlight. Like the moment she broke through the boundary of the Star Realm and finally made it home.

Gallen's hand grasped hers, his eyes steadfastly staring into her own.

"But even time does not let you forget." She barely heard his words over the sound of her pulse gaining pace, his fingers brushing her exposed leg.

They remained there for what felt like an eternity, her heart lodged nervously in her throat, before Gallen finally stood.

"If you ever need to talk. To grieve. To rest. I am here."

With that he nodded and walked back toward his tent.

Malinar stilled, processing the short conversation. She had known Gallen to be kind, yes. But she had not anticipated this sort of sensitivity. He was gentle. Reassuring. Honest.

It was likely just the generous words of a leader, encouraging a younger warrior to stay the course. Nothing more. Nothing deeper.

Still, it had been a long time since she knew such vulnerability.

When Malinar finally rose from her place near the lake, her feet pruned from their place in the water, all she wanted was to coax Gallen into speaking further truths to her. To lull her to sleep with sweet thoughts of sincerity. But she thought better of it.

Instead, she reentered her own tent, scooping the book into her hands, and letting Gallen's kindness finally settle her aching heart.

Malinar turned to a story of triumph, a tale she read often:

Queen Malindra of the Meadows

A woman of low birth from the Meadows of the Star Realm, Malindra understood with great certainty the importance of opportunity. She often paced in her tent at night, seeking a way to care for her family. Her sickly father and her young brother both stayed in the far corner of their tent, the segments of the rooms separated by sheets of dark fabric. One day in her nineteenth year, Malindra set out to work for meager pay, with little knowledge of skills that would provide her with more. And, on that day, opportunity arrived in the form of a daring knight bursting into their small town, lit torch in hand.

Malinar adored these words—the hope of an opportunity existing just on the horizon when one least expects. She remembered reading through the lines on this very page when she achieved a place amongst the Night Flyers. The news made her feel like Malindra. A queen. Brought up from nothing yet achieving so much for her family. A family that relied on her. That believed in her.

She sucked in another deep breath, internalizing that thought. This quest could be the one to propel her even further, give her a place amongst the strongest of the Night Flyers. Solidify her position in the kingdom soon to come after this damned war. Then her family could join her. Then they would see that all they endured was worth it.

6

Sol

For Sol, the first night of their journey passed in utter silence. She settled in her own tent as soon as she could and did not leave until the night stars silenced and the morning constellations awakened.

As if more attune to the call of the morning, Sol was the first to emerge, hugging her arms to keep the chill of the morning air at bay. She did not appreciate the warmth of her tent until the cold pricked her skin. She pulled her silver cloak close to her body, the embroidered moths dancing along the collar.

Determined to make a better impression on her companions, Sol set out to find wood for a fire. Her boots crunched the small pebbles underfoot as she strode around the edge of the lake toward a grouping of trees. The lake looked just as still in the morning glow as it did the night before. A layer of fog hovered just above the surface of the water. Serene. Sol could almost forget the war in a place like this.

But that she could not do. Her life was tied to this cause.

She reached the trees and began searching the forest floor for dry wood. The bark was a light brown that matched the color of the straw mingling amongst the pebbles. On her walk back to the camp, she swooped low to grasp small handfuls of the straw to use as kindling.

Hunching over a pile of wood and straw at the center of the three tents, she struck two smooth stones together to coax a spark. The fire blazed within minutes, the flames radiating a comforting warmth that immediately eased the chill in her bones.

"Some things never change." Gallen yawned as he passed through the opening of his tent.

While he always appeared relaxed and carefree, Sol had never seen him more at ease than how he looked now, likely still too sleepy to register the many responsibilities that constantly churned in his mind.

She faced the fire, her palms reaching as close as the heat would allow. "What do you mean?"

Gallen chuckled as he sat to her left, close enough that she could easily set her hand on his knee yet far enough away to suggest such a gesture would be unwelcome.

"You were always the first to rise on quests. Alcor would say you could coax a fire from water if you tried." He shook his head, his hands fidgeting with a piece of straw.

Sol's eyes never left the fire, her hands soaking in the warmth like it was the energy she needed to survive the day. "Like writing or reading or breathing. It just came naturally."

Gallen nodded. "It must be nice to attempt these skills in nature. You never had to do such things at his estate, did you?"

As if not expecting a response, he quickly rose to his feet before she could think of something to say. "I will gather food," he nodded toward the lake, "then we should begin to decamp and pack the horses."

Sol watched him as he strode off, walking hastily toward the lake She watched as he stripped his shirt from his body, the pale blue of his skin glowing in the starlight. She watched as he unbuttoned his trousers and pulled them lower...

Sol quickly shifted her eyes back to the fire.

"I am sure it is nice to be able to look upon the body of someone you care for." Even in the morning Malinar expressed her disdain with veracity.

The comment hit its mark. Sol slightly shifted her weight as she pulled her legs to her chest in front of the flames. "Good morning to you too," she said weakly, ignoring the reminder of the recent past.

Sol noticed that Malinar never spoke *of* Ranor but rather *around* him, like the ghost of a person haunting her every word. If any person brought the topic to light, Malinar immediately removed herself. She certainly avoided the topic with Sol, leaving the Keeper of Records unaware of who the couple were before her capture. Unaware of what Malinar lost.

Malinar remained near the fire, soaking in its warmth while ignoring Sol completely.

Sloshing footsteps joined the sound of the crackling fire, breaking the uncomfortable silence that settled between the two women. "This should be sufficient for the day's journey." Gallen plopped a pile of fish on the ground near the fire.

Gasping, Sol looked at Gallen, his blonde waves still slightly wet from his dip in the lake. "How did you manage to yield such a great catch in minutes?"

His only response was a shrug of his bare shoulders, his shirt stuffed beneath one of his arms. Three streaks of pink lined his side just above his waistline, his pants thankfully covering his lower half. The scars moved slightly up and down as he breathed, glistening with beads of lake water.

He gently laid his shirt by the fire before turning toward the tents to start working. "Malinar, can you cook them? I will begin gathering our tents. Sol, could you tend the fire?"

As Gallen completed his tasks, quickly disassembling the tents and folding the fabrics, Malinar obediently flaked the scales from the fresh fish. She grasped the crimson hilt of her knife in her left hand with an intimidating and impressive confidence. As if the dagger was an extension of her hand, so natural in its movements, so seamless.

The scales that scattered along the pebbles between them looked beautiful in a way, creating a blanket of glimmering turquoise gradients. Sol stared at the scales in the glow of the firelight, lost in thought. The rhythmic sound of Malinar's knife against the fish faded into the background as Sol watched the fire dance across the scales. She quietly braced herself for a long, long journey.

It seemed like only minutes, but somehow also hours, until the fish were cooked, the tents packed away, and the pegasi fed and prepped for another day of flying. "Eat quickly. We should attempt to reach as close to the border of the realm as possible." Gallen gestured his hand toward the pile of cooked fish. "We will need to stop frequently, to rest the horses and reassess our position."

"Are the pegasi not suited for long travel?" Malinar questioned as she brought a filet to her lips. "I do not recall such stops the last time."

"The stars, while gorgeous, do not offer the best light for the horses to see any…disruptions. It is best we spend spurts of time in the sky rather than full days." He coughed a bit as he answered.

The vague explanation gave Sol pause. She had a familiar feeling, as if someone was hiding something important. Something life altering.

She knew Kinsle well enough to know he could ride for at least a half day with no rest. Their journey from the Ice Realm to Celestra used those metrics- a half day of riding, then a break, then another half day, and so on. Sol took a fish in her hands, the skin still warm and charred. She stared at the white flesh, considering whether to confront Gallen or allow the silence to eat away the last minutes on land.

Fortunately, Malinar seemingly never shied from confrontation. "Is there something we should be aware of, Gallen?"

Sending a silent message of thanks to Malinar, Sol sunk her teeth into her food, the fish surprisingly flavorful. Her eyebrows lifted as she looked between her companions and awaited a response.

Gallen sighed, holding the bridge of his nose between his fingertips. "Malinar, it is nothing to be concerned with…" His baritone voice petered out slowly as if he thought to elaborate, yet he did not appear willing to say more.

"I understand. Perhaps it is not my place…yet." Malinar tossed a small fishbone to the side. "If there is danger, we deserve to know."

Sol crunched the fish in her mouth, allowing Malinar to take the lead. The tension wafted through the air like poisonous gas. Gallen fidgeted with the fabric of his shirt, the tips of his ears growing a deep shade of pink. He cleared his throat several times yet refused to elaborate. His eyes met Sol's with perhaps a plea, or was it an apology that sat behind that look? She remained still, the notion of speaking against either of them making her nauseous.

Malinar pushed once more, bolder than Sol believed she could be. "If we are flying to our certain death we should be prepared."

He sighed once more. "When I returned to the Ocean Realm," he began slowly, as if convincing himself to hold the words close as he spoke them into the eager air between the three, "I heard rumors of a violent weapon used in the skies. A weapon that can light ablaze at a moment's notice."

Fish tumbled from the women's hands simultaneously. Sol's mouth popped open while Malinar's eyes grew painfully wide. The shock was palpable, replacing the tension with something heavier.

"I did not want to inform Alcor quite yet." A slight choking noise left Malinar's throat as Gallen continued, his eyes practically begging Sol for empathy. "I knew there was a great likelihood that he would postpone the quest, and I know how much this meant…"

Meant to Sol? To him? Sol could not determine which as she sat slack-jawed at the confession.

"What do you know about this weapon?" Sol finally squeaked out.

Gallen's eyes shifted to his boots. "Well, that is another reason I decided to keep the information contained. My mother's sources could not verify the creature nor its abilities. They only know it flies and bursts into flames. My mother claims the creatures could turn the tides of the war, if Rostair uses them to his advantage."

His mother was the most vocal supporter of Alcor in the Ocean Realm. If she expressed genuine concern, the creature must have been a true impediment to the cause.

Kinsle nuzzled the back of Sol's shirt, taking advantage of the now empty camp to shuffle closer to his rider. He seemed to sense her confusion and discomfort and concern. She barely registered his nose until he nuzzled again, more forcefully the second time. She leaned into him, placing a gentle hand on the bridge of his head.

The silence that followed was new. Not one of disdain or annoyance or distrust. A silence borne of fear.

It took a moment before Malinar reacted. "How are we to proceed? Fly blindly?"

Gallen gulped. "If either of you wishes to turn back, I would not force you to stay the course. But I must find this weapon."

His intentions weighed heavily in the air. "Was this the purpose all along?" Sol stated tersely.

"As I said, Alcor knows nothing of-"

She did not allow him to finish. "Not my brother's purpose. Was this the reason you wished to come? The reason you pushed for this quest?"

"I believed the opportunity could serve more than one purpose. To find the beast and your memories." He explained.

Sol considered the options before her: Return to Alcor and await a new time to venture to the caverns. This was a reasonable solution. Yet, the timing would never be so convenient as it was now. The war still raged, and Alcor would soon need everyone at his disposal.

Alternatively, she could stay the course and reach the caverns. Regaining her memories could potentially solve so much in her life: the conflict, the relationships, the mistakes, the broken promises. If the pools of magic cured her, reversed the effects of the poison Mairette served her all those weeks ago, it could change everything.

Or there was an emerging third option. One that Sol wished she felt less connected to, less driven toward as she lifted her hand to run her fingers through Kinsle's mane.

"We should find it."

She had never seen Malinar become so pale, her skin depleted of any warmth. The red flames danced in his golden eyes as Gallen nodded solemnly.

"I considered requesting an audience with your former master in the High Realm. He might provide knowledge regarding the creature. I do not want to place you in an unfortunate position, Sol. But they will likely know. They know everything that happens in the sky."

Sol thought back to the many nights Asha described their time in training together. She said their master was "serious, powerful, and stuffy." Could he hold the knowledge they now needed? There was only one path that would offer an answer.

"For King and Sol?" She whispered the call of rebellion, the phrase of Alcor's supporters. She looked at Gallen for validation.

He grinned a bit, the first sign of positive emotion. "For King and Sol."

They both turned to Malinar, her face motionless in the waning firelight. Her eyes looked vacant, yet Sol could see her contemplating the options. Her black hair waved in the slight breeze that whipped stray sparks away from the quieting fire. Malinar knew the implications of this quest. The risk. But a Flyer who returned from an incomplete quest faced consequences. No warrior wanted to lose the trust of the king.

Kinsle's nuzzling kept Sol grounded as Malinar cleared her throat, calmly whispering, "For King and Sol."

THE FLIGHT WAS FAR LESS peaceful than the day before. In addition to the stress of her interactions with Gallen, Sol could not help her mind racing with anxious thoughts of deadly creatures stalking the skies. Fortunately, the wind whooshing past her cheeks blocked out any unexpected noises for her mind to fixate upon. Unfortunately, that left the interim moments, where her fear faded to a small hum in her chest and left room for her mind to replay the conversations with her companions.

Gallen was the most important, and most concerning. She relived their discussions in her mind. His expression of dissatisfaction, of disappointment, somehow stirred more fear in her heart than the mysterious dangers ahead. His opinion of Sol apparently affected her more than she originally thought.

The Flyers continued in a staggered formation—Gallen flying in the front, followed by Sol, and Malinar protecting the group from the rear. While they remained close enough to stay in view of one another, the winged horses maintained a safe distance apart, allowing their riders to enjoy some space to privately process the fireside confession.

Sol wondered aloud to Kinsle as they flew through the clouds, "Do you ever wonder what roams the skies, Kin?" She ran her hand through the coarse hair of his neck, his wings thrumming near her arms as she dipped her face closer to him.

"None could truly disappear amongst the stars," she continued, attempting to quell her fears through manufactured rationalizations. "And if they did, I would protect you with all I have."

Kinsle whinnied, his head slightly leaning into her arms in response. The gesture gave her some solace; however, the logical part of her mind knew thoughts and feelings could not prevent the perils of this world. But, in this moment, Kinsle's support was enough.

Hours and hours and hours passed. The group descended and ascended every so often, just as Gallen suggested, giving the pegasi time to rest and the riders moments to eat and regroup. The stars continued to guide them away from Celestra and toward a new place of old. Sol's simultaneous past and future. She continued her conversation with her pegasus, thinking through who she might meet and what she might say.

The farther north the trio flew, the lighter the sky became, the constant deep blue so quintessential to the Star Realm fading into lighter shades of tinted with pale purples and pinks. It was to Sol like a perpetual sunrise. The sky a beautiful kaleidoscope of colors and twinkling lights. The moon followed them like a loving mother, almost beckoning them a sorrowful farewell as they neared the border of the Valley Realm. While Sol knew the moon would remain in the sky, unseen in the bright light of the sun, the thought of its disappearance caused her a sort of grief. Almost as if the moon protected them from above, warding off any evil that lurked in the realms.

The purples and pinks, while admittedly gorgeous as they swirled together amongst the clouds, were a signal that day would soon dawn and the Star Realm would truly be behind them. For Sol, it felt like the first time leaving home, though she knew it was not. The pit in her heart remained all the same. She only wished she could pull the paper and ink from her satchel to put the feelings to words. Writing always provided her with a sense of relief, giving her a story she could control.

She tangled her hands into Kinsle's mane again as they soared toward a clearing, Gallen signaling to stop. The turquoise grass reflected the pale colors in the sky as the sun peeked through the clouds ever so slightly. The horses landed gracefully, barely disturbing the long, wild grass. As Sol dismounted, the bluish blades grazed her calves as she walked toward the other two Night Flyers.

"Shall we set camp?" She looked to Gallen for direction.

He nodded, taking stock of the location. "I will walk the perimeter of the field if you both could begin setting the tents."

He barely looked at his companions before his boots crunched the soft grass, leading him toward the edge of the clearing.

Sol took stock of the scene. The long grass in a lustrous shade of turquoise spread for a few miles in a wide oval shape, speckled by small wildflowers in shades of white and pink. Thin, treelike plants surrounded the field, like shoots that protected the grass from whatever awaited in the rest of the realm. The sunset colors painted the ground, providing enough light to see but not as much as the sun. Sol looked up to see the stars, still twinkling above yet more muted than before. As she walked through the windswept grass, she could almost hear Celestra calling her home, begging her to remain safe.

After a few minutes, Malinar sighed. "We should set camp near the edge."

The young Flyer reached for Storm's neck, leading her toward the wall of trees.

"Of course," was the only response Sol could provide as Malinar continued headstrong toward the trees.

Sol noticed the redness in Malinar's eyes, her cheeks and nose chapped from hours of flying. Concern itched at Sol's mind as Malinar worked. The Flyer was almost a blur, her dark hair swaying over her shoulders as her thin form rushed to set the tents upright.

The two women took less than thirty minutes to plant three tents in a triangle formation, facing a small fire in the center. The pegasi found a comfortable place to rest a bit farther out, munching on the long strands of grass as they enjoyed the sun's short farewell. Gallen emerged from the far side of the clearing just as Malinar laid the last strip of fabric across his tent frame.

"What did you gather from your patrol?" Malinar's voice was hoarse with exhaustion.

Noticing her clear discomfort, Gallen suggested, "all is well, Malinar. Try to sleep some. Sol and I will attempt to gather food. We will inform you when we have something substantial."

Bleary-eyed, Malinar shuffled through the grass to her tent, the fabric flaps closing behind her with a gentle swoosh.

"Shall we, then?" Sol lifted a brow as she turned to Gallen. Feeling the breeze against her neck, she pulled her cape to her chin, hugging her body to maintain some warmth.

A bit disheartened, he returned her gaze. "We appear safe in the clearing here. I believe there may be some fruits or berries we can eat. Unfortunately, I found little water. There is a stream we may use for drinking, however no fish to eat."

"We have preserves aplenty," Sol pointed out gently. "Enough for the journey initially planned."

Gallen huffed a sigh, "I would prefer fresh foods to supplement. Though you speak truth. Let us try to gather at least something of substance."

He gestured for her to walk with him toward the tall shoots of plants. Drawing closer, the plants or trees or something in between appeared strong while flexible; the deep green highlighted by lighter shades that created vertical patterns around each cylinder. As they reached the thick wall of green, Gallen moved some of the sturdy shoots aside to provide a path for them to follow. Her leather boots squished as they moved, the ground similar to a moist forest floor. As the two warriors pushed plant after plant aside, the greenery became less dense. Eventually, Gallen and Sol could walk side by side, looking for anything edible in the dim light.

"Did you enjoy the flight with Cotton?" Sol's voice seemed to echo through the woods.

Gallen shrugged. "I enjoy Cotton, and I enjoy silence."

The words hit like a punch in the gut. Sol instinctively folded her arms in front of her chest, her breathing coming quickly. Suddenly, the world tilted. Sol noticed every inch of her body. The way her braided brown hair lay slightly off-center behind her back. The crinkling of her silver cloak. The rubbing of her thighs together as they walked. The stark red of the scar lining her right cheek.

Sol spied a patch of mushrooms and took the opportunity to create distance between herself and Gallen. When she returned with a bushel of food in her satchel, he breathed in deeply, as if preparing for an arduous task.

"Sol, we do not need to be disdainful toward one another."

The statement validated her fears. "I did not think we were. At least, I do not wish to be."

Silence again.

"I enjoyed the flight." Sol trudged forward. "It provided space for me to consider my thoughts and my past actions."

"We need not do this." He reached for a few fruits hanging from the sturdy green plants. Placing them in his own bag, he continued, "I believe we need to begin fresh. We cannot pretend we are the same as we were before…"

The thought trailed off and Sol felt the bruise in her gut once again. She wanted to avoid this very thing. To avoid Gallen learning too much and hating what he saw. She realized, especially in that moment, that his silence hurt worse than the risk of rejection. His refusal to even consider reconciliation a thinly veiled façade of a deeper reality. Starting fresh seemed to Sol a simple way of saying ending gently. Ending what they were. Ending what they could be.

"There are moments when I wish I was her," Sol started hesitantly, "then there are moments when I wish to be only myself. Myself as I am now."

Gallen did not respond, yet remained in step with Sol, looking toward her curiously.

She continued, "I cannot change our past, nor my betrayal. However, I can attempt to make my amends to you as I am."

Gallen sighed. "Sol, you know nothing of the pain you caused."

"I know I hurt you. I hurt you and Alcor and Asha. I hurt those I care for so deeply."

"It does not change that when I look at the scar on your face I think of that night when you abandoned my bed for a foolish mission." His words were terse, harsh, raw.

Another bout of silence billowed between them.

"Sol." He stopped, pulling her hands into his own and looking down into her eyes. The movement made her breath falter. Her knees trembled slightly as they stood together in the wood.

"I would like to know *you*. Not who you were. You. That is what I mean when I say start fresh." Gallen swept his thumb over the top of her hand as he spoke.

"A fresh start would be greatly appreciated." Sol breathed. "As long as it is truly fresh. Pure. A pure start."

He considered the semantics a moment, wringing the strap of his satchel in his hands as they continued walking.

"I know you have changed; you are not the Sol I knew. The Sol I loved. And that is not negative. Not wholly." He paused, clearly working through his next thoughts carefully. "It is different. We are different. And I do not want to place any unfair expectations on you."

The sentiment was a kind one, generous even.

"I would like to be your friend, if I could. If that is what you still desire," she offered.

At this he nodded. "A pure start."

When Sol and Gallen returned to the camp, Malinar was tending to a small fire. She appeared more alert and refreshed. The pegasi gathered nearby, Cotton and Kinsle munching on the long grass while Storm lay near the tents.

"Were you able to find anything?" Malinar poked the small flames with a green branch, not looking up as she questioned her companions.

"A few morsels to tide us over. We shall use some of the preserves as well." Sol walked toward the fire, noting a few places that would assist in increasing the size and power of the flames. "Do you feel better?"

With the encouragement of a new start with Gallen, Sol hoped she could convince Malinar to give her a chance as well. Unfortunately, the wounds that plagued Malinar were far deeper than Gallen's. She merely rolled her eyes and pushed a stray black hair from her eyes.

Gallen stepped forward, providing a reprieve from the palpable tension. "We filled the satchels with food and the flasks with water. We should boil it first."

He handed three flasks filled with water to Malinar who accepted them with a slight grin. "I will begin the process for us."

Sol settled near the fire across from Malinar. She reached into her satchel and pulled out a handful of berries, plopping one into her mouth.

Gallen joined her, retrieving berries in the bag, "This will be our final night in the Star Realm." He threw a berry into his mouth.

Malinar furrowed her strong brows. "Are we not out of the realm already?"

Gallen explained through a mouthful of berries, "the magic of your realm blurs at the border. We may have seen remnants of the sun, but trust me, it will become even brighter."

Sol looked into the starry sky, as if searching for such confirmation.

Gallen gulped and continued, "I appreciate you both continuing forward."

"Do you truly not know what the creature is?" Malinar still refused to look toward the others as she boiled the water in the fire.

Eating another few berries, Gallen shook his head. "I do hope answers will emerge in the High Realm."

This answer did not appear to satisfy Malinar, yet she quieted all the same. And, once the water was prepared and the food divided, she stood and quickly returned to her own tent, leaving Sol and Gallen alone once more.

Sol could not help but fill the silence. And, in the spirit of a new start…"Tell me about yourself." She said with a hesitant grin.

He chuckled a bit and munched on a mushroom. "What is there to know, truly?" The deflection pained her as deeply as rejection, though Sol attempted to ignore the wound.

"You said it yourself. I am not who I once was." She twisted a small, purple berry between her fingers. "Shall we be friends? Friends know one another, correct?"

The tone was one of jest—she hoped so at least. It was only when Gallen chuckled once more that she could breathe.

"Well, Sol," he turned his body to face her, the embroidered moth centered on his blue tunic shimmering in the firelight. "I am male. I was born in the Ocean Realm on the Coral Estate of Eckral."

He spoke in a playful tone, one that ignored so many reasons the two should not enjoy this moment. Sol nodded along and smiled, truly smiled.

"My mother is the strongest person I know. And the ocean is the most beautiful place in the Nine Realms." His eyes beamed with pride.

"Why did you leave?" Sol wondered aloud.

Gallen's mischievous smile turned somber. "I met a woman on a beach, and she dragged me into a war of moral implications."

There was a bit of a smile in his words, as if remembering a happy dream.

"Shit." Sol breathed the thought to herself.

Silence seemed to stalk this group, even the most innocent of moments victims of its cruel arrival. This was no different. Sol could only cough to fill the void.

"Well, I am glad you arrived. Alcor needs you."

The sentiment, while avoidant, was true. Gallen was an essential part of expanding Alcor's reach and gaining the support of other realms. From the few weeks she spent in the Star Realm, Sol could already see his charisma. The way others confided in him and relied on him. While Zeffra was Alcor's First, his second-in-command, Gallen served as his confidante. And, in a more practical sense, his upbringing came with essential skills—languages, tactical planning, diplomacy.

"I am merely satisfied with being helpful to a noble cause," he said. He was also notoriously awful at accepting praise.

The fire faded to a slow burn as he smoothed the creases from his tunic. "This is an important position, one that I believe in whole-heartedly." He continued, "In my thirty years, I have not experienced anything like it. The realms have never had a king. One *true* king. As if we have been waiting for Alcor all along."

The words sank in as Sol looked at the man before her. In this light, his skin looked a cooler shade of blue, and the thick lines of dark blue kohl accentuated the flecks of gold in his eyes. His figure, hunched over as he fiddled with his clothing, was long and formidable. Not broad and built like Alcor, yet strong, sturdy, dependable. His blonde hair, a bit disheveled from a long day, was still plaited in two braids that reached his shoulder blades. His skin's soft shade of blue accentuated the bright gold of his eyes. And, even more, he was genuine and loyal and good.

Before him now, Sol desperately wished she could reclaim whatever it was they had. Because, Gallen.

He was…astonishing.

7

Malinar

Malinar fumbled through the camp, once again unable to quell the noise in her head as restlessness pushed her from the comfort of her tent. She shuffled past the remnants of their campfire before walking across the grass beneath the stars. Her mind reeled, constantly worried about her family. Her position. Her heart.

To her surprise, Storm followed her path, keeping a distance while trotting behind all the same. Horses were never Malinar's chosen companion, never mind horses with wings. Though, it would be foolish to pretend Storm's concern did not warm her heart ever so slightly.

She breathed in deeply, her lungs filling to capacity before finally letting the air escape through her lips. The practice usually helped calm her nerves, yet thoughts of Ranor instantly made her mind an anxious mess.

Thankfully, as she walked further from the tents, the silhouette of a man and a pegasus came into view. Gallen lay peacefully on Cotton's belly, his face filled with thought as he worked with a needle and thread on the hem of his tunic.

"Sleep evades you once again, I see." Malinar's voice seemed to put Gallen at ease. He turned his head, smiled slightly, and patted a patch of grass at his side, a welcoming invitation for her to settle near him. She gladly obliged, nestling close to Cotton, who provided a sweet warmth in the increasingly cold night. Storm stepped close enough to keep Malinar in her eye line, the white of her mane nearly luminous under the moon.

Gallen completed a few more stitches before carefully poking the needle through the thickest part of the hem. He looked at the stars, their twinkling like a salve for his still pained soul. "There is much to consider, and it often keeps me awake," he whispered.

The two simply sat for a few glorious moments. Their breathing synchronized as the wind gently cooled the air between them. Malinar could not remember feeling so natural with another person. Not even Ranor.

"Do you still love her?" Malinar was unsure where the question originated nor why she necessarily cared, yet she was curious all the same.

From the corner of her eye, Gallen's expression seemed understanding. "I loved who she was, yes. The Sol I knew was adventurous, dazzling, and decisive. I so admired those parts of her. Particularly for someone who merely does what he is told." He scratched his head awkwardly. "But it was that same decisiveness that often turned to recklessness. And I do not know quite how I feel about that still."

Malinar considered his response carefully. She should be overjoyed to have a comrade who also blamed Sol for the issues in the world. For the decisions she made with no input or guidance. Her decision to run completely counter to the plans established by her own brother, her future king. Her ignorant belief that she alone could face Rostair. That she held the key. That she was invincible.

Prompted by her positioning as the face of the future. *For King and Sol.* How Malinar had grown to abhor the statement that once brought her pride. Since that night, it would never be the same.

Strangely, as she listened to Gallen, Malinar felt nothing but pity for Sol. The insomnia and emotional turmoil must have been truly affecting her. She attempted to tap into her usual store of disdain for Sol yet fell short. Malinar could hardly drum up the anger against her. Just compassion for a woman who likely did not anticipate the fallout of her actions. Who likely did what she thought was right.

"As a decisive person myself," Malinar said, pulling at the leather straps of her boots, "I know that I only make many of my own reckless decisions to protect those I care for."

Gallen's eyes widened a bit before he nodded. "A wise response."

She beamed. "I know what it is like to have a world of expectation thrust upon you. It forces you to become assertive. Protective. Decisive. We do what we think we must, you see."

"And you see the same in her?" He questioned softly, not a reprimand as much as a consideration.

Pulling at the blades of grass, Malinar pondered the notion. "We are not similar truly," she said, even as her own words left her unconvinced, "not in ways that matter."

"How then?" He mused, "I suppose you have both loved, both lost-"

"Rather," she interrupted, hoping to avoid the dreaded topic of Ranor with Gallen of all people, "rather, I believe we both carry expectations of our birth. Hers far more pressing than my own I am certain. But it is heavy, knowing the lives of others rely upon your success."

Malinar pulled her hair behind her ear, still too embarrassed to look Gallen in the eye after her defense of her enemy. Or could it be her *former* enemy? Perhaps neutral acquaintance.

"I am glad to know this side of you, Malinar. It helps me better understand so many things." Gallen breathed. "About you. About Sol. Even about myself."

A blush rushed to her cheeks as Gallen's hand gently pressed against her own. She halted her fidgeting.

"I would love to know more," he continued, squeezing her hand slightly. Though she refused to meet his eyes, she could feel the expectant look. She laughed; she could not help herself. The scene in this picturesque clearing was almost comical: lying near a handsome warrior, resting upon a mighty pegasus, and sharing intimate details of her life. Neither Tress nor her sisters would believe it.

"I do not jest!" He nudged her arm with his elbow. "You said you make decisions for those you care for..."

She paused. "Yes?"

It was Gallen's turn to chuckle a bit. "Well, who are they?"

She sighed. She did not share too much about her life with the other Flyers. Not even with Tress or Ranor. Just the bare minimum, enough for them to know she was more than a ghost. So why was she so tempted to completely bare her soul to this man?

"I am the eldest of ten children." She paused, as if this information were enough to garner judgment. Yet his face lacked the usual gasps or side glances when others learned of her family. Instead, he continued to look at the stars, unfazed. Or maybe just willing to listen.

More confidently, she continued. "My father knew I would be great. He would wake me before the morning stars and tell me over and over how much I needed to be strongest version of myself. For him, for my mother. Mostly for my siblings."

Gallen's thumb slowly rubbed her hand, a kind gesture.

"When my family learned of the potential to become a Flyer, they were overjoyed. We did not have much when I was a child. Yet, hopefully, if I became great, they would be taken care of."

Speaking the words aloud, she was almost amused. A dark sort of comedy in which she found herself the central character. Of course, she loved her family. Or at least, she knew she should love them. Regardless, each payment she received, each contact she made or jewel she obtained, she sent back to that small town to the west.

Gallen considered her words carefully, expressing a verbal "hmmm" of contemplation. "No person should be forced to bear that burden," he began, still looking at the stars, their reflection twinkling in his eyes. "You should find who you wish to be, not to be great but to be satisfied. To be whole."

The words took a moment to sink in before Malinar could truly appreciate them. No person had said something so counter to what she internalized her entire life. Most Night Flyer recruits wanted to rise through the ranks. To become a part of the elite group closest to Alcor and his friends. She assumed the goal was shared by all. What else could make her whole?

Almost sensing her disbelief, Gallen restated, "I believe every person in the realms has greatness within them. Yet, if they are not happy with who they are, that greatness is dimmed."

He seemed so confident in his words, so sure.

"Also, who determines one's greatness? Who can define what makes a person 'great'?" Gallen waved his free hand in the air for emphasis, the other remaining in Malinar's.

"What I am attempting to say is," he continued, growing flustered, as if wanting to say a million thoughts at once, "every person can be great in their own way. Yet, I believe that it does not matter, their greatness, if they cannot enjoy it. You understand?"

"I believe I do." Malinar sighed. "No person has voiced such an idea. Not to me, anyway."

Her response prompted Gallen to rip his gaze from the sky, concern lining his brow.

"I hope you never believe that you are anything less than great, Malinar." His words were gentle and low and sweet. "I barely know you, yet I already know that you are far more valuable than a hundred 'great' persons."

Gallen pulled her hand closer as he looked into her eyes. Their heads moved up and down with Cotton's breath.

Her thoughts ran wild. Certainly, this was a bout of chivalry, of Gallen saying nice words to ensure Malinar would stay the course. It was what Alcor would do, surely.

Gallen replied again, almost as if knowing her doubts, "I do believe it."

Redness tinged her cheeks, and she nodded against Cotton's surprisingly smooth fur.

"Perhaps on another night I may share with you a part of my story." Gallen gave her hand a last squeeze before rising to his feet. "Though, as an only child, I am certain it is nothing compared to the excitement of a full household." He began walking toward the tents, his steps slow as if waiting for her response.

"I would like that," Malinar said softly, almost to herself.

She thought he had not heard her until his smooth voice called over his shoulder, "then we shall meet again on another sleepless night."

He walked to the fabric flap of his tent and disappeared.

LAYING IN HER BLANKETS, Malinar felt more restless than when she stalked through the camp. Though now, the insomnia was not due to nervousness or fear but a sort of eager anticipation.

How could Gallen, the son of a lady and the right hand of the king, want to know more about her? The daughter of a nameless citizen. The eldest of a host of children with little prospects and even fewer connections. The warrior in her twenty-second year, with little experience in both warfare and life and romance.

Perhaps he was being kind. Kindness is important in leadership. Malinar's book said as much numerous times. Yet, there was such a transparency, a vulnerability that could not be mere kindness.

He treated her like a friend. Like an equal.

Guilt stabbed Malinar's heart. While she cared for Ranor, she truly did, she could never claim to have loved him. Not in the way he claimed to love her.

And Gallen, he truly loved Sol. Malinar saw the depths of sorrow behind his eyes when he admitted his conflicted feelings. Though he claimed to only love Sol's former self, she could see hope in his features. Hope that this quest was successful. Or maybe hope that he could fall in love with this new version of who Sol was.

Malinar could understand falling in love with this Sol.

She was genuine and kind and thoughtful. She sought not only who people were or what they did, but their dreams, their fears, their most precious moments. As a woman raised to believe that a person's worth was dependent upon their position, it was interesting to see Sol toss a career to the wayside to record histories. To invest in a community. To dedicate one's future to the immortalizing the past.

She tugged a blanket over her side and pulled the worn pages of her book toward her, hoping the stories of formidable, ferocious, and decisive women could convince her mind to rest.

Though the stories sparked more curiosity about who Sol had chosen to be. She barely knew *Sol the Warrior*. That Sol appeared inaccessible. Stern. Driven. Intimidating.

This Sol—the Sol sleeping mere feet away—was almost too open. Too compassionate. Still extraordinarily driven, yet to a different end. Not for glory or success. But to aid others, those in the present and in the future.

In the same breath, Sol exemplified all the characteristics that Malinar despised. Sol's pedigree. Her talent. Her thoughtlessness and ignorance and pride and—

"But that was the *old* Sol," she scolded herself quietly.

Would the new Sol make a rash decision, a selfish decision, to put others at risk as the old Sol did? Would she go off on her own and leave her companions behind to merely wonder and plan for her rescue? Would she look at the face of a dead warrior and feel nothing?

The line of questioning in itself was selfish, Malinar understood this. Yet, it was so tempting. So tempting to hate Sol for killing Ranor, when it was herself she should blame. Not for his demise but for his shame.

It was not Sol who chose Ranor for his position. It was not Sol who remained coupled for her benefit. And it was not Sol who stayed with him despite knowing the emptiness of their future. Despite preparing to break his besotted heart. Despite her selfish indifference.

No. That was not Sol at all.

Malinar rolled her eyes at the realization that was now too clear to ignore: She could no longer hate Sol.

8

Sol

The following morning took Sol by surprise. She had almost forgotten that the sky lightened in the day, although the morning light at the edge of the realm was still rather dim. The fading stars forced her to action, slowly folding the silver fabrics of her tent and placing them gingerly into bags across Kinsle's back.

The pegasus appeared well-rested and well-fed—a slight tinge of turquoise lined his light grey lips. Sol giggled when she saw the coloring on her friend's snout.

"Would you like to pack some for the remaining journey?"

Though said in jest, she pulled a few handfuls of the strangely-colored grass from the soil and stuffed them with the fabrics.

"Quite considerate."

The smooth voice caused Sol's heart to skip a beat as Gallen walked toward them. Cotton had been prepared to leave long before Malinar and Sol readied their own steeds.

"Kinsle enjoys a treat now and again." Sol gently petted the horse's head as he leaned into her touch.

Gallen smiled. "He's fortunate to have such a thoughtful rider. Do not forget to feed yourself this morning," he said with a smirk before plopping a few berries in his mouth.

"I will enjoy these very delicious preserves!" Sol noted confidently as she pulled a jar from one of Kinsle's packs.

Gallen chuckled softly then turned to survey the broken camp, checking for items left behind or evidence of their presence in the clearing. Though Gallen appeared upbeat, Sol still could not help but worry about the mysterious words she said to him in Celestra, the barrier that kept them apart. Between bites of food, Sol continued preparing Kinsle for another long day of travel, eager for any distraction. The group planned to fly from border to border, across the entirety of the Valley Realm in one day.

Malinar pulled the final strap tight around Storm's back. She appeared slightly better than the night prior. Her purple eyes were not surrounded by red and the bags beneath her lids were less puffy. The warrior emerged from the night far more graceful and alert, her light skin basking in the sun's rays as she huddled close to Storm.

"Did you rest well, Malinar?" Sol asked.

Sol's daily attempt at friendship lingered in the air before Gallen offered another question: "Will you be able to make the full day's trip?"

This question brought her to attention. "Of course!" She straightened her spine and focused on the sky.

Gallen only nodded as he climbed atop Cotton's velvety back. "Be sure to eat before you fly."

Malinar nodded, pulling a bit of wrapped fish from her satchel.

Sol looked at the tips of her brown boots, knowing that the next few hours would be spent replaying her words to Malinar over and over in her mind. Perhaps she could conjure a question that would elicit a more positive response. There must be something.

~

As the journey continued, the pegasi and their riders grew more comfortable with the flight. Even Malinar looked tranquil on Storm's back. The winged beasts pulled closer together, and Sol and Gallen and Malinar shifted positions as they raced through the air. Sol found herself flying not far behind Malinar and soon noticed the young Flyer's mannerisms as the sky grew lighter. Her posture was naturally impeccable, chin high and chest forward. Every so often she hunched her shoulders forward to stretch or whisper into Storm's ear before returning to her stoic state. Whenever the winds grew rough, she shivered rapidly, attempting to maintain her composure. The sharp lines of her hair swished left and right as the flight continued on and on.

Another constant from Malinar was a whistling that floated through the air as the group forged ahead. When they flew in the darkness before, Sol assumed it was the winds themselves who sang. However, in the light she could see Malinar's shoulders move slightly up and down with each whistling tune. It was mesmerizing, like the calming sound of the ocean just after a storm. It dulled the pain of leaving home, leaving Alcor and Asha and Piré ever so slightly.

As the cool air of the Star Realm dissipated and the sun in all its glory rose to dominance in the sky, Sol could hardly keep her eyes from squinting. She almost forgot its heat and the blinding brightness that followed its arrival. The silver cape wrapping her shoulders became burdensome, her hair damp with sweat. She immediately missed the moon and the stars and the shadows in the sky. But it did feel satisfying to have one leg of the journey complete. One realm left for another.

The thrum of Kinsle's wings soothed Sol's worries. Malinar's whistling mingled with the warm gusts of wind delightfully. Toward the end of the flight, her heart lightened, her head cleared, and her body eased into the pegasus.

Sol reexamined each of her previous words with Malinar—well *to* Malinar. Perhaps her approach with Malinar was too familiar, too casual. It was possible the young Flyer wished for more formal discussions, or at least more direct than one's sleep. If only Malinar approached Sol as she did Gallen. The two appeared to have such a natural rapport. Nothing forced. Nothing overthought. Sol considered other options to try when the group stopped, filing away two or three alternative questions to ask as she rolled the emerald ring around her finger. She wished Malinar would face the situation between them, even negatively. That she would yell or scream maybe even cry. Something to indicate that Malinar was at least dealing with her hateful feelings toward Sol.

During their first stop, Malinar insisted upon taking a nap rather than converse. Gallen seemed more focused on fishing than chatting, gathering another load of food to keep for the day ahead. Before Sol realized, he prepared the pegasi to fly again.

The second stop yielded no words of note. The three built a fire and ate some of Gallen's catch. Though Sol did not drum up the courage to share her thoughts directly, she noticed a softness in Malinar that was lacking before. It gave her hope to see the younger flyer gain her footing on this important quest; to see that the pressures in the Star Realm dissipated as they strayed farther and farther from home. When the food was eaten and silence spent, the three swiftly joined the clouds once more.

So strange the clouds appeared from so high, like pillowy platforms of white and pink and blue. With Kinsle steady and the wind calm, Sol reached her hand out toward the soft forms, passing through the air like a goddess of the skies. Pastel colors swam around them, caressing the hooves of the pegasi as they ran. It almost forced her to forget her panic, forget the weapon that they sought, forget it all.

After a longer stretch of flight, Gallen looked back at them and pointed his arm downward before leading Cotton toward the ground. The women followed, their pegasi swooping beneath the clouds and near the realm below.

The valleys were magnificent. All that Sol knew of this realm she learned from one of Asha's romance novels. Between the scenes of fiery love, the characters described colorful fields of grass and grains, each estate separated by thin brick walls. From a bird's-eye view, Sol could see the sharp variants in color that marked the estates in the realm. Over the centuries ladies and lords altered the textures and shades of the ground to mark their territory, leaving a wondrous mixture of yellows and oranges and greens that created a patchwork quilt throughout the realm and linked several villages of wood and brick.

Gallen led them past several squares of yellow and orange before settling Cotton's hooves just outside a village of wooden lodges. Sol could feel Kinsle's muscles relax as they landed.

"We must be vigilant." He patted Cotton's mane and led them toward the entrance to the village. "The Valley may declare its allegiance to Alcor, yet there are dissidents in any place beyond our borders."

Sol looked at the stark silver coat wrapped around her shoulders, barely disguising the shimmering red moth embroidered boldly at the center of her Night Flyer uniform.

"I did not consider bringing a disguise," she noted as Malinar looked down at her own uniform.

Gallen laughed heartily, his baritone voice practically melodic. "Sol, there is no disguising when you arrive. Your presence alone demands attention. You are the brightest of all stars."

His words were matter-of-fact, spoken in a seeming moment of transparency. Sol could feel the blush creeping along her neck toward her cheeks as he turned and continued walking. Malinar rolled her eyes before following behind him, Storm shadowing her steps.

"Have your knives at the ready—that is all I ask. Never relax when we are in public. Always aware, yes?" Gallen strode ahead.

Kinsle nudged Sol slightly with his nose and Sol, still speechless from the compliment, stumbled forward to catch up with the others. She muttered a thank-you under her breath to her loyal pegasus.

Several enormous buildings made of large tree trunks dominated the skyline, surrounded by slightly smaller wooden structures. As the three Flyers walked closer, the details of each building came into focus. The wooden planks were etched with intricate designs and words. The massive dwellings loomed high above Sol as she walked. Like an insect scurrying beside flowers or babes playing in towering forests of old. Even the entryways rose many feet above her head, built for beings far taller and wider.

Though, the village itself appeared off. Not like the descriptions Sol read. The streets were not filled with merchants nor musicians nor families. Rather, each individual held a weapon—a sword, a bow, a spear. The buildings once meant for trade were now used for storing armor; the arena once meant for performance now used for forging chainmail. The ongoing war touched all corners, and even in the shadows Sol could see posters pasted to wooden walls reading: *Come all who are able. Come fight for your King.*

The squabbles she had between Malinar and Gallen appeared so small when Sol remembered the stakes of this journey, the importance of this knowledge. A sober reminder. There were so many things beyond their control, so much evil for which they remained powerless against. With such realities before them, how could they possibly remain at odds? They were all on the same side, after all. Sol hoped her companions wished the same.

After walking only a few minutes, a large man on the side of the path waved wildly for their attention.

"Gallen! The horses are more impressive than Alcor intimated!"

His booming voice reminded Sol of her brother, and his wide, mischievous grin certainly mirrored Alcor's demeanor.

Gallen hastened to meet him, reaching up to grasp the man's arm in his own in greeting. "Mawl! The Valley is beautiful this time of year."

Standing near Mawl, Gallen looked like a child. Mawl stood a full foot taller than Gallen, with broad shoulders and dark brown skin. His eyes shone an astonishing white as they frantically looked from Gallen to Cotton to Storm to Kinsle. When his gaze found Sol, his eyes grew wide, and he immediately threw his arm forward while bowing his head low. "Warrior Sol. An honor."

Sol grinned and nodded. "An honor to meet you as well."

The large man flashed his teeth at this, his smile wide and inviting. He returned his hands to his side, pulling on the thin fabric of his sleeveless tunic as the muscles in his arms glistened in the setting sunlight.

"I have prepared stalls for the winged ones and rooms for you three." Mawl wiped a bead of sweat from his bald head, his muscles flexing as he reached up.

Gallen nodded, the loose tendrils of his windswept hair landing briefly over his gold eyes before he pushed them aside. Malinar sighed at the mention of a room, clearly spent from her time in the sky. Noticing her weariness, Sol reached for Storm's reins.

"If you would like, I can settle the pegasi in their home." Sol smiled slightly. "Mawl, is there a place to clean before we sully your clean beds?"

The large man howled in laughter, a sound that seemed to shake the earth beneath them. "Of course, Warrior. A wooden tub is in each room. Ask ahead for warm water."

Malinar looked at Sol and offered a brief, "thank you," before rushing toward the wooden inn.

When Sol successfully grasped the reins of each pegasus, she marveled at those words. Such a simple sentiment, *thank you*. Yet, to Sol, the statement offered her something deeper. Perhaps Malinar, too, realized their differences paled within the context of the broader conflict. Perhaps she, too, wished to quell any tension that remained within their control.

～

Mawl graciously prepared two rooms for the Flyers to stay for the evening. Malinar and Sol in one and Gallen in the other. Gallen encouraged Sol to rest and bathe while he discussed matters with Mawl. The two appeared to be quite close. Mawl slammed a large hand on Gallen's back before inviting him to eat at a round table at the corner of the common room.

"Come along, young buck! What did your mother tell you under the water?"

The voices faded into the background as Sol turned the doorknob of her shared quarters. Like everything in the building, the room was large. The bed looked double the size of her normal sleeping blankets and was raised a few feet off the ground. On each side were two large tables meant for books or water or other trinkets. Also like the rest of the inn, the room was built from robust panels of wood in varying shades of brown. A sizable window offered Sol a glimpse at the open stalls where Kinsle's nose sniffed the air. Across the room, hidden by a screen of linen and bamboo, Sol could see the silhouette of a bathtub and a woman inside.

Clearing her throat, Sol turned to see an impressive amount of sunshine from the warbled glass.

"Malinar? It is Sol." She called over her shoulder, waiting for a few moments before continuing, "it appears we are sharing quarters, if that suits you. If not, I am certain we can make a different arrangement."

Nerves rushed through Sol's body, a tingling sensation pricking her skin. She did not want to feel Malinar's rejection, not after hearing the softness of a "thank you." She certainly did not want to ruin any headway she may have gained.

She stared outside the absurdly large window, gazing at the elegantly etched wooden panels that framed the glass as she strained to hear a response. She wondered if there could ever be a way Malinar would forgive her. If they could ever truly enjoy friendship.

Awaiting Malinar's voice from the other side of the panels, Sol examined the arches. A story emerged within the etchings. Fields of wheat surrounded hills on both sides of the windows. A farmer, toiled with a scythe in hand, working the wheat with experienced precision. On the top panel, a bright sun blinded the farmer, forcing him to abandon his craft. In the next scene, the sun concedes its power to the moon who basks the farmer in an ethereal glow. And from the beams of moonlight, a woman appears, stepping from the stars to the earth to assist the man in his labors. In the final scene, she holds the scythe, smiling as the man raises his hands to the moon, a thanks for all that was granted to him. The story touched something in Sol, a longing for the same provision. Wishing that she too could be gifted the moon in her times of turmoil.

Minutes passed in forlorn stillness, the silence Sol had grown accustomed to in their days of travel. Just as she abandoned hope, determined to request another arrangement from Gallen, even if it meant sleeping in her tent for the night, Sol heard the water slosh in the tub behind the screen. A brief look over her shoulder confirmed the petite shadow of Malinar stepping carefully on the wooden floor.

"No need to alter the plans." Her voice smoothly floated over the barrier between them.

Sol let out a deep sigh of relief, staring at the window once again.

"Do you need privacy? I can step out while you prepare for the night—"

"Please. Stay." Malinar stepped forward, each footstep joined with drips of water.

Sol sensed her moving closer and closer, the water drip, drip, dripping on the wood beneath her. A sudden impulse consumed Sol as she listened to the trickling upon the floor; an urge to turn and see Malinar standing, drying her body, slipping on one of the nightgowns Mawl provided for them both. An unexpected desire, one Sol refused to indulge. Instead, she stared and stared and stared at the couple in the windowpane, the etched wood almost swirling together as she desperately refused temptation.

She was shaken out of this downward spiral with a touch of Malinar's hand on her shoulder. Jumping back, she heard a genuine giggle from her travel companion. The sound was surreal and fantastic, so unfamiliar and promising. Turning her head toward the smaller Flyer, Sol thought perhaps the weeks of apologies softened the Malinar's sharpness towards her. She hoped at least.

"Apologies. It was not my intent to startle." Malinar folded her arms over her chest, the thin cotton of the nightgown crinkling slightly. Sol nearly fainted. *Two apologies within the hour?* "You seem completely lost in thought. Three days of flight is too arduous for the legendary Sol?"

Well, perhaps they were adversaries still.

Sol wrinkled her nose and attempted to ease the tension with a laugh. Malinar seemed to notice the awkwardness in her response, as her next words were far softer, gentler. "The bath was refreshing. I am certain changing the water will take little time at all."

Before Sol could agree, a knock rang through the room. Two tall, heavyset women opened the door, assessing the scene before moving toward the tub. As Malinar presumed, changing the water took mere minutes, the women adept at the task. Grunting for the Flyers to move, the women worked swiftly. Their strong arms dragged the wooden tub to the window, dumped the contents, then brought warm buckets of clean water for Sol to enjoy. With a final bow, the women left.

"Do *you* need privacy?" Malinar's words, an echo of Sol's earlier query, were not in her usual tone, not malicious or sarcastic. The genuine care took Sol aback.

Sol shook her head. "I actually do not wish to be alone, if that is alright."

She walked toward the screen, stepping behind the wood and cloth that blocked the bath from the rest of the room. Sol could see Malinar's silhouette slowly walk to the bed before jumping to sit atop the sheets.

Sol stripped the Night Flyers clothing from her body and threw it to the ground with a soft thud. Wringing her hands together, she considered removing the ring from her finger but could not stand the notion of parting with it for even the briefest moment. Naked, a film of grime coated her arms and legs, the smell of dirt and sweat once hidden beneath the blue tunic now wafting through the air. She wrinkled her nose at her own stench, a condition that oft accompanied a warrior's quest. As she dipped her feet into the warm water, calm radiated throughout her body. It was a glorious feeling. The stress of the journey and the fear of an unknown weapon mixed with the personal anxiety over what she said to Gallen in the Night Streets and the reality that she may never reach the magic of the Ice Realm caverns to create a toxic concoction.

She wished Asha were here. Asha always knew either what to do or at least what to say.

Sol dunked her head beneath the water, warm suds trickling down the sides of her face as she rose to a seated position.

"Do you ever feel afraid?" Malinar sounded meek, completely different from anything Sol had experienced from the young woman. It took her a bit to process the words, to recalibrate to such a drastic shift.

"Afraid of what?" Sol rubbed the back of her neck, soap lathering splendidly between her fingers.

Malinar breathed in deeply. "Afraid we may fail? Afraid to step into your past? Afraid to return to the Ice Realm? Afraid…

afraid..." She paused, the weight of her words like a rock in her throat. "Afraid that we may succeed? Afraid that you may despise who you were? Who you become?"

The questions sent Sol into another spiral. Of course, this was a possibility she considered. Countless were the nights where she lay awake thinking through these very possibilities. Fearing who she was. Fearing who she could be. Fearing she would hate the memories that reappeared.

However, there were so many things she needed to know. So many uncertainties she needed resolved.

Sol ran her hands over the surface of the bath, focusing her vision on the ripples that formed from her touch, the glimmer of her ring seemingly at home in the water. "I live in a constant state of worry. Worrying over what may be. Worrying over what may never be. Worrying over being alone. Worrying over having no time to myself."

She saw Malinar's shadow through the screen, her body resting comfortably on the large bed. Listening. Empathizing.

"What I worry of most, though..." Her heart thrummed in her chest, unsure of whether to divulge her largest shortcomings, her consistent struggles, with Malinar of all people. Yet, there was a whisper that helped soothe the anxiety, a calmness that emerged just knowing she was there listening, caring. "I worry that I may let others down. I do not care if I fail to gain what I want. I worry that my failure will irreparably impact my family, my friends."

Tears fell from her cheeks, plopping into the water. With each drop, she felt lighter, as if sharing such notions restored her. It was cathartic, an outpouring of the emotions she left stowed away in the shadows of her heart. There was an ease between Sol and Malinar as they spoke between the screen. An ease that was impossibly reassuring. This woman who supposedly hated her now spoke as a friend, a confidante. Why did she feel so comfortable, so raw, so...herself?

"I understand," Malinar stated, her words compassionate.

Sol's eyebrows raised. *Who was this woman?* She thought incredulously, *How did two nights in the wilderness encourage such empathy?*

"I feel similarly," Malinar admitted, shifting her body slightly to face the screen. "It is difficult to constantly monitor others' expectations in hopes that you exceed them. It is an albatross, such a terrible weight that can consume you, body and soul."

Sol's tears continued, growing violent and difficult to mask, the sniffles surely loud enough for Malinar to hear. Self-conscious, Sol reached for the edge of the tub and pulled herself up. She looked desperately for fabric to dry her body before slipping the nightgown over her head.

When she emerged from behind the screen, Malinar rested comfortably on her side, facing the window. Whether her intention, it provided Sol the space she needed to process her dramatic reaction.

Sol walked to the other side of the large bed and buried herself into the sheets, tears still streaming down her face. She attempted to stifle sobs and calm her nerves, though she could hardly stop her shoulders from shaking. Lying between Malinar and their window, Sol should have felt far more embarrassed, far more invested in maintaining the countenance of a leader, the sister of a king, a warrior of the Star Realm. But she did not.

Why was she crying? Why did she care? Why did Malinar make her feel so nervous yet simultaneously calm?

She turned the ring over and over and over around her finger, clutching to the metal as if it could provide the answers to her confusion. The ring was like a lifeline. Sol had no reason to feel such a way, but it was as if the ring called to her. A remnant of something deeper. She pulled her hands close to her chest as her quiet tears continued pouring over her cheeks.

The two lay there a while, the serene silence a sanctuary between them as Sol cried. Rather than nervousness or indignity or shame, lying in the wide bed with Malinar, all Sol felt was freedom.

9

Gallen

Mawl was an old friend, and Gallen always loved visiting his cozy home. Importantly, the Valley Realm host was a loyal supporter of Alcor and would sacrifice anything to see him vanquish the many evils of the Nine Realms. The people of the valley were well-acquainted with the strife that accompanied exploitation. As the most naturally productive of Nourels, other realms consistently poached their resources with little care of reprimand. Some believed looting was an unfortunate fact of life, while others, like Mawl, believed thieves should be held accountable. That the old ways should die and a new era arise.

For Alcor, Mawl was a trusted manager of the growing army soon to be stationed in the valley. For Gallen, he was an asset for accurate information in the central realms. His charismatic and intrusive nature made it possible to develop key connections throughout the surrounding realms. People trusted Mawl and Mawl trusted Gallen. The partnership was useful and honest.

Stepping into the large entryway, Gallen rushed toward a seating area with tea and food prepared for the expected travelers. His boots clicked on the wooden floors as he hastened toward sustenance, unaware of his hunger until he smelled the chicken, bread, and greens prepared. He quickly hopped onto a chair and began scooping food into his mouth. Delicious, as always. The Valley Realm always had the freshest foods and knew the most delectable recipes. He could never admit such to his mother, but he far preferred the warm taste of fresh bread to anything else he ate at home.

That is certainly a discussion for another day, Gallen thought as he took another bite of meat. Mawl lumbered toward him, swiping a piece of bread before sitting on the bench across from Gallen.

The room was prodigious to Gallen's standards, yet for the height of those in this realm, it was modest, yet was constantly filled with people. Mawl was known as a great host, someone who enjoyed the company of others and did not discriminate against those who needed a place to rest their head. As the two sat at their corner table, people continuously filed in and out of the hallways and entrances. Some brought food and drinks to the various visitors. Others tidied rooms for wayward travelers. Gallen, Sol, and Malinar fit right in with the crowds of people from bordering realms. No one would ask any questions about three travelers in a home for wanderers.

"Ah, my friend. I nearly forgot!" Gallen wiped his mouth and reached into his satchel.

He placed an embroidered patch on the wooden table between them, grinning as he watched Mawl look at the piece, eyes glimmering with appreciation.

"My first moth," he whispered, folding the fabric carefully before stuffing it in his pocket, "I shall keep it close, of course."

Gallen nodded, the hours spent were well worth it.

Mawl leaned in. "Any recent reports?" He was consistently direct, ideal for an informant.

Gallen took a moment to swallow his food, then sipped the cup of tea to wash down the meal. "A weapon has emerged. Ocean informants seem to believe it originated in the Desert Realm, but we cannot be certain. Especially considering I have not seen the beast with my own eyes. It is a magic born of fire and supposedly controlled by the enemy."

Gallen shook his head. This newest wrinkle in this war was stressful. He wished he knew more while also wishing he could be blissfully ignorant regarding such perils. And, while he recognized its comparative unimportance, he could not help but be constantly concerned by the situation with Sol.

Mawl appeared contemplative yet calm. "I will reach out to our allies throughout the realm and see if there have been unusual sightings."

Nodding, Gallen rattled off the few details he knew of the weapon: It emerged in the sky, it controlled fire and could destroy any living being in its path, it was far larger than any beast that flew, and it threatened their success.

"Have you heard word of anything, friend?" Gallen barely finished the final word before scooping another spoonful of veggies in his mouth.

Mawl's strong jaw clenched slightly, remaining silent for a moment as a man dropped off two glasses of mulled wine for them to enjoy.

When the server fell out of earshot, Mawl returned to the conversation at hand. "There are rumors around these parts. Rumors that spark new fears amongst those who've wavered in their support. Rumors of your warrior companion."

Gallen reached for a glass of mulled wine nonchalantly, unsure of the damage such rumors could unleash on Alcor's cause.

Noting the nonreaction, Mawl continued, his typically booming voice muted slightly, "Warrior Sol. She is not unwell, is she?" His voice cracked in pain at the mere thought of her injury.

"She is more than well, my friend!" Gallen sipped the wine

cooly. "She wanted to be a part of this important aspect of the war. She wants to find this weapon and seeks a way to work around it, perhaps destroy it."

Of course, she only realized the existence of the weapon after their quest commenced, yet Gallen was not lying. Not technically. None of the allies in other realms knew of Sol's condition, of her forgetting. Even those who attended Rostair's damned ball were told to believe otherwise. And Alcor wanted the information to remain within the confines of only a reliable few. Not even his own mother knew of Sol's memory loss and her shift to Keeper of Records. The Night Flyers knew that if questions regarding her unusual behavior left the Star Realm, they could play it off as some sort of strategic information gathering. Sol was always known for her unorthodox way of planning, and this would fall in line with that reputation. However, the concept of an ill warrior. An ill leader. That was dangerous.

Ladies. Warriors. Kings. They were figures that united entire realms to their cause. Without Sol, a woman who represented a light in the darkness of the world, the support of many would waver. Gallen caught only bits of Piré's story and, even from the little he knew, he could piece together how deeply the Keepers of Endoneth loved Sol as an ideal.

Even if she would never fight again in this life, Sol needed to remain a figure of intelligence and might and optimism.

Gallen took another long sip from his glass. "Do not fret, friend. Sol will continue to represent the power of the Star Realm and the hope of Alcor. For King and Sol."

"For King and Sol," Mawl breathed, clearly relieved.

Mawl reached between them for his own glass of wine, draining its contents in one swig. He slammed the cup on the table, his body shuddering as the alcohol moved through him, and emitted a satisfied belch.

The two men talked for hours that night—from more serious reflections on the current state of the realms to light gossip about common acquaintances. As each glass emptied, a replacement was set before them by one of the many people milling about the room. With each new glass, the two became less concerned about serious matters and instead laughed about the joys of the world, as two friends often do.

When the room itself finally quieted—the various travelers and locals heading to their respective rooms—Gallen stood and bid his friend good night.

∼

Rather than immediately seeking comfort in the room prepared for him, Gallen walked to the stables. He needed to see to it that Cotton received proper care. The pegasus was a loyal steed and, while small, was valiant. Gallen fell in love with her wings as soon as he set eyes on her on the roof of Endoneth the night of their grand escape. While the other pegasi had traditional colors marking their coats and wings, Cotton was complex. He held a kinship with her that he could not fully explain.

When he reached Cotton's stall, the pegasus neighed joyfully, the pastel metallic of her wings fluttering open then closed. He guided her toward the main path, walking slowly through the sleeping village. The Valley Realm itself was far smaller than the Star Realm, an amalgamation of tiny villages connected by miles and miles of fertile farming land. In fact, the three central realms combined—Valley, Sun, and High—were still smaller than any other realm in Nourels.

Gallen always appreciated venturing to these regions during his quests as Star Realm ambassador. While all three existed in a symbiotic state, each realm providing essential needs for the other two, the people were so vastly different. Those in the Sun Realm valued beauty and pageantry above all else. The buildings there sparkled in the brightness of the blazing sunlight, the specks of gold and jeweled embellishments seen from miles away as if by magic. Their leaders were well-versed orators, skilled in speaking to others and forging deep-rooted alliances, deals, and plans. The leaders of the three sister cities, the major metropolitan areas of the region, provided diplomacy. Through their many connections, the lords and ladies of the Sun Realm provided building materials, weapons, and other essentials for their neighboring realms.

The High Realm provided security as its main contribution. Housing the most impressive training yards and masters of warfare, the armies and assassins protect those in the Sun and Valley Realms. A common jest amongst the central realms was that no person was truly a native of the High Realm, with a reputation that boasted diversity. Another was that only certain folk had the privilege of calling themselves so. Only those with the proper permissions could enter. Gallen never tired of the famed marble buildings of the High Realm when he received the honor.

Settled between the massive twin mountain ranges called the "Protectors," those in the Valley Realm were arguably the most essential to the trio. Their people, while far meeker and simpler than their counterparts, provided sustenance. The land was an ideal location to grow and harvest an assortment of grains and fruits and vegetables.

Gallen smiled as he thought of those who called this beautiful land home. Holding Cotton's reins, he guided her through the dirt paths of the village, passing a mixture of lodges, tents, and stone dwellings. The people of the Valley were resilient. And he valued resilience.

The people would certainly need such resilience now. Gallen's heart fell as he saw the evidence of what was to come. The outlines of tents to be constructed, the posters plastered along the street calling for refugees to flee south, the lack of music and bustle and joy. He missed that element of this place, the joy. After this war, that would likely take decades to return.

The man and his horse walked the length of the village and back before heading toward a small patch of grass near Mawl's hostel home. It was the perfect place to sit and stargaze, and Gallen eagerly partook, resting atop the soft soil. Cotton knelt by her rider, enjoying the peaceful silence outside of the crowded stable. She stretched her wings wide before tucking them by her side, providing Gallen the perfect place to rest against. The two looked idyllic. Cotton's pastel mane stood out against the dark night and Gallen's blue skin blended in beautifully with her yellow fur. The stars twinkled above them, reminding Gallen of his duty to his realm, his people, his king.

"They look different from here, do you not agree?" Gallen gently laid his head on Cotton's side. "The Star Realm is perfect in all places for stargazing, yet our city is the ideal. The farther from Celestra, the more vague the stars appear."

Cotton whinnied in response, then laid her head on the cool grass as Gallen continued, "what if this is a mistake, bringing these two warriors on a dangerous and unknown mission? They both trust me. And I..." He contemplated his intensifying affection for them both. Sol and Malinar, so different yet beautiful in their own ways. "I appreciate them both."

Cotton huffed at this notion, clearly hearing the hesitation in Gallen's tone.

"Well, it is true!" Gallen returned his attention to the stars. "They are both precious to me. I do not wish to place them in harm's way."

This was the case, in fact. Although they had only traveled a few days, the openness Gallen experienced with Sol and Malinar was akin to his trust in Alcor. Appreciation was the appropriate term for a word he could not possibly place yet.

Rather than question the extent of his feelings, Gallen looked at the stars. The constellations were always something Alcor studied; he knew the various positions of planets and moons. Yet, to Gallen, they were beautiful mysteries, songs sung in another language. Empty vessels for his many ideas and stories and dreams. At times, the dreams were optimistic, filled with intention.

Yet, as he leaned into Cotton's comforting presence, lifting his eyes upward, he could not envision a pleasant dream.

He could not completely verbalize what pained him. Perhaps it was the many struggles that contributed to his insomnia. His desire to please Alcor or his mother. The fear of the mysterious and powerful creature. His consistent gravitation toward Sol who likely wanted nothing but peace. The confusion of his growing friendship with Malinar. The guilt that racked his chest as he remembered the war being fought, the soldiers being slaughtered, the innocents being cast aside.

Despondent as Gallen was, he knew it would help no one to succumb to the aching in his soul. He found himself lying in the grass for hours looking at the stars and leaning on his trusted pegasus. While he told himself it was due to the particular beauty of the sky, he knew he was waiting for someone. Hoping that someone might wander out of Mawl's home.

Wishing that Malinar would join him on another sleepless night.

Or that Sol might help him create a happier story to project into the skies.

10

Malinar

Sol's crying filled the empty air like solemn pleas for support. Each shiver of her shoulders, an appeal. Each whimper, a hesitant request. Malinar remained static, facing the grieving Keeper of Records. She warred internally, uncertain whether to offer comfort or allow the woman to grieve. Now that she was less focused on making Sol her enemy, Malinar saw a person she admired. Her softness. Her aura. Even with Sol's back turned, her beauty filled the room. Sol's dark hair was still dripping from her bath. The water created streaks of transparency down the nightgown clinging to her thick curves.

The sight tugged at Malinar's stomach.

Was this still the woman she blamed for her internal strife? The woman she once refused to speak to? To look toward? To think of?

Yes and no. This was a woman she misjudged or perhaps judged too harshly. A woman more similar to herself than she initially wanted to admit. Someone she could befriend. Someone she could...

The thoughts swirled through her mind as Sol's sobs pushed her shoulders forward and back. Malinar simply lay next to her, wanting to do something, anything to help. Regardless of their recent past, of the decisions she made and the destruction she caused, Sol was still a fellow Flyer. At the end of all things, they both wished to help the people of the realms. Malinar knew that.

She reached a wavering hand toward Sol, her fingertips meeting the bare skin of Sol's shoulders with a satisfying spark. The feeling served as a blessing, the reassurance Malinar needed to continue. She wrapped her arms around Sol's stomach, pulling her flush against Malinar's chest. They remained in this position a while. Sol's sobs became calmer, slower, before dissipating altogether. Even when her last tear fell, Malinar refused to let go.

If a mere hand on her shoulder offered comfort, this soothed even the deepest wounds in Malinar. She immediately numbed to the anxieties of the realms, of their quest, of her hesitant fondness for Gallen, of her confused emotions toward Sol. It all melted away as she held this woman close. As she internalized Sol's pain while simultaneously easing it. As she relished the silken smoothness of her skin or the brush of her curves.

The two women—the warrior and the writer—huddled close together in the bed.

They fell asleep in each other's arms.

THE FOLLOWING MORNING, Malinar awoke still clinging to Sol, the two sharing a blanket on the edge of the bed. She breathed in deeply, the smell of Sol's clean skin filling her lungs as their bodies pressed together. For a moment, Malinar wished they could stay here. Avoid the responsibilities ahead. Ignore the realities of her increasingly complicated relationships.

Thoughts of Sol and Gallen and the time they all still had together made her jump from under the sheets and roll away from Sol's still-sleeping figure.

Malinar looked for her clothes. She saw her boots near the door, yet the tunic and leggings were noticeably missing. Before admitting defeat, Malinar cracked open the door just enough to peek into the common room. There were a few people awake and enjoying warm cups of coffee or tea as the early morning sun shone through the windows. She looked down to see a basket sitting in front of the door. Without thinking, she pushed the door open a bit wider and pulled the basket inside. When she opened the basket lid, the smell of clean linens wafted into the room. She wrapped her hands around the familiar fabric of her uniform and let out a slight sigh of relief.

Malinar pulled the Valley Realm nightgown above her head and replaced it with her navy-blue tunic. The fabric immediately anchored her, setting her mind toward the task at hand: getting to the High Realm.

Malinar prided herself in her ability to compartmentalize and, in this moment, it was a welcome skill. Rather than ruminate on Gallen or Sol or her family or the prospect of failure, she instead creaked the door open and slipped out quietly. She surveyed the common area, filled with tables and chairs of various sizes and colors, and chose a small square table near the far corner. Her stomach growled angrily, begging for attention. Almost immediately, a young man popped into view holding two mugs of liquid.

"Coffee or tea?"

His wide eyes glowed with glee as he offered Malinar her morning brew of choice. She thought for a moment before gesturing to the dark cup of coffee. The man nodded, his tightly wound braids bobbing as he handed her the drink before slinking away to the back of the home.

She breathed deeply, enjoying a serenity that the Valley Realm seemed to provide. Malinar curiously watched several people work throughout the home. The cleaners, waiters, and attendants seemingly cared for the home day and night, yet they were treated like guests when they finished their work. She took another sip. A couple entered the space, settling on a sleek bench nearby. The same young man who provided her cup attended to another traveler, a gruff-looking gnome with pointed ears and a long, purple beard.

The quiet of the morning was a welcome reprieve from the constant concerns that plagued her mind since leaving the Star Realm. A short, stocky woman placed a plate filled with fruit and pastries gently upon the wooden table. Without a word, only a nod, the woman rushed back to the other side of the room, leaving Malinar with only the sweet smell of strawberries. The aroma alone sent her stomach into spins. And the first crunch of a fresh tart consumed her thoughts, pulling her into a world of syrupy goodness.

Just as she reached for a second treat, the door to her room opened wide. Sol appeared far better than she did the night before, her hair combed into a tight braid that pulled any wayward strands from her face, highlighting her round cheeks and bright smile. And, as she scanned the room for a familiar face, Malinar rose to her feet in response, leaving the remaining coffee and food behind.

Sol's smile broadened as Malinar approached. She clutched the hem of her Night Flyer tunic in her hands, fidgeting with the fabric with ink-stained fingertips.

"Malinar, it is lovely to see you in the light of day. I spent some time working…" Her thoughts trailed off as she clutched her hands together. "Would you like to see the pegasi? To prepare for the day ahead?"

Although Malinar's heart pounded at the invitation, she took a moment to appear less eager. She eventually nodded and walked briskly toward the door. Sol followed, her hands still clamped by her sides.

The morning light warmed Malinar's cheeks as she walked outside, the scent of fresh grass and soil accompanying the glorious heat. Though her eyes took some time to adjust to the sun, so very used to the pale blue lights of the Star Realm, she confidently strutted the pathways that connected the disparate dwellings throughout the village. Birds chirped overhead, filling the skies with a sense of promise.

"Thank you for last night." Sol's voice mingled beautifully with the birdsongs.

Malinar was not sure how to respond. It was difficult to reprogram her mind to ignore the hatred she once held for Sol, yet she yearned to be close to her. To trust their future friendship.

"I understand how it feels to be overwhelmed. There are times when I cry for seemingly no reason," Malinar began. "Then there are times when the reasons are too vast to face and the tears help clear the fog."

Unsure if she was making any sense at all, Malinar kept her head low as she spoke, watching her leather boots crunch the soil underfoot.

"The burden of leadership is difficult for any person." Malinar looked up slightly to meet Sol's eyes, shocked at her attentiveness.

The moment seemed to last longer than a mere glance, their legs continuing to move them forward while Malinar lost herself in Sol's blue eyes. The older Flyer broke the tether, looking forward as she spoke again.

"I greatly appreciate you, Malinar. I want you to know this." She sighed deeply before continuing, almost as if considering how honest to be with her companion. "I am unsure how aware you are of my current relationship with Gallen."

This piqued Malinar's attention. Had he spoken of her to Sol?

"He and I are beginning fresh. You are likely more knowledgeable of who we were to each other before than I am. I do not know yet what I want, truly. But I hope to have a friend in you both when we finish this quest, if it is what you desire as well?"

Malinar considered the question, although she knew the answer long before Sol offered the olive branch verbally.

"I have honestly considered this the past few days." Now it was Malinar gauging how honest to be. "I once harbored anger for things beyond your control. However, I now fear I am too tired for hatred."

Sol's shoulders relaxed, clearly satisfied with the trajectory of their conversation.

Emboldened by her ease, Malinar continued. "Do you believe you care for him? Gallen, I mean…"

As the words tumbled out, Malinar hesitated. Sol stopped in her tracks, her hand hovering near her chin as she thought carefully. The question was out, floating between them both like some sort of ghost, or an omen perhaps.

Malinar clarified. "Do you care for him as more than a mere friend?"

The clarification seemed to fluster Malinar further, her heart fluttering in her chest as she waited for Sol.

Had Malinar misread the tension between the three Flyers during their short time together? Perhaps she should have waited. They would have days left together and Malinar may have placed herself in a precarious position—from the tension of hatred to the tension of discomfort. Malinar would far prefer the former.

Yet here they were. There was much left unsaid, yet almost too much being voiced.

Sol looked back down toward Malinar; her eyes were not filled with unease or even self-consciousness. There was a glimmer of something. Joy? Hope? Mischief? Malinar wished she knew her superior better. Wished she could understand her thoughts with just a look. Yet, she waited for Sol to speak before she could breathe once more.

"My heart is conflicted." Sol was earnest, which helped Malinar think a bit clearer. "I feel echoes of my past, but I want those closest to me to care for who I am now. As I further learn who I want to be, I want to surround myself with those who encourage me to not merely mirror my former self but to become confident in who I *could* be."

Sol continued, clearly feeling the same comfort that encouraged Malinar's boldness to first ask the question. "I do care for him. Though I want to be sure it is the present me rather than the past. Does this…am I—?"

Malinar placed a steady hand on Sol's arm. "I understand, friend."

The word friend stuck to Malinar's tongue as if unwelcome there. Not because she hated Sol anymore. Quite the contrary.

As the two women walked slowly toward the pegasi, toward reality, toward Gallen and quests and uncertainty, Malinar tried to understand this feeling. A flurry of something curious. Something sweet.

For the first time since leaving Celestra, she felt eager to fly. To daydream of a new future with people who cared for her as Sol cared for Gallen. As Gallen cared for Sol. As she hoped they may also care for her.

THE FLIGHT from Mawl's home to the High Realm drifted on like a dream. Storm drifted atop fields of clouds, galloping into the sunshine. While the threats of travel remained, Malinar was significantly calmer than she had been thus far on their journey. She leaned into Storm's movements, embracing the title of flyer as she never had before. Throughout the hours in the sky, she oscillated between replaying her discussions with Gallen in her mind and attempting to look over her shoulder to catch a glimpse of Sol's smile. A few times she even felt comfortable enough to glance downward, in utter awe of the vast fields of crops and grazing grounds. When fright threatened to steal her newfound spirit, Malinar stared forward at Gallen's slender build. Each time she did, he seemingly sensed it, looking back with an encouraging smirk.

As the sun set before them, Malinar saw the grassy landscape shift. The lush fields became dark and rocky, completely depleted of plants, trees, or wildlife. The greens, blues, and yellows of the valley grass were overcome by shades of black and grey. Her heart sank. Desolate. Horrific. Utterly lifeless.

In the distance, the barren landscape sat in shadow. Malinar craned her neck upward to see rocks that sat leagues into the sky, hovering in mid-air. Closer and closer the Flyers sprinted. Before them, the High Realm emerged in its glory.

Gallen whistled to Malinar and Sol, waving his hand upward before launching higher into the sky. Storm dashed after their guide, galloping up, up, up until Malinar could finally see what only a privileged few ever had.

Her first time seeing the High Realm was enchanting. Malinar knew of the lore, yet, no story could have prepared Malinar for her first glimpse of this world.

Dozens of islands sparkled in the sky. While the ground below appeared desolate, the realm above was gloriously green. Large bushes of palm leaves and golden roses lined the marble walkways. Large vines of greenery climbed the walls of the white marble buildings. Patches of grass provided training grounds for warriors of all realms, young and old. As Malinar flew above each group, she noticed their discipline. No person looked at the sky as they hovered nearer; instead, each warrior in training focused on their respective tasks.

Sol flew ahead, nodding to Gallen as she passed him. Malinar assumed the shadows of her memories were leading her somewhere safe. She hoped so, at least.

A few warriors took notice as the hooves landed in a grassy yard near a towering marble building. Malinar dismounted, her boots crunching the short blades of green as she surveyed the area. The building itself stood three levels tall; imposing and dignified and brilliant. The home had no glass windows or wooden doors. Instead, rounded squares were drilled into each massive slab of shimmering stone, leaving the inner home open to the fresh air. Each dwelling mirrored this architecture, the arched openings, the polished stone, the sharp corners of the square roofs.

While Malinar gawked, Sol and Gallen began talking as soon as they landed, discussing where this master himself trained and which building would be most important to visit. Gallen pointed ahead, leading as he did so well while Sol wore her usual expression of embarrassed confusion.

They walked forward, pulling their pegasi behind them. Malinar trying to place the fragrance of that swirled around them. Only subtle notes of aromas. Crisp lemongrass. Delicate rose. Stone. Soil. Fountains of fresh water.

She craned her neck up to examine the building more closely. The white marble looked ethereal, as if Malinar sauntered into the heavens. Although she heard no animals—no birds or horses or even insects— running water provided a calming soundscape. Malinar took a few precarious steps forward, reaching for the nearest fountain.

Before her hand touched the glistening marble, an older man walked through the large opening of the building ahead. The man's stature oozed authority. His white, satin robes billowed behind him as he moved briskly toward Gallen and Sol, both of whom stood wide-eyed and tense.

"Master Zelan." Sol spoke with a shallow confidence. She fell to one knee as he approached her, displaying a reverence Malinar had never seen before from the experienced Night Flyer. "We request counsel."

The older man stopped before her, his long beard hanging low and braided into an impressive design below his pointed chin. His head was completely clean of hair or dirt. His visage highlighting the Flyers' own filth.

The world appeared to freeze in time as Sol lowered her head.

Malinar held her breath, nervously fidgeting with the hem of her tunic as the man stalked closer and closer to her friend. Rather than turn Sol away, Zelan grasped her face in his hand, lifting her eyes to his own.

"My child. You are most welcome here."

11

Gallen

While Gallen visited the High Realm on a few occasions, he had never gained an invitation to feast at Master Zelan's table. The honor was presented to a select few, even amongst those who trained in the realm. As a former apprentice—and, according to Asha, one of Zelan's favorite students—Sol's presence afforded them the opportunity. The sight of pegasi alone took Zelan away from his daily responsibilities. And, when Sol came into view, the master immediately requested they join him for a meal.

Within minutes, the pegasi were ushered away, the Flyers shepherded into the Master's abode, and a feast spread before them. Malinar protested as they ripped Storm's reins from her hands, though they assured her of the horse's wellbeing. The realm's warriors would surely care for his charming Cotton in the ways she was due. They better had.

The stone chairs were cold beneath Gallen's leather leggings, the three quietly sipped small glasses of white wine as they waited for Zelan to speak. The old man, seated at the head of the long marble table, looked unapproachable. He had barely spoken, had barely shown expression at all, since the three arrived. He sat on the marble throne, his tanned face stoic and hands clasped in his lap. His yellow eyes held multitudes of knowledge yet revealed nothing. Even Gallen, a warrior trained to interpret the thoughts and motivations of others, could glean nothing from the man's disposition. Master Zelan wore white silk robes that matched the walls and the floors and the furniture The scene gleamed brightly in varied shades of white marble, almost too clean for Gallen's taste.

Before her stay in Endoneth, Sol explained bits and pieces of her life here, allowing Gallen a glimpse into her training. Each aspect of life acted as a lesson. Each child served food, laundered clothing, cut the grass and sheered the bushes. *We learned to put provision above comfort,* Sol once said.

The young children that set several bowls of food onto the table, were no older than seven years. Zelan remained still.

Gallen looked across the table where Malinar and Sol sat close together, whispering to each other as the food appeared before them. He wondered what they discussed. He had not truly spoken to either woman since yesterday and relished in the shock of their closeness. He lifted his hand to hide a smirk that lifted his wind-chapped cheeks as he admired their growing friendship from afar. Their amiability would present a far more positive experience as their journey continued.

Gallen reached toward a plate filled with seeded bread. He locked eyes with Sol and nodded toward their host.

"Master, thank you for your hospitality," she began hesitantly. "We arrived at your doorstep with the hopes of sharing information and perhaps requesting your expertise."

A positive beginning. Gallen looked at the man, his eyes still paradoxically vacant yet brimming with understanding. It must have taken decades to train his mind in this way, to hide his intentions from others so seamlessly. To convey both nothing and everything.

Malinar munched on a forkful of vegetables. Gallen pulled the bread apart, twisting bits between his fingers. Though hungry from a long day of travel, his nervous energy made him nauseous, and each second they awaited Zelan's response, the worse his stomach hurt. Sol seemed to share his sentiment, her plate empty and her hands grasping the edge of the table in anticipation. Malinar's crunching on leafy greens remained the lone sound echoing through the dining hall for quite some time. *Crunch. Crunch. Crunch.*

Each excruciating second increased Gallen's frustration. He wanted to know what Zelan knew. He wanted to explain the importance of their visit. He wanted to expedite this process, to formulate a plan and execute it. Yet, timeliness did not appear to be Zelan's way.

He coughed forcefully. Both women whipped their heads toward the sound. Malinar appeared concerned, Sol exasperated.

"All things in due time, young Ocean lord."

Zelan's mouth remained closed, as if his serpentine voice existed solely in Gallen's mind. Gallen looked back at Sol to register her response, but her expression was unchanged.

Was it in his mind? Did he hear anything at all? Gallen looked toward the master quizzically.

"There are more skills than those of the physical." Again, his face remained unmoved.

"Do you jest?" Gallen could not help but voice his frustration, as if a child being scolded by an overbearing parent.

"Gallen!" Sol slammed a hand on the cool surface of the table.

"You are here regarding the phoenix, yes? You wish to gain knowledge from our realm to understand this creature, to best it, hmm?" Zelan queried.

The words rang through the space, no longer confined to

Gallen's impatient mind. He contemplated responding, yet the anxious tapping of Sol's boot convinced him otherwise. Instead, the room returned to its eerie silence; even Malinar was too stunned to continue eating.

Zelan's voice absorbed the silence. "The guardians of the High Realm sensed your arrival. We have planned accordingly. There are three rooms prepared and baths drawn. We have the option for a massage, if it would suit you all. I teach all apprentices that the body and the mind must be at ease before an effective plan can be formulated."

He stood, the silk fabric reflecting the setting sunlight that passed through the round windows lining the far side of the room. Sol rose to her feet, encouraging the other two Flyers to stand as well, as the aster slowly floated to an arched exit. Gallen strained to listen as the cryptic Instructor walked through the hall. The three released a simultaneous breath when the light tapping of his feet could be heard no longer.

Without the master sitting at the head, an air of ease settled in the room. The Flyers returned to their marble seats.

Gallen looked at Sol in confusion. "Master Zelan knows of the weapon?"

"Creature, he said." Malinar corrected, pulling the bowl of bread to her before taking another bite.

"Creature. A phoenix, he said." Gallen tapped his fingers on the edge of the table. "Sol, what do you make of it all?"

Her face lingered upon the arched exit where her former master made his leave.

"From what Asha has shared, this reaction is not surprising. I suppose we must rest before we form a plan. I imagine Master Zelan will not meet with us again until we do."

Malinar gulped the last of her white wine as Gallen continued tapping his fingers anxiously, his heart rate increasing as he desperately fought the urge to run after Zelan and force him to answer their questions immediately.

The war. The creature. The danger. Pressure and urgency and tension wound into a toxic knot in her chest. Why did this "wise" man refuse to strategize? To share his knowledge? Was there something to hide here in the heights of the High Realm?

Sol stood, looking at Gallen as she spoke. "I believe I will venture to our living quarters."

Before she even finished the thought, Gallen stood as well. "I will as well. Malinar, would you like to join us?"

She shook her head gently. "I will finish my meal and perhaps take Master Zelan's advice to rest. Please, retrieve me if the group wishes to discuss our plans."

Gallen nodded before following Sol into the hallway.

If the home itself appeared large from the outside, it was even larger as Gallen paced over the marble. The halls were disorienting. The same arcs, same windows, same blinding white stone. Gallen followed Sol into a wide hall that opened into a common area marked by a large skylight overhead. A massive door loomed to the left, leading to a yard of manicured greenery. A young apprentice walked briskly from another hall, her silky tunic and slacks swishing. Her small features spied the two Flyers standing in the entryway, utterly lost in this world of polished stone. Without a sound, the warrior graciously led them to their proper quarters.

As Zelan stated, three rooms had been prepared, the doors stationed close together along the same wall of a corridor. Gallen clutched the marble doorknob before stepping into the room. The space was quaint and cold, with a small desk, chair, and bed. He breathed a sigh of relief to see neatly stacked blankets atop a feather mattress.

Placing his satchel delicately on the floor, Gallen's boots clicked as he reached the edge of the bed. However, before he could begin unfolding the blankets to rest, a small knock stopped his task.

"Enter!" he called out, too tired to open the door himself.

The door creaked open and Sol's round face popped into view.

"I believe Master Zelan requested the masseuses to prepare in only one room." Her face was a bit flushed, her voice fluttering as she spoke. "If you're interested, you may come to my room."

Then, just as quickly, Sol disappeared, leaving Gallen still standing near the edge of his bed staring at the closed door. A full day of travel coupled with the frustration of Zelan's refusal made his mind sore. Yet, the thought of releasing the tension of his aching muscles pushed his feet toward the door, into the hall, and into the adjacent room.

The scent of lavender beckoned Gallen toward a raised table covered with a sheet and guarded by a woman in a striped robe. A second bed lay close to the first, just fitting in the small bedroom space. The masseuse lifted the blanket and gestured for him to lie down. Sol's body rested on the nearby bed, the sheet pulled down to reveal her back covered in oil as her own masseuse pressed firmly on her shoulder blades.

"Please do get comfortable." The woman still held the sheet in her hands before he grasped the silk himself. "When you have disrobed, please lie face down."

At that, she turned to face the window while Gallen slowly pulled the Night Flyer tunic over his head. He tossed the shirt on the floor before tearing the pants from his tired legs. The table was surprisingly warm, welcoming him into a state of peace. Or, closer than he had been in weeks.

The massage itself transported him to heavenly bliss. Places he did not even know were in pain suddenly relaxed. The hands of the masseuse were magic. Or perhaps true magic was involved, a potion laced in the oils that she lathered along his bare skin. Gallen cared little. He allowed the smell of lavender, the sensation of relief, to guide him into utter and euphoric mindlessness.

∽

"Gallen?" A gentle hand rubbed his arm. "It seems you have fallen into a deep sleep. Master Zelan must have recognized how acutely you needed to release the tensions within you."

Gallen rubbed his eyes with his palms as he rolled from his stomach to his back. He noticed Sol, holding the thin sheet with one arm above her chest while the other rested on the massage bed. He also noticed her eyes lower and widen a bit, smile growing, before moving back upward. Shifting his body to lie on his side, he felt the pressure of what she must have seen.

If this was before, he would rip the towel from her voluptuous body. He would rest her quivering thighs on his lap. He would rapture her with kisses, on her lips, her cheeks, her neck. He would take her here on this bed, in these sheets. He would not leave her be until she screamed his name through these sanitized halls.

But Sol was not who she once was.

Gallen's head rested on his arm as he stared and stared and stared at the woman near him. Sol shifted, moving her body closer to his. The thin sheet clung to her curves, and the indent of her nipples pushed against the silk. Gallen could not help but notice her strong thighs slightly rub together, almost as if she wanted to feel him just as much as he wanted to feel her.

Leaning toward him, Sol's breasts nearly fell from beneath the sheet as she reached a hand to push a stray wave of blonde hair behind his ear. Her touch lingered on his neck, then his shoulder, down his arm. Her nails scratched ever so slightly upon his skin, the subtle pricks of pressure fanning the flames of his lust. She placed a gentle hand on his side, sending waves of shock throughout Gallen's body. Mist bless him, he wanted her. Needed her.

Yet, even as her grasp on the sheet loosened before him, his moral compass took control.

He remembered Malinar encouraging empathy, helping him recenter and refocus on what he wanted. Who he wanted. In that moment, he wanted Sol. But, he had to be sure it was a future with her and not just a recreation of their past. He had to be certain the pain of her words from days ago in the Night Streets were more than mere intoxication. Then, there was Malinar.

Gallen leaned his head back. "We should meet Master Zelan."

His heart sank as she quickly retreated, casting her eyes low. "Of course."

Sol walked swiftly toward the edge of the room opposite the door. She barely looked back toward Gallen as she said, "I will meet you in the hall after I bathe."

A gentle request to leave. Gallen rose from the bed, and the silk sheet awkwardly shifted in his arms as he pressed it tight against his stomach to keep his body covered. His bare feet were like lead as he gathered his filthy clothing and shuffled to the door. His mind reprimanded him for hurting her. For rejecting her advances. Yet, another part of him knew it was appropriate. He did not wish to ruin the fresh start of their relationship.

But, as he closed the door, he could not help but glimpse the curve of her bare back as the thin sheet fell to the floor. Sol's voluptuous body dazzled in the light of the room. Her olive skin glowed, surrounded by the luxury of the marble as if she herself were cut from rich stone.

Sol was a galaxy incarnate. A goddess amongst women with a tenderness about her that was foreign to Gallen, far from the harsh determination he knew of her before. And it was that tenderness that now drew him in. He thought of it as he walked to the adjacent room. As he dressed. As he waited in the hall.

He thought of Sol and the memory of her hand on his side.

THE NOTE SLIPPED under Gallen's door instructing him to meet in the outdoor field where the group landed hours before. Master Zelan sat cross-legged on the grass, a small mat beneath him as he hummed melodically as Sol and Gallen approached him. The trains of his long robe were carefully folded by his sides. The three pegasi were also present, kneeling alongside the master with their eyes closed, as if pleasantly dreaming or partaking in his meditation. The night sky housed a massive galaxy that swirled in saturated purples and pinks and blues. The stars winked at the Flyers as they approached the resting horses and their newest friend.

Sol rushed to see Kinsle, whispering questions into his ear as he provided a mixture of nods and neighs in response. The other pegasi peered over to investigate the interruption. Cotton nearly ran into Gallen as he walked into the grass while Storm whimpered at Malinar's absence.

"These creatures are magnificent. Masters of the air. We knew of their existence yet have never seen one grace the skies of our realm."

Zelan's eyes remained closed as he spoke. Although his face retained his usual lack of emotion, his voice was more tender. Perhaps the pegasi loosened something within the aged warrior.

Sol stroked the top of Kinsle's speckled head. "During my months in Endoneth, I witnessed many pegasi fly. Though they contain the strength of twenty horses, they are trained to never leave the Ice Realm. Forced to serve the realm at whatever cost, to whatever end."

The two were irrevocably close; the winged horse served as a true companion for her. Gallen saw the black ink lining the tips of her fingers, evidence of the few pages of notes she managed to write before they walked over. She was dedicated, that much was certain, a fact that comforted him. His mind drifted from Sol to Malinar, as it was apt to do.

Gallen could not help his curiosity. "Have you seen our travel companion? She deserves to join in these discussions."

Storm waved her head in agreement, concern laced in each strained whinny.

Malinar was elusive. Her room was empty and the dining hall

cleared. With the note gone from her floor, Gallen and Sol assumed she would manage her own way.

"There are many important ways to prepare oneself for an adventure. Uncovering a new part of one's being is often the most important." Zelan stated.

The cryptic response did nothing to ease Gallen's concern. Cotton's sweet nuzzle pushed against his arm as his heart rate rose. The pegasus soothed him with her presence, the metallic sheen of her pastel wings flicking in and out of his peripheral vision. It was only when his heart settled that Zelan continued, almost as if the elder warrior sensed anxiety, sensed grief or sadness or anger.

"The younger Flyer is in the tactical room, if my ears hear correctly. She shall return to her own steed soon enough."

Sol leaned on Kinsle. "We shall wait to discuss our plans until she arrives."

It was rare that Sol reminded Gallen of her old self, yet she was more assertive with this declaration than he had seen her since her return. It was not cold or forceful, merely pragmatic. As she sat near Master Zelan, crossing her legs and pulling a book from her satchel, Gallen noticed a confidence in herself, in her determination, in her protection of her fellow Flyer. Master Zelan's only agreement was resuming the rhythmic hums of meditation.

Gallen followed her example, plopping down between the master and his former apprentice, pulling a small needle and thread from his satchel. He considered adding a few patterns to the silken attire, though thought better of it.

Instead, he leaned nearer Sol, attempting to read the words on the page from over her shoulder as they waited. She smiled as they sat, shifting slightly so he could gain a better view. Gallen was typically impatient, a character flaw his mother pointed out often. Yet as he sat near Sol, reading a few lines of her romance novel every so often and stifling a chuckle here and there as he glimpsed the notes scribbled in the margins, he felt at ease. He missed Malinar, but he also soaked in this feeling with Sol. After the embarrassment of earlier, she was seemingly letting him in. Or at least maintaining the peace.

Gallen wanted it to be the former. Which revealed more about himself than it did Sol.

But letting him in meant transparency, opening up to her completely. Perhaps they would reach that point. For now, he enjoyed the closeness, her sideways glances, and the promise of their pure start.

12

Malinar

The house was a glorious maze of mysteries, one Malinar wished she could explore for hours and hours. Though a bath sounded glorious. When she arrived at her designated room, at least the only room left with the door wide-open, she stepped in and set her possessions on the bed before slipping off her uniform and climbing into the marble tub. She braced herself for cold water—at least half an hour had passed since Master Zelan told them the baths were prepared. Yet, as she hesitantly held her toes above the water, she could feel the warmth wafting from its surface. Malinar submerged into the perfectly warmed water, suds clinging to her skin, seemingly scrubbing the grime of the day from her body without her lifting a hand.

"Enchanting," she breathed to herself, eyes wide as she stared at the bubbles working their way over each inch of her.

It took but a few minutes before the suds dissipated, her skin practically shining. The constant heat soothed her. The steam floating through the air eased her into a state of contemplation. Had it only been a few days since leaving Celestra. To Malinar, it appeared more like months.

Despite the start of their journey, she was growing to enjoy her companion's company, often wishing the three could sit and talk together rather than risk their lives flying between realms. However, the realities of her life, of those she left in the Star Realm, caused such immense guilt it pained her. She hated that she was enjoying an adventure while her family suffered through uncertainty. That she was able to see the world while her younger siblings could barely leave their small village.

She traced her fingers along the edge of the marble tub, staring at the light refracting under the water's surface. While she was accustomed to the distance between herself and her family since moving to the big city, it was nothing like these extended quests. Of course, she experienced such in the past—the longing for home. But such quests were with dozens of people, Ranor amongst them, with tasks and worries distracting her. Yet here, with the daily flights where she had nothing but the wind and her mind, there was almost too much time to ponder.

With a groan, Malinar slipped out of the water, her bare feet leaving a trail of wet footsteps on the marble floor as she sauntered to the bed. A stack of blankets seemed to beckon her to sleep before the harrowing discussion with Master Zelan where they would truly realize the threat looming in the skies. The thought alone pushed her away from the bed and toward the door. She slipped a silk dress over her head and soft flats on her feet as she went. So desperate to clear her head, she nearly missed the note settled on the ground.

Meet in the grass to discuss the future.

Pointed. Simple. Authoritative. She had only known Master Zelan a few hours, yet the note clearly held his voice.

Malinar folded the paper and tucked it in the pocket of the dress before swinging the door open and walking into the hallway.

Candles lined the space, suspended from above as if flying in the air. The flames illuminated the marble walls and floors and ceilings. Dreamy colors of orange and yellow against the striking white and grey.

She strutted to the open space where the hallways met. Rather than turn toward the main entrance, she felt obliged to explore. Perhaps it was selfish, but Malinar wanted to linger in this place of pleasant ignorance, avoiding threats and weapons and plans.

The hallway that sat opposite of the guest hall led to the dining room where Malinar ate her fill of house-made pastries. She turned to the third hallway, the curved archway almost coaxing her to enter. And enter she did.

On either side of the wide hall were a mixture of archways, windows, and doors. Every so often, a skylight offered a better glimpse of the stars. As her silken flats tapped on the stone floor, Malinar looked into each archway, outside each window, through each slightly ajar door, noting the slight details that differentiated one space from the next. The practice provided her with a familiar satisfaction of finding her way. Memorizing. Mapping.

As she neared the end of the long hall, ready to return, the last room caught her eye. Not the room itself, rather, a piece of furniture at its center, the first she had seen made out of a material other than pure marble. The table, carved out of an ancient wood, had papers strewn across its surface. Some appeared as old as the table itself, while others were still wet with fresh ink.

The table stood in stark contrast to the room, another four walls of marble. Diamond cubbies were chipped into the walls in diamond patterns. In each compartment, more scrolls sat in wait for a scholar to unlock their secrets, discover tales set aside, appreciate mysteries hoping to be solved.

She steadily approached for a better look at the table, her hands tingling with the need to hold the papers, to examine them more closely. Each page, regardless of its size or age, pictured various maps. Maps with paths and geographic markers. Maps with colors and shades of black. Maps with ancient scripts and descriptions on the edges.

Malinar's eyes grew wide as she soaked in the scene: the beautiful array of maps stacked haphazardly atop one another, holding abounding knowledge. She wanted to absorb the images, to capture the pictures and paths and scripts to hold in her mind forever. Just in case. Her hand reached for a small map of Nourels. While she could not read the script, written in an unfamiliar language, she recognized the shapes of the realms and their boundaries. Her realm. Her home.

She could pinpoint her family's tent. Where she trained with her father before the morning stars shone bright. Where she taught her youngest sister how to swim. Where she begged her mother not to leave.

"Are you meant to touch these tools?"

She jumped back as a lanky man dressed in milky-white slacks and a loose-fitting sleeveless tunic emerged into view. His dark eyes were black as night as they stared at Malinar unflinchingly. She shrunk back into herself, hugging her arms tightly around her midsection.

"Master Zelan goes to great lengths to keep objects such as these in their rightful positions."

His gravelly voice scraped into Malinar's serenity. The man reached a pale hand toward the maps, straightening the sheets as he maintained his deathly glare. He stalked too close.

"You are a guest in this home, an honor which is given to few. Do not overestimate your value, young one."

This warrior's tone was harsh, far harsher than any of the other High Realm trainees shuffling around. Certainly harsher than the master's himself. Malinar stood stunned. She walked back a few steps, attempting to slip away from the negativity of the warrior and any consequence for her untimely curiosity. Just as she reached the door, her back barely over the threshold of the arch, the soft hand of another reached her shoulder.

Startled, she jumped back into the room with the still-frowning warrior before her, his dark cropped hair hanging in his face as he grimaced.

"Do not allow Lemntz to intimidate you, Flyer. He fears competition and craves the master's admiration."

This voice was the foil of Lemntz: affable and smooth and marvelous. They pressed Malinar further into the room, the hand presenting an assurance of her belonging in this place. When Malinar reached the table once again, she turned to see her new ally, a petit warrior with deep brown skin and blonde curls styled close to their scalp. They wore similar clothing to that of the man, the slacks and tunic looking more ethereal on their body in comparison.

The smoothness of their voice calmed Malinar in a way she could not quite place. As if transported to a dream. "Lemntz, I believe the master instructed you to gather a few scrolls?" The words were presented as both a question and an instruction.

Malinar could not help but smirk as Lemntz's aggressive eyes rolled upward. Clearly conceding defeat, he grasped with his thin arms a pyramid of scrolls hiding in the walls. It was only then that Malinar realized how full of knowledge the room truly was; each wall of marble was carved into cubbies filled with wayward papers, leather-bound books, and scrolls. She could only imagine how much information was held here.

Having found the objects of his task, Lemntz briskly walked to the archway in a huff, his elbow pushing against the other warrior as he passed them. Malinar and the nameless friend waited for his rapid footsteps to recede before speaking.

"Do not allow men like Lemntz to scare you away from your calling."

Their voice placed Malinar in a trance of tranquility. She could almost fall asleep, the tension from her memories of home, her guilt, her obsessive thoughts of Gallen and Sol all falling away. A delightful distraction.

"Thank you." The sentiment was meant for both the collision with Lemntz but also for this peace that seemed to ooze out of this being in front of her.

"I do mean what I say." The stranger's deep blue eyes bored into Malinar. Unlike the man's black stare of contempt, this look was careful, meaningful. "The maps call to you, do they not?"

Malinar looked down at the table, her hands pressed against the edge of the wood, drawn again to the patterns and words and spaces. She nodded to the strange warrior who grinned.

"I am Avelia, a potions apprentice of Master Zelan. Those like Lemntz often dismiss the value of intuition. The value of anything other than traditional combat." They continued to look deeply into Malinar's eyes, as if reading her like one of the scrolls lining the walls. "The master teaches us to look at all areas of life as equal. There must be a balance between the rough and the soft. The harsh realities and the moments of joy. Some take longer to internalize such notions."

Avelia certainly sounded like Zelan, with their words both wise and confusing, meaningful and vague.

Malinar settled her hands on one of the parchments. "Yet you understand such notions?"

Malinar often forged barriers between herself and others, and was successful at keeping others at bay. Avelia's presence almost warred with her instincts. Malinar wanted to both maintain her distance while also divulging her innermost thoughts. Of course, this was likely a part of Avelia's training. And Malinar prepared herself for such mental strategies, a lifetime of keeping others closed out helped her recognize when others were attempting to get in.

If Avelia knew the extent of Malinar's reluctance, they did not express it in their features, which glowed a beautiful purple hue as they walked to the opposite end of the table.

"I have been told that I hold a gift of awareness. I see the souls of others just as I see their faces, their weapons, their clothing." At those words, their blue eyes scanned Malinar's body from head to toe and back again. "You are an interesting warrior…"

Instead of elaborating, Avelia looked instead to the maps. "You should invest in this gift of yours."

Their slender hand ran over the ink of the small Nourels map, enticing Malinar to feel it as well, to study it, to internalize it. Avelia suddenly snatched the map into their hand and extended it outward, arm outstretched over the table. Malinar met them in the middle, the two arms like a bridge, an alliance of sorts.

"We should meet the master in the grass as he commanded," they noted, still clutching the other end of the map. "Would you join me there, Malinar?"

The map sent a spark through Malinar, like lightning running from her fingertips to her chest. A bolt of something unknown. She released the map as if the parchment itself was on fire before staring back at Avelia. The warrior stood still, dazed as if struck by an unseen foe. Seconds later, they opened their eyes and looked at Malinar, arm still outstretched.

"Take it, friend."

Malinar could almost taste the sweetness of these words and immediately obliged, taking the small map and stuffing it inside the pocket where Zelan's note remained.

Avelia's small figure stepped toward the archway, their hand still held out, beckoning Malinar to follow. And so she did.

When Malinar arrived at the rectangular segment of grass before the home, Avelia by her side, she noted the eerie tranquility of the scene. It almost convinced her that this *was* all a dream. That there was no war. No weapon in the skies. No family relying on her. That all there was to life was sitting amongst friends and enjoying the stars.

Gallen's smile broke the deception. "Malinar! We have been awaiting your arrival. Did you rest? Are you well?"

His concern lifted her spirits as they descended into reality, followed swiftly by Sol's knowing glance. She nodded to Malinar as if understanding her need to wander before returning to responsibility.

Malinar sat in the grass nearest Sol, stretching her legs and crossing her ankles before leaning back on her arms. Storm settled her head in Malinar's lap immediately, as if she were jealous of the other pegasi and their riders.

"Did you not enjoy the grass?" Malinar joked quietly.

Storm only blew a strong puff of air onto Malinar's bare legs, which she took to mean a definitive *no*. She rested one hand between the horse's ears. She hated to admit such, but she appreciated the animal, another wandering soul wishing for a place to land. A place to be.

Avelia stood carefully behind Master Zelan, whose eyes were still closed from hours of meditation.

"Now to the task at hand." Gallen spoke firmly with the confidence of a Night Flyer.

Malinar's heart to stalled, a ridiculous reaction to a tone of voice, but one she could not shake as he continued.

"We have less time than appropriate, I am certain. My mother knew little of the weapon, only that its effects could be devastating. We must form a path forward. We need your guidance, Master."

While Gallen looked rested, even a bit more even-keeled than usual, he remained ever the planner. Zelan opened his eyes and turned his head slowly to meet Gallen.

"This creature. It will be devastating to all realms. All but those who breed them. Or so they believe."

So much expressed in so few words. Malinar pressed her hand into Storm's soft mane. Sol clearly sensed a similar foreboding as she voiced the concern ominously: "Do you mean to say this beast is invincible?"

The elderly man pulled his hands together in his lap, choosing his words carefully. Malinar could see Gallen tapping his fingers on his knee while Sol clutched the edge of the silk tunic she wore. Both looked utterly terrified.

"We have only known of its existence for but a month now. There is little information, only myths from long ago. Yet, we believe the source is in the North. Either the Realm of Mountain or Ice or Desert."

Gallen looked exasperated. "How can you not find the source? Do you not have warriors guarding the skies? Could you not search from above?"

Sol shot a warning glance to Gallen before clarifying, "I believe warriors in this realm would need far more than a single month to search the three northernmost realms in their entirety."

"We must also consider the use of otherly elements," Avelia chimed in.

Malinar squinted at the word. "You mean...magic? That is a skill of the fairies, correct?"

"There is magic both natural and conjured," Gallen corrected.

Sol nodded. "Yet we know that the upper realms are not above manipulating such magic for their gain."

Sol's eyes grew cold, the pale blue of her eyes misting over as if in another place, a memory perhaps. Malinar shifted far enough to feel Sol's hand in hers. Sol blinked away the memory at Malinar's touch, leaning into it.

Avelia leaned down to whisper something into the master's ear before returning upright. "We are exhausting our every resource here to learn about this beast, to understand it. To find a solution. However, we admittedly need the assistance of another."

They looked at Gallen who immediately returned a glare, as if sensing the attention back on him.

Avelia continued, "Flyer Gallen. We need information from your home realm."

"From the Ocean Realm?" Gallen questioned. "What information could possibly be gleaned there that you have not learned?"

"We may be a wealth of knowledge, yet these are from written works. Tomes of history. Guides to warfare. Drawings. Depictions. The Ocean Realm traces their past through voice alone, is that not correct?"

Avelia's words held true to Malinar's knowledge. Any story of the Ocean Realm was often told by another realm.

"Words and murals..." Gallen nodded slowly. "What do you intend I do?"

"Find the answers. You know where they lie, as do I." Avelia stated plainly.

Zelan spoke with eyes still shut, "it is best."

Gallen sighed, rubbing the back of his neck before conceding to this new path, "I may swim to Somov, gain an audience with our Past Holder, and return with the knowledge you see—"

"Avelia shall accompany you." Master Zelan's voice cut through any sound in the courtyard. Even the bugs and trees seemed to whisper as he spoke.

Gallen appeared undeterred by the master's authority. "The lords and ladies of the Ocean Realm only permit certain visitors to enter. This is not the way. I would need to procure the proper equipment for you to accompany me below the tides. I am born to breathe underwater—you all cannot."

Avelia held out a vial of a strange, blue liquid.

"We have liquid air for the swimming journey." They tucked the glass back into the pocket of their silk pants.

Potions. Malinar did not realize the extent of their power. And an apprentice to the greatest of masters? Stronger than brute strength indeed. Malinar saw the warrior in a fresh light, as if Avelia obtained the power to control them with little effort at all. A wary piece of new information.

Gallen pushed back. "Master, you should empathize more than most. Visitors, meetings with the Seers of our world, they take time and planning and—"

Avelia cut in again. "You said yourself that time is of the essence. And, in times of chaos, of warfare, and ruin, there may be exceptions to the way of things."

"Allow me to journey alone." Gallen grasped a fist full of grass in his hand, "Sol and Malinar shall be safer here, amongst warriors."

"Not with you, Flyer Gallen?" Avelia questioned.

"This is beneath you both." Zelan's eyes flitted open in frustration, "the journey shall begin. The warriors shall travel together. The knowledge shall be gained."

THE REMAINING hours of the night flew past Malinar. Avelia conveyed the plan as if it had been conceived weeks in advance. Perhaps it had. Those of the High Realm seemed to convey a sense of knowing, of understanding their roles in the world and merely contributing their part. Malinar could not live in such a way. She readied for sleep, carefully spreading layers of sheets over the mattress before resting.

Malinar stared at the wall. A magnificent star was expertly carved into marbled stone, golden and radiant. One would assume the events of the day would elicit a swift and sound sleep. Yet her eyes stared at the carving, following the steady lines of its pointed edges.

She heard a knock at the door before Gallen's voice whispered, "Malinar?"

At the sound of her name, she jumped to her feet, reaching for the doorknob. Gallen stepped inside and sauntered to her bed. "May I sit?"

Malinar nodded, a blush creeping through the silk collar of her dress. Before she could think too deeply of the implications of Gallen resting on her bed, he rubbed his eyes wearily, sighing heavily as he contemplated their earlier discussions with Master Zelan and Avelia.

"Does it worry you that Avelia is to join us? Should we be worried? Should we venture forth upon this mission at all?"

Why Gallen thought to ask Malinar of her opinion, she was unsure. However, just as she conjured a response, another knock rang through the room. She stepped back to the marble door and opened it to reveal Sol, her hands folded together and eyes downcast. When she peered into the room, shock replaced her meekness. Gallen chuckled and waved a hand to welcome her in.

"We were just discussing the precarious position we have found ourselves thrust into," he said.

In Sol's presence, Malinar could sense Gallen relax a bit more.

"Gallen, you must understand. Master Zelan would not make a decision such as this rashly." Malinar watched as Sol sat beside Gallen on the bed and placed a steadying hand on his leg. "We must trust him."

Gallen scoffed softly. "It is difficult to trust a person who wishes to exploit your home."

Malinar stepped forward. "Sol, should we not consider the king? Should we not find your memories first and foremost?"

Sol considered this, then shook her head slightly. "As I said before, this weapon is greater than our previous plans. Greater than me."

"Then we must at the very least inform Alcor of this shift. He must know we are changing course so severely. I mean, if you both agree." Malinar did not intend to sound controlling, but she knew she was correct in this.

Gallen nodded, validating her fears. "Indeed. A letter to inform him of our intent to see my family. But not of the phoenix, not yet. That is information to be spoken, not written."

"But it is what's best for the realms, is it not?" Malinar questioned.

Sol spoke softly, "we would not wish for this information to reach the wrong hands. They cannot know we are searching for a way to destroy these creatures."

With a reassuring glance at her friend, Sol pushed herself further onto the bed to make room for Malinar.

Gallen shook his head. "I feel torn. You both understand such a plight. To feel a connection to yourself and to your realm, your family."

The two women huddled closer to Gallen as tears began staining his blue cheeks. His blonde hair, usually so pristine in tightly woven plaits, now frayed as he continuously ran his fingers through the waves.

Sol's words brought light into the darkness of Gallen's despair, of his fear and worry: "We are here, Gallen. Always. You know this."

Malinar nodded her head as it rested on Gallen's shoulder. Just past his chest, she could see Sol looking toward her, an expression of deep gratitude and affection.

As his tears continued to pour, Malinar admired his honesty and transparency. Admired his willingness to defend his family, his realm. And, in a way, admired his tears, his humility, leaning on them for strength. Malinar hoped their warmth could soothe him, could keep at bay the thoughts of terror that surely plagued him in this moment. She knew if it were her family being asked to assist, being thrust into this dangerous and utterly unknown position, she, too, would be terrified. That thought alone made her lean in closer. She gently took Gallen's hand from his hair and pulled his arm close to hers. Sol followed suit, coming to his other side to gently hold his other arm in hers.

In time, the tears slowed and Gallen cleared his throat, not daring to move the women from his sides. "Thank you, both. I did not anticipate this turn in our journey. It is difficult for me to endure what I cannot foresee."

Impatient as Gallen was, Malinar always knew him to have a plan. A plan he was certain he could accomplish.

"This shift in our quest is for us all. I see no other way without you both." Malinar held her other hand to Sol who accepted, their fingers lacing together as if two pieces of a newfound puzzle.

Gallen's eyes widened, a smirk curving his cheek upward. "I suppose my journey home was only one shift I did not foresee."

Sol laughed. "There is much that escapes your sight, I'm afraid."

He ripped his hand dramatically from her hand, placing his palm against his tunic with a sarcastic gasp. "Our fair Keeper of Records, you harm me so."

Giggling, Malinar said, "there is still much to learn on this journey, to be certain."

"Am I now outnumbered?" He pulled his hand from Malinar's playfully. "Well, I suppose we must remedy this immediately."

The three Flyers sat together, talking for a long while that night. And these talks—of jubilance and fears and life and pain—led to a mutual recognition between them. That they were together in this. Not just in the quest but in something much deeper. Malinar felt it as the two others rose to leave. She felt it as Sol offered a warm hug followed by Gallen's own soft embrace. She felt it as their warmth lingered even in their absence.

MALINAR MET the following morning with more zeal than usual. She was thoroughly prepared to fly to the Ocean Realm, to enter into the deep waters and explore a new place with two people she had grown to enjoy, even to trust. Two people and Avelia, whose blonde curls bounced slightly as they prepared to mount Malinar's pegasus.

Avelia insisted upon riding alone, stating definitively that they knew better than the three Night Flyers of the ways of the skies. Much to the distaste of Gallen—who continued to suspiciously eye Avelia from Cotton's saddle—Malinar reluctantly agreed, offering Storm's reins and joining Sol on Kinsle's back for the journey. She was sure to give Storm the tightest hug, scratching behind her ears in just the right spot before allowing the potion master to take her place.

It was far too early to debate, and the sooner the four entered the skies, the sooner Malinar could be safely on the ground. She reached her arms around Sol's stomach and laced her fingers together, clinging to Sol as they climbed into the sky.

As the shining buildings of the High Realm disappeared in the clouds, Malinar sighed softly. It was strange how much a night could alter one's trajectory. The morning hues painted the sky delightful shades of pink and purple. She looked up at the final remnants of blue night sky, the moon slowly fading into the light of day.

"Are you faring well after last night?" Sol whispered over her shoulder.

While the air whirred by their ears, Malinar could hear her companion well enough if she pressed in close.

"It was a shock to see Gallen in such a state," Malinar admitted. "A shock and a blessing. I am not sure if that is sensical. I felt the three of us were...we were utterly—"

"Aligned?" Sol finished for her as they flew, her head shifting slightly, causing Malinar's lips to barely graze her cheek.

She did not turn away, placing her chin on Sol's shoulder as she answered, "it was comforting to me. I have not had people in my life whom I could truly rely on."

The statement did not linger, swept away by the rush of wind. Yet the two let it settle over them as they flew, the sky shifting into a pale blue as the morning sprang forth.

"I understand if you still feel disdain toward me. I would understand, I..."

In Sol's voice, Malinar could hear the shame. Shame for an event Sol could not even control. For how it impacted Malinar herself. It reminded her that she never cleared the air, not completely. And perhaps now, as they flew hundreds of feet above distant realms, the two could establish clarity.

"I hate myself," Malinar uttered, hoping her voice could be heard above the wind. Or maybe hoping the wind would take the admission far from the two women as they went. If Sol heard, she did not reply.

Though she knew the words already—statements she said to herself in the middle of the night—they struck deep into Malinar's heart.

"I hate that I could not tell Ranor the truth before his passing. That I wanted more. I suppose I still want more. Yet, bearing the weight of my family's future, the worries of how I am perceived, how I perform. It requires that sacrifice, I suppose. It was far easier to find another to blame."

Sol turned her face enough to meet Malinar's tear-filled eyes. Their souls almost whispered to one another as their eyes locked. The deep purple of Malinar's gaze searched for a place to land and Sol's icy-blue eyes offered a sanctuary.

"It is honorable to admit such a thing," Sol said. "And I could never hate you for doing what you needed to grieve what was lost. Even if it was not what you wanted, in the end."

A pressure lifted from Malinar's chest at Sol's patience, her grace, her willingness to understand.

Malinar felt the tears fall onto Sol's tunic, "That is most kind."

"I do hope you learn to love yourself, Malinar," Sol continued, "for I can see that there is so much to love."

How the two arrived here, Malinar was unsure. She could trace her growing openness to Sol— a woman she once looked up to, then despised, and now strangely empathized with. Perhaps it was her discussions with Gallen or Sol's obvious emotional turmoil. But, whatever the reason, the past few days forced Malinar to see

Sol differently. Not as just a stunning spectacle, but someone of substance. Someone she admired. Gods. Malinar was thinking of her constantly. Just as much as she was thinking of Gallen.

And this closeness, the two women suspended above the world, Malinar's arms woven around Sol like a cincture pulling her into place, it was natural.

When Sol looked forward again, Malinar clung to Sol more tightly. Tight enough to sense Sol's heartbeat, thumping wildly. Tight enough to hear her sighs as the wind whipped past. Tight enough to feel like a part of her. And feeling a part of Sol was more than joyous. It was effervescent.

13

Sol

The hours of riding passed far more quickly when talking with a friend. Sol could not remember the last time she was so unabashedly excited, particularly in the face of such danger. Yet, she was flying to see a realm beneath the seas, the home of someone she cared for. And such a journey was to be made with another that she wanted to grow closer to.

"What was it like there?" Malinar said as they galloped over a misty cloud.

Sol knew what she meant, and she hardly wished to discuss the matter. Though, maybe in speaking aloud what she experienced she could finally write it.

"Breathtaking at first," she began, harkening back to all those months ago. "Endoneth itself was a dream. Majestic. Luxurious. Filled with decorations and artwork and beauty. There were many parts of my stay I could confidently call pleasant."

She paused, the wind whirring past the two women as Malinar

tugged at her stomach, a gentle reminder that she listened, she cared.

Sol continued, "I witnessed a host of visitors. Old and young from nearly each realm. It was glorious, that world of dancing and dining and gossip and pleasure. It was until it was not. When the guests of Endoneth betrayed me. When he betrayed me…"

Sol never meant to share more than a few tidbits from that part of her life, though once she began, it was as if a flood of words fell from her mouth, uncensored, uncontrolled.

"Rostair," the name on her tongue made her gag, "he was an evil man, cruel, amused by the suffering of others. So much so that he took and took and took anything he wanted. Any*one* he wanted. And I was merely another object to lay claim. To possess. To use."

Another pause as Sol caught her breath. Malinar's grip never faltered, firmly pressing her cheek against Sol's cape.

"You need not continue if you do not wish," Malinar finally spoke, her words pained though sure, "but, if you need an ear, I am here, Sol."

A tear fell from her cheek, Kinsle glancing back as Sol gripped his reins.

"He took me once. Not all of him, but…he violated my body. And I did not know who I was."

Now it was Malinar who whimpered softly against Sol's shoulder.

"I will kill him." She whispered through gritted teeth.

Sol shook her head, "There is no need to—"

"No, Sol." Malinar cleared her throat, her voice stern as she stated, "*I will kill him.*"

Sol wished she could share more with Malinar. Of Mairette poisoning her mind and removing her memories. Of her worries returning to their realm. Of her trepidation in ever finding safety in romance again. Traveling with Gallen and Malinar, her immediate optimism melted into a confusing mess of calmness and caution.

Sol saw Gallen gesture to land, waving his arm toward the ground. She wiped her cheeks and whispered as much to Kinsle, his ears perking up at the thought of rest.

Just as his nose dipped forward, a scream permeated the sky. A stark scream that pierced the somber air that surrounded Malinar and Sol. Sol's stomach flipped as Kinsle turned quickly to investigate. The riders hurled forward with him, Sol grasping Malinar's hands to ensure she remained safely seated. The wind carried with it a sickly smell, like that of scorching cinders or burning flesh. Another scream rang through the clouds, followed by a call.

"IT IS HERE! IT IS HERE! LEAVE NOW!"

Avelia's voice quivered as they yelled their warnings. Yet, just as Gallen pulled beside Kinsle, Sol refocused on what they faced.

Flashes of light sprang into view, followed by waves of heat that shot through the air like menacing arrows of death. It was a mass of flame and ash and smoke. The once blue sky now bled, the sun dwarfed in its dominance to this rush of orange and red. The flames demanding in the sky's deference to their sovereignty. The creature's feathers shimmered with beautiful terror and beak sharpened to a lethal point at the end of its head. Storm and Avelia appeared dwarfed by its size. And, as Avelia quickly realized their circumstance, they raised their voice again, turning to the three Flyers in a desperate plea.

"LEAVE! YOU MUST LEAVE ME!"

They pushed Storm to fly, turning right to avoid the beast that now enveloped the sky. Sol's heart thumped in an erratic rhythm as the bird stalked Avelia.

Turning to Gallen, Sol begged, "we must save them. Avelia and Storm. We must."

Gallen shook his head, his blue skin growing sickeningly pale as he witnessed the battle unfolding before them. "There is no way to defeat it. You heard the master..."

"We may not defeat it," Malinar chimed in, squeezing Sol's waist, "but we may help our new friend escape it."

With that, Sol pushed Kinsle to move, to rush after Storm and her rider and find a way, any way, to save them. As they gained speed, the air grew hot, steam rising from the sweat of their arms and Sol's throat growing dangerously dry. Smoke stained the sky, overtaking the white of the clouds like spilled ink staining parchment. Sol could hardly see let alone steer. Billows of grey and black grew thicker as they tried to push through clouds of smog.

Then, in a brief and terrible moment, the darkness cleared and Sol saw the flames of the beast, its wings barely alight as it chased Storm. The sight of the pegasus immediately eased some of Sol's worry, though the monstrous phoenix rushed toward her with malicious intent. Bursts of flames flew from its beak, the smell of sulfur scorching the heavens.

Malinar pressed into Sol. "Get us to Storm, then we can lead them away."

Sol guided Kinsle quickly below Storm, praying to any goddess listening to pull the bird's attention up rather than down. Malinar let one arm ease from Sol's stomach and into the air, waving wildly in hopes Avelia would see.

However, the warrior was far more focused on avoiding fire than looking down. Sol shook her head. "We must ascend."

Malinar said nothing, yet Sol sensed her reaching low before returning her hand to its former place, a dagger now clenched in her trembling hand. She clung to Sol as Kinsle flew higher, the air nearly suffocating as they grew closer to Storm and Avelia. Yet, as they rose, the fire of the phoenix became faster and more precise. Storm herself appeared tired, perhaps fearful of this monster attacking her mid-flight.

Sol could empathize with such terror. The closer they came to the creature, the clearer its horror became. Its feathers glowed an unearthly hue of oranges and reds and yellows, flickering disturbingly with menacing flames. Where feathers could not reach, its form was nearly skeletal, its bones barely hidden by a thin layer of black skin. Its eyes—wide and foreboding—were lakes of sickly yellow surrounding a slit of black. The sight curdled Sol's blood as the creature flung its body toward her companion. With each burst of heat escaping the phoenix's sharp beak, she fell into further despair.

Such discouragement appeared absent from Storm. The pegasus nimbly skittered from side to side as the roars of fire threatened to singe her white wings. Her impressive shifts, dodging flame after flame, could only last so long. They needed a diversion, something to keep the beast's attention while Kinsle and Storm flew to safety.

As Sol wracked her brain for a solution, anything to keep them from leaving Avelia and Storm in this perpetual battle alone, a deafening cry cursed her ears. Through stinging tears, she watched as Storm's wing took to the flames, its pure white engulfed in blackness. Avelia heaved, pulling their tent from one of their packs to assist in quelling the fire. Storm, through the pain, continued flapping, keeping the two afloat in midair as the phoenix shot again and again and again.

Malinar's tears soaked into Sol's shoulder, her sobs quietly adding to the madness. They needed to act. Needed to do something.

Gallen appeared at her side, Cotton neighing sorrowfully. "They must jump."

The thought broke Sol. They could not leave Storm, not this beautiful creature who sacrificed so much for them. No, they would save her. They would.

Frozen in indecision, Sol sat, Malinar sobbing on her back as Gallen rushed to assist Avelia. "JUMP!"

Sol heard the words yet could hardly register their meaning as she watched the High Realm warrior leap from the back of the pegasus, then clutch Gallen's arm. Grimacing, he shot Sol a glance and nodded toward the ground, a silent command to run. To leave.

Storm remained in the air, wings still flapping against all odds. The phoenix sprayed another spurt of fire toward her, the flames now consuming her other wing. Sol refused to look away. She wanted to stay there with Storm. To be there when she...when she...

"SOL! FLY NOW!" Gallen's voice was coarse, stern, and tenacious. The voice of a leader, a commander.

As his warrior, she followed, pulling her eyes from Storm's bright body and toward the safety below. Though they rushed further and further from the turmoil above, Sol could hear the screams for miles. The pegasus wailed as the phoenix consumed her in light.

Soon, the others found their way onto solid ground. They quickly hid in a refuge of trees, hoping for any sort of haven from the beast. Without a word, a movement, a thought, they remained stuck in place until the wailing ended.

The shrieks were soon replaced with a sickening nothingness. No burning, nor gasping, nor yelps of pain. Nothing left of Storm.

The fire's light faded, and the stench of sulfur became just another scent in the woods.

⁓

The remaining trip was solemn, tainted by the brutal reality the group faced. Haunted by the echo of Storm's screams.

It was difficult to manufacture cheer in a position such as theirs, to return to the nervous excitement of before as they trudged through the trees of a beachy forest. The terrain was a mixture of soil and sand, the roots of barely visible and greenery sparse. Sol's boots slid over the shifting sand, her hands fumbling for the trunks of palm trees for purchase as they went. Despite her need for balance, she refused to let go of Kinsle's reins, refused the possibility of losing him.

Looking at Kinsle's saddle, Sol caught a glimpse of Malinar's sullen form. She had yet to breathe a word since the altercation, only offering slight nods and subtle glances when others spoke.

The display was as salt to a bleeding wound. Sol winced as she noticed Malinar's face, her pale skin streaked with soot and dirt and tears. She appeared undone, this relentless warrior now broken under the weight of dread and death.

Gallen led Avelia and Cotton through the thinning forest, leading the group at a gracious pace. Rest was what they needed, surely. A time to process the scene, for their bodies to register the trauma they endured. But, it would have to wait until the warriors reached the beaches, until Gallen himself could see the ocean.

When the forest finally dwindled to but a few passing trees, the sky had deepened to a rich navy, the stars beckoning the warriors to rest. The group set up camp in silence, almost avoiding the inevitable affirmation of their greatest fears. The sound of the waves was like a lullaby for Sol's already exhausted body. Yet, she could not sleep until the group solidified the morning's aim. Gallen and Malinar sat beside a roaring fire while Avelia stood aloof near their designated tent.

Avelia was the first to speak: "Shall we acknowledge the severity of this creature?"

The reference to the beast began a barrage of memories flashing through Sol's mind. The feathers, the beak, the fire, Storm. Tears pricked at the back of her eyes as she relived the horror over again.

"It is fiercer than I imagined—" Gallen whispered.

"And why did it not attack the rest of you when given the chance?" Avelia interrupted. "Why allow us moments to escape?"

Sol considered this, though ultimately she could not move past the reality that some did not escape. That Storm's corpse, or whatever was left, lay somewhere in the fields of the High Realm.

Malinar cleared her throat before speaking, "it appeared smaller than what we assumed. Is it possible there are more?"

Gallen had described the beast as "larger than any in the skies." Yet, the creature they faced was hardly larger than Storm herself.

"Perhaps you were incorrect in your knowledge," Avelia chided.

Sol looked at them, a sense of protection rising in her chest. "Or, as Malinar claims, there is something larger at work here. What if the animal we witnessed was not fully grown?"

Avelia swore softly to themselves before stating, "if so, then we must act."

Gallen nodded. "We may swim below tomorrow. The travel will be comparatively light. We must bring only the essentials."

Gallen pushed kernels of sand with a small piece of dry wood as he spoke, Malinar following his hands with her eyes. The two Flyers looked comfortable, as if they had traveled together for months rather than days. Sol walked close to the others, soaking in the fire's warmth as Gallen detailed the needs of the following day.

"With the liquid air, you all should be able to successfully swim from the shore to the nearest town, Anthozoa. I fortunately know a cousin who settled there and should be able to procure us a place to stay while we contact my mother."

Avelia perked up at the mention of the High Lady. "And you shall gain an audience with her tomorrow. And we shall meet the Past Holder, I assume?"

Gallen scoffed, the tension in the air palpable. Sol set her head against Malinar's shoulder as they witnessed the mental battle between these warriors of two different realms. Both Avelia and Gallen were accustomed to leading such quests, and it seemed each word served as a way to assert authority.

"I am afraid that is not the way of things. I will swim to the main city of Somov myself, discuss these new revelations with my mother, then proceed from there."

As Avelia raised their head to protest Gallen's response, Sol voiced her main concern: "What of our pegasi? I need to know Kinsle is safe."

Gallen nodded, his eyes dipping low as the thought of their companions only reminded him of all that was lost that day.

"The pegasi do need to remain on land. There is not enough potion for them to safely make the journey beneath the water, if they would even attempt to venture in, that is." He turned to set his eyes on Cotton, as if reassuring himself of the steed's safety. "These creatures were bred for air."

Sol looked toward her own flying companion, a pet she had grown so very attached to while in Celestra and certainly on this quest. With the dangers so tangible, she needed him to make it to safety. She refused to leave the beach without such a promise.

"I can ensure the beasts make it to whatever location you believe best." Avelia's tone evoked a sense of confidence despite the ridiculous nature of their words. "It must be a place they have flown before. The High Realm or your own Celestra, perhaps?"

The furrowed brows lining Malinar's forehead encapsulated Sol's incredulous reaction to Avelia. Yet, the options proved slim.

"I could remain with them," Malinar suggested. "I could lead them back to Celestra—"

"There is no need, truly," Avelia interjected. "I promise, the winged horses will arrive just where you need them."

Sol turned toward Gallen to gauge his reaction. He scratched his chin with his hand, the stubble lining his jaw catching on his nails as he thoughtfully considered their proposal.

"How can we be certain?" he asked.

"You must trust, I suppose," was Avelia's response.

While Sol could not fully trust the warrior, she certainly did not want the group separated. She also believed Kinsle could provide for himself; he was smart and stubborn. But she could not help but worry for the worst, particularly with a phoenix scouring the skies. Perhaps more than one.

Gallen looked to the women sitting near him, the crackling fire filling the moments of silence as the night trudged on. "What do you both think? Shall we send our steeds back home or lead them to the Ice Realm?"

Taken aback, Sol spoke freely, "why ever would we consider completing our original quest? With so much at stake, should we not abandon it and focus our attention on the present evil?"

Malinar's hand settled on her thigh, a token of support.

"It is truly your decision, Sol," Gallen stated plainly.

His golden eyes looked with such affection toward her, as if the concerns of the following day, the dangers that lurked in the realms, as if none of it truly mattered if Sol were unhappy.

He continued, "I will gladly see this quest through to its dedicated end if it is what you desire. The plan is set, though we know plans can be broken if necessary."

Malinar's hand squeezed her thigh again as if in agreement.

Tears lined Sol's bottom lashes before brushing them away with the hem of her cape. "May I have the night to consider?"

Gallen looked to Avelia who nodded.

Sol rose to her feet and bid the others good night. Pulling her coat tightly around her collar, she allowed the cool breeze of the salty air to brush through her loose hair, easing her concern with each step. Rather than retire to her tent, she walked to the edge of the water, pulling her boots from her aching feet and basking in the salty sea.

"May I accompany you?" Malinar's voice whispered into the wind.

As Sol turned to greet her, she saw the Flyer already seated in the smooth sand. She nodded, leaving the comfort of the water to join her friend. The two remained still a moment, listening to the hoots of owls and the lapping of the waves along the shore. The warmth of Malinar's hand neared hers as they both stared ahead. The touch was as desperate as it was kind. Malinar seemingly needed Sol as much as Sol wished to comfort Malinar.

Looking forward, the darkening night offered an obscured view of the shimmering water ahead. Though tired, Sol could stay awake a bit longer. Especially now.

"How are you, truly?" Sol whispered.

"It was not a loss I expected." Malinar admitted, "Though I will endure. Storm was…she was…"

Tears slurred her words as she searched for the ways to express what the pegasus meant to her. Sol saw it herself, the ways the two bonded. She pulled Malinar closer.

"Just," Malinar whispered, "just help me forget."

Sol's heart cracked, rubbing her friend's arm.

"Tell me, Malinar, what do you want in life?"

Sol remembered the moment distinctly when her own brother asked her a similar question. Alcor's heartfelt offer to Sol placed her desires before his own—perhaps the first time the choice had been given in such a way. It was liberating to have an idea of one's future, or at least know one's desires. She wanted Malinar to experience the same freedom. Of choice. Of thought. Of desire. To know that such freedom existed, even in the darkest of times

Malinar pressed her cheek into Sol's silver cloak, her nose sniffling before she responded. "My mother gifted a book to me as a child. In it are the stories of strong women who made the most of their circumstances. Some leading armies, others creating tapestries. Each with a distinct purpose, a passion. I have always envied these figures, women of the past. I keep the book with me wherever I travel, turn to it for guidance or reassurance." She breathed in deeply. "I realize it is ridiculous. But I honestly wish to be a Flyer. It is what I have always wanted, I suppose. To reflect the confidence of those women. Though, if I am honest with myself, there were never many moments in my life where I considered if this path was my chosen way or if it was the way of convenience. Not because becoming a Night Flyer is easy—quite the contrary as you know... *knew*..."

She paused, awkwardly avoiding any mention of Sol's condition. Then Malinar continued, "becoming a warrior is natural to me. I tend to understand tactics and movements and locations. And, for better or worse, I will sacrifice anything for my family. If being a successful warrior is what is necessary, it shall be so."

Sol considered Malinar's words, this woman of six years her junior holding the responsibility of so many with such grace and determination. She was more than admirable, she was inspiring.

Yet Sol knew that burden all too well, the need to be a vision of strength to hold the world together. And such a role was difficult to carry alone.

"I do not believe you answered the question truly," she told Malinar.

Sol smiled toward the seascape, the moon and stars sparkling in its reflection.

"I suppose it is an answer I have yet to find myself. No person has truly pushed me to know myself in this way," Malinar answered carefully, as if speaking the words for the first time.

Sol pulled her closer, wanting the words to sink in as she spoke. "If we continue growing closer, I will surely challenge you to consider what makes you happiest in life. And, perhaps, help you achieve that happiness, if you will allow."

She could barely hear Malinar whisper a gentle response: "I would like that."

The women huddled near one another, ignoring the fears that certainly plagued them both. Ignoring the responsibilities that faced them tomorrow. Just two women, looking at the ocean, breathing in the clean air of the sea, hoping for happiness.

In a matter of minutes, Sol could hear Malinar's gentle snores against her shoulder. She looked at the woman so close to her now, brushing the strands of hair from her stunning features. She was a vision. A dream. A reminder of something pure and worth fighting for.

Everything within Sol wished they could sleep beneath the stars, yet she knew they would both need their strength for the journey ahead. She gently shook Malinar's shoulder. "Shall I help you to bed?"

Malinar offered a muffled murmur of acceptance and allowed Sol to lift her from the sand and guide her to her tent. "Until morning," Malinar whispered, her eyes still half closed.

"Of course," Sol replied, walking to her own bed for the night.

When she entered her tent, the fabrics shimmering in the

moonlight and the sound of the waves filtering pleasantly through the folds, she immediately lay on her blankets and shut her eyes.

She hoped in the morning she would know her decision. Hoped she would awaken with a solid sense of what she wanted.

With that hope, she breathed in the clean, salty air and allowed the relaxing sounds of the ocean whisk her away to sleep.

SOL WOKE the following morning feeling even further from a confident decision. Although exhausted, she tossed and turned most of the night. Flashes of fire, echoes of screams, visions of Malinar's face stained by grief. She was shocked she managed a minute of sleep. Even in the brief moments of peace when the cries faded and the images calmed, her mind warred with itself.

If she decided to venture to the caverns where she may be able to regain her memories, was she rejecting this version of herself? The version that valued history and identity and empathy? Though this question was not a recent concern, it took on a more crucial meaning now. Now that she and Gallen established a friendship, an affection. Now that Malinar opened herself to Sol. What would her future be as her former self? How would the three Flyers retain the friendships they have, the relationships they could have?

The thoughts that haunted her through the night weighed on her as she prepared for the day.

"Sol?" Gallen's whisper interrupted her internal struggle, pulling her to the present.

"Gallen," she sighed, "is it time to venture forth?"

A pale blue hand pulled back the flap of fabric, and he stepped into the small travel tent. "To wherever you decide."

Nerves bubbled in her gut, her head throbbing in indecision.

"I do not wish to let anyone down," she whimpered.

Gallen kneeled by her side, one hand reaching to pull her tangled hair from her face. "You could never."

The statement was sincere, though it did little to ward off her continued frustration. He offered another statement: "What do you want at the end of all things? What is your ideal ending to this extended quest of ours?"

He stroked her face with his hand, his other tucked behind his back. Sol thought deeply about this. What *did* she want?

"I wish us to be safe," she breathed. "I wish for us to have the answers we need. Not of me...not yet."

He offered no indication of his preferred response, though he gave Sol a grin of affirmation.

"In that case," he pulled a turquoise rectangle from behind his back and presented it to Sol, "I wanted to gift you something important before our journey underwater."

As she grasped the gift in her hands, she noticed the details of a tightly woven bag.

"I could not sleep for much of the night." He motioned to the satchel. "The kelp is waterproof and should keep your papers protected, though it will not hold all of what you have brought. I believe Kinsle should carry the rest to wherever the horses venture."

Sol looked at the bag in disbelief. Gallen wove this in a mere night, mere hours. And to protect her work. Work that she admittedly had not considered when thinking of swimming through the ocean. Heat flushed across her cheeks.

"Thank you, Gallen. It is wonderful."

He smiled, placing a hand delicately on her arm as she continued to stare at the bag. The touch sparked Sol, a shudder of desire flowing through her as Gallen's golden eyes studied her reaction, perhaps experiencing the same sensation. The same lust. She wanted to pull away and maintain a bit of distance between them, wanted to establish a proper platonic connection after agreeing to their pure start. Yet, this connection, the magnetic draw the two had toward each other, was difficult to ignore.

"I want you to know that what you do for the realm is important; it is essential. There are so many people, so many stories, that are worth telling. Worth keeping alive," he told her.

His hand slowly moved down her arm to her hand as she clutched the gift, a precious symbol of his care. The touch left a trail of goose bumps in their wake, a warming thrill settling in her stomach as her heart rate heightened. The intensity in Gallen's eyes was now electric, the energy almost palpable.

"What if I chose to avoid the ocean?" Sol asked innocently, refusing to look away from Gallen as he raised his other hand to stroke her cheek. The gesture was enough to fracture her resistance. She reached her hand from the thoughtful favor of his affections to cradle his cheek, grazing her thumb over the short pricks of his stubbled face. He sighed loudly, perhaps also wrestling with his desires to move further, hold her closer, breathe her in.

"The bag could work in ice as well." His mouth curved into an intoxicating smirk, the creases in his cheeks deepening as he leaned in.

"When shall we set forth?" Avelia's smooth voice broke the trance.

Sol and Gallen jumped backward leaving a strange distance between them. The air itself seemed to realize what they refused to accept, wanting them to join together once more. To share more moments like this.

Gallen cleared his throat and answered, "momentarily."

He reached to grasp Sol's hand a final time, pressing it to his lips, before returning to camp.

Sol was undone. Her mind was thoroughly muddled and thoughts flying. While Gallen's advances were not unwelcome—quite the contrary—Sol still believed something missing. Or perhaps someone. Regardless, his impromptu visit and thoughtful gift solidified her decision for Kinsle and Cotton.

She walked steadfast through the fabric entrance, her boots sinking into the sand with each determined step. Seeing the three others hovering near a newly forged fire, she presented her choice.

"I believe I would prefer the pegasi return to Celestra."

The others looked toward her.

"There are written works, histories of our realm, that are too important to risk. I also would not want these friends to be harmed in the midst of all that is unknown."

Though the phrase offered clarity, Sol knew the others recognized the truest reason: Sol enjoyed this life. These memories. These relationships. And, even as she fidgeted anxiously with her emerald ring, her past was something she was more than willing to sacrifice for the potential of a future she believed could emerge.

Malinar stepped toward her, pulling her body into a tight embrace, the younger Flyer's body nearly half her size yet certainly just as strong. "We shall support your choice, of course."

"We should ready ourselves to leave," Gallen stated, looking on in joyous awe at the two women.

Avelia asserted their voice in the mix: "I will convey this request to the creatures."

Sol merely nodded, looking toward Kinsle and the others rolling in the sand. "I will fold the tents."

"Quickly, then. The swim will take an hour or so and we may need to rest for a bit on the way." Gallen began pulling the fabrics from his own tent as he spoke.

Avelia took the opportunity to explain their potion before they moved to the pegasi. "While the liquid air will allow you all to breathe underwater, the sensation requires great adjustment. Your mind will convince you of the dangers, that you are assuredly drowning. Yet, you must resist such thoughts."

Sol had not considered the mental strain of such a venture. And, as she began truly thinking about the swim ahead, the anxieties of all that could occur rose to the surface. The unknown was always uncomfortable. And Sol was experiencing it in both the skies and the seas.

"One more detail of the journey." Gallen cleared his throat. "We will need to send our Night Flyer clothing with the horses as well.

The wet clothing will make the journey even more difficult, as if we are swimming with weights strapped to us."

Sol looked at Gallen, attempting to gauge the motivations of this suggestion. She raised a brow. "Necessary? Shall we roam into your mother's home in nothing save our skin?"

A blush splattered across Gallen's pale blue cheeks. "Avelia initially packed wetsuits for the journey. They were stored in their pack, which had been strapped to..." He paused slightly, a grimace shading his features as he rushed through the remaining explanation. "We shall find sufficient clothing before we reach mother, I assure you."

Malinar chuckled, a sound of positive fortune for a sensitive journey ahead. Sol would keep that sound with her as they ventured forth.

14

Malinar

Malinar stood with bare feet at the edge of the ocean's tide. The cool water lapped against her ankles as she watched her friends bid farewell to their pegasi. Cotton's glowing wings stretched wide as Gallen hugged her pale-yellow neck. Nearby, Sol touched her forehead to Kinsle's, whispering words of encouragement as the horses prepared to fly.

Turning her head to the horizon, Malinar crunched her eyes closed, scolding her tears as they threatened to fall. The disappearance of the white pegasus was stark as the others offered their tearful goodbyes. Their companions were far more than horses, more than magical creatures who transported them between realms. They were family. Though Storm would never see home again, she hoped that the others would.

The warriors shed their clothing as they prepared the horses for their journey home, sending their supplies—boots and all— back to Celestra. Malinar shivered, her arms hugging her body.

The cold steel of her twin daggers stung her skin, their copper hilts belted safely on her upper arms. Never had she been so exposed in a public space. Her home village expected modesty from their citizens. Such expectations largely followed her into adulthood. Even in amorous moments, the most intimate of spaces, Malinar rarely allowed her body to be seen beyond her tent. The other warriors' exposure diminished her bashfulness, replacing a bought of hesitancy with growing confidence, even if slight.

Sol was a vision. If Malinar believed her to be stunning before, seeing her in almost nothing proved that it was not the clothing or the colors she often painted across her face that made her so. Malinar was enamored with the woman as she tenderly pet Kinsle's mane, the emerald ring she refused to leave behind catching the dim light of the morning. The thin black fabric hanging on her chest barely covered her sizable breasts while her generous curves held the tiny undergarment in place over the intimate space between her large legs. A belt held one of her knives in place in the middle of her thigh while her other weapon was settled into a leather holster belted over her shoulder. The tanned olive tone of her skin radiated in the sunlight, a sight that Malinar certainly never noticed in the darkness of their home realm. Her dark hair, tied in a single braid, flowed down between the blades of her shoulders.

Then there was Gallen. His chest was exposed, revealing the allure of his pale blue body, the shimmer of his skin and the cut of his muscles. His twin blades were strapped comfortably around his torso, slung like a satchel. Malinar wished she could settle comfortably into his toned arms and place her cheek onto his soft stomach to rest. His undergarments were thin, black, and short, the wide bulge between his legs leaving very little to the imagination.

"They are beings of beauty, your companions." Avelia's smooth words shook Malinar from her lustful trance.

She was unsure how to respond to Avelia, this curious apprentice of the High Realm.

"Are you prepared to enter the water?" Malinar queried, shifting her eyes painstakingly from Gallen and Sol to Avelia.

Unlike the Night Flyers, Avelia wore garments that completely covered their midsection, a piece of clothing that offered covering from their shoulders to their mid-thigh. Malinar hoped the fabric would not impede them from swimming effectively. Based on what little she knew of Avelia, the warrior was likely unbothered by the challenge.

"If you Night Flyers are prepared, I would say so."

Malinar nodded, taking all her strength not to roll her eyes at the arrogance. Rather than engage in a battle of will, she sauntered toward Sol and Gallen.

"I believe Avelia is prepared to start our swim," Malinar stated plainly.

Sol turned away from Kinsle, a few wayward tears finding their way down her cheek. "I was moments from beckoning you over. Was there anything you wished to include in our letter home?"

She extended a piece of parchment to Malinar. Their hands touched briefly at the exchange and time itself seemed to offer reprieve. Malinar became brutally aware of the breeze cooling her naked skin. Even more aware of Sol's naked skin.

"Alcor shall know of our altered plans." Sol continued, "Gallen prefers we keep word of the creature to ourselves. He assures a message could be sent by an Ocean Realm messenger when they arrived at his mother's estate in the city, one far more secure."

Malinar briefly glanced at the note, though could not think of an item to add to Sol's thorough letter.

Clearing her throat, Malinar said, "appears sound."

"There is also something I wish to ask." Sol slipped the parchment in a satchel of turquoise and smirked, "you told me of a book you keep with you. I have made enough room if you would like to bring it."

Sol opened the top of the bag to reveal several papers, a book, ink, and quills. Gallen walked from Cotton's side to set a hand on Sol's shoulder. He smiled at Malinar, eyes red from a tearful farewell.

"It will protect anything inside from the water."

Her heart leapt into her throat as the two warriors looked intently toward her. She was fortunate to be traveling with two wonderful beings, two beautiful people both body and soul. She nodded, retrieving her book of strong women from the satchel on Kinsle's back. Then, another thought crossed her mind. She reached into the satchel and revealed the map from the High Realm.

Malinar gasped as she examined the page.

"Malinar, what—" Sol began.

"Can you read these words?" Malinar asked them.

Confused, they huddled closer.

"This is an ancient language. There are few who understand it, so I am told." Gallen offered.

Sol's gripped Malinar's arm. "Why do you ask?"

Malinar shook her head, the markings that just yesterday were incomprehensible swirls, symbols with no meaning, were now words. Places.

"I can," she gaped.

Avelia clomped toward the group. "I believe the sun is gaining an advantage upon us. While rest is necessary, sloth is tawdry."

Gallen turned on his heel, prepared for another crusade for control. Before he could respond, however, the High Realm apprentice faced the tides, squinting as they looked to the horizon. Sol still held Malinar's arm, and she used her free hand to grasp the book from Malinar and delicately place it inside the protective bag. Malinar grinned as Sol drew their faces close together, her lips brushing against Malinar's ear.

"I will protect it with my life."

Malinar wanted Sol to remain near, to keep whispering in her ear, to keep stroking her arm with a warm hand.

But the moment passed as Sol whistled for the pegasi to fly homeward before turning toward the sea. Avelia pulled the glass vial of glowing liquid from a chain around their neck, pulling the cork from the top. The liquid fizzled as they exposed it to the salty air.

"We each need only a sip. The effects of the potion will last for half of a day."

Malinar stepped forward. "Are you certain it will last?"

Avelia smelled the potion slowly, as if enjoying this moment. "Of course, young warrior. Years are spent developing such concoctions as these." They raised the potion in emphasis, giddy with pride.

Sol stepped near them and reached for the blue liquid.

"Only but a sip," Avelia warned as Sol allowed the glowing liquid to slide down her throat.

Malinar followed suit. The blue glow was sour, first freezing her throat and lungs, before burning like an inferno in her ribcage and arms and hands. The sensations lasted only a few seconds, literally one breath in Malinar's screaming lungs, then the warmth settled. The soreness in her torso was a the last evidence of the potions potency. The air tasted salty and clean and…normal.

"The potion should begin its effects immediately," Avelia informed them.

Gallen walked steadily toward the water, his eyes filled with anticipation as he spoke.

"Let us find out."

BREATHING UNDERWATER WAS A CONFUSING SENSATION. Malinar focused her entire being on convincing her body she could not drown. She drew in water as if breathing air. Rather than the taste of salt and seaweed and fish she expected, the water was neutral, lacking anything both off-putting and pleasant.

Though the transition was tiresome, swimming through the Ocean Realm with Gallen and Sol was otherworldly. The water swirled into various shades of blue that glimmered in the beams of sunlight from above. Small fish moved in mesmerizing schools, their scales splashing dashes of vibrant colors into the blue seascape. While her eyes adjusted well to the saltwater and the pressure in her head tolerable, Malinar could hear nearly nothing. The swooshing sound of their movement garbled as she strained to catch any sounds nearby. Gallen led them down into the depths of the ocean.

Once the group swam past a drop-off of sand, Malinar avoided looking below at the never-ending darkness. The occasional creature faded in and out of her peripheral view—a reminder that the warriors were far from alone as they swam. When a fear pricked the back of her mind, thoughts of what lay in the darkness, she reached for Gallen on her left or Sol to her right. Their presence, only an arms-length away, allowed her mind to wander away from fear and toward awe. As they traveled deeper, marine life began to glow mystical shades of oranges, yellows, and blues.

They slowed halfway, allowing the group to catch their breath and soak in the wonder. Malinar was weightless as she floated in the deep, her arms and legs spread wide. The ocean water smelled like her bath in the High Realm, though mixed with kelp and coral. It was like nothing she had ever experienced. A treat for the senses. Sights, smells, sensations. All otherworldly, as if in a dream.

As they swam on, Malinar spied a glowing light in the distance, one that grew stronger and stronger as they continued forward. Nearly an hour of swimming truly passed like minutes and soon the darkness of the deep was illuminated in an orange glow. Soon Malinar was floating before an entire town encased in a massive bubble of air suspended in the middle of the water, a sphere that shimmered with enchantment. Swimming beside the bubble made

Malinar feel like a speck of dust within this endless ocean, so minuscule near the grandeur of this bit of the Ocean Realm. Near the middle of the sphere, a golden platform stood before a gilded archway. The doorway wavered, like a translucent wall between them and all they saw beyond the barrier of orange. Moving closer, Malinar saw the intricacies of the arch. Shells and jewels and coral were embedded in the gold in a wavering pattern, mimicking the look of the water around them.

She followed behind Gallen as he waved them toward the shimmering archway. Standing before the towering doorway, swirls of pink cast rainbows across Malinar's skin. She raised a hand before her, eyes wide in awe.

Gallen faced the entrance head-on, straightening his body and taking a step into the light. Avelia followed quickly behind. Sol looked at Malinar and grasped her hand, linking their fingers together as they faced the portal. Malinar kicked her foot forward, adjusting to the density of a bridge on the other side. She and Sol pushed through the archway together, a trail of water following as clean air washed over them. The taste of true air was like a treat for Malinar's lungs and she gulped it greedily as she reoriented herself.

As soon as their bare feet stepped through the portal, all liquid disappeared from their bodies, as if the town itself sucked the moisture from every fiber of their undergarments. Shivering in the cool air, Malinar hugged her arms over her chest, clinging to her shoulders as they walked through the city. While whatever magic existed here left her dry, nothing could shield her now exposed body from strange onlookers. Uneven coral pressed painfully into the soft heels of her feet. Sol and Avelia carefully paced forward, perhaps also missing the thick leather boots stashed on Kinsle's back somewhere in the sky.

As the warriors walked on the bridge of coral, a cozy sea town came into view, filled with dozens of buildings, bustling carts, and hundreds of people. Sand and stone and shell forged the town's infrastructure, which was essentially a series of bridges between platforms of various sizes, some with buildings and some meant as gathering places.

Unlike those on land, the sea town was filled with a delightful mixture of people—some mer, some mortal. Gills and fins and sharp teeth were sprinkled throughout the small crowds that filled the central gathering area. As Malinar passed through, she noticed the vast majority of townsfolk wearing thin, bare clothing made of rope, small linens, kelp, and beads. Their half-dressed group blended in seamlessly.

"My kin live nearer the other edge of town, not too far." Gallen appeared utterly unfazed by the shift from swimming to walking.

Malinar wished she could say the same. Her legs wobbled as her body readjusted to gravity's pull. Still holding Sol's hand, the two followed Gallen clumsily while Avelia silently walked behind the group, looking in amazement at the sudden existence of the town in the depths of the Ocean Realm.

"Anthozoa is just as other smaller villages," Gallen stated as they reached a large platform of buildings and carts, "it is within only one pocket of air. Though larger cities required three, even four, to house the sprawling buildings, streets, and people."

Malinar perked up at the smell of fried meats and breads. Carts lined the pathways, merchants calling the names of various street foods. Malinar assumed so, anyway.

The buildings stationed behind rows of carts evoked shapes of water—the rippling effect of waves, the movement of sea plants, and the sleek shapes of sea life were clear inspirations. Stone and shells, held together by a sort of sanded plaster comprised most homes. Each was smooth; the roofs domed at the top with a few small, circular windows to allow the filtered sunlight in. To Malinar, the town itself seemed an extension of the sea floor, though there was certainly farther to explore, deeper to swim.

Some enchantment held the town in place; the platforms suspended within the massive orange orb. Patches of coral thrived throughout the town, like vibrant flowers. Street lamps lined the bridges and platforms. Unlike those from the Star Realm, which emitted a calming blue aura into the everlasting night, these raged an aggressive orange that filled the town with an abundance of light. Shadows could hide nothing here.

Gallen slowed his pace as they approached one of the many nondescript buildings. He knocked on the curved wooden door and signaled for them to wait.

"Gallen?" a small voice chirped as a female of average height and build opened the door, "when did you arrive?"

The woman did not appear much older than Gallen and looked every bit his kin. Bright purple freckles speckled her pale blue skin and crowded her face. Thick lines of navy-colored paint outlined her jawline and impressively crisp wings of glitter framed her eyelids. Her blonde hair was plaited into several tight braids that fell down her shoulders, reaching well below her waist. She was dressed in what Malinar could assume was typical attire for the town, a delicate tunic woven from purple seaweed cropped to reveal the underside of her breasts. She wore a skirt made from the same sea flora, with small beads threaded into the hem. The woman looked past Gallen's shoulder to see his three companions, still standing on shaky footing.

Her breath caught in her throat, and the smile she wore upon seeing her cousin dissipated as she connected the pieces.

"Your mother will reprimand you harshly for bringing unwelcome strangers to this realm." The high pitch tone of her voice was less cheery and more alarming.

"Neva, take a moment, please." Gallen held out his hand as he attempted to reach his cousin.

Unamused, Avelia stepped forward, despite Gallen's look of disapproval.

"There are matters far more important than tradition, I am afraid to admit," they stated frankly, the charm in their tone wooing even Malinar to acceptance. "Shall we discuss such matters in the safety of your home?"

Less a question, more a demand.

The woman looked back to Gallen, aghast. "You must fix this. Whatever it is you have done."

She turned her back to him and walked inside, leaving the door ajar as a reluctant invitation to enter. Gallen pinched the ridge of his nose with his fingers in frustration but weakly followed, waving the others to enter as well. Avelia needed no encouragement, confidently walking into the space with their chin held high.

The home contained no sharp corners or edges, only smooth curves and open archways. The walls mirrored its exterior: sandy plaster holding together the various pebbles, shells, and treasures. The designs appeared far more deliberate on the floors, walls, and ceilings than on the outside. Malinar noticed a plethora of pearls decorating the space in various swirling designs. The first room was sizable and filled to the brim with furniture and trinkets and art. Most things were made of wood and basic metals—wooden chairs, iron tables, and the like. But there were a few notable exceptions: two chiseled blue stone carvings of a traditional mermaid and a delicate swan.

Sol and Gallen took places on a large bench, and Gallen gestured for Malinar to join them while Avelia continued to slink in the curved corner of the room.

"Do tell, dear cousin." The dissonance of Neva's natural brightness and the revulsion in her voice caused Malinar to shift uncomfortably.

"My companions, Sol and Malinar, and I," Gallen began, an unnatural meekness shading his face, "began a quest, and it has led us quite far from our intended goal."

He appeared flustered as he drummed up the courage to continue. "There are dangers above, Neva. If we do not assist in their demise, all realms will suffer."

Neva scoffed at the mention of any "above" world dangers and became especially agitated at notions of their realms being tied. "First talk of a king and now this? What has the upper air done to your seabrain?"

She was clearly unwilling to acknowledge that the dangers that lurked above may well impact those below. Sol, Malinar, and Avelia remained silent during this interaction. Malinar considered leaving the two to discuss matters alone; yet, as she began shifting her weight forward, Gallen placed a tender hand on her leg.

"Neva," he begged, "you must understand the value of life, even if that life resides out of your reach. There are people in the above world, families, animals. You must resist these fantasies of isolation. The Ocean Realm is powerful, capable. It is irresponsible to stand aside."

Neva crossed her arms across her chest. "The way we remain powerful is to remain isolated."

"Mother would say differently—" Gallen began.

"Kattegat is tainted. Tainted by the fantasy you conjured of uniting the realms. And do not for one moment think I have forgotten the source of such foolishness, such danger." She shot a callous look at Sol.

Gallen placed his other hand on Sol's leg, assuring his support. "There is so much you do not know, Neva."

"Call your mother, then leave my home. You have one hour."

With that, the woman stood, the freckles of her face besmirched by a look of menacing disgust.

GALLEN USED one of Neva's messenger jellies to call on Lady Kattegat. The process of whispering to the glowing jellyfish momentarily pulled Malinar from the intensity of their precarious position. Thoughtfully, carefully, Gallen instructed the small creature to swim to his mother and relay a message he hoped would bring support. Its delicate arms swished in graceful waves through the air, flowing from its domed body like ribbons of light. And, in a flash, the jelly zoomed outside Neva's oval window and into the world beyond. Malinar wished to see more beings of this realm, the graceful and the glowing and the utterly glorious.

While Sol and Malinar remained glued to their respective places in the room, afraid to further upset Gallen's cousin, Avelia took the opportunity to closely examine the home, looking through every trinket, inside every box, and analyzing every painting.

"This is truly an extraordinary opportunity to learn about this realm," they whispered gleefully. "The realm itself has remained isolated for centuries. Though some venture in to see sights and enjoy its pleasures, nothing substantial has ever been revealed. This look into their world...it is priceless."

Malinar assumed the apprentice meant well. As a lifelong student, they likely could not help the opportunity to learn. Yet, as Malinar watched them scurry from one spot to the next, she kept a watchful eye on the doorway, in case Neva came to reprimand them. She eased slightly when Gallen returned to the room. He ignored Avelia's continued intrusion of his cousin's privacy and settled between his two true companions. He pressed his palms against his eyelids.

"The message should reach Mother soon enough." His voice sounded weighted.

Malinar examined his stray strands of blonde hair and affectionately combed them back with her nails. "What should we do?"

She looked at him eagerly, coaxing back the former fervor of the leader she'd ridden behind the entire journey. Gallen appeared more downtrodden than usual, deeply affected by his cousin's rejection, her absolute hatred of anything above the ocean's tide.

Gallen extended his arms around the two women, pulling them close to him for a bit of comfort, perhaps to remind himself of who he was and why he chose the life of a Flyer. The hug extended far longer than any platonic expression of appreciation, one that even shook Avelia from their snooping around the room. They watched the trio embrace, sighing loudly before turning back to the treasures lining the walls. When the three separated, Gallen exhaled deeply.

"My mother should arrive soon, I am certain. Then we shall—"

A booming knock reverberated through the room. A tall woman stepped over the threshold, clothed in cords of silver woven with glowing beads and shining shells. Her lavender hair fell over her shoulder in hundreds of tight braids accented with tiny golden charms. She demanded attention from the Flyers, from Avelia, and soon from Neva who rushed back in. The woman ignored their stares as she stomped into the room, her bare feet jingling with various anklets. Gallen took a quick breath in.

"Mother."

15

Gallen

The scene could not have been more concerning: his mother, three land dwellers, and her son disheveled and completely off course. It was a living nightmare for Gallen. He wished he could take Sol and Malinar and whisk them away from this uncomfortable reunion. Perhaps show them what he loved about the Ocean Realm. Not the harsh and judgmental people who despised what they could not understand, but the joyful folk, the beauty of the buildings, the magnificence of the ocean itself.

Instead, he stood to his sore feet—the calluses that once protected him fully from the many rough, shell-lined roads not quite as thick as when he was a child. He bowed deeply.

"Many thanks for your swift arrival—"

His mother scoffed, "When the jellyfish flew through my door, my intuition screamed to see with my own eyes this...situation."

Gallen knew this tone, and it was not good.

"Tell me, dear son, what you expected from this sudden and

unsanctioned visit? Last I was aware, you were deliberating with our future king about a certain...obstacle."

Kattegat swept her golden eyes over the room, pausing over each person, only stopping her examination when Sol leaned into view. Her demeanor shifted immediately, a bright smile completely lifting the disappointment from her face.

"Sol, my sweet! I am glad to see you held together by your courage." The lady swished toward the bench to grasp Sol's hand in her own, pressing it to her forehead.

Sol blushed, holding the wooden plank with the other hand hard enough to whiten her knuckles. Gallen knew his mother meant well. The two women shared a strong bond before Sol ventured to Endoneth. Hopefully, they could again.

The sight of Sol certainly lightened his mother's mood, her voice amenable.

"Now. I have arranged transport for your guests. We may need to meet with members of the city council for their retroactive approval, yet I am certain circumstances will dictate necessity."

She turned to Gallen knowingly, a woman altogether commanding in her decisions. Her fortitude in full display.

"Shall we?"

Leaving Neva's home was bittersweet. He loved seeing his cousin, someone he was raised alongside, yet he hated the isolation that bubbled to the surface when he visited places like Anthozoa. Many in the Ocean Realm held older views of those who lived above. Believed other realms cared nothing for their people or interests or cultures. Believed they would never know how to care even if they wished. And when Gallen, a figure believed to hold great power in the realm, decided to join the Night Flyers of the Star Realm, it was not well received.

Gallen sullenly followed his mother's formidable figure as she rushed through the cobbled walkway from Neva's home to a golden chariot sitting a few steps away. The chariot was a familial heirloom, a magical transport that sped from one end of the Ocean Realm to the other in a snap. When he was a youth, Gallen recalled riding the chariot with his grandfather at the helm, chasing pods of whales and searching for treasures. The memories brought a smile to his face.

He led his friends toward the magnificent work of art. The gold was nearly blinding as it reflected the orange lights, the etchings curling in fine lines throughout the structure. The delicate, winding metalwork stretched as each rider climbed into the structure, making ample room for the group in its entirety.

Sol and Malinar sat on either side of Gallen, and he pulled their arms toward him.

"You may want to hold my arm."

Sol grabbed hold of his outstretched arm while Malinar gave a look of confusion.

The lady of the realm sat at command, the lines of glittery purple painted across her cheeks shining in the sea light. She grasped the reins in her hands before the chariot flew through the air, toward an upper portal outside, and into the ocean. The women at his sides clutched onto Gallen's arms as they gained speed, the rush whipping them back into the padded seats of the chariot.

Gallen knew the sensation, the strange view of the ocean at breakneck speed as magic propelled them forward. While the chariot shielded its riders from the water, it did nothing to prevent rushes of pressure as it gained speed. But, even with the inconveniences, it was the fastest form of transportation in the realm.

The chariot drove further and further away from the bubble, and deeper and deeper into the ocean. And, like Gallen knew it would, it took mere minutes to reach Somov, the City of Dreams.

As they pulled through a massive arched portal into the city, he pulled the women closer, whispering encouragement as they attempted to remain composed. Malinar's face was a crude shade of green as Sol breathed rhythmically in and out. Avelia jumped out of the chariot as soon as it slowed, apparently unfazed by the trip. Gallen could not help but be impressed.

His mother also took notice.

"A warrior with a stomach of steel." She beamed.

The comment was meant as a compliment, yet Gallen could see Avelia did not quite understand how to respond, offering a brief nod before looking at the unmatched beauty of the city.

He found it unmatched, at least. Gallen had traveled throughout the Nine Realms, once as a noble heir, then as a Night Flyer, setting foot in at least one region of each. While there existed appealing locales, nothing he had witnessed could compare to his home. To Somov.

The smell of salt and sweet clementines surrounded him as they landed on a glimmering platform made of glowing corals. The chariot was settled between three enormous castles with golden, swirling turrets and asymmetric windows. Similar to the use of shells and jewels in smaller towns like Anthozoa, the buildings throughout Somov were decorated with intricate designs using impressive treasures, evidence of the immense wealth of the city, cultivated over centuries of exploration. The sister castles were the most ostentatious example of this. They sported jewels the size of whales surrounded by the most minuscule diamonds and sapphires and pearls.

The walk from the coral platform and the golden chariot to Eckral highlighted the most stunning aspects of the realm itself. Gallen never understood the true impact of the realm's isolation until he stepped above water. The architecture, the food, even the way individuals approached life were all vastly different here. Though Gallen had often told his mother of the ways other realms valued their culture—adopting their fashions more than any other realm in Nourels—the lady was slow to believe the realms could work in harmony. Convincing the people of the Ocean Realm to consider joining Alcor and partake in the concerns of the realms above took painstaking effort on his part. Though, once his mother became an avid supporter of the cause, largely thanks to Sol's investment in the realm, other lords and ladies began to take notice.

Sol and Malinar were still shaky from the hastened journey from Anthozoa; they retained their hold on each of his arms. He whispered to them, hoping his words would offer a welcome distraction as they steadied their stomachs.

"The murals represent ancient lore of the realm."

He pointed to the castle on their right. "Here is an image of Mist, the goddess of water and life, breathing our protective bubbles into being."

Mist's form took shape with iridescent turquoise gems that shined orange in a certain light. Her face, gentle and calm, effortlessly created the pearlescent balls of air where cities, towns, and estates found home.

He continued, "then, our left castle showcases the earliest-known pilgrimage to Somov. Groups from throughout the future Ocean Realm came together on this auspicious day, brought by the aura of Mist and integrated into one society, one people. The mural represents the importance of unity, that despite our ancient origins, each people group truly belonging to Somov."

A semicircle of luminous pearls portrayed this event beautifully in the mural. On one side of the barrier, different jewels were used for the various groups, set into the golden walls of the castle. Some outlined by red rubies, some brown topaz, and others black onyx, swimming toward the city from divergent sides toward the semicircle. On the other side of the pearls, striking emerald stones made up the people.

"Then, there is the largest castle, placed at the center as it is the most important aspect of our people, our destiny." Gallen motioned to turrets that sat slightly higher than the others.

Unlike its sisters, the golden walls of this castle displayed no mural, no captivating story of Somov's past. The walls were instead bare save a singular emerald, settled above the asymmetric entrance of the magnificent building.

"I was taught that the central castle represented the future of Somov, a blank slate for the citizens to dream." Gallen grinned as his golden eyes reflected the green stone, "my grandfather claimed that these castles once housed powerful beings. Members of the community who could hear the voice of Mist herself. Now the buildings largely served public uses: a neutral location for ladies and lords of the twelve estates to meet, a welcome home for those fallen on difficult times, and a central site for the city's festive celebrations."

Gallen loved watching the women absorb the marvelous sights of the realm. They gasped as the group passed the castles, their eyes wide as they watched various chariots of disparate shapes, colors, and sizes exit through a portal ten times the size of the archway of the other town. What warmed his heart the most was seeing Sol gaze in admiration at the coral that paved the pathways throughout the realm. Though the material was by far the simplest of any in the realm, to Gallen it held so much more meaning than the gold and jewels. Without these platforms, the city would crumble. And, while the coral glowed in various shades of deep purple, red, and blue, it was the color green that captured Gallen most.

They continued to follow the path passed the sister castles. And, just beyond the three strongholds, stood the Estate of Eckral where Kattegat asserted her influence on the people in Somov and throughout the Ocean Realm. The coral estate belonged to his family since the founding of the city and, like all other buildings, the estate was fantastic. Forged from a mixture of metals—gold, silver, iron, and rose gold—all twisted into impressive shapes throughout its exterior. Within the swirls of metal were shining precious stones, some newer, some ancient. As the warriors walked through the rectangular doors, memories of his childhood warmed his heart. His grandfather. His mother. His late father. All helping Gallen to become his best self.

"This is marvelous, Gallen," Malinar whispered. "You spent your childhood in this place?"

Sol looked at him eagerly, her curiosity unmistakable. The three walked in unison, like a united front against the world. Peace enveloped Gallen.

"This was home," he replied with a smile.

"You must give us an extensive tour," Sol stated, her eyes soaking in the entryway, then the first major hallway, then the sitting room.

Gallen's mother noted the four sets of clothing crumpled on a long table at the front entrance. Kattegat waved a hand toward them.

"Dress so we may begin untangling these knots of information."

She must have sent for linens—always like his mother to prepare even given the shortest of notice. The group reached for the clothes, and Gallen noticed Malinar's hesitancy as she clasped the thin fabrics native to the realm. He grinned as he watched Malinar and Sol slip the short dresses above their heads and down their torsos, their undergarments still somewhat visible through the threads.

Kattegat, walking at a determined pace, led them toward a study. The room was impressive, as Gallen's mother preferred. She fitted the room with four couches covered in silk placed around a circular table. An ornate tea set sat atop the wood, steam filtering through the small spout of the kettle, ready to pour and enjoy. The lady of the house waved the group of four to sit on the couches as she sauntered over to a desk and chair positioned at the far end of the room. In this position, the power dynamic on display, Gallen understood his mother's intentions. She needed answers and they would not leave the room without providing them.

"Gallen."

With one word, Kattegat could convey multitudes. Gallen

stood near the edge of the farthest couch, perhaps to use the position as an excuse to look at Malinar and Sol, respectfully waiting for the debrief to begin.

"The weapon is far more concerning than we initially believed."

Flashes of Storm's scream rang in his mind. He shivered, the memory of the bird's eyes boring into his soul. Sweat beaded along the back of his neck as he continued, "those in the High Realm believe—"

Avelia cut in before Gallen could fully explain, "we believe the Past Holders of your realm may hold the key to their demise."

This warrior of the High Realm was beginning to wear thin on Gallen's patience, which was at baseline quite limited. His mother appeared equally unimpressed by the interruption, instead looking to her son.

"Continue." She stated.

"Master Zelan of the High Realm explained that there are those in the Northern realms who hold these creatures, phoenixes, as another measure in the fight for power."

Kattegat listened carefully as Gallen explained, nodding intermittently.

"As Avelia stated," Gallen cast a stern glance their way, "the master believes our realm holds the key to preventing this creature from gaining control of Nourels. As you feared, this phoenix, the first of many it seems, is as much a threat to those in the Ocean Realm as those above."

Gallen looked to the others. Malinar offered him a supportive nod as Sol scrunched the fabric of her dress in her hands, eagerly anticipating Kattegat's reaction. Avelia, shaken from the silent reprimand from the lady of the home, stared ahead at the bookcases lining the walls of his mother's study. The group awaited a response from his mother, though, as Gallen was well aware, she often took her time to fully contemplate the implications of information. And this information was realm-altering.

"We must inform the Twelve. It is what is right."

She stood, her hands firmly planted on the desk before her, as she definitively stated this objective. Gallen could only watch as his mother stomped toward the door, her long braids swinging from side to side as she moved confidently outside. Before she left the four warriors alone, she added, "you all may stay as long as is necessary. Gallen will show you to the guest halls."

With that, the Lady of Coral disappeared into the depths of the estate.

Gallen turned as the decision passed over the others. He saw Avelia working through the meaning of his mother's words, their eyes shifting from side to side as if reading some invisible transcript of the former conversation. Malinar and Sol sat near each other on one of the couches, waiting for Gallen to offer guidance.

"If you wish, I may escort you to visiting quarters." Gallen swung his arm toward the room's exit and Avelia was the first to oblige, stomping away from the quartet of couches. "Perhaps provide a tour?"

"Take me to a place to rest. I must be at the peak of attentiveness to absorb all that your fair realm has to offer," Avelia demanded.

Relief overtook him as Malinar stifled a laugh.

"I am certain Malinar would enjoy a tour," Sol said, smiling meekly, "The offer has certainly intrigued me."

Malinar nodded eagerly. Reassured, Gallen quickly ushered them from the study, through open walkways and gathering spaces, and to the visitors' hall. The wing of the estate dedicated to guests began with a large living area filled with various tables, chairs, and bookcases for visitors to enjoy. The floors and walls were made of green, glowing coral sanded down into smooth surfaces, the natural holes in the material filled with gold and silver. The effect was transcendent, a lovely mixture of natural beauty and luxury.

Gallen spread his arms wide, "I present you the guest suites."

The others searched the space quizzically. Gallen smirked as

Avelia searched for a door in vain. He pushed upon the wall, knowingly. Suddenly, an arched door pushed inward, part of the glowing green and gold wall moving aside to reveal Avelia's quarters.

"Astonishing," Malinar breathed. "How many rooms are connected to this gathering place?"

Gallen beamed. "Only three in this wing. Though other quarters contain more."

"Enlightening, Flyer Gallen." Avelia nodded, "Farewell, for now."

The door shut with a thud, disappearing once more in a camouflage of coral. Malinar chuckled as the three Flyers were left alone in the spacious gathering area, "They are an enigma."

Sol laughed as she looked to Gallen. "A tour, if you will?"

Gallen looked at her with a grateful smile, excited to share the objects that shaped him.

"After you," he replied.

THE WOMEN WERE MORE than gracious as Gallen pointed out every detail of Eckral that held meaning to him: the largest carpet depicting a jellyfish, his most beloved animal. The painting he almost destroyed playing with a slingshot at age eight. The bookcase his grandfather built for his twelfth birthday. The burnt photograph of his father, the only picture of him remaining in existence. The two women eagerly soaked in even the most minute aspects of each artifact. Each piece of his past offering another link that tethered the three together.

They walked through the halls of coral, the more vibrant colors fading subtly into a calming natural hue. Artifacts filled the rooms, keepsakes both set on display and hidden away in trunks, cases, and files. Each new room led Gallen down partially forgotten parts of his past—memories tucked away for safekeeping and rarely pulled to the surface of his consciousness. The three entered a room painted a striking white, with bookcases sunken into the walls and displays scattered throughout the floors. With no seating in sight, the purpose of the room was clear: a showcase of sacred items.

They began walking through the space, stopping every few steps for the women to request information from Gallen regarding the most unusual pieces.

"And what is this piece?" Sol asked, pointing to a shard of glass bejeweled with red stones along its pointed edge.

"My grandfather chose this for my mother. He gifted it to her when she came of age as a reminder that even the most beautiful objects have sharp edges. He always saw a fierceness in her."

He appreciated Sol's interest, her kindness as she gently touched his back and examined the glass shard intently. She seemed to know exactly what to ask to reveal the most important aspects of his life. The Keeper of Records at work.

He heard Malinar's quiet gasp as she stood before another object of familial significance. She examined a small, rectangular parchment, no larger than the size of Gallen's pearlescent compact. He joined her there, standing near a pedestal upon which the parchment lay. The page displayed an image of a map. Gallen recognized the spherical bounds of Somov immediately.

"Would you like to see something truly enchanting?" he asked her.

Like a giddy child demonstrating a magic trick, Gallen waved his hand over the parchment. The paper responded, gleaming with a pale blue light that mirrored his skin tone. After a few moments, the small rectangle grew twice its size, the map of the single city now including the Ocean Realm in its entirety.

Malinar's purple eyes grew wide, a smile brightening her already stunning features. Gallen's heart soared.

"Is this map truly enchanted?" The excitement burst through her words.

Sol grinned as she watched Gallen and Malinar's interaction. Another reason for his heart to take flight.

Nodding, Gallen waved his hand over the parchment once more, acting as a guide for the vibrant lights that slithered around the various cities and towns and passages in between. The paper became sturdy and wide. When he lingered over Luiosh, a city on the outskirts of the realm, the bubble grew to encompass the entire parchment, the intricate details within becoming more visible. Homes akin to the coral mansions seen in Somov came into focus, connected by baroque iron paths. Malinar squinted as she focused on each detail.

"Are they moving?" she asked gleefully. "Is this a view of what is happening at this very moment?"

"It was a particular day in the past. A particular day at a particular time, yet each session is never the same," Gallen explained. "The map is a unique form of art. One that sees the beauty in the known yet unknown. The wonder of seeing the Ocean Realm as a space united by so much, yet each small segment so unique. The enchantment will allow only glimpses of life, not enough to be used maliciously. Only enough to appreciate."

Sol stood close behind the two as they spoke, peeking her head over Gallen's shoulder. Malinar reached for his arm as her eyes scanned the city.

"Magnificent," she breathed quietly.

"Utterly stunning," Sol replied.

A wave of pride fell over Gallen. That his realm produced something wondrous that both women could appreciate. A work of art that could inspire. He continued explaining its origin.

"The artist had the gift of Seeing, unique in its manifestation. He could conjure what has happened before. This is just one of his enchanted works."

They stood silent as they watched the figures turn to and fro before Malinar looked at Gallen and said, "do say more."

WHEN THE THREE moved on to the next room, Malinar still presented the occasional question about the map and its view of the world. Then the next room. Then the next.

Though the day of exploring proved lovely, Gallen remained taunted by Sol's admission that night in Celestra. While the journey gave Gallen a different perspective of Sol, the words she said in the Night Streets continued to replay in his head. As if his mind sought to protect his heart any moment the two grew close. The impact of the dreaded phrase led him into spirals of confusion and hurt and anger. Speaking with Malinar was a pleasant surprise, her levelheaded empathy opening his eyes to another view of their mutual friend. He knew the only way to move forward, to shed the final barrier between himself and Sol, was transparency. Voicing frustrating and painful truths.

At the end of the tour, a whistling sound signaled the start of dinner. The three Flyers almost ran to the dining hall. Gallen had not realized the impact of the journey on his hunger until he smelled the sweet pineapple-coconut bread, the salty fish stew, and the savory spiced meat surrounded by grilled greens. Avelia was nowhere to be seen, likely resting and regrouping after the discussion with Kattegat. The lady herself was also absent, leaving Malinar, Sol, and Gallen to enjoy the feast alone.

Once the food was largely gone, Gallen summoned the courage to approach Sol. "Would you mind a private walk?"

Sol looked up from her soup, slurping the final spoonful before nodding nervously. Malinar looked from one of her friends to the other, curious about Gallen's request yet still enjoying another plate of vegetables. Sol stood cautiously and followed him away from the table and toward an area close to Gallen's heart: his personal quarters.

The scent of his room immediately settled Gallen. The walls and floors were a dazzling shade of pale blue that reminded him of

Sol's eyes. At the center of the space, a large, circular bed was prepared with silky white sheets. Sol walked to the bed and sat on its edge facing Gallen, waiting for the purpose of this impromptu meeting to become clear.

"I realize I may have initially acted rather distant toward you, and I believe you deserve to know the reason."

Sol straightened her spine, a look of intrigue written on her face.

"The final night in the Star Realm we gathered with the other Night Flyers, do you recall?"

A slow look of realization crept onto her face as Gallen continued, "You said something to me that night. Away from all but Asha. The words...I am ashamed to say that they have remained in my mind since that night, taunting me with a reality I have tried desperately to dispel."

She looked at him, her eyes brimming with tears as she nodded. She never broke her stare, her icy eyes looking into Gallen's with unbridled emotion. Gallen could not say if it made him more confident that she cared for him or less confident that this was the correct course of action.

"What were the words? I—I desperately wish I could say that I knew. I was—I had a good amount of alcohol that night."

The confirmation did little to quell his nerves, yet he forged ahead. "You told me that you preferred it there. With him. And that you missed the way he *felt*."

Her mouth opened in disbelief, as if the statement was so far from the truth that she could not understand the reasoning of her former self. Another confirmation that did little to settle him.

"Gallen," she reached for his hand and pulled him closer, "I apologize. There are no words. I...there is truly nothing I could say to justify words so vile. So insensitive."

Gallen took her hand as an invitation to sit, and so he did. She pulled him closer, winding her arms over his shoulders to fully embrace him.

"I do not know why I would say such a thing. I do not know why."

The guilt seemed to sit heavy in her chest, as if she could not manage a deep breath.

"Everything feels...wrong." Gallen could only watch as her mind tumbled through an endless sea of catastrophic possibilities. "I cannot fathom a world without you. Without Malinar. Without the Flyers and Celestra and the place we built within it."

As he pulled back, Gallen could see the barrage of thoughts swarming Sol's mind. They were written on her face as clearly as her records. Gallen watched as Sol ran through her entire range of emotions: Shock, hurt, confusion, disbelief, shame. Once she settled, she addressed Gallen with a brazen honesty he appreciated.

"Perhaps it was an attempt to hurt you. To hurt you for being so cold to me. For all I have wanted, truly, is to be close to you."

The look of utter turmoil in Sol's eyes melted the cool barrier between them. It was as if Gallen could no longer recall the hurt that once plagued him when he stared into the pools of salty tears lining the corners of her blue eyes. His heart warred menacingly with his mind. Memories of his abandonment, of her spiteful drunkenness, of her admitted intimacy with the Ice Lord, all pushed against his desire to forgive her. Only a fool would.

But Gallen never claimed to be wise.

The idea of further rejection loomed above him viscerally. Perhaps he did not want to believe she could ever love him as she once did. This new Sol. This enchanting, generous, and considerate version of the woman he once knew so well. Because to care for someone so dearly meant there was far more to lose.

"In truth, even if you yearned for that time—for a time where you were treated like royalty by a powerful lord—I could not fault you."

"Gallen..."

"Listen," he pressed his thumb against her hand, "I do not mean to say you want him. Who you know him to be now. Yet, I understand the desire to want a feeling you once had. A yearning for a time you may not fully understand or a place that may not have been reality. It is not a shameful feeling, to want to feel loved. Adored. Desired."

Sol considered his words as they sat together, staring as Gallen's heart thudded faster and faster.

She again pulled Gallen closer, not in a rush of emotions or in an attempt to convey her apology, but gently, lovingly. He thought back to their night in the High Realm, her invitation he turned away. If only he could turn the clock back. If only they could have the moment once more. He placed a shaking hand on her thigh, hoping this time she would not refuse him as he refused her.

She whispered in his ear, and the feeling of her cool breath sent a shiver down his spine. "There is no other place in all the realms I would want to belong than with you. You and—"

A knock at the door startled them, still clinging to one another as if their bodies would not survive separation. Malinar's petite form opened the door, the coral creaking and the sound of her bare feet shifting. When she saw them on the bed, Sol's arms wrapped around Gallen and Gallen's hand creeping up Sol's thigh, she did not turn around. Did not run away or even hide her face. Instead, she gazed longingly, intrigued and enticed.

Sol looked at Gallen, a look that he understood instantaneously. He reached his hand out toward Malinar as Sol voiced the desire they both felt. A desire they perhaps felt for days.

"Would you like to join?"

16

Sol

ould you like to join?"

THE WORDS TASTED like the first fruits of a season – a satisfying sweetness after patiently awaiting harvest. Malinar's arms trembled as she hugged her stomach, taking deliciously slow steps toward the bed. Sol shifted her legs against the sheets, her bare thighs reveling in the sensation of the silk. Gallen drew a sharp intake as they both eyed Malinar, her small frame almost gliding over the pale, coral floors, the translucent fabric of her dress providing brief glimpses of her luminous skin.

When she finally stood before them, her head lowered, shifting from one set of lusting eyes to the other. Sol's body demanded she reach toward the woman, to pull her into the bed with them, to feel her body heat on theirs. Instead, she watched as Malinar reached her hand to rest on Gallen's thigh. Sol took the moment to appreciate his body. The feel of his skin beneath her arms. The sleeveless tunic made of loose fabric laced in a circular pattern that left more than half of his body open to the cool air of the room. She saw bumps rise on his pale blue skin as Malinar's hand slinked up his thigh.

In the midst of so much uncertainty, so much struggle and grief and shame, Sol's body begged for something hopeful. Something genuine and beautiful and wholly hers.

Gallen grasped Sol's thigh, his grip light yet intent, as he used his other hand to pull Malinar on the bed beside them. Her laughter sounded like heaven, a blessing for their future together.

Together. Sol enjoyed that thought.

Sol leaned into the center of the bed, the circle large enough to comfortably fit the three warriors with room to spare. Though she did not want room between herself and these figures. She wanted them near.

"Touch me."

Sol voiced the thought as if the barrier between what she pondered and what she expressed barely existed. It was the comfort, like Malinar with the map or Gallen with her drunken statement. The sensation of this comfort compelled her to share her true self. All of who she was. All she wished to be.

As soon as Sol spoke, Malinar shifted from sitting to crawling, inching toward her with a bewitching look. Leaned over, Sol could see the shape of her small breasts hanging within her dress, swaying slightly as she moved tantalizingly toward Sol. Gallen watched from behind Malinar, eyes looking from her ass to Sol's body as she lay back on her arms, utterly welcoming.

When Malinar reached her, she was practically salivating, wanting the small hands to hold her like that night in the Valley Realm.

As if reading her thoughts, Malinar hovered directly above Sol, their bodies sickeningly close to touching, their breath heavy with want. Gallen shifted as well, following Malinar to the center of the bed. Rather than join the women, he remained inches away, observing, yearning, waiting.

"Go on, Malinar. Touch her."

His words were less a command than a plea. An overture for himself as much as them.

Malinar lifted her delicate hand and cupped Sol's cheek, tenderly brushing a stray strand of brown hair from her red scar. A warm shiver tingled down Sol's spine. Malinar indulged the woman before her, swiping her thumb in gentle strokes over Sol's cheek and jaw and neck. Her smile pressed her cheeks upward, her eyes squinting in pure bliss. Over Malinar's shoulder, Sol saw Gallen grin deeply, a bulge in his pants growing as the women drew closer and closer.

For such a harsh woman on the surface, Malinar's touch was like that of a feather, delicate and tantalizing. It swept over Sol's skin like a promise of what was to come. An invitation to demand more. Malinar pressed her hand where Sol's jaw met her neck, pulling her head upward with a fluid and forceful movement. A soft gasp escaped Sol's lips, her thighs trembling as she remained caught between the mattress and Malinar's lithe form. A willing prisoner to the alluring snare of the woman's touch. Her breath. Her being.

Unable to resist any longer, Sol reached forward and pulled Malinar lower, their bodies crashing together magnificently. The moment their lips met, Sol melted into the kiss, enthralled by the knowledge that this woman wanted her. She wished to store away each sweet second, each euphoric heartbeat, each flutter of Malinar's lashes, so tantalizingly close.

Though she dared not tear her eyes from Malinar, Sol heard Gallen's uneven breathing as he watched their connection. She could sense him admiring them, cherishing them. His breathing hitched with every swipe of Malinar's finger against Sol's chin, as if he warred with himself, wishing to ravish them yet also to watch the women enjoy each other.

Malinar broke the kiss, leaning her mouth to graze Sol's ear, sending another thrilling shudder through her body. Malinar's hand explored with amorous intent, her fingers roaming up Sol's thick thighs toward the hem of her dress.

"You have gone out of your way to make me feel safe these past days."

Her fingers swirled in seductive circles up Sol's thigh as she spoke, deftly pulling the thin undergarments aside.

"Let me make you feel safe."

She pressed two fingers against Sol's body, running them against her entrance, toward the sweet center of her thighs. Sol arched her back, moans of pleasure escaping her in short bursts.

Gallen moved closer then, as if beckoned by her call. The silk shifted beneath Sol as he observed Malinar's hand continue consistent pressure on the most sensitive spaces of Sol, the fingers pressing in on her clit in a glorious rhythm. As her hand worked below, Malinar kissed her neck, then her chin, her cheeks, her brows, and her forehead before easing into another passionate kiss on her lips. Sol affirmed her pleasure, swiping her tongue against Malinar's as the rhythm of her fingers continued. The two moved in a harmonious cadence, a dance that was both exciting and comforting. Malinar pulsing against her, Sol tugging at Malinar's hair. Malinar caressing Sol's breast, Sol cupping Malinar's ass.

Sol sensed herself growing closer to that final release and she wanted it. That freedom. The waves of pleasure easing the growing tension in her stomach. Yet, as she climbed toward the edge, she placed a hand on Malinar's. A gentle request to pause.

Sol turned her eyes from Malinar to Gallen before stating through heavy gasps, "I want us all to reach it together."

They looked back toward Sol, a wicked grin shared by the two as Gallen swept in to claim his own kiss. While Malinar's kiss was slow, deliberate, and soft, Gallen's was impassioned and eager;

both were desperate to please her, to care for her, just in different ways. That knowledge alone emboldened Sol. She reached her hand to cup Gallen's growing bulge thinly veiled by his ever-tightening shorts. As she stroked him slowly, his sighs encouraged her to move more and more quickly as his tongue dragged along Sol's.

Sol pulled her lips from Gallen's, opening her eyes to see his own- focused and fiery. As Sol continued the tempo of her hand along his growing shaft, she watched as Malinar spread her legs open toward Gallen before beginning her circular motion against Sol once again. With an invitation, he combed his hair back and leaned his head forward. The tip of his hardness peeked below the bottom hem of his garments as he shifted his position. Taking advantage of the opportunity, Sol pulled the linen away completely, revealing his bare, throbbing skin. As he began licking Malinar's legs, his head disappearing under her dress, Sol grabbed him fully and began the movements again, working to match the tempo of Malinar's fingers which slid wonderfully along the top of her clit.

Sol could hear Gallen lapping at Malinar's folds, licking her at a similar pace. Malinar groaned and soon slid into Sol's entrance, thrusting her thin fingers in and out. The pressure mounted as Sol focused on the sounds and smells and feelings.

She wished this could last a lifetime. That the three warriors could remain in this bed of pleasure for hours. Days. Decades.

The thought of Malinar and Gallen joining Sol in such a way, with such passion and commitment, led Sol to the edge once again. She could sense the other two nearing the same place.

The pumping quickened. Their breaths and moans and sighs filling the air. Sweat mingled with the scent of clementines and linen. The silk brushing past Sol's skin cooly as her body warmed with the heat of Gallen and Malinar, the warmth of exertion and ecstasy. Sol begged aloud for more and more.

"Keep going," she gasped, "please."

Malinar took the command in stride, swiping her thumb

against Sol's clit as fingers curled to reach Sol's most sensitive place.

Thrusts and swipes and licks. Over and over until a light burst from her core, the tingling sensation traveling through her arms. Her legs. Her mind.

Tension met by satisfying release.

And she could hear the other two enjoying their own arrival. Their own tension and release. Grunting and laughing and steadying of breaths.

The evening was a dream, a mingling of souls as much as bodies. Malinar and Gallen crumpled onto the bed, utterly spent. Sol's eyelids were heavy as her head found the comfort of a feathered pillow. Lying in the center of the circular bed, she heard the sheets rustle as her lovers found a place on either side of her body. Malinar snagged one arm and snuggled close while Gallen pushed his sweat-laced body against the other side. She turned the emerald ring around her index finger as she breathed in deeply the smell of salt and sweet citrus.

Her eyes scanned the room, Gallen's heritage on display. Dim streams of light cast wavering shades of pale colors along the walls, the art, the bed. A sickening familiar feeling tugged at her heart as she saw glimpses of him in the darkness of night. She wished she recognized the trunks of his belongings, the silken feel of his sheets, the vanity set against the far wall. Squinting her eyes, she noticed canisters of face paints, like those worn by others in this realm. It was difficult to see the shades, though she tried to imagine Gallen with lines of pale green or vibrant yellow across his chiseled face. As a Flyer, he wore the trends of the Star Realm— simple lines of colored kohl that followed the upper and lower eyelids— but she could see him favoring the former.

Malinar stirred slightly, her eyes closed but perhaps not completely asleep. Sol pulled the bedsheet to cover Malinar's shoulders.

This had been the first time since Endoneth, since Rostair. Sol once dreaded this day. She feared that all forms of trust, of intimacy, of joy were utterly unattainable. That she would live out her days in uncomfortable loneliness. For it was far better to be alone that to be deceived. Humiliated. Broken. There were times, in the nightmares that plagued her sleep, that she heard Rostair's words to her, the ripping apart of her being:

You, Lady Sol, are far more arrogant than I understood.
Southern whore.
You are all dead. No realm will follow you.

The cursed words of a fool, yet words of weight, words with bite. At times, she heard them whispered in the corners of her mind, mixed with the vision of his silver hair and evil grin. And at times she believed him. That she knew nothing and that no one would ever follow them into a kingdom of realms. That all she would ever be was a southern whore, caught up in her own fantasy of romance amidst warfare. That she was far too arrogant to love or be loved.

But, as she enjoyed the closeness of her companions, as Gallen held her and beckoned Malinar to join, Rostair's glare never entered her thoughts. Instead, the two only brought with them an all-consuming feeling of calm. A feeling that she wanted to bottle up and keep with her forever.

Gallen's arm gently pressed against her side. A flood of appreciation nearly brought Sol to tears. His gracious nature, his willingness to move beyond whatever compelled her to speak to him that alcohol-induced night, it was far more than she deserved.

And, as the two phantoms of her past merged together—Rostair's disgusting stain on her psyche and her own mysterious drunken confession—Sol finally faced a truth perhaps she wished to ignore: She did miss her time in Endoneth. But it was not the company of Rostair, nor the guests of his estate that she desired. What she truly missed was the ignorance. A situation that once frustrated her now appeared to her a welcome escape from the horrors of reality. The hatred, the exploitation, the fear. In her chambers in Endoneth, Sol never wondered of the enslavement of those in the desert nor the harnessed powers of the fairies in the woods. She never considered if the pegasi that lived in Rostair's stables wished to remain. Nor if those who graced his halls visited out of a sense of friendship or obligation.

Such an admission—the wish to forget the cruelties of this world—brought her the deepest sense of shame. She crunched the sheets in her fists as she chided herself for such selfishness. The privilege she held to even consider avoiding the struggles of others, their suffering, their hopelessness. All while she fretted over her responsibilities, her loneliness, her position.

Malinar's hand rested upon her arm, delicately brushing her skin until she reached Sol's tightened fist. Sol immediately relaxed, looking to offer a smile of gratitude, and meeting Malinar's warm eyes before they closed once more.

Sol wanted so desperately to talk to Malinar. To bear her anxieties and realizations and shame. Asha would never believe this turn of events, Sol's closeness to someone they both believed so cold and unfeeling. It was strange what a journey could shift in a person, in a connection. Strange how facing a fiery death could help refocus what was truly important.

Compelled to record these thoughts, Sol wished to put ink to parchment and detail these surprising truths and personal discoveries. Yet, the warmth of Malinar and Gallen, of their nearness and care, encouraged her eyelids to fall. Sol conceded, her eyes closing. Such concerns would be for another day.

The final memory of this night was Sol's contentment. Her unbridled joy. Though she was imperfect, at times selfish and privileged and desperate for affection, the warriors at her sides still wished to have her. To console her. To forgive her. Cascades of contentment rushed through Sol, easing her body as she allowed her mind to rest.

It was in that mental place that ushered her into a deep and serene sleep.

17

MALINAR

Malinar watched as the two flawless figures rested atop the silk sheets in the darkness. She was not certain how the sun could reach this far beneath the ocean's surface, or if strategically placed artificial lanterns provided light during the daytime hours that softened at night. Either way, the streams of flowy lights delicately kissed the skin of Sol and Gallen as they slept. Malinar could not rip her gaze away.

Though Malinar's body was tired, her mind was at peace. More at peace than it had been in a long while. She looked around the room, Gallen's room. The space was ethereal in the nighttime air, the pale blue of the walls and floors reminiscent of the skies above. Along the edges where the walls met the ceiling were strokes of painted gold. Framed landscapes from each realm hung around the room, tokens perhaps of his many travels. Malinar lingered on the tents and stones of the Star Realm, the blue lanterns so realistic she could nearly see them glow. She sighed, remembering their purpose here, her reason for agreeing to this quest. She wondered if her sister lay awake at night. Wondered if her father sensed something amiss in the air. Or did her family remain as unknowing as the rest of the realm? She hoped so.

Trunks and cases around the space contained an entire childhood, Malinar imagined. She wanted so badly to jump from the bed and rummage through the clothing and books and trinkets to gain a better sense of who he was. Rather than give in, she continued scanning the room with her eyes alone, spotting Sol's knitted satchel on the floor. She gently shifted to the edge and lightly traipsed toward the bag. She glanced toward the still sleeping couple before grasping the sling. Pulling the bag close to her chest, she glided toward the bed once again.

Settling back into her place, she reached in the satchel and felt for the familiar spine of her book. A comforting warmth settled in her heart as the cover came into view in the dull light. She flipped through the familiar pages, the words she'd read over and over floating through the room, surrounding her like a weighted blanket. Though she was glad to see her companions sleep, especially Gallen who had such restless nights as of late, she wished she could read to them her favorite passages. Just as Gallen proudly explained the various pieces of his past, she wanted to share more of herself through this book. Like her own display of artifacts that she could point to. The words that guided her through the worst days of life. The pages she turned to in moments of bliss. The scene of battle she read before her first quest as a Night Flyer. The story of sorrow she read when her mother left.

Turning page after page, Malinar realized even more deeply how this book of historical remembrance and legend truly reflected so much of her past. Her approaches to life.

Her eyes settled upon a name she knew well: *Kahlee the Enchantress*. Malinar read through the familiar passages, her eyes squinting to soak in each word in the dim night:

Enchantress of the Stars, Kahlee began this life in ignorance. Nobility incarnate.

Betrothed to a man of great fortune, Kahlee learned to love the partner of her parents' choosing. Her trial was hard, though Kahlee persisted. In time, she grew to love him, this betrothed, before one fateful day, in a state of internal strife, he took his own life.

Pain of loss plagued Kahlee. Such loss pushed her to learn her craft, gaining knowledge of magnificent enchantments. She sought the answers to life's questions and perhaps find a solution for those who suffered as her love once did.

Born of grief, her magic harnessed the long dormant powers of the stars above to cast indefensible spells.

Kahlee grew stronger and stronger in the years following her partner's death. Her reputation stirred intrigue throughout the realm, lords and ladies alike seeking the power of the stars. A high lady of the Star Realm requested Kahlee live amongst her people to utilize her skills for the betterment of her sprawling tented estate. In due time, Kahlee realized the lady brought her there to do no more than exploit her skills to bolster her hostess's authority.

Wanting to stand for justice, for egalitarianism, for lesser beings, Kahlee abandoned her post, leaving the hostess with a parting gift: a spell that would limit the lady's authority in the realm.

To Kahlee, her parting gift was no curse. 'Twas a blessing. A blessing to those who walked into her tent to present her wine. To those who carved her elaborate chairs and wove her illustrious blankets. To those who were never given the right to be in her presence. The blessing was to them.

While the story began in tragedy, Kahlee represented so much more than her brokenness. A tear wet the corner of the page, seeping into the text as many had before.

"I have never seen you quite so emotional." Gallen's voice was weak with sleep, his head barely lifted from his plump pillow. "Why hide such a divine side?"

Malinar quickly wiped the wetness from her cheek before closing the book and facing him fully. With Sol still sleeping soundly between them, she whispered her words.

"There are parts of myself best kept for the hours alone. Because it…it just…"

She attempted to articulate the reason, the mental shield firmly placed in the recesses of her being, protecting the parts of her best left untouched. The places of vulnerability that would certainly lead her to attachment, to immovable ties that could bind her heart, her soul, to another. Opening parts of herself to Gallen and Sol, it was never an aspect of her plan. Never what she anticipated from this long-awaited quest. The culmination of a career in warfare.

And, as her father reiterated over and over and over again, sentimentality had no role in warfare.

Perhaps he was correct. That the only road to success was emotional isolation. But, for an irrational reason, a reason she could not fully comprehend, she could no longer see the validity in such a notion.

Malinar looked back at her companions. Gallen's eyes now laced with concern as he lifted his body and walked delicately to Malinar's side of the bed. He rested on his knees as he looked up to her, his expression so genuine, so open.

"You need not dull yourself for us, Malinar. Flyers can be more than their brute strength, more than their cunning. I understand protecting yourself. But know you are worthy of self-expression, even if you believe it will be poorly received."

Gallen looked softer; it seemed the atmosphere of the Ocean Realm set him at ease. While he exuded confident command in the Star Realm, it was different here. He remained headstrong, yet the subtle furrow in his brow had lifted. The determination that often focused his gaze was somewhat muted. He no longer appeared to be awaiting the next action or moment or plan. Rather, Gallen looked still, peaceful. For a moment, the shift in the Flyer unnerved Malinar; she had become so accustomed to his command, even in moments of intimacy, as she learned that night. However, as the two continued to look at one another, as Gallen rested his hand on Malinar's arm, her own hand still clutching the book by its spine, the softness was infallible. The lift of his brow befitted his true character, perhaps saved for solely those within this room.

It was then the words truly fell into place in Malinar's mind. Indeed, Gallen said them to quell her insecurities but also his own. As it dawned on her, she placed her free hand on the shoulder of the man kneeling before her.

"I understand, Gallen. We all deserve to express our truest selves. If not to the world, then at the very least to each other."

His eyes glimmered with delight, the concern from moments before melting away as she spoke truth into existence. The solidifying of something so pure. Sacred. Something Malinar never understood before. Not with her family. Nor Tress. Not even Ranor. Her truest self on display. Accepted. Nurtured. All this she witnessed in Gallen's eyes. A future she could not have imagined before this quest. Before their flight from the High Realm. Before this night.

But with that came the inherent fears that Malinar often attempted to lock away. Fears that pushed her from exploring relationships beyond the surface. Fears that this future she could now see vividly in Gallen's delightful gaze and could hear in the soft sounds of Sol's snores could be taken from her. Just as her father pushed her away from her home. Just as her mother left their family. Just as Ranor died.

Rather than entertain such worries, to succumb to her natural instinct to hide away, to seek a graceful exit from this situation, Malinar set the book to the side and pulled Gallen to rest near her. She relished in the contentment of her position, her body nestled between her two friends, and left her fears for the morning.

THE LIGHT that sparkled through the round window of Gallen's chambers shone just as brightly as the sun above the waves. Malinar squinted as she slowly woke to find herself alone in the sheets of the massive bed. She reached a sleepy hand to the side where Sol's body once lay, though only blankets met her grip. The disappointment did not last long, as a voice broke through the waves of silence.

"Good morn, Malinar. I do hope you were able to rest last night."

Sol appeared in Malinar's blurred vision, her voluptuous figure barely hidden by a fresh outfit provided by their host. As Malinar blinked the sleep away, she noticed just how amazing Sol looked. The tunic, made from numerous beaded braids of silver twine, covered her neck wholly yet ended just past the midpoint of her chest, leaving the lower portion of her large breasts bare. The same material created the skirt which hugged her stomach, thighs, and bottom nicely. Malinar knew the Ocean Realm valued the beauty of the body, and she enjoyed that fact in this moment. Sol seemed to realize the length of Malinar's stare as the tips of her cheeks sported a crimson hue.

"I also hope you enjoyed the night," Malinar stated, blushing as well as she recalled the night's events. And yes. She did enjoy them. "Of course, it is wise to know one's traveling companions. Especially on a quest such as this. Do you not agree?"

The once mean-spirited jabs that plagued Malinar's speech were now flirtatious and fun. She wished they could remain in this literal bubble of the Ocean Realm. That the three could explore one another in body and mind and soul. She wished that with every fiber of her being.

Yet, her mind turned to Alcor. To Tress and Asha and the Flyers in the Star Realm. To her father and sister. To the war. The wishful thinking of avoidance was unfortunately impossible.

Malinar pulled the covers from her legs and stood.

"Why, of course," Sol answered as Malinar searched for her own change of clothes. "Knowing one another *is* essential."

It was as if Sol sensed the sudden shift in Malinar's thinking. Like Gallen, it was as if this warrior could read her mind. Or perhaps, like Gallen, Malinar, too, was beginning to soften her typically reserved exterior when around them. That her face revealed far more than she usually allowed.

Surprisingly, the thought brought her joy rather than shame.

As Malinar began preparing for the day, Sol pulled a book from her bag and scribbled notes as she read. Malinar kept her within eyesight, the frequent glances not seeming to bother Sol, who continued diligently reading page after page. When looking again at Sol's clothes, Malinar's gown was modest by comparison. The dress was one piece of green, silk fabric with an opening in the middle where she pulled her head through. The sides of the dress were completely open, save the thick, golden rope that cinched the gown together, leaving a sliver of each side slightly exposed. Once dressed, Malinar reached for her book, carefully searching for a place to keep the precious piece of her past. She settled for a trunk on the far side of the space, more shrouded by shadows than the rest of the room.

Placing the book on its lid, Malinar wondered about the remaining day aloud: "Do you know of a plan in place for the remaining days spent here?"

She turned to see Sol looking up from her book. "I have yet to hear. Gallen was leaving to meet his mother just as I was waking. I imagine we will learn more at lunch."

Malinar gasped, "lunch?"

Sol laughed, the sound like sweet honey. "Yes. I know it is unusual for you, but it seems you overslept."

Shocked, Malinar ran to the adjacent wall and peered through the window. The streets were bustling with people, the sunshine—or essence of sun—beaming as the bubble above lit with radiant shades of yellow and orange. It was indeed midday. She heard Sol shut her book and walk toward the window.

"It is wonderful to provide the body with what it needs every once in a while." Sol softened her voice as she spoke, her hands brushing against Malinar's waist. "Do you not agree?"

Sol's touch reached from Malinar's waist toward her stomach, pulling her into an embrace. Malinar breathed Sol in, her heart thudding against her chest and a tingling sensation moving swiftly from the source of Sol's touch down lower. She could feel her legs begin to tremble as thoughts of last night flashed into her mind. Her mouth salivated at the thought of Sol sinking to her knees and taking her again.

Instead, Sol squeezed once before pulling away. "We should find the others and join for the midday meal," she said.

Malinar nearly groaned with disappointment, though instead nodded and followed Sol into the hallway, down the corridors, before reaching the dining hall where Gallen and Avelia sat.

As the women walked into the room, Gallen burst into a deep smile that exuded excitement and longing and relief. Avelia continued discussing their recent discoveries as they explored Gallen's home city, their beautifully dark hands gesturing through the air with emphasis, undeterred by the sudden presence of the others nor by Gallen's abundantly evident disinterest.

"Eckral is filled with such specialties, is it not? I discussed the power of the Mist with a few eager citizens on today's pass through town. Unlike yesterday's exploration of the grounds of the estate, I found that…"

They continued discussing the particulars of their latest jaunt as the women walked to the opposite side of the table. Sol pulled one of the many chairs from the coral-topped table for Malinar to sit before taking her own place on the adjacent chair. As Avelia remained undeterred from their chatter, Gallen raised his voice above theirs, "How was your rest, Malinar? I do hope you are feeling ready for the journey ahead."

Gallen lifted the corners of his lips as he spoke, a bit of humor slipping into the genuine comfort of his words. He seemed reassured by her ability to sleep into the day. Silenced by Gallen, Avelia crossed their arms across the teal silk suit chosen for their day in the Ocean Realm.

"We have planned another journey?" Sol questioned, avoiding the ice-cold glance from Avelia as she reached toward the mountain of food arranged in the center of the table.

Malinar followed her example, filling the empty plate in front of her with a mixture of fruits, breads, and smoked fish.

"Indeed. My mother spoke with the Twelve. It appears members of the Ocean Realm elite are more willing to end this era of isolation. They were quite receptive to my mother's call to action. We will leave tonight to meet with the Past Holder of our great city."

"Ncheeldon." Kattegat's bare feet clicked along the coral floor as she paced vigorously toward the warriors. "He is the oldest of the Past Holders in this realm. He holds his meetings at night."

She strolled behind Malinar's chair toward the head of the table. Her black hair whipped to the side as Kattegat passed, a cold shiver of intimidation slinking down her body in response. While the lady of the Ocean Realm was a woman she respected, Malinar was certainly fearful of her tenacity. Yet, the strength of the leader reminded Malinar of the women in her book. So bold yet so evidently caring for the needs of others.

Avelia watched Kattegat with a keen eye as well, eager to interject their opinion on the matter. Malinar noticed them sitting on their hands, almost as if to keep themself from appearing too eager. The self-control did not last. "We are all able to contribute queries to this holder of knowledge, yes?"

Kattegat slid her eyes to Avelia. "I will speak on our behalf. The Past Holder is a creature of tradition. Gallen can explain any questions you may have before we leave." Her body barely hit the chair before she stood to leave. "Be ready to depart our estate at last light."

With this command, the lady dashed from her position in the room, behind Gallen and Avelia's chairs and through the dining hall entrance.

When his mother left, Gallen could no longer hide his amusement. He chuckled slightly, eyeing Malinar and Sol with a glimmer of mischief. Though at times the competitiveness between himself and Avelia appeared childish, Malinar adored this side of Gallen. Looking at Sol's reaction, her eyes rolling dramatically to the back of her head while wearing a sly grin, Malinar could sense she shared the sentiment.

"We should ready for the journey." Avelia pushed their hands on the edge of the table, the chair legs scratching the coral floor. "I shall rest in my chambers."

The silken teal of their suit caught the light as they walked into the hall. When the other Flyers could no longer hear their footsteps, Malinar burst into chirping chuckles. Sol giggled in turn, followed by Gallen. The three relished one final moment of happiness, of certainty, before the reality of the world slipped in. And, as they sighed deeply, the final bits of laughter easing their way out, that dreaded reality stepped completely into view.

"I suppose there is no more hiding from this. The phoenix. The war. It is real." Sol sounded as defeated as Malinar felt.

"We can always alter our course, Sol," Gallen responded. "Shift the path. Swim to the Ice Realm and find your memories, then return to concern ourselves with warfare."

Gallen looked toward Sol, his face reflecting a solemn seriousness, as if the fate of the Nine Realms fell second to her well-being. While Malinar recognized the irrationality of such a notion, she admired Gallen's affection for Sol. And, as Sol shook her head, wringing her hands together nervously as if the decision was far more difficult than it should have been, another pang of admiration struck Malinar. She settled her hand atop Sol's, offering a small gesture of support. The slight trembling of Sol's intertwined fingers slowed at Malinar's touch.

Gallen cleared his throat. "I should also rest before the journey. Would you both like separate quarters to spend the remaining hours of daylight? I certainly do not mind sharing my own space as we did last night. I mean, when we fell asleep. Not that what occurred prior to falling asleep was not enjoyable. It was. It was indescribable, really…"

The two women allowed Gallen to ramble on far longer than what was courteous.

"If you both would like to rest in a space of your own…I would certainly understand. Yet, my chambers are always yours, if you would like them. What would you both like to do?"

When Gallen finished his long-winded question, patches of red flushed his pale blue skin.

Sol was the first to respond, ending a silence that filled the dining hall with a palpable tension.

"Gallen, it is gracious of you to offer your space to us. I cannot speak for Malinar, but I can say that being with you both is the most at ease I have felt since waking in the snow of the Ice Realm all those months ago."

Sol pressed her hand in emphasis. She looked back at Gallen, whose face had grown only redder.

"I echo Sol in this. You both provide a sereneness I have yet to experience. One I cannot fully place," Malinar said smoothly.

She looked at her hand in Sol's, the connection only reassuring her words.

Sol's smile in return sent a jolt of bliss down Malinar's spine. Gallen's eyes did nothing more than elongate the sensation, the two warriors melting away the walls Malinar carefully forged over years of pressure, strain, and stress. It was as if her movements, her choices and actions, were no longer under the harsh ridicule of a superior. Rather, the loving glances of her peers, of the Flyers who ushered her into the fold so quickly and seamlessly, were nothing more than affirmations. It was a position Malinar rarely found herself occupying. To be observed, not for her inherent faults or mistakes but for her positive attributes. Her intelligence. Her thoughtfulness. Her beauty.

Such attention left Malinar enthralled. Exhilarated. Eager.

It was strange to be certain. In a foreign realm with two highly ranked and respected Night Flyers, warriors she looked up to during her training. Gallen, a man who defied the odds and created a place for himself among the ranks of Zeffra and Alcor. And Sol, a person with a more complicated story that proved her resilience.

The three walked back to the large room with the circular bed and their respective belongings. The women huddled on the sheets together, books in hand. Gallen lay near them, threading a needle and thread to begin a new project. Malinar breathed in deeply, the crisp air of the Ocean Realm easing the anticipation of their future. Of what was known and unknown. What the three would face. And, perhaps, if this would be their final moments of peace before the true storm.

18

Sol

Though Sol adjusted well to flying on the back of the winged pegasi, the enchanted chariot was another beast entirely.

The flight from Kattegat's Coral Estate to the Past Holder's cove left her queasy. She steadied herself using Gallen's arm, and though he showed no sign of discomfort, she imagined her grip was painful on his bare skin. She focused her thoughts on her heartbeats rather than the wind chapping her cheeks. Fortunately, unlike the smooth rides on the strong back of Kinsle, the chariot seemed to bring the group to their desired destination in mere minutes. While the city's portals existed toward the top of the bubble, the archways glowing in the faux night, the chariot led them downward, below the platforms that held Somov's many buildings. The lower the chariot fell, the dimmer the light became, until darkness engulfed the warriors and their host. Sol noticed Avelia shudder as they descended further and further into the abyss, clearly unaccustomed to the lack of brightness. For Sol, however, such darkness was welcome, a reminder of home. The chariot emitted a dim orange shine that provided just enough light to see directly ahead, above, and below. And, as the group of five sank deeper, the air became clearer, untainted, utterly pure.

Kattegat sat at the helm of her enchanted chariot, the portrait of regality. Her suit of choice for the night's journey was a pair of stately silk pants that billowed in the rushes of wind coupled with a woven cropped top of kelp. She provided similar clothing for the younger warriors: Sol and Malinar wore short dresses of silk while Gallen and Avelia sported longer pants with matching vested tops.

The lady's massive cape established her definitive authority. Sol distracted herself by looking at the work of art strapped to Kattegat's neck. The piece was made from ropes of various sizes woven in an intricate pattern that formed a gradient of colors. The ropes were garnished with a mixture of gold chains and jewels with shells and coral sewn in as well. The various stones glistened as the chariot flew through the air. The shells jangled together in a delightful melody as the cape wavered in the wind. It was enough to calm Sol's nerves ever so slightly.

Soon, the chariot found the ground, or at least the bottom of the large protective bubble surrounding the city. Sol took a shaky step out of the chariot, following Kattegat and Avelia onto a bed of tan. The sand passed through Sol's toes like liquid, the grains minuscule in comparison to the beaches above.

"The Past Holder will speak only to those native to this realm. It is the way of things."

Kattegat locked eyes with each of the visiting warriors individually, assuring the severity of her words effectively reached each of them.

"I would like a verbal confirmation." Her gaze held on Avelia, "no person is to speak directly to the Past Holder. I am pushing the limits by allowing those from above into this sacred space."

Malinar immediately spoke up, "I understand."

Sol nodded as well. "Of course, Lady Kattegat."

Kattegat smiled at Sol's response before turning again to Avelia. They paused for a moment before conceding, "I understand as well."

"Good." Kattegat turned, her cloak of rope and shells jingling behind her as she took a steady step forward into the darkness.

Avelia looked at Gallen and whispered, "you will still voice our questions for us?"

They motioned to Malinar and Sol as well, though the question was clearly for themselves.

Gallen rolled his eyes and took a step to follow his mother. Puzzled, Avelia sought affirmation from the other "above" visitors. Sol shook her head and squinted to keep her eye on the fading figures of pale blue falling into the shades of gray darkness. She took Malinar's arm in her own before also stepping ahead.

The bottom of the city was utterly empty save the occasional plant lying dead on the dry sea floor. Coral did pop up every now and again in Sol's peripheral vision, though she dared not take her eyes off of Gallen and Kattegat. Before long, the group stood before a trench, a large, black lake within the sandy surface. Kattegat stood with her toes on the edge of the drop-off, examining the void below. Gallen joined her as the others fell behind, keeping a safe distance as they awaited instruction.

Suddenly, the lady of coral began wailing into the darkness, her shrieks not of pain or caution but of something more. Like a solemn prayer, a call of surrender and reverence. Of respect for something greater than the five supposed great figures. Warrior and apprentice and lady. Those titles seemed to slip away into the blackness of the cove, leaving the guests as mere mortals in the wake of a being far larger than themselves. Was this the power of the Mist? The power that breathed all things into existence, that ushered in this great civilization?

Perhaps so.

The wailing continued. Kattegat's voice shook with effort as she screamed rhythmic lines into the emptiness. Holding his hands behind his back, Gallen bowed his head with his eyes closed, offering silent prayers that synchronized with his mother's vocal chanting.

Malinar stood stunned, her eyes wide and mouth slightly agape. Slowly, Sol reached her hand to tap Malinar's shoulder, a gentle reminder to respect what they witnessed, though she understood the awe. To Sol, this was more than a mere presentation of passion, it was a holy ritual, a privilege to witness.

Minutes passed. Kattegat's cries, joined by arm movements and stomps, echoed in the cavern below. The warriors each watched on, Gallen whispering indiscernibly as the ritual continued. Finally, the lady's cries quieted. Her stomps slowed. Her eyes opened and breathing steadied.

Kattegat called out. "Now. We descend."

She led the group a few steps to the right where a rope ladder hooked into the sand. With no other words of direction, she threw her cape over her shoulder as she took step after mighty step down into the darkened cove. Gallen trailed his mother into the darkness, followed by Avelia who eagerly grasped the ladder with trembling hands. The grin on their face denoted excitement rather than hesitation, their body vibrating with anticipation rather than unease.

Malinar grasped Sol's hand, gently leading them both to the edge of the cavern. The black hole before them left everything to the imagination. And, unfortunately, Sol was never one to imagine happy things.

"Together?" Malinar asked, calmly stepping her bare foot toward the ladder.

Sol nodded as she watched the warrior take another step onto the rope. She followed, the scratching threads cutting into her bare feet as she went. The air grew colder as they descended further, chills creeping down Sol's arms. The climb down stretched on for miles. At least, Sol convinced herself as much. Her fingers occasionally grazed the walls of the cavern, even the slightest touch scratching against her skin, scratching her hands and knees and toes. The wall was built over centuries and centuries of life, packed with shells and bones. Hearing Malinar's huffs of effort acted as the gravitational pull Sol needed to keep lowering her body down, down, down.

Above them, the light faded into a fine point in the distance as blackness fully engulfed Sol. In the complete darkness, an incredible sense of serenity consumed her. As if looking at the cavern from above was far more daunting than living in it, breathing the cool air, grasping the itchy rope with her hands.

When Sol finally stepped onto a cool surface, the entrance was just a small sliver of light. She turned her back to the rope, squinting her eyes in the total darkness. Suddenly, a rush of light illuminated the ground beneath her, the floor glowing a bright shade of green. The walls that once resembled dirt were now made of a translucent crystal that reflected the light of the smooth stone ground. A few steps forward, Sol could see a large mosaic in the center of the circular chamber, delicate shards of glass, stones, and shells arranged in an unfamiliar pattern.

Kattegat sat at the center of the swirling mosaic, rocking back and forth as she hummed a haunting tune. Gallen stood to the side of the swirling design in silence, his hands folded as they were at the edge of the cavern. Solemn. Deferent.

The remaining warriors gawked at the scene. A glimpse into a world otherworldly and righteous, entrenched in the magnificence that lay at the depths of the Ocean Realm. A soft whisper hummed into Sol's ear:

A summons was requested, and so a summons will be received.

Sol scanned the space, though no person save the five who climbed down were visible.

Beware the one who controls all fate. Who leads in shadows as all abate.

The voice continued the soft whispers into Sol's mind, as if the source needed no introduction, no physical manifestation to relay their cryptic message.

Tread lightly, warrior of the quill. For futures bend only to her will.

Sol continued in her confusion to search for a source, yet no being emerged in the green glow of the cavern. Kattegat's humming remained the sole sound reverberating through the cave. The only movements were her body pulsing back and forth.

Then, another flash of light burst through the center of the room. Kattegat's pale blue skin shone brightly as a small figure emerged by her side. Sol could see nothing of the mystic, the forest-green cape consuming the diminutive figure. The lady stood to her feet and offered her place to the hooded stranger.

"Ncheeldon," Avelia breathed, the yellow in their hair luminous as they looked on.

Kattegat kneeled before the stranger, still hidden by the hood of the green cape, as the cave grew painfully silent. "Past Holder," she whispered, the words a sign of reverence for the figure. "We visit to gain answers."

The hooded figure reached out a dark blue hand to Kattegat who brought the feeble fingers to her lips. As soon as her mouth touched Ncheeldon's skin, her eyes paled, misting unnaturally as her head tilted back to stare toward the entrance far above them. Her lips parted slightly, as her breath came in short spurts, her chest spasming up and down with effort. No other person moved, none willing to break the trance.

Minutes passed like hours.

Kattegat's body floated barely above the floor, pulled into the air by a power beyond Sol's comprehension. She watched in curious terror as the lady's knees barely grazed the smooth surface of the ceramic, the tiles slightly speckled with wayward grains of sand from the world above them.

Her cape shuttered with her effort, floating behind her as she remained linked to the Past Holder by the hand. Sheer power emanated from both figures, so palpable Sol believed she could harness it in a bottle. Power pulsing from the giver of words to the receiver.

Ncheeldon's pale blue lips moved quickly, whispering indiscernible chants in a language unlike any Sol knew. She could not look away from his mouth, so softly staining the air with puffs of pale blue. His words could be any manner of phrases. Were they a promise or prophesy or omen?

Kattegat twitched her head as the ritual continued; her thick braids fell in a glorious waterfall down her arched back. From the corner of her eye, Sol noticed Gallen still at the edge of the mural, his head leaned forward as if waiting for his mother's call to assist. Sol wondered how much he understood, if he, too, could hear Ncheeldon from inside his mind. If he, too, was warned of something unseen. Something dangerous.

Then, just as the Past Holder entered in a flash of light, a sudden flood of darkness settled into the air, extinguishing the green glow and the slight light of Kattegat's mystical gaze.

Then, quiet.

Sol reached for Malinar's hand, grasping for anything to anchor her in reality as darkness consumed them. The two women shivered, the cool air returning to the bottom of the cavern in the light's absence. As they shuffled closer together, Kattegat rose to her feet and spoke in her authoritative tone:

"It is complete."

CLIMBING toward the light was not nearly as frightening as walking down. Perhaps it was the view of Malinar's bare legs that settled her, the younger flyer having insisted on leading Sol to the surface. It could have also been the knowledge of Gallen's view just below her, again insisting he be the final warrior to make the climb in case the others slipped. Both warriors appeared less impacted by the glorious ritual they witnessed, though Malinar rarely expressed her emotions and Gallen knew what to expect.

Sol was not certain if she knew what she expected.

The seemingly endless journey below passed far quicker on the ascent, which provided little time for Sol to consider the ritual and its implications. Instead, flustered footholds and small glimpses of Malinar's tight bottom filled the time. Sol indulged in the view, reminiscing on the previous night.

With the importance of the quest, she had not considered what they were, the three warriors. What she did know was this: She did not want it to end. And that notion scared her far more than any weapon of fire roaming the skies.

As the group rode the enchanted carriage swiftly to Kattegat's coral palace, Sol contemplated the wonder and the pain of the ritual. Kattegat, a feminine force of such renown, offering a sacred seat in the center of the cavern, bowing low to something more tremendous than herself. Offering her body as a vessel to incur a mystical promise or vision or call.

Providence.

Destiny.

These were the things Kattegat cried for. Though the words were unknown to Sol, she recognized the need to understand one's current place in the world. And what place would later emerge. The whispers of the all-seeing Past Holder tickled Sol's memory:

Beware. Tread lightly. Beware. Tread lightly.

After the deception of Rostair, the wicked Ice Lord who imprisoned her with a charming smile, Sol constantly felt the need to tread lightly. Perhaps this was Ncheeldon's warning for Sol to distance herself from Gallen and Malinar. The two warriors did not appear to intend ill will, even Malinar who seemingly shifted her perception of Sol in the weeks of traveling. In the soft silences of flight. In the crackling of campfire light. In the embraces of comfort and whispers of assurance.

Yet, was that not what a villain did? Did they not persuade, manipulate, and ultimately fool those whom they deemed lesser?

Sol's breaths began coming in rapid succession, her nails clawing against her arms as she hugged her chest. Perhaps Sol had been hasty in her desires for Malinar. Perhaps she ignored the signals of danger. The young Flyer was clever and ambitious; Sol would be the perfect partner to claim a title in the realm, a position at the end of the war.

And Gallen? Perhaps Sol had been too hasty to return to the life she could not remember. To offer her body and heart to him as if their realities were not unimaginably altered by the choices of her past and the dangers of the present. What if he were playing the part of a forgiving friend while harboring resentment? Could he be waiting for his moment to humiliate Sol, to break her heart in cruel and spiteful ways?

The thoughts spiraled in her mind, her heart growing heavier in her chest as she considered each new possibility, each new potential horror.

As the chariot grew nearer to the citrus glow of the Somov, Sol's mind continued reeling. Two words, "tread lightly," had seemingly turned her world on its head, reminding her of a moment of similar grief when all she thought she knew was wrong. Where her friends were enemies and enemies were family.

The chariot flew through the barrier as her mind continued its fall. The presence of both Malinar and Gallen on either side of her did nothing to quell her thoughts. Could these relationships truly mean nothing?

Idiot. Fool. Naive child, Sol chided herself.

When her feet touched the textured paths of coral leading to the estate, Sol refocused her thoughts. She would dedicate her energy to the quest at hand. She would seek out this threat to her realm and her family. She would help Alcor win this war. With each step, the anxieties that plagued her quieted as these resolutions took full form in her mind.

When Kattegat led them to her study to debrief, the warriors each found a place to rest on the chairs strewn throughout the room, and Sol found her first opportunity to prioritize the cause.

"Where is our heading, Lady Kattegat?" Sol's voice cracked with anticipation, a need to put her fears of betrayal behind her. To hide them behind a desire to defeat a common threat. "What did the Past Holder impart?"

Kattegat sauntered to her desk, settling down into the wide chair before considering her words.

"The wise Ncheeldon presented a confounding picture," she began, scratching the tips of her fingernails carefully against the golden paint on the edge of her chin. "This weapon is invincible, of this I am now certain. As Lord Rostair of the Ice Realm guides the beast, we cannot wage a war against something so powerful."

Avelia piped in as soon as the lady completed her thought: "How did the Past Holder speak to you? Did pictures appear in your mind? Did you hear his voice?"

Kattegat ignored Avelia's queries and continued, "The visions he provided certainly shifted my approach. I will need to contemplate our future."

"This will certainly convince the other Ocean Realm leaders to join the cause?" Gallen said hesitantly, a deep frown lining his pale blue cheeks.

His mother shook her head. "Of this I am unsure. Shall we risk lives of our warriors? It appears far less secure than I previously assumed."

Gallen rose abruptly to his feet, concern and frustration evident in the furrow of his brows and the clenching of his jaw.

"Years of effort! Of toil and discussions, and for what?" His voice strained as he implored his mother to do her part as she promised.

"We will continue to petition their support. Alcor will be king, my child. We just need to ensure the proper preparations take place to ensure the position of *our* realm and of *our* people."

The room stilled; even Avelia stood silently in place. Gallen maintained eye contact with Kattegat, his fists still clenched tightly by his sides. Malinar stared awkwardly at her feet as Sol looked from Gallen to his mother and back. Moments passed as the two Ocean Realm elites held their ground, each waiting for the other to concede in this game of willpower.

While Gallen was headstrong, his mother was tenfold, refusing to bend to his will. After a few minutes of painful tension, Gallen turned on his heel with a huff and left the study.

Sol looked toward Kattegat as his footsteps faded. The lady sifted through some stray papers on her coral desk.

"What must we do?" Sol's words left her chest as a whisper, tumbling into the space as Avelia began pacing near the back wall of the study.

"Nothing. Go to the Star Realm where your king awaits," Kattegat commanded.

The lady's words were confident and firm, as if instructing a soldier to do her bidding. Confusion wracked Sol's gut. What did this mean for the war? Would those of the ocean not fight with them? Would they help solve the mysteries of the phoenix? Fear struck deep in Sol's chest. Though, when she rose to confess her anxieties, Kattegat turned her chair away, waving a hand for the remaining three to leave.

Malinar remained glued to her chair, her eyes still staring at her toes. Sol placed a soft hand on Malinar's shoulder, causing the smaller Flyer to shudder, before nodding toward the door.

Sol's voice remained quiet as she turned toward the entryway. "Let us go then."

They left before Sol had the chance to watch Avelia attempt to gain further insights into the Past Holder's visions of the future. Sol did not want to know.

MALINAR REMAINED quiet as she and Sol walked hurriedly through the halls. She refused to meet Sol's gaze, her eyes remained locked on the coral floors as they walked. When the two women reached Gallen's chambers, he was nowhere to be found.

Sol turned to her friend, her fingers nervously twisting in the silver silk of her dress. "Shall we search for him?"

Malinar remained silent, shaking her head before shuffling into the room. Sol watched quietly as the Flyer retrieved the map along with a few sheets of blank paper. She barely acknowledged Sol as she retreated back into the halls.

Stunned, Sol stood in the entryway a moment before she, too, searched for something to calm her. She reached for the turquoise satchel almost instinctively. The moment the binding of Asha's book touched her fingertips, her nerves settled briefly, as if its existence alone served as a reminder of those she could trust completely.

Reading Asha's words scribbled casually on the edges of the text provided Sol a respite. Though she completed the book in the first few days of the quest, she continued rereading the words lining the margins, finding space throughout this journey to enjoy her friend's rambling. The story also assisted, the romance offering an escape of sorts—not of warfare or danger but of love and frivolity. Sol was enticed by such simplicity.

As Sol rested on the cozy covers of Gallen's bed, sifting through the pages, she allowed herself to live in this fantasy, losing herself in this reality just for a little while. In the reality where she need not consider the ill intent of others or fret over betrayal. One where Malinar and Gallen and she could run from their responsibilities to create an uncomplicated life in a harmonious realm. Where their biggest worries were of choosing their attire or creating a guest list for an illustrious ball. The thought was so enticing and fantastic and pure.

No war. No phoenix. No mistrust or confusion. Just herself and this book and her fantastical dreams. Just harmony and hope and a future of possibilities. Perhaps even love.

The only drawback of indulging in the story, in losing herself in the concept of romance, came when the space was gone. When the book closed and Sol braced for realities of the world rushing back in, flooding her mind with an exhausting intensity. And, on this day, when Sol closed Asha's book, she found herself more downtrodden than usual. She rested her head in her hands as she sat alone.

Unfortunately, this was no fairy tale. No harmonious period of unity and romance. She *was* a Night Flyer, the sister of a king with a mission to find her memories with a realm to consider and innocents counting on her success. And now the phoenix. The destruction it may wrought. And now a warning: *Tread lightly. Beware.*

And so, she would close the book and face reality. She must.

Sol delicately placed the book back in her sack before pulling out blank paper and her ink quill. Rather than focus on what could be, she would do her duty to the realm. With this in mind, she began to write of it all: the phoenix, the High Realm, Kattegat and the Past Holder. She would ensure the details would live in infamy. That this evil they faced would be known and remembered and honored.

That the truth, as she knew it that day, would be safely inked into her pages.

Not only for the Star Realm but perhaps for all realms. For the kingdom they would become.

Black ink stained her fingertips, a comforting reminder to Sol of her work. She wrote pages and pages into the morning.

19

Gallen

Gallen's bare feet paced back and forth between massive pillars of dark gray. His rage led him from his mother's study to the Coral Estate's armory, a small building housing weapons of both steel and strategy; racks of spears and cases of scrolls. The armory itself was never a place Gallen particularly enjoyed frequenting. It was cold and dark and gloomy. His grandfather occasionally brought him into the building to encourage an interest in military strategy, one that Gallen did not entertain until much later in life. He much preferred the halls of artwork and shelves of leather-bound books. The enchanted maps and gilded murals.

It was the last place others would look for him, a building he visited only once of his own volition. A place where he once sobbed and screamed when he learned of his grandfather's passing, now where he vented his frustrations of all he could not control.

"How dare she undermine everything I've worked for. The reason I left my home. The only chance for the damned realms!"

He screamed at the lines of columns, unconcerned by the notion of those nearby or perhaps not caring if they heard.

"Was this all a plan of her own making? That she would feed me this unthinkable information, encourage my deception to our king, and *then* have me continue on as if nothing has happened. As if the winged beast that haunts the upper world will not find its way here too! The fires surely could not abide at sea, yet the consequences will be far-reaching. None are safe. Not even those beneath the water. Mist! She cannot be so thoughtless as to ignore the impact on politic, on trade, on…on…what is right!"

He stomped on his heel in emphasis, ranting to the empty air his many concerns. Of course, Gallen was content to help Sol retrieve her lost memories. Or at least attempt to. Content to continue their course to the Ice Realm and face whatever swirled in those magical pools in the far-off caverns.

However, was it not strange that they would learn so much only to feign ignorance?

This is what he could not reconcile. He needed to act. To warn Alcor or return to the High Realm and convince Master Zelan to fight alongside them. To search for the source of this weapon and eliminate the threat.

Realistically, he knew his mother's wisdom could never lead him astray. Harsh as she could be, her priority was the realm. Yet, the feeling of coming so close to unattainable knowledge, to learn the origins of a mysterious being plaguing the skies, it drove him mad.

And so, he walked back and forth. Back and forth. Walking past the same grey walls adorned with military armor of the Ocean Realm. The same weapon stands displaying the might of various shields and spears. The same paintings of famous battles—water and blood framed in menacing scenes immortalized in art.

He walked and walked and walked until the lantern's day rays peeked into the small windows of the room.

After a while, Gallen slumped against one of the large pillars, dragging his body to the floor. He sat contemplatively, the words of his mother mingling with another phrase he heard that night—the words of the Past Holder himself. At first, Gallen thought it was a hallucination, created by his mind as his mother convened with the worn and sacred being in that cavernous pit. But, as he sat and considered, perhaps it was real. A voice in his mind that was a mere whisper:

Circumvent the plainer path, as those with power cling to wrath. When clouds of red stain the sky, then you shall find a true ally.

Gallen could not claim to understand the meaning, though he also could not shake the feeling of its significance. The notion of red staining the skies did not present a positive image of the future, though a true ally would be most welcome. He had never been one to understand riddles or omens; languages were something he learned easily yet used poorly. Sol was the true wordsmith, always had been.

Rather than dwell on the omen for much longer, Gallen rose to his feet, the day's light now confidently streaming through the small, circular windows lining the top of each wall. He caught a glimpse of purple jellies floating to the surface, holding a message from his mother. The jellyfish, angelic and reliable, floated in and out into the morning, Kattegat likely communicating with the Twelve of her revelations.

The way the light filtered through the windows and rested on his bare arms reminded him of waking just yesterday in such a vastly different circumstance. Closing his eyes, he imagined both Sol and Malinar close to him. Leaning into his torso, still glistening with evidence of their passion. The thought made him gleeful, like a lovesick child. They would likely be wondering where he disappeared to for so long.

This in mind, Gallen swiftly left behind the grim armory. The daylight bathed him in warmth, thawing him from his angered state to a place of tranquility. Or, at least, as calm as he could muster. The women he cared for, whom he was beginning to truly treasure, were waiting steps away.

When he wandered further into the halls, he could hear the manic rustling of papers and rapid pacing that mimicked his own panicked state. Peering into the striking white room of Eckral artifacts, Gallen spied Malinar moving quickly around the enchanted map he presented her on their tour. Though his body screamed to rush toward her, to hold her in his arms. He instead stood in the archway of the space, allowing her to continue in her task. He followed her with his eyes alone, tracing the creases of thought that lined her forehead. Her fidgeting hands. The way she subtly bit the inside of her cheek. A stunning display of a woman dedicated to her task.

She moved at a frantic pace—pulling sheets of papers, making notes, peering at the map and its visions of the Ocean Realm. The scene was beautiful, like an inventor in the thralls of making a world-defining discovery. Like a dancer performing the solo of their career. He could not stop her. No. Not as she tinkered with the intricacies of the map and its contents. A broad view of the Ocean Realm that—

Gallen audibly gasped when he noticed a significant alteration to this fixture that he knew so well. The artwork that displayed so many facets of his home realm was now not displaying that at all. In fact, it was now showing…

"Tents." The word escaped his lips as a whisper, yet Malinar's steps stopped all the same.

"Gallen?"

A glimmer of delight burst in his chest.

"I wish not to disturb you." Gallen grinned as he spoke, taking careful steps forward as he took a closer look at the map diorama. "What is this?"

A blush spread across Malinar's cheeks as she looked shamefully toward the pages in her hands.

"I did not mean to ruin anything I just…the thought consumed me as I looked over the map of the realms. And I…wandered into this room and the map just glowed in the darkness like a beacon."

Her words were hurried, the pages crunching in her hands as she attempted to explain the altered piece of art. Gallen reached for her hands.

"Malinar. It is no worry." He noticed her eyes tilt upward slightly, reacting to his tenderness as if caught in an act of indiscretion. "Art is meant to inspire."

He continued holding Malinar's hands as his eyes shifted to look at her handiwork. The map still illuminated light, holographic figures that moved across the sturdy parchment. But the map was no longer of the Ocean Realm. Instead, the representations moved across what looked like the Star Realm. Gallen recognized the major cities and their associated landmarks. He noticed the swirling pattern of tents organized exactly like Celestra. He could even point out his own tent if he looked close enough.

Impressed as he was, Gallen was confused. This map was enchanted by an artist of great notoriety, someone with the gift of Seeing. A gift not seen in this realm for decades. Nor in other realms for even longer. His head snapped back to her.

"How were you able to shift the enchantment?" He thought out loud.

Malinar looked meek, scared even. "I cannot fully explain how…I just. I knew." She turned her eyes toward his. "Please, do not be upset."

Gallen nearly laughed, but instead he pulled her into an embrace, the pages drifting to their feet. "Dearest. It is as I said. This is art's purpose. I am certain the man who made this map would feel overjoyed to see it has inspired this."

He breathed in her vanilla scent, an even deeper sense of calm seeping through him. She returned his embrace with her own tight hold, pulling their chests close.

"What are you mapping, then?" He whispered into her hair, his breath gently blowing the loose strands. Mist help him, he could watch those wisps of hair for hours in her arms. To his great pleasure, she remained close as she answered.

"I thought I would begin with a place I knew, somewhere familiar. Just to see if I could."

She gathered the silk of his vest in her hands as she spoke, pulling him even closer.

"If I could push it further."

This certainly piqued Gallen's interest. "Further?"

She nodded against his chest. "Imagine if we could see everything. If we could see the whole of the Nine Realms."

He attempted to remain close to Malinar while still peering at the map, where the images of lanterns and people and tents constantly moved. If she could manage to see everything and control the moments individually, it could change everything. They could track this beast. They could gain an advantage that no one in the Ice Realm—no one in any realm—could detect or replicate.

"Imagine," he whispered.

Gallen could hardly stop his mind from reeling. This skill, this map, this woman, could solve many issues plaguing the war effort. The Flyers could anticipate movement, yes. But they could also communicate from realms away. No longer reliant on their most trusted warriors to travel to relay messages. With this map, it could all change.

Malinar explained her process, or at least attempted to, as Gallen tried to follow along. A whistle rang through the estate.

"The morning meal," he stated, still squinting at the enchanted map.

Malinar nodded, flicking her hands over the parchment to

suddenly fold it closed. Gallen grinned at her confidence, as if the map was hers to command.

She crinkled her nose. "What's that look?"

"Oh nothing, my little enchantress," he said smoothly. "You just never cease to surprise me."

Her smile in return lifted his spirits even higher, if that were possible. The rage toward his mother. The Past Holder. The potential of failure. It all seemed to melt away, paling in the presence of Malinar's smile. The way she blushed slightly. The way her short dress skittered along her bare thighs as she turned to leave. She turned back to him with a hand extended, beckoning him to walk with her, beside her.

They sauntered hand in hand through the halls of coral and brightening lights, though Gallen wished he could dance. What a difference one conversation, one interaction, could make. Did this make him impressionable? Perhaps. Though he wasn't in the state of mind to question the implications.

Malinar seemed similarly inclined to ignore the realities facing them. She pulled his arm close to hers as they rushed through the halls, beams of light fading in and out as they walked past the circular windows. None of the harsh truths they learned, or the inevitable consequences, mattered. No, none of it quite mattered as much as this: her hand in his.

All that could improve the scene, all that could bring Gallen even greater joy would be…

"Sol!" Malinar's bright voice broke the silence as Sol's form appeared near the dining hall. She had changed out of the silvery silk dress into a pair of sleek, green slacks that hugged her thighs and flared out toward the ground. Her hands fidgeted with the hem of her cropped tunic, a trail of ink blotches staining the golden threads. She appeared refreshed, reminding Gallen of his own filth. A bath would have likely offered him greater relief than an entire night of pacing and raving at stone walls.

"You must see what we have found, Sol. It is. Well. It is mystical." Malinar continued describing the scene she and Gallen witnessed, the scene she created with her enchanted hands. Sol's eyes widened as Malinar spoke, moving her arms wide with emphasis. Gallen spied Avelia eavesdropping near the doorway, their blonde curls bobbing up and down as they nodded along with Malinar's vivid descriptions.

Placing a tender hand on Malinar's shoulder, Sol unleashed a bevy of questions, matching the energy and fervor of her friend. As Malinar addressed each query—Avelia waiting eagerly for more information—Gallen ushered the group into the dining area to enjoy their meal, his face surely shining at the auspicious turn of events.

The food looked inviting. Variations of cooked fish, crustaceans, and vegetables filled the center of the table and the four warriors each scraped mounds of food onto their waiting plates. Servers brought goblets of bubbling water as Gallen sank his teeth into a bite of fish. The salty taste of seafood always brought him warmth and satisfaction. It reminded him of his days as a young boy, enjoying a wonderful meal with his family.

Speaking of family, Gallen scanned the dining hall. He swallowed the food with a gulp.

"Have you seen my mother today?" he asked the group seated at the table, though he slid his eyes to Avelia. They must have sensed his intent as they returned his glare.

"I have yet to hear of her," they stated, bringing a singular grape to their mouth with a fork. "After the three of you left last evening, the lady of the estate indulged little more regarding the Past Holder and his visions. The tradition is so very fascinating. To harness such an ability would allow the realms to accomplish so much. If only Master Zelan could see for himself—" Avelia continued on as Gallen rolled his eyes. They could speak on the topic for hours, surely.

"Did she mention the Twelve?" he interrupted. "Anything at all about the future. Any plans?"

The other women looked to Avelia as they shook their head. Gallen breathed out slowly, suddenly uninterested in eating. The disappointment of the previous night came crashing back into him.

"Your mother seems to believe you three should venture home. And that I..." Avelia stopped a moment, pushing the fruit around their plate as they spoke, "that I should return to my realm."

"I believe I said, 'return to where you belong.'" Kattegat's voice rang out in the hall, booming and authoritative. "No need to censor my words for your companions."

Gallen saw his mother's figure slide through the door out of his periphery. She wore her cape, the tangle of fibers and shells emanating a regal aura that trailed behind her as she walked to the center of the table and placed both hands deftly on the edge of the coral surface. The tips of her blue ears glistened with multiple rings and the large stone necklace resting on her bare chest shone an exquisite green. The Lady of Eckral often appeared majestic, but today something had changed. Gallen had never quite seen his mother so stern, so sure. Not since his grandfather's passing all those years ago.

"And Gallen, my son. Take your friends home. I hope earnestly that they will find how to avoid catastrophe."

The look in his mother's golden eyes sent a cold sensation down Gallen's spine. He often yearned to hold the confidence and authority that seemed so natural to her. He looked up to her as a model of leadership, one that he could never quite match. And now, as the warriors sat sullenly in her shadow, memories of his childhood played back in his mind, moments of reprimand and guidance. Of Kattegat establishing a hierarchy of power that always set Gallen low. Oft as he tried to live up to her expectations, he could not help constantly falling short.

But, greater than his disappointment and shame, he admired his mother more than anyone. For enduring. For leading when all was against her. For pushing for change when necessary. For supporting tradition if possible. For always fighting for her realm and the people she cared for.

And thus, this request to abandon their quest caused a stirring in his chest of something more cutting than mere disappointment. It was perhaps a crack in her commitment to the cause, a cause Gallen had sacrificed his life in the Ocean Realm for. And, despite his love for his home, he would follow Alcor into the fire. He would burn if need be.

Avelia rose to their feet, shaking their head as they stalked into the halls. Gallen looked to Sol and Malinar, still struck by the finality of Kattegat's words. Sol lifted her eyes to meet his, the icy-blue color intensified by glistening tears. He nodded to her before standing to his feet.

"If that is what is best," Gallen turned to look at his mother once more, "then we shall."

"This must not be the intent of the Past Holder. I know it," Malinar said as she slumped onto the sheets of the circular bed where Gallen and Sol sat. Sol rubbed her eyes wearily, whimpering softly as Gallen gently stroked her back.

Clearly, a night of agonizing over his mother's schemes alone did little of consequence. He was eager to hear their opinions, forge a path forward as a unit. Malinar was the most vocally confounded, verbally considering the many explanations to rationalize what was said at the dining table.

"You do know," Malinar settled near Gallen, resting her head on his shoulder as she spoke, "it is entirely possible that the Twelve will understand the urgency of our situation. That they will see the danger such a threat poses to us all."

Gallen rested his free hand on Malinar's knee while continuing to gently scratch at Sol's tense shoulders.

"I am afraid my mother may convince them to remain neutral

as well, considering the unyielding nature of our foe…" he said weakly.

"What can we do?" Sol added, her voice muffled as she kept her head nestled in her hands, "what can we possibly do to convince these leaders of the weight of our circumstance? The horrible weight of this knowledge?"

Gallen looked at Sol with an endearing sympathy, but it was Malinar who spoke next: "This will have far-reaching ramifications." Gallen saw her eyes grow cold. "This could be the end of us. Of our realm. Our people." Her final words left her as a mere whisper. She pressed her fingers to her temple and groaned. Gallen wondered if there was more to this fear. More than what they each knew regarding the phoenix.

Gallen turned to face her directly.

"What leads you to believe it so dire? Have you seen something more in the map?" He asked.

Malinar shook her head. "No. No, it was in the Past Holder's cavern. I heard a voice. It spoke to me."

Sol's head lifted from her hands. "A voice?"

Drawing in a short breath of surprise, Gallen took their hands in his.

"Did you hear one as well?" Malinar asked quietly, though not soft enough to mask the quiver in her voice.

Gallen held his breath until Sol's nod of affirmation solidified his suspicions.

He squeezed their hands in his. "We must share, all of us, what we heard."

"We?" Sol queried.

"Ncheeldon appeared before us all. Such warnings are a natural part of rituals." He thought through the implications as he spoke, "Though, the Holder's was willing to reach you both, those of the land, those so foreign to this realm. There must be something grander at work, something only Ncheeldon in his wisdom could ascertain. Omens are gifts of the divine, a sacred sight into the voice of one who is beyond this world.

The women were motionless, the words washing over them. Gallen persisted.

"It is a curious gift to be sure, yet a gift nonetheless."

Nodding slowly, Sol shifted from the bed's center to its edge, reaching her hand down to feel along the floor until she pulled her satchel from the shadows. She swiftly retrieved a few blank sheets of paper along with a quill.

"Recording what we recall may be useful," she stated.

Gallen smiled. "Astute."

"Malinar," Sol licked the tip of the quill and tested the ink on the corner of the page, "what say you of the Holder's speakings?"

"Omen," Gallen corrected, his cheeks still lifted.

Sol nodded. "Omen. What say you?"

Malinar pulled her eyes upward, as if the phrase appeared neatly etched into the coral ceiling. Gallen tapped his newly freed hand on his knee while Sol, the red scar on her cheek nearly blended into the red smudges left by the pressure of her hands, shifted to examine Malinar's face more closely.

"The voice…I have yet to shake it since climbing the ladder of the cavern. It was…dreamlike yet strong. It frightened me. And its words. Its words frightened me further. It said, *Approach shadows of hidden pools as streams of red outpace the cruel. A sacrifice of one's own, the stars above to atone. Through fire's burn, you all shall see the path that builds eternity.*"

Gallen considered the omen. "A sacrifice from stars…" No wonder poor Malinar fretted so over their collective fate.

"Gallen, do these omens…are they things that *will* be?" Malinar attempted to steady her voice, though the words still quivered as she spoke.

Before he could respond, Avelia's short frame burst through the door of the room. "Flyers of the Night, I believe this is a path even Master Zelan did not quite anticipate. Well, not entirely."

Avelia barely glanced at the three warriors crowding one side of the bed. They fiddled with a vial of green liquid that bubbled as it sloshed from side to side. Their voice was calm, yet, as they turned the vial over in their hands, Gallen could see an uncharacteristically frenetic energy to Avelia. The shift was unnerving.

"Flyer Gallen. What say you of this shift in your mother?"

Gallen did not move to speak. In fact, he was unsure of what to say to Avelia. Malinar's admission still loomed thick in the air, and Gallen hardly wanted to discuss such personal matters with the High Realm's potion master.

"Did she make mention of meeting the Twelve?" Gallen questioned.

Avelia shook their head. "The lady appears resolute in her decision. She worries of the danger, claims it is too much to face at present. She did make mention of Sol several times. That Sol need return. That Sol may hold the answer. She has requested an audience with her...alone."

Gallen rolled his eyes. This was typical of his mother, a woman obsessed with Sol since she first arrived in the Ocean Realm all those years ago. Sol crept forward to the edge of the bed before sliding her feet to touch the ground.

"Perhaps I should discuss the circumstances with Lady Kattegat," Sol said.

She looked at Gallen and Malinar each before moving past Avelia.

"Is this wise?" Malinar questioned.

Sol waved away her concern. "I shall attempt to perhaps build a bridge. We were once close, no?"

With all eyes looking to him for affirmation, Gallen glumly nodded, providing Sol the validation to continue down the hall. Gallen pushed away the impulse to follow her. He knew better than to insert himself into business between Sol and his mother. The two shared something intangible, a bond that constantly drove them together. Unfortunately, both women were also known to be rather headstrong, especially when discussing two topics: matters of their home realms or, Mist forbid, Gallen himself.

Gallen fought against the barrage of thoughts that immediately flooded his mind. He knew Sol could hold her own, yet the worry remained. She was not the same Sol who visited the Ocean Realm monthly as a seasoned warrior. Not the Sol who spent hours discussing military strategy with his mother over wine. Though she kept her daggers strapped to her thighs, she was not the Sol who spent every waking hour practicing her aim. And while he favored this Sol, possibly succumbing to the early flitterings of love, he knew his mother would appreciate the former far more given the choice.

Avelia, perhaps sensing his unease, adopted a much calmer tone. "Would you both like to be alone?"

Gallen turned his head to Malinar whose brows were knit together in deep concern.

"I was actually wanting another look at the map," she said slowly, "if that is alright with you, Gallen?" Her purple eyes pleaded with him as she asked.

"Of course," he whispered back, running his hand over her bare calf before she leapt forward toward the door.

She beamed a bright smile toward him before disappearing into the hall.

Gallen sought his own escape, mustering any excuse to be on his own. For alone with Avelia was the last possible place he wanted to be.

∽

GALLEN GRASPED the hilt of his dagger's blade before flicking his wrist, hearing the satisfying thunk of metal on wood. As Malinar and Sol each went their separate ways, anxiety churned through him, begging for some form of release. Such thoughts led him to a series of targets in a small plot of seagrass beside the armory.

Each wooden circle displayed a mixture of patterns meant to challenge warriors. A few were marked with thin red circles that ended in a singular dot in the center. Others contained several oddly shaped marks meant to offer a variety of difficulties. Gallen mastered them with ease, a vast improvement from his years as a boy.

The daggers sat heavy in his hands as Gallen threw them with deadly precision. Their visit to the Ocean Realm had distracted him from his daily practice, a task of all Night Flyers on their travels. His shoulders and wrists grew sore as he tossed his twin blades over and over and over.

When a half hour passed, Gallen could feel the difference as he thrust the second of the pair through the air, barely missing his desired spot on the wide, circular target. Frustrated, he wiped his palm over his tired eyes before retrieving the blades, contemplating the form of his wrist.

"It is an impressive show." Avelia popped into view from the armory's path.

Sighing heavily, Gallen barely masked his disappointment as they sauntered toward the targets.

"Truly." They pulled at one of the blonde curls that settled close to their scalp. "I am impressed. I do realize there are warriors of high caliber elsewhere in Nourels. Usually, they are ones trained by the High Realm, yet I concede others prosper."

It took all of Gallen's self-control to hold his daggers to his chest rather than fling them toward Avelia.

"That is high of you to say," he managed to spit out as he walked back to the edge of the grass, readying his hand to throw.

Avelia stood aloof, their fingers laced together in front of them as they observed Gallen's movements. Another dagger flew through the air, this time sinking deep into the very center of the target.

"Any notes?" He smirked.

They shook their head in response. "It is impressive, as I stated."

Gallen shook his head and tossed the other dagger to meet its mate. Another hit. The practice was truly helping his form.

"Your mother, is she also so stern? I have studied much of this realm and its leaders, yet there is little written."

"Studied?" Gallen's confusion read easily on his face as he walked to retrieve his daggers, "why study this realm?"

Avelia walked a bit closer, still maintaining a few feet between them. "Master Zelan is blessed with the power of premonition. He cannot see the complete future. Yet, his visions are extraordinary. Far more accurate than any other recorded mortal. He is certainly the most divine human I have witnessed. That is, before our meeting with the Past Holder."

Gallen stopped in his tracks and turned to meet Avelia's eyes. "Visions?"

They nodded. "He knew I would accompany you and your warriors. He knew we would learn what needed to be done."

"And was there more?" Gallen prodded, inching his way toward them.

"Ice. Darkness. That is all."

Gallen considered the words. "And you trust him."

"As you trust your own mother."

Turning the blade over in his hands, he said, "there are few bonds more sacred than blood."

"He is the closest I know to it." Avelia gracefully sat on the path nearest the grass.

Flinging the blade toward the target, Gallen continued, "I understood that warriors were given to the High Realm by their kin, then returned in time."

He knew this secondhand, from Sol then Asha. Yet, both warriors knew their families. Cherished them.

"Most, yes. There are also those born to High Realm. Born in ash and soot and stone."

With these words, Gallen lowered the knife in his hand, though he remained facing the line of targets as Avelia continued. "Those like my mother, with children who exhibit promise early, they may offer their babes to ascend into the warrior's keep. There, those like me are raised together, with only other trainees as kin."

Avelia paused a moment, breathing in and out slowly as they spoke. "Only those with the most promise may enter into training with a master. And, further, only those with exceptional potential work under Master Zelan himself. I was ordained. Lucky."

The final word seemed to discount all they had achieved, the hard work that must have driven Avelia to gain so much.

"It certainly could not be only luck. Of that I am certain." Gallen raised the dagger again to throw.

"I do not mean to make an enemy of you, Flyer Gallen." Avelia's words came out quietly, a little louder than a whisper yet not their usual ostentatious tone. "Even in the enlightened High Realm, evil endures. Exploitation of those most vulnerable...I have not known many males I trust."

They did not elaborate, yet anger bloomed in his chest all the same.

"Master Zelan claims it is my greatest stumbling block."

Gallen stared at the two daggers stuck in the wood. Silver framed the translucent hilts which glimmered in the fading light. He was not sure how to respond, what even to think of such an admission. He turned his back to his twin blades and held a hand toward the blonde warrior, who was now shivering slightly. Never had they appeared so unnerved, so...shaken.

"Trust is to be earned." He offered them a hand and pulled Avelia up from their spot on the path. "I appreciate your willingness to place faith in me."

A part of their story. A harrowing set of memories, Gallen was sure. They nodded to Gallen, a show of thanks.

He looked at the warrior, their dark skin gleaming as the day wore on, "I do understand I have been less than cordial. That we both contain our own…opinion."

"Strong warriors tend to oppose." They said with a grin.

Gallen shrugged. "Another of your master's wise maxims?"

"No," Avelia pulled at their curls, "this is my own."

He laughed. True and boisterous and refreshing.

The two walked back toward the halls of Eckral together.

20

Sol

The walk to meet Kattegat struck terror in Sol's heart. She was certain it was not the first of their personal chats. Gallen admitted to her many times that his mother far preferred her to himself.

"*You* did not abandon your realm," he would say on many a drunken night in the Night Streets. "*You* did not forsake your inheritance."

Surely the Lady's love of her son superseded such a decision, especially one so noble.

Sol spun the ring on her index finger, the emerald stone pricking her skin slightly as she pulled it toward her palm then away again. The practice centered her as she walked, like the picture of her mother nestled in her silver locket. A keepsake that surely meant the world to her in another life. In *her* other life.

The thought of what was missing merely added to her growing anxieties as her bare feet pressed delicately against the coral halls with each step toward Kattegat's study. So strange that the lady of the estate would not desire an audience with her own son to discuss matters such as these. Nor could she imagine herself serving as the solution to the phoenix conundrum. If anyone were more capable, it would be the potion master, Avelia, or even Malinar, who was showing some sort of affinity for enchantment.

Though, as she neared the threshold of the dreaded meeting place, Sol resigned herself to the responsibility of this discussion. To speak on behalf of her companions, her friends. With such confidence in that alone, Sol knocked on the frame of Kattegat's door.

"Enter."

Kattegat sounded exhausted and resolute. Though the lady did not look one bit out of sorts as Sol entered the room and found a seat on a lush chair. The cape that billowed through the seas on their journey now rested on the back of her chair as she stood staring through the window on the far side of the room. Having changed clothing, Kattegat appeared more approachable. A simpler gown of brown cotton replaced her typical grandiose attire. She wore no jewels, save silver rings lining the edges of her pale blue ears, and her hair was styled in long braids tied behind her back. The glitter that lined her face drew the eye to her sharp cheekbones before disappearing into her braids. Simple, yet striking.

While she did not look as extravagant as before, she remained as regal as ever. Her posture never wavered as Sol rested her back against the chair.

"I have admired you a long time, young warrior." She refused to even glance toward Sol as she spoke, her eyes instead glued to the window. "Since you entered the edges of my realm, I have understood you. Formidable. Ambitious. Like myself as a younger woman. Once a woman of great renown, to be sure…"

Sol twirled the ring over and over and over as Kattegat spoke. With each word, the tension between the two grew. Could the lady of Eckral know of her memories? Of the truth of her time in Endoneth?

"Purposeful, you once were. A force." Kattegat's voice rang through the space as she spit out each word. "Imagine my distress when I placed your hand to my temple and felt...a shift in your being."

The air evaded Sol, her lungs suffocating from the tension. She squeezed her hands against her knees, trying desperately to ignore the tightness in her chest as the lady continued. "Now, Gallen did inform me of your capture and escape. Brave. Courageous. As I would have guessed, truly. Though, the scar, it tells a different story."

Sol reflexively pressed her hand to her cheek. A flush of heat stained, though the image of the blemish remained. The scar, she knew, was a signal of shame, though she never confirmed its origin. When Rostair revealed himself a villain, she assumed the scar was his doing. However, could Kattegat surmise something more?

Alarm seized Sol, and suddenly the welcoming home of a friend transformed into a tightrope. She pulled the emerald ring from her finger, scraping the gold with her fingertips before pressing it tightly to her palm like a lifeline. Like her only source of safety during a tense conversation, one that gained more significance as the seconds passed. She considered asking the lady for an explanation. Yet, Kattegat allowed her no spare moment to voice concern.

"Protection is my purpose. To enact choices that protect the people of this realm."

Kattegat finally turned her head, her nostrils flaring as her golden eyes pierced into Sol, pinning her to the chair with one look. The woman could gain unimaginable information with her manipulative presence alone. Though her voice was harsh, her eyes were soft and her manicured brows curved into a sympathetic arch. The contradiction made Sol's heart beat at an uncontrollable rate, confusion swirling through her mind as Kattegat took step by painfully slow step toward the center of the study.

"I am afraid you must leave. Today. Do not speak to another as you go."

The words settled uncomfortably onto Sol, her breath now coming in gulps as she desperately sought something to help free the knot in her chest. Kattegat continued her stroll toward her. Sol remained frozen in the padded seat, feeling for the first time more like a prisoner than a guest. It was only when the lady stood before her, setting two strong hands upon the arms of the chair that her demand registered in Sol.

"Leave...?" The whisper barely left Sol's lips, the voice barely her own. If Kattegat heard the query, she ignored it.

"Ncheeldon presents his visitors with the foresight to see possibilities. Futures both possible and inevitable. It is the responsibility of a leader to decipher which is most likely."

Thoughts spun chaotically through Sol's mind as the lady continued, snarling toward Sol as if ridding her home of a pest.

"Why? I wondered to myself. *Why is this woman before me such a threat?"*

Kattegat tightened her grip on the arms of the chair, the fabric crunching viciously beneath her sharp nails.

"Then I recalled a notion told to me by a man of Ice. I recalled rumors of a woman who lost herself yet put on airs..."

She refused to finish the sentence, yet Sol perceived the knowledge she contained. Understood that the lady of Eckral knew of her circumstances. Knew and was not amused.

"I owe you no explanation. You are no longer welcome here." she spat out, the venom in her words striking with delicate precision. "There is a chariot waiting. Go."

Kattegat pushed the arms of the chair as she said these words, regaining her straightened posture before returning to her place near the window.

Sol's heart fell, thinking of Gallen and Malinar in the room nearby. "I must tell—"

"No!" Kattegat's voice boomed. "Leave at once. A soldier will escort you as you exit."

The words stunned Sol, hardly able to stir up the courage to refuse. Instead, as she shakily rose to her feet, she relaxed her hands, hearing the satisfying clattering of metal on coral. Kattegat resumed the glaring into her city. She never looked back to Sol as the Night Flyer walked out of the study and suddenly broke into a run. The attempt to escape did not last, a guard ripping Sol violently toward the door. The soldier dragged Sol to the chariot, grunting profanities as she fought. Her throat burned as she screamed for them. For the only two people she knew she could truly trust.

Her neck cracked to the side as the soldier struck her, pulling her body onto the chariot and shutting the door. Try as she might, the door refused to budge as she pulled and screamed and sobbed. The chariot began its flight away from safety and control and certainty. Away from *them*.

QUESTIONS SWARMED Sol's mind as the enchanted chariot rushed away from Eckral Estate. Away from Somov. Away from Gallen and Malinar.

Why am I not welcome at Eckral?

Why could I not tell the others of my going?

Where is this damned chariot taking me?

A violently sudden turn sent her stomach into a most unwelcome summersault. She reached for her arm, still sore from the altercation with the guard.

Kattegat saw something in the Past Holder's vision that pushed her to this. It was the only explanation that made a modicum of sense. It was more than possible that the vision—the omen—that Kattegat witnessed poisoned her against Sol. But, why only Sol? Why not Malinar or Avelia?

The blue water rushed around the magic of the chariot as Sol ascended at a rate that could not be safe. She held her head in her hands as the pressure increased incrementally. The rushing water dulled her senses as loud roars pounded against her ears. The journey lasted far longer than their previous journeys. From Anthozoa to Somov. From the city center to the Past Holder's keep.

It was nearly impossible to ignore the frustration of being so out of control. Sol crushed her eyes shut and thrust her mind somewhere far, far from here. She focused on Celestra. The flickering blue lights. The fabric settled neatly upon her tent. She saw Asha, laughing on a cushion in the corner, turning the page of a book. Her blond hair grazing the side of her cheek. The light brown of her skin glowing in the moonlight. The sound of her cheer, even in a memory, was enough to make Sol tear up.

She saw Piré, her quiet friend, describing her latest baking endeavor. Her curls waving to and fro as she whisked away to find her newest ingredient or help Gramma Ishpa clean pots and pans. She saw Alcor, offering a thought-provoking poem to their friends. She saw Luminor, sipping his cup of tea between his well-intended lecturing.

The chariot took another sharp turn, shaking Sol from the memory of her friends. She reached for the railing that lined the front of the carriage, gripping the cold metal in an attempt to steady herself.

She needed to ignore the ache building in her head or the metallic tinge in her mouth or the quivering of her thighs.

Sol longed for them. She longed for Gallen's arm hugging her waist, encouraging her to hold him, laughing a bit at her reaction to the enchanted journey. She longed for Malinar to mutter words of flirtatious affirmation, claiming the two needed to reach the surface to ensure they could read a story together.

She thought back to Gallen's room: The silk sheets. The smell of sweat and citrus. The taste of Malinar's tongue. The heavy breathing of the three warriors. Sol lost herself in this recollection. That moment that she wished would last a lifetime. Gallen's soft skin and Malinar's warm fingers. She relished the thought, coaxing it to push away the pain of this flight upward from the depths of the Ocean Realm.

She wondered if she would ever enjoy such moments again.

As the thought assailed her, warmth cradled her cheeks. The rushes of water calmed against her ears. She opened her eyes slightly to see beams of light streaking through the rough waves.

Orange light. Faint yet present. Present yet fading.

The surface was near. Yet, rather than rush upward to the surface, the chariot slowed, the enchanted glow fading around her. The lights that shone so brightly when near the city now flickered dimly. Sol's body relaxed.

The chariot whirred to a stop, still submerged a few feet from the surface. Sol noticed the rail grow warm. Not just warm. Steaming. Water bubbled around the entire chariot, boiling as she scrambled to escape. Sol ripped her hands from the now scalding heat of the chariot's rim, pulling them away just before the heat could sear her bare flesh. The chariot floor grew dangerously hot, burning the sore soles of her feet.

Suddenly, the chariot lost its enchantment, Sol flying forward into the open ocean. Startled, struggling, and without the hold of magical protection, she began sinking into an abyss of darkness. She swallowed a mouthful of saltwater that burned her throat and nose.

The shock pushed her to swim. To swim as fast as she could to the surface. Though her head still ached and her hands and feet burned, she willed her body up, up, up. Her lungs pleaded for air, her eyes stinging as she fought to keep them open. To keep her vision focused on the light above her. The light that was fading too fast. Far too fast.

She was so close, so close to the surface that her mouth watered for a taste of fresh air above. Her arms wobbled against the effort of pulling her body upward. The muscles in her legs shook with pain. A darkness faded into the edges of her vision. Her head grew heavy. Her legs numbed, begging for reprieve.

But she was so close to the surface. Only a few more strokes of her arms. She could reach it.

When she was almost spent, the darkness hovering dangerously close to the center of her vision, her fingers burst through the surface of the water. Her head emerged with a tremendous gasp. Sol squinted at the setting sun as she coughed up gulps of water. She steadied herself as she waded, focusing on her breathing. In and out. In and out.

Sol indulged in the ability to breathe freely again, lingering in her personal triumph. Adrenaline seeped from her pores as she treaded water. Sensation returned to her limbs as her heart settled into a neutral rhythm. And, as her vision returned to focus, Sol believed she escaped a severe fate.

Then the cold set in. Cold was perhaps a euphemism. This was hellish, icy, piercing cold. The water pricked every inch of her body, like hundreds of needles prodding her flesh. The daggers that often provided sentimental comfort now served as just another conduit for the frigid water—the blades stinging against her skin. Panting, she pushed puffs of white clouds into the air just above the waterline as her teeth chattered.

She needed to move.

Sol searched desperately for an deliverance. If not, she would die. Freeze to death in the middle of the ocean.

Better than drowning, she thought cynically.

The sun shrank like a coward in the sky, the bright orange dimming into pinks and purples on the endless horizon. At the very least, she would die in the elegance of the setting sun, as the stars glinted marvelously above her. But then, just before she resigned herself to begin swimming blindly, the disappearing sun in the distance revealed something more. A white blur.

Sol cared not what it was nor where it was. She sucked in a deep breath and plunged forward toward the unknown.

If her body was screaming as she swam to the surface, it was in utter agony now. She could hardly feel her bare feet as she willed them to push her body forward, could hardly sense if her hands were clenched into fists or spread wide as her arms moved over and over and over her head.

To her great excitement, the white blur materialized slowly before her. She dared not let up to look more closely at the details, to consider what she was swimming toward. The only thought that flooded her mind was land. Warmth. Dry land and warmth.

The sun refused to pause its descent, the air growing more frigid by the second. By the time her stomach skimmed the banks and her hands found a place to pull her body onto land, her fingers were so numb that she could hardly recognize the texture of the sand. Either way, she clawed up bit by desperate bit until she could no longer feel the wet cold of the water. Even then she continued forward, crawling away from the freezing water until she could barely hear the crashing of the waves against the harsh banks.

Only then did she turn over to rest on her back, her eyes searching the stars as she assessed the damage. Her body ached from the sudden journey. Taking a deep breath, Sol pulled her elbows behind her and tried to lift her head. The movement alone dazed her. Pain radiated throughout Sol's tired body. She settled on her forearms, looking down at her bare skin and pushing away the persistent impulse to rest her eyes. She could not faint, not in her state.

It was then that Sol noticed the sand. No. Not sand. Snow.

Snow surrounding her for miles and miles. And a trail of red leading from the water to her hands. She took a closer look. Blistered and bleeding. The tip of each finger tinted blue, a few showing specks of black.

Damn.

First drowning, then freezing, and now frostbite.

The pathetic ropes and rags that barely covered her skin provided no protection from this hellscape. Kattegat gave Sol no time to bring warmer clothing, despite surely knowing the chariot's destination. Kattegat could not have known. Surely, she could not have anticipated.

Sol pushed the present confusion and frustration aside to attend to the wounds that spread across her body, the cold continuing its unrelenting barrage against her vulnerable skin. Blisters along her fingers, stomach, and thighs. She noticed a similar coloring on the tips of her toes.

Damn. Damn. Damn.

She needed to find shelter and find it fast. Taking another massive breath—and praying to any god there was to provide her some energy—Sol moved to her knees. She clenched her teeth as she pressed her weight into her right foot before lifting to a standing position.

Agony. Sol experienced the purest of agony as her legs threatened to fail her completely. Her jaw ticked as tears froze to her chapped cheeks.

She could do this.

Sol turned her head gradually to minimize the throbbing in her skull, then scanned her surroundings for anything resembling a shelter. She saw something to her right, barely visible in the growing darkness of night. In the distance, a blot of blackness in a sea of snow.

You are brave. You are bold.

Sol took one step. Pain shot through her spine. Her breath hitched as she struggled to stay upright.

Another step. More pain.

Another. Then another.

With each solemn step forward, Sol was more determined to live. Determined to make it to shelter. She ignored the bitter wind that scraped past her cheeks and the burning sensation ripping at the soles of her feet.

The clattering of her teeth set an ironic rhythm for her feet to follow. Step. Step. Step.

Finally, the blackness formed something substantial: a cave. Thank the gods. And behind it, more black mounds making clusters of sanctuaries. She heaved her body forward, the allure of an escape from the wind and the snow encouraging her broken body to continue on. When Sol set foot on the stone floor, her legs gave in. She barely felt her body crumple to the ground, her knees crashing into the stones with a sickening crack. And, though it remained cold and misty inside the cave, relief swelled within her.

Her eyes took a few moments to adjust to the darkness, though the eerie glow of moonlight reminded her a bit of home. She noticed tools for fishing: baskets, hooks, rope. If her throat were well, she would have screeched with relief as she spied a pile of clothing sitting against the cave wall.

Sol's shallow sighs echoed through the cave. She shuffled toward the side, finding her balance against the smooth surface of the cavern wall. She pulled what remained of her wet clothes over her head, wincing at her stiff muscles. Shedding the Ocean Realm garb was like a weight off of her shoulders, as if the burden of betrayal fell to the ground along with the shimmering threads. The cool feel of her daggers was all that remained as she straightened her spine. The relative warmth of the cave helped thaw her hands; the tingling sensation returned feeling to her legs and feet as well. She moved further into the space, using the wall for support. To Sol, the mildewed and well-worn clothes sitting on the ground looked like sumptuous, her rescue from the bitter cold that swept through the cave's entrance. She slid inch by inch until her feet brushed against the pile. Taking a brown tunic in her hand, she dried her hair as best she could, ignoring the faint scent of sweat and soil in the cotton fabric. Once her locks quit dripping, she looked at the remaining clothing.

Sol quickly found something substantial to protect her frigid form: long, woolen pants, a rustic tunic, and a thick coat of fur. The hem of the pants fell well past her feet, serving as soft coverings for her toes as she found a dry place to sit.

The baskets served as sufficient kindling to spark a fire, though the task took nearly an hour to accomplish. And fire. Fire was her true savior.

Huddled against a pile of worn fisherman's clothes near a makeshift fire, Sol's body finally gave in. Her lids closed and muscles relaxed. Sleep came swiftly and lasted well into the morning.

～

"Well, how fortunate I am."

Startled awake, Sol jumped to attention, her muscles screaming in protest at the immediate call to move. The voice at the mouth of the cave was menacing. Like a viper spitting venom into its intended prey. A shiver slithered down her spine. The voice was one she recognized.

Cold fear sliced through her chest as memories of the Greentime Ball flooded back. Rostair's betrayal. Asha's torture. Gallen's pain. And his minion. The lord's true lover with bloodred lips and a heart of stone.

"We heard a whore washed onto our shores. In fact, you could say we *expected* such an arrival."

Helzaf's words cut through the air like arrows, aimed to attack

Sol at her core. Helzaf would say anything to hurt her, though the words caused Sol to pause. *Expected?*

The woman was horrifically ravishing. The daughter of a great lord of the Desert Realm, hailing from the estate of Tselm, she was accustomed to taking exactly what she wanted at any cost.

Helzaf sighed, pushing the bright blonde hair away from her cruel eyes. "As I said, I am quite fortunate. I have always dreamed of the moment I would rid the realms of you and your kind. Your parents were the beginning."

She stalked toward Sol with wicked intent, drawing a blade in her small hand.

"Rostair has claimed Alcor as his prize," she pouted before her crimson lips lifted her chiseled cheeks, "but you? He afforded me that honor."

Sol reached to her thigh, where one of her twin daggers sat dutifully in its sheath. Her fingers wrapped around the onyx hilt, the movement familiar, though she feared not familiar enough to defeat Helzaf. She prayed the lord's child was not as competent with her sword as she was at slinging insults.

Helzaf raised the large blade above her head before plunging it downward to meet Sol's waiting dagger. The sound of clashing metals pierced the air, ringing sharply as it echoed from wall to wall. The dagger in her hand shook with effort as she ordered her arm to hold steady.

Sol, weak and blistered and cold, would not die here.

At least, not without a fight.

21

Gallen

Malinar stood near a long table hovering over the enchanted map like an artist admiring her craft. Gallen paced back and forth across the coral floor as she worked, looking over his shoulder every so often to answer her questions or occasionally monitor her progress.

"Tell me of the path between our realm and the Sun Realm. What lies there?"

Her voice was angelic, so different from the Flyer that began their quest. She was open to learning. And, despite the occasional jab—well, more than occasional—she was kind. Warm. Affirming. It was a welcome shift from the standoffish girl from the boundary of the Star Realm.

"Ignoring is not the way to a woman's heart," Malinar quipped.

Gallen smirked. "Apologies, dearest. It is easy for the mind to stray when looking at you."

Malinar laughed and rolled her eyes, though Gallen noticed a blush rise to the small apples of her pale cheeks.

"The gap, here. A description of such a place would help." She pointed to a blank space on the glowing map.

Pulling a hand through his blonde waves, Gallen considered.

"We tend to avoid this path. You see, just beyond the Valley Realm are bogs. Swamps between the valley and the Green Realm beyond. It is far simpler to travel on solid ground."

Gallen tried to recall what the swamps looked like, yet he had only seen distant glimpses. Malinar nodded.

"Good. Good."

The two worked like this for hours, Malinar asking Gallen key memories about the many places he had visited throughout the Nine Realms until they created a rudimentary blueprint of Nourels itself. Some regions were far more detailed than others, yet the existence of the map was remarkable.

Malinar sighed, concentrating on the far corner of the Green Realm.

"I may need to rest my eyes. Are there regulations against raiding the kitchens?"

Gallen ripped his head toward the nearest window, where he saw the wavering rays of afternoon dimming into evening. The time passed so quickly. And, while Gallen enjoyed talking with Malinar immensely, he wondered what became of Sol's discussion with his mother. He wondered what topic could take so long to explore.

"We must have missed the lunch signal. You did not hear anything, correct?" Gallen walked closer to Malinar as she delicately folded the map into a compact square.

She shook her head. "I heard nothing. Is that unusual?"

He rubbed the side of his jaw, the small stubble scratching at his fingers. "My mother is quite prompt with such instructions, even if she arrives to meals late."

It was more than strange. Certainly, the chimes for mealtime were varied, but they were never absent. Fear gripped Gallen's heart.

"What was it that Avelia said of my mother's request?" He held out a hand to Malinar as she walked toward him, as if drawn to his voice.

As she took his hand in her own, she crinkled her nose. "That it was Sol who could save us all. Only Sol. A variation of that notion at least."

Their fingers tangled together and Gallen pulled Malinar close to his side. He smiled halfheartedly. "Let us see what my mother has done with our sweet friend."

Malinar returned the slight smile, appearing just as nervous as Gallen. Though, it was likely one of his mother's many attempts to wield control over a dire circumstance. Another way to show Alcor and Sol that her allegiance was true to her people and her responsibility to the realm.

The two walked toward the study, anticipation rushing through Gallen's chest as they did. Each step brought more unease. Each corridor more concern.

Had Mother learned of Sol's memories?

Flashes of foreboding spread through his body at the thought. If Kattegat knew, it meant she knew his deceit. A lie of omission, yes. But one that certainly could shift her choice to join the conflict.

Gallen pulled Malinar to move faster as the thought took root. If that happened, if his mother learned that Sol was not the same warrior she had known before, who knows what his mother would do. Not to punish Sol alone, but to punish him. To punish Alcor. To punish this rebellion.

"Gallen, what is it?"

Gallen could not answer. He looked ahead, pulling at Malinar's hand to move from a brisk walk to a light jog. She stayed with him, her eyes wide with worry. It did not take long for them to reach the study doors, which were open wide.

Between ragged breaths Gallen managed to call out, "Sol?"

Malinar ran into the space, echoing his call, "Sol? Sol?"

The desperation in her voice was like a knife to Gallen's heart, his dismay increasing twofold. He surveyed the space. Empty. The night's light flowed through the windows, inking eerie blue swirls along the floor and furniture. Gallen's heart raced then sank as Malinar looked up at him, purple eyes frightened and dim.

"Where is she?"

Gallen lifted his shoulders. "Perhaps. Perhaps she is back in our room. Let us see."

The two ventured back out again, running as the halls wound their way to his curved doorway. Gallen placed a heavy hand on the door before pushing. A figure stood at the window, still as stone.

"Mother?" Gallen stepped inside swiftly, stopping by the edge of the bed that sat at the center of the room. "Where is Sol?"

The question should have proved simple enough. Gallen prepared himself for an explanation to ease his anxieties. That his mother and Sol talked long into the night and that Sol needed to walk the length of the fields to clear her head. That she and Sol found a solution to their impossible circumstances. That Sol was eating. Sleeping. Breathing.

He hoped.

Kattegat turned her face slightly toward them, harsh pity marking the edges of her eyes and brows and the turn of her mouth. Gallen's heart fell.

"The warrior is one of habit, I am afraid." She paused dramatically before dismantling Gallen's final hope. "She has left."

Malinar gasped. Gallen gripped the edge of the sheets in his hands, channeling the tension that built in his body into wringing the silken threads. Kattegat paid little mind. Instead, the lady swept her cape to the side to face the two completely.

"Yes, my child. She absconded with my chariot and flew toward the surface. Howling something of saving the realms." Kattegat flung her hand in the air for emphasis. "She begged for you both to return to your home. To the stars, she said."

Gallen stared blankly at his mother. This did not make sense. No, not at all. Kattegat did not wait for their response before taking her leave. "You both should think upon your next steps. You are welcome here, of course, for as long as is necessary."

With that, the lady of the estate took her cape in both hands and marched toward the door. The stomping of her footsteps slowly quieted until they dissipated into the recesses of the halls. Even in the complete silence, Gallen could not move. Could not speak. He did not feel angry, as he thought he would if this happened again. No, he only felt sheer, cold dread.

He jumped as Malinar's hand rested upon his waist.

"What...what do we do?"

Gallen reached his hand to meet hers, unable to move his eyes from the spot his mother once stood.

"I am. I..."

He wasn't sure. The last time Sol left him like this she nearly died. He nearly died. Ranor *did* die. It was too much to consider. He stroked his thumb across the top of Malinar's hand. He wondered what she thought of this. Was her mind racing as his was? Did she think back to that morning at the Night Flyers' camp as the warriors filed into the center of the tents just to learn of Sol's absence? Bile threatened its way up Gallen's throat as he debated the possibility of Sol running away, of thinking she could face the phoenix alone. Just as she faced Rostair alone. Just as she nearly cost them all the war.

"I believed she had truly changed." The dismay that sat cool in his veins quickly turned into fiery anger. "Yet, here we are once more. Like a vigilante she has fled. And what did she believe us to do? Did she mean to keep us here? To await her fate like before?"

He squeezed his eyes shut as sorrow and rage and exasperation washed over him in waves, the memories of waking in his tent alone flashing over and over and over in his head. A faded pounding in his temples rattled in the background of the repetitive images, serving as a tortured soundscape. He wished he could find comfort in the present, to shake him from this cursed nostalgia. But his eyes refused to open, refused to recenter him in reality. The only anchor was Malinar's hand grasping his waist.

But even that too slipped away as her hand fell away. He heard her soft footsteps move across the room. His shoulders moved dramatically up and down as hand clutched the place on his waist where her hand once lay, desperately seeking some sort of comfort as he spiraled. Malinar knew more than anyone how this ended the last time Sol recklessly faced evil on her own. Gallen let his other hand guide his body onto his bed, crumpling into a ball of anguish as his mind continued its tortuous run through a barrage of memories. As the silk sheets caressed his cheek, he heard Malinar shuffling around the bed.

"I am unsure," Malinar whispered. "Gallen. I am unsure."

Frustration grew within Gallen's chest as he selfishly wanted to wallow in his depressive state. Why was Malinar not also infuriated? Was this not the same woman who spewed hatred toward Sol for months after her last heroic stunt?

"Gallen!"

Malinar pushed his shoulder fervently. When he finally opened his eyes slightly, the edges of his lids lined with tears, he noticed her clutching a book to her breast.

"She did not leave of her own accord." Malinar stated defiantly, "she did not."

Her confidence pulled Gallen from his position on the bed, looking at Malinar for a further explanation.

"Think of all we have been through together. Think of the woman we have grown to…"

She reached for Gallen's hand, her purple eyes filled with affection.

"That we have grown to care for. She is not who she once was. I have reckoned with this myself. To realize my hatred for her was not warranted. It was a hatred of *myself*. And it was Sol who helped me realize this. I *needed* a person to blame, you see. And Sol, she... she allowed me the space to hate her if I needed to. That was enough to show me who she was. Think of it, Gallen. The person you know. The person *we* know."

He had never heard Malinar so affectionate and assured. And, despite the pulsing that continued to plague his temples, he knew her rationale held merit. Sol was not who she once was, though it was difficult for him to completely separate those memories of loneliness and apprehension and vexation.

Malinar pointed to a stack of parchment neatly organized atop his trunk. "She has worked tirelessly to record our every movement. And this," she squeezed his hand as she held out a leather-bound book, "Asha's book. Sol would not leave it here, not without good reason. Perhaps that is silly to think. But I know how much it means to her, the book, her writing. I cannot imagine her at the very least ensuring we take it back home."

Malinar set the book delicately on the bed in front of Gallen. He chuckled slightly, using his other hand to trace the worn spine.

"I know the old Sol would care not of such trifles. However... leaving something behind..."

Gallen could not finish his thought, not with the idea blazing through the panic and fury that still settled deep in his gut. He rushed off the side of the bed, like a man hellbent on validation.

Straining to see even a slight glimmer of gold along the bedding, the floor, the curved corners, or within Sol's braided satchel, Gallen huffed in disappointment. Yet a still small voice in the recesses of his gut told him to continue. Told him to hope. To trust. To search.

"Come." He stated softly as he continued eyeing the floor.

He grabbed Malinar's hand in his and led them down the familiar hallway toward the study. The two burst into the room where they stood not so long ago. This time, Gallen looked more closely throughout the space. His eyes traced each piece of furniture, each shelf of each bookcase, every crevice of the coral floor until—

"Malinar!"

His heart leapt. The anger that once plagued him melted into something different. Guilt. Remorse. Unfettered joy.

He reached beneath one of his mother's upholstered chairs. His hand closed around a small token of affection, a piece he hadn't held in months. He turned to Malinar with his hand extended. Now it was Gallen who presented his own evidence of their partner's loyalty.

"She did not leave on her own accord, indeed."

Malinar looked at the ring settled neatly in the crook of Gallen's palm.

"Her ring," she noted, a smile growing on her face before fading just as fast. "Where is she?"

"My question precisely." He placed the ring on his pinky finger.

Malinar began pacing, a shared trait of the two, Gallen noticed.

"Could we approach your mother? Convince her to tell us if she knows more?"

Gallen shook his head. "If she knows more, she clearly did not want to indulge that information to us. There is no indication she would share such now."

"Even if we insisted?"

"Unfortunately." Gallen grazed the emerald ardently.

She exhaled, "there must be a way to learn something."

The pacing continued and Gallen watched as Malinar moved from one side of the study to the other, considering their options when an idea manifested.

"If only we knew a potions master." He beamed slyly.

Soon, Malinar and Gallen stood before Avelia's door, waiting for them to invite the two inside. Gallen grinned broadly as he entered the room. It certainly did not match Avelia's more serious personality, and he wondered how comfortable they were with the accommodations. Avelia's guest room looked much brighter than Gallen's. The coral walls were painted a pale shade of yellow that nearly matched Avelia's tight curls. The furniture also evoked a positive energy: the bedding another bold yellow shade, embroidered with pastel coral reefs and the lone trunk painted with intricate pictures of vibrant fish.

If Avelia was bothered, they did not show it. Sitting on the small bed, they swirled a bottle of liquid in their hands. The entire room smelled of soil and florals. Gallen wasted no time with pleasantries.

"We need your assistance," he said.

"And what of it, Flyer Gallen?"

The two warriors quickly explained their situation: Sol's visit with Kattegat. The lady's curious admission of Sol's valiant disappearance. Their realization of Sol's hidden message in leaving her ring. And finally...

"We need a way to find our friend." Malinar gasped for air as she finished the lengthy explanation.

Avelia's eyes were wide, like two mountains of volcanic sand surrounded by pools of blue. Their expression was difficult to discern as they looked from Malinar to Gallen and back. They continued to swirl the liquid round and round, their golden brows creasing and relaxing as they considered various options.

"Do you believe the lady of Eckral knows her location?"

Gallen slowly nodded. "Or may know her heading at the very least."

Avelia set the bottle upon the bright pink rug that lined the floor.

"There may be a way. A potion. Tonguesoother."

Malinar nearly leapt forward at the mention of any chance to find Sol. "What do you need to forge such a concoction?"

Avelia tapped their nails upon the seam of their silk slacks.

"I believe I've spotted suitable ingredients on my walks. I will need some time, perhaps thirty minutes. I wish speed was my gift. Alas not."

Gallen's brow raised slightly, impressed by Avelia's talent and humility. Malinar heaved a sigh of relief. Before either warrior could thank them, Avelia rushed to their feet, pulling together a collection of empty jars and cups, many of which Gallen recognized from the estate —a cup from the kitchen, vases from one of the art galleries, a jar from the armory, amongst others—before leaving the room in a rush.

Malinar turned to Gallen with renewed positivity. "Let us prepare to leave."

She pushed Gallen through the doorway to gather their own supplies. Malinar crouched to pull a few pieces of clothing from a trunk. Gallen took the turquoise satchel, still weighed down by a stack of blank pages. He pressed the kelp close to his chest. Disgrace fell heavy on his shoulders once more. Then the earlier trepidation followed close behind.

"If my mother cannot inform us of her whereabouts…will you join me still?" He asked faintly.

He turned his golden eyes to hers as she dropped a tunic and rose to her feet.

"I would follow you to the ends of Nourels," she spoke with a tender assurance, "especially to find Sol."

She walked closer, cupping his jaw in her pale palms and pulling his face down to touch her forehead to his. Her lips so close, her nose barely grazing his own, her hair teasing his cheek put Gallen at ease, even just for a moment. For a moment of ease, the terror that threatened to choke his lungs eviscerated with her nearness. A moment. A moment where they were together and Sol was safe and his mother was wise and true. A moment.

He looked down at the ring still settled on his finger, the emerald shining against the satchel between them.

"I gave this to her, you know."

His words were hushed as he recalled another time. Another man. Malinar stroked his cheeks with her thumbs encouragingly.

"I forged it for her. A symbol of both worlds, the emerald of our oceans and the pink diamonds of the stars."

The ring shone brilliantly, as if acknowledging Gallen's grief. The halo of diamonds dazzling amidst the rich green of the center stone.

"Before our last quest together," he continued, "I presented her with this ring as a symbol, a promise, if you will. I asked her to live with me for the rest of our days." A tear trailed viciously down his face, "and she accepted."

His heartbeat hastened as he remembered that night. Sitting outside the city, the primroses swaying auspiciously in the breeze. The emerald stone shimmering in the light of the stars. Mist, he was nervous that she might reject him. That she would find their romance as a mere distraction from her true purpose. Instead, she kissed him fiercely. She assured him of her priorities, her steadiness, her loyalty. A crack in her typically rough façade. Perhaps a glimmer of who truly hid underneath.

Malinar continued stroking her thumb against his cheek as he reminisced. He looked back into her eyes.

"When I saw her donning this ring the first day of our quest, I nearly wept at the sight. I could not articulate whether it was due to the grief of what I lost or the even greater grief that she likely did not know its meaning."

Stray tears stained his cheeks, falling toward Malinar's waiting hands. He dared not move away from her nor drop the satchel. Instead, he merely remembered. Remembered all that they were and all that they were becoming.

He ached for Sol to be here, to be safe.

"We will find her." Malinar's words sent a shiver down his spine as her warm breath touched his lips. He looked toward them, the thin line of lips slightly plumped in the center waiting to be kissed.

Her hands, still holding Gallen's cheeks, conveyed a soft confidence. So sure.

He wanted her hands to grip his neck, to pull him in. Their lips were so tantalizingly close that it would take a small movement forward for him to feel her. To suck at the pout on her bottom lip. To repay her for her affirmation and attention and affection. And her eyes, the purple hue blazing with passion, echoed a similar sentiment.

Her chest press against the satchel in his hands as she eliminated the small gap between them.

"Let us, Gallen. Let us find her."

With those words, Malinar crushed her lips into his, sucking the breath from his lungs as she swept her tongue inside. The caress of his cheek transitioned into a firm hold, keeping him there with her. Her possessiveness sparked a longing within him. The kiss was ravenous, as if the two needed something, anything, to alleviate panic and dread that pained them.

Gallen kept one hand clutching the satchel while the other found the nook of Malinar's waist, pulling her even more tightly against him as they kissed. Malinar moaned as the friction between their bodies increased. Their lips rarely parted; their heads synchronized as she slipped her hands from Gallen's face to his neck.

A rap at the door interrupted as Avelia swooped into the room. Though Gallen and Malinar rushed apart, the scene was obvious. Looking the two up and down, Avelia's dark cheeks flushed a deep crimson. Gallen instinctively held the satchel in front of his groin, eager to avoid the awkward admission of his inconvenient arousal.

"Have you found a solution, Avelia?" Malinar cleared her throat nonchalantly, though a flush marked her chest and face.

Avelia smirked slightly, raising a jar of greenish-orange liquid.

"I have indeed. A varied version of the Tonguesoother. I must admit, the quest to discover ingredients in a new locale caused a bit of a conundrum. However, as Master Zelan says, *We will it with what we have.*"

They spoke with confidence, turning their attention to Gallen. "How shall we administer it?"

Gallen was admittedly unsure of a way to incite his mother to action without drawing suspicion. Guards were surely stationed at her bedchambers, and she would likely not trust a mysterious drink from any of them...unless.

"I may have a plan."

"Why have you summoned me at such an hour?"

Kattegat's frustration was written on her face as she sat squarely in her study chair. Gallen flashed a somber smirk.

"I could wait no longer before discussing this latest wrinkle in our grander plans." He sat beside his mother. "I believe, I wish to wed."

The look of confusion lining his mother's features was visceral.

"To whom?" she demanded.

"Whomever you wish," he admitted, tossing the ring on her desk, the emerald stone shimmering in the light of the sea-time night. Kattegat placed a shocked hand on her chest.

"My word. Gallen. You are quite serious?"

"Mother," Gallen continued as he readied glasses of wine, "with the world so uncertain, I know that I must solidify our position in the only way I understand how. The people may not trust me as I am. A warrior of a far away realm. Though, to wed an ocean dweller..."

He handed his mother a goblet.

"...perhaps it will garner the trust I need."

Her stern face refused to reveal any reaction. No contemplation, no excitement, no disappointment.

She huffed, squinting at the glass of wine. "And I am to believe you would abandon young Alcor and this whole scheme of rebellion."

With each syllable, Gallen screamed internally, maddened by the lack of trust his mother held in their cause. After all this time. After investing so much.

"You were correct about Sol." He continued, wearing embarrassment like a mask, "she is tainted. Quite so. Alcor will surely understand my predicament. He is an heir. He holds the weight of that expectation just as I."

"And you would entrust me to choose on your behalf?" She swirled the red liquid casually.

"You alone understand the intricacies at play here, mother." Gallen tipped his glass in emphasis, "who else shall I trust *but* you?"

The lady of the house looked intrigued. The ruffles lining her nightgown wrinkled as she repositioned herself in her chair. Gallen continued his act, unwilling to relent until she drank the wine. He placed his own cup to his lips, gulping the wine in meek deference to his mother's will.

"Perhaps this last betrayal is a blessing, my son." She stated, a bit of her harsh exterior cracking under the tender support of a mother's care. "You hide your truest emotions from me,"

Gallen's heart faltered.

"...though I know it is due to all you have endured, all you have lost." She finished.

He released a wavering breath, "it is difficult to hide much from you, mother."

She winked knowingly, "she is waste, dear son. One of us will serve you better, indeed."

With a triumphant grin, she raised the glass. "To an auspicious future."

"Indeed," Gallen whispered, taking another sip as his mother drank her fill.

When their glasses were empty, Kattegat rose to her feet.

"This is a shock, my dear. I must consider our many possibilities for your glorious future."

Her words began to slur as she spoke, the potion setting in motion an internal series of events. Gallen whistled sharply, a bright and alarming tone. As Kattegat crunched her brows in confusion, Avelia and Malinar emerged from the hall. Taking nearly no time to assess, Avelia stepped forward.

"Where is Sol?" they asked clearly, raising their chin in delightful defiance as they spoke.

Kattegat scoffed, a small hiccup escaping her mouth before she responded, "it is laughable. The thought of the warrior alone in the Ice Realm. Laughable."

Alarm struck Gallen at the words.

"Why did you send her there?" He asked forcefully, attempting to steady his voice, his body quaking with wrath.

"The Lord of Ice awaits. He promised. Promised to spare us. For her. A worthy trade."

His heart pounded in his ears, heat rising to his chest at his mother's foolishness, at her heartlessness.

"You have sent her to slaughter!" Malinar wailed, Avelia holding her back from an indifferent Kattegat.

The lady shrugged. "I believe so. It was what is best."

Avelia and Malinar appeared stunned into silence, mouths agape as the confirmation fell upon their shoulders. Gallen, however, was left to rage at his mother's side.

"Tell us her heading. Now! Provide us with a chariot and tell us her heading!"

He had never been so forceful with his mother. Never to any person in authority over him. But a beastly anger rose from his neck to his face, threatening to consume him if he did not act quickly. Sol was out there. In the snow. Being hunted by those who held her prisoner. Being tortured, most likely.

And they were here.

He felt nauseous at the thought. The overwhelming dread

subsided slightly as his mother called for a guard to bring a chariot. Her eyes never left her son as she gave the orders, concern and perhaps pride laced in her golden gaze.

Gallen snatched the ring from the table and handed it to Malinar.

"Look at me no more," he seethed to his mother as he turned to leave.

He thought he heard Kattegat reply, though he could ascertain little with the pounding that resumed in his head. He did not care to know her response. Not as much as he wanted to leave. Not as much as he wanted to find Sol.

22

Sol

Sol cringed at the sound of metal scraping against metal as she pushed Helzaf forward with a thrust. Adrenaline and trepidation mingled treacherously in her veins, blocking the excruciating pain in her body. Her legs allowed her to stand, to face her foe on equal footing. Helzaf snickered, taking a step backward and taunting Sol as she regained her balance.

"Whatever the Ocean Realm did to you is nothing compared to what is to come."

The words left Helzaf's mouth like venom. The sickly smile that pressed against her pale skin caused Sol's blood to boil. She would not play games with this bitch.

Sol flung her body forward, her dual daggers swishing through the air with a lethal intent. Helzaf moved quickly, the white fur coat that hid her spry figure swirling as she circled through the cave. Sol's oversized clothing also followed as she leapt toward her enemy again, the murky brown of the fabric blending into the faded grey of the cave walls. Though Helzaf dodged the brunt of the attack, Sol heard the satisfying sound of squelching flesh, the slight contact flashing droplets of scarlet onto the cavern floor. Helzaf growled, a fresh tear in the thick coat revealing a shallow cut in her arm. Sol grinned as she witnessed red seeping into the white fabric.

"Do you not wonder why you are here?" Helzaf circled Sol as she spoke, trying to pull her focus from the battle. Sol refused to bite. "Your former friend, the lady of Coral? She is no longer enslaved to your brat of a brother. No. It seems her Past Holder revealed the true breadth of our power here in the North."

The further betrayal of Kattegat came as little surprise considering her enchanted chariot left Sol to her own devices in this icy hell. Though, the confirmation of the lady's complete desertion from their cause, from the salvation of Nourels, stung. Sol shoved her suffering down, pushing the disappointment to the back of her consciousness where her physical pain desperately pulled at her nerves. She would not provide Helzaf the satisfaction of crumbling before her. Sol remained stoic, her eyes focused on the blade Helzaf lazily flipped from one hand to the other.

"No intelligent retort? Well, this is unlike you, Warrior Sol. How I often think back to our sparring of words in battle. But, oh dear," her red lips fell into a satirical pout, "you are not the Sol I once knew, is that correct? Rostair did warn me of your naiveté. Who knew you would abandon your skill with blades altogether."

She gripped the wooden handle of the large knife, raising the weapon above her head as she squinted her eyes to Sol's figure.

"Pity…I wanted this to last."

Sol held her own onyx hilts in her hands. The weight of the daggers settled comfortably in her palms, even if their tactical use was less obvious to her.

You are brave. You are bold.

The words encouraged her, even if they were written for a former version of herself. She needed to let go of hesitation, to move as naturally as she could. She hoped some of her former training lay somewhere deep within her subconscious, that her arms and legs would recall her years in the High Realm, her many quests as a Flyer, and her hours of personal practice Gallen insisted upon.

As Helzaf's blade swung upward, the difference in height worked to Sol's advantage. She dashed to the left, ignoring the soreness in her knees. The blade smacked against stone as Helzaf growled in frustration. With a tired grin, Sol ran toward the opening of the cavern, hoping the light of the sun might assist her aim. As she reached the arch of stone, Sol planted her right foot in front and turned quickly to see Helzaf jumping through the air. She emitted a screech that rang through Sol's already pounding head as she swung the blade down onto Sol's shoulder. Sol veered to the side, but not fast enough, and a searing sting erupted at the side of her right arm. She reached her left hand to assess the damage and nearly fainted when she saw blood gushing through her fingers.

Laughing, Helzaf moved to strike again, yet Sol shook herself from her stupor in time to fling one of her daggers toward the blur of white and red. The blade struck true, sinking deep into Helzaf's thigh. The ice warrior wailed as Sol took the chance to hit again, flinging her other dagger in the air with a flick of her wrist. Helzaf stepped to the side with manic speed, landing onto the ground in a heap of sweat and blood. The sound of the dagger skidding across the stone echoed through the cave. Sol rushed her crumpled figure, thinking she could gain the upper hand. Though, as she lifted her leg to kick Helzaf in the stomach, the ice warrior swung her body forward.

The world turned upside down as Sol landed on her ass. Hard. She could hardly catch her breath as the pain she worked so diligently to ignore crept back to the edges of her consciousness, threatening to pull her into an abyss of suffering. Sol shook her head in protest, yet the movement only furthered the thudding in her ears followed by an insistent ringing that clouded her thoughts.

Focus, she chided herself. *Focus or die.*

She lifted her arms to block her face from Helzaf who hovered over her body, hatred oozing from her pores.

"You will pay for that," Helzaf spit out, clenching her hands into a fist and thrusting them toward Sol's center.

Sol cried to the snow as it began to fall. Helzaf punched with her entire weight. Relentless and precise and rabid. Sol's ribs ached as Helzaf continued to pummel into one side, then the other. Sol shielded her face from the woman above her, grunting from each consecutive blow.

She had to get out of here. She needed to run. She needed to be *able* to run.

Sol risked lowering her hand for a moment, grasping for the familiarity of the dagger's hilt. Her fingers grazed the cool of onyx that stuck grotesquely from Helzaf's thigh. She smirked, ignoring the cracking of bones and bruising of skin. The bitch did not realize the shift until Sol hunched forward, twisting the knife further into the leg before wrenching it out with any strength she had left.

Helzaf screeched, shuttering back and falling onto the snow. Sol took the opportunity to run. Her thoughts also ran wildly, seeking shelter while considering her many wounds. Wincing at the harshness of the snow, she saw that damned blackness cloud the edges of her vision. But she continued on. Pushing her bruised body forward one painful step at a time. As she gained distance from Helzaf, her legs groaned, the adrenaline dissipating with each step.

No. No. No.

Soon, the pain reemerged in its full form. The force of it nearly knocked Sol from her feet. It began in her ribs. Then her arm, the blood still trickling down her hand leaving a red trail from the cavern's entrance. Her entire body burned, begging her to stop moving, to rest.

But she could not, *would not*, concede. Not now.

She pushed ahead, shuffling forward, deliberately, torturously. Tears poured from Sol's eyes as she went, the hope of leaving this conflict alive dwindling as her feet slowed their progress.

Then she saw something on the horizon of the blinding snow. The sun, now high in the sky, dominating the clouds, surrounded the figure as a halo, highlighting the image that offered Sol a final bit of optimism. The flapping wings stirred her heart. A figure of speckled sunshine. Kinsle whinnied loudly, concern lining his voice as he neared Sol's position. She was unsure why the pegasus was here, but she could not muster up the effort to care. What mattered was reaching him. He could fly her to safety and there she could mend. The sight of Kinsle reinvigorated Sol, gave her body a spark of resilience.

She needed to live. She needed to see Asha and her brother once more. She needed to tell Gallen and Malinar that it was more than just one night. She needed to write everything down, to inform Nourels of the evils in the world. She needed to love. To want. To live.

She needed—

A slicing noise silenced her. Sol looked down to see silver peeking out from the brown fabric covering her stomach. The knife felt like just a prick in her side, simply another pain to add to her compounding suffering. The darkness in Sol's eyes threatened to close in, though she continued to fight.

The world tilted on its axis, the bright sky filling her vision as her body fell to the snowy ground. Helzaf's wicked figure loomed over her, blood leaking from the side of her temple as she lifted the large knife above her head.

"This," Helzaf choked out, "this is the end."

Before Sol succumbed to unconsciousness, she heard another slice of flesh.

"Sol, hold on!" Malinar's words were the last she recalled as blackness consumed her.

23

Malinar

*B*lood cast gruesome designs on the snow. Malinar's heart thudded violently at the sight of Sol's limp body. Her skin was a pale hue, contrasting the bright red cuts and purpling bruises. Her legs were in a sickening position on clouds of white. The surrounding sounds faded. Gallen and Avelia lifted Sol's arms as Malinar stood frozen. Red spread like a contagion, consuming flecks of snow in its wake. Soon the scene was a war between red and white, the former moving further and further as signs of rescue faded.

Malinar's own blood left her face, her skin pale and head light. She barely felt the tears in her eyes as she looked on as the others attempted to save Sol. Save her friend.

"Malinar?" Avelia's soothing voice barely registered. "We must find a place to go. We must assess her injuries."

Her injuries? Malinar looked at Sol once again, the blood pulsing from wounds in her arm and stomach.

She could. She could...

Malinar couldn't finish the thought as she followed the others, refusing to lose sight of Sol's face. They led Sol to Kinsle's waiting back. The winged horse whinnied, moving his head back and forth, his mane rustling through the chilled air. His neighs seemed desperate and intentional.

"I will fly with her. Someone needs to hold pressure on her wounds." Gallen's voice cracked in pain as he forced the words out.

Avelia nodded. "Indeed. Fly where?"

"To the shadows..." Malinar whispered, recalling the omen. "The pools. We must take her there. Certainly Kinsle knows the way."

Gallen shook his head quickly. "Avelia, please. Tell him."

As Avelia relayed their request, another pegasus flew into view, then another, then another. Malinar gasped at the sight as hundreds of winged beasts filled the sky above them. She clung to the satchel stationed upon her shoulders, her knuckles growing white as she squeezed.

"Heavens..." she whispered to herself.

Kinsle rushed from his position on the ground as a pegasus of pale yellow landed near Malinar and Avelia.

Cotton.

Malinar jumped toward Cotton, hugging the beast by the neck before launching onto her back.

"Avelia!" She shouted, offering a hand to pull them up.

She watched as a woman's lifeless figure grew smaller and smaller as the pegasus rose into the clouds. She focused fully on Kinsle and Gallen and...Sol.

The ride to the caverns took mere minutes, though to Malinar it felt like centuries. Her mind flooded with only the worst outcomes. Sol could die before they reached the pools. Rostair could be waiting for them to return. Kattegat could send guards to force Gallen home.

Her thoughts turned more and more irrational as the seconds

passed. Every nerve in her body screamed for her to move. Her brain worked with intensity to find a way to make things right. To save those she cared for. Was this not the reason she became a Flyer in the first place?

She thought of her family back in the Star Realm, ignorant to her own strife yet fully dependent upon her success. And Alcor, he needed Sol to become king. To save the Nine Realms.

And she...*She* needed Sol.

Searching for something, anything to anchor her aching mind, Malinar searched for the cool metal of Sol's ring on her hand. Though, as her thumb scraped across bare skin, the motion causing further distress. The ring must have slipped from her hand during the rush toward Sol. Lying somewhere amidst the ice and blood and tears.

She attempted to steady her breath as her heart raced. A sinking feeling wrenched her gut into a sickening twist that caused her to double over, but Avelia steadied the rider before she fell from the sky. Losing Sol would mean losing a part of herself.

Malinar did not know to which god to send her pleas, yet she spoke them all the same. "Please. Please. Please. Save her."

The horses landed swiftly at the mouth of a large cavern, one of dozens that lined a mountain of caves. Despite the pull of the enchanted wood or the glimmering beauty of the snow, Malinar refused to remove her eyes from Gallen and Sol. Kinsle's grey and white fur was unrecognizable; layers of dried blood caked his sides. Gallen, too, was soaked in red, his hands trembling as he carefully slid along the side of Kinsle's wing.

Malinar did not remember leaving Cotton's back, nor did she recall the dreaded steps into the dark and damp cave. She barely felt the weight of the satchel lift from her shoulders or heard the bag land with a thud on the ground. She only remembered the sadness in Avelia's eyes as she passed them. Remembered the terror that struck Gallen's face, heightened by the glow of blue that emanated from the pools of water. Remembered the paleness of

Sol's skin as he clutched her body close to his chest. Remembered kneeling beside the water, pressing her hands at the edge of the pool.

Then, Malinar remembered holding her breath as Gallen waded into the closest pool, dragging Sol's motionless figure with him. The swirls of blood mingled with the glittering blue water, steam hovering above the waterline in whirls of heat. He called to her, his voice muffled and warped, as if in another world.

"Malinar, come."

She saw his figure grow closer but could not recall her feet stepping forward or sensing the temperature of the water as she plunged into the pool. She whimpered as Sol's body came fully into view. Malinar's toes barely rested along the floor of the pool as her arms slipped beneath Sol's back. At the touch of her body, Malinar immediately calmed, as if the still figure of her friend contained a power over her. Gallen's hands gently held her arms, the two cradling Sol, surrounded by a mixture of blood and fog and blue.

Malinar took stock of every inch of Sol. Her sides, purple and blistered. Her legs, worn and cut. Her fingers and toes tinted a terrifying black. She noted her wounds, the blood still oozing from cuts of varying depths. Thinking of the pain she must have endured hurt Malinar to the core.

She wanted to commit every line, every curve of Sol to memory. She looked at the red scar on her cheek, the vibrant kohl that etched her eyes. She traced the curves of her hair as the various strands swam through the pool.

She wanted to remember every piece of her. In case…In case…

The two stood in silence for hours, holding Sol between them. Avelia slipped out to gather tools for a fire, their voice a garbled message of sympathy and patience. Malinar noted the setting sun in her peripheral vision but dared not remove her gaze from Sol's broken body. She heard the fluttering of Kinsle's wings as he lay on the floor of the cavern. She heard the whistling of the wind as a storm brewed just outside.

But nothing, no one, could take her attention from Sol.

Gallen also said nothing, his hands clutched Malinar's arms as they swayed.

As the sun's eventual descent sent darkness into the cave, Malinar began to weep. The emotional toll of the quest thrust upon her, as if the stars' light reminded her of who she was and why she was here.

And she wept for Sol. With every passing moment, the chances of her survival, of a miraculous remedy, diminished.

She wept, the droplets of water passing over the grime that clung to her face, falling from her cheeks and chin before plopping into the clean, still water below. She heard Gallen join her, his wailing filling the curves of the cave, echoing through the various chambers that went on for miles and miles and miles. The wind drowned their cries, perhaps nature's own gift to the warriors, an added layer of protection as the they grieved. Though, thoughts of enemies and warfare were far from Malinar's mind.

Sol's body bobbed up and down as the two warriors crumpled under the weight of their shared sorrow. Yet they held onto each other, held onto Sol. Crying and screaming and shaking. Yet they held on.

Kinsle whinnied as well, a crackling, ghastly sound that broke Malinar's heart over again.

The sky, too, cried its own tears. Malinar listened as the wind became roaring thunder that rolled through the realm, sheets of rain and hail and snow pounding the cavern rock. Lightning cracked through the skies, sending streams of light skittering through the mixture of crevices and smooth stones.

The pool glowed beneath Sol's body, as if power from the sky's bolts of light brought magic to life. The water bubbled around them. The ground where Malinar's toes barely touched shook as waves pulsed. For the first time, Malinar looked up from Sol to see

Gallen's face, flushed and puffy from tears. Lit with the glow from the water's surging power, his golden eyes were dazzling.

Then, a warmth settled along the skin of her palms and the tips of her fingers. She jerked her head to Sol's stomach, the dark brown cotton cloth clinging to her exquisite curves. A sudden force pushed the limp body upward, her back forming a concave arch as it lifted from Malinar's hands. She rushed to grab ahold of her friend, but Gallen held her arms in place beneath the growing waves. The water pushed Sol toward the ceiling, the stalagmites that looked down shining with hundreds of incandescent lights that burned Malinar's eyes as she tried to keep Sol in her view. Gallen pulled Malinar close to him, the feel of his chest pulling her rational mind back to the present.

Sol hovered as the water roared and rioted within the small space. Fog surrounded Sol, as if drawn to her. The rain continued to ravage the sides of the cave, its intensity increasing as Sol's back strained, her body now parallel to the water below.

Malinar could barely hear Kinsle's neighs above the noise, yet Malinar saw him desperately running back and forth, rearing his hind legs up to the ceiling as his rider rose. Avelia attempted to soothe him, yet even they could not help but focus on the miracle before them.

Soon, Malinar could barely see through the waves as they crashed. She spewed gulps of water as she choked in the onslaught. It tasted earthy and warm, almost vibrating within her, shocking her senses and bringing her renewed energy. The noise rose to an unbearable level. Malinar braced herself against Gallen's shaking torso, closing her eyes so tightly that her head began to spin.

Then, without warning, the cave fell silent. The water stilled. The noise stopped. And, as Malinar hesitantly opened her eyes, she saw only darkness. A darkness that fully enveloped the small cave and all inside.

Malinar could still feel Gallen's chest rise and fall in confused and stuttered movements. She strained her eyes as she searched for any sign of Sol, lifeless or not. She reached a hand into the darkness, splashing the water before her in blind desperation. Gallen's hands kept her steady as they stood.

Then, a dim light sent a spark of hope through Malinar's spine, her heart lifting as she saw Sol lower ever so slowly back into the pool before them. Her skin radiated a faded shade of pink, as if Sol had swallowed the stars. The luminous color tinged her face, her arms, her feet. Malinar looked, lips pursed, as Sol's voluptuous hips kissed the water, followed by her hands then her hair, her head. As her body settled into the pool again, floating like a lantern in the sea, Gallen's hands slackened as Malinar waded toward Sol. The rain calmed, a mere drizzle compared to the downpour from before.

Malinar squinted as she neared Sol's body, refusing to look away even as the brightness stung her eyes. The water rippled around her as she reached out a cautious hand toward Sol's still skin. But, as soon as Malinar touched her skin, she sensed the purest feeling of indescribable peace. Her shoulders fell, the ringing in her ears silenced, the worry, the despair, the hurt, the quivering, aching, hopeless, restless, constant pain.

It...left.

Gallen stretched a hand to cup Sol's cheek, the tension in his jaw relaxing.

It was glorious. Inhuman. Enchanted.

And, as Malinar shifted her eyes to look at that beautiful face, the face she had dedicated to memory, Sol's eyes opened.

GALLEN AND MALINAR each held one of Sol's arms in their hands, pulling her body to rest on the grey floor of the cave. Malinar hugged her head to Sol's shoulder, waiting for any sign of movement. Any sign of...

"Sol?"

The sound of Gallen's voice, of anything pure and good, sprung new life to Malinar. As if air reached her lungs for the first time in hours. Sol's bright blue eyes were rimmed with a glowing pink light that faded slightly as she raised her head.

Then she smiled. And with that smile, Malinar nearly burst.

Gallen flung his arm around her, hugging her neck with a fervent desperation.

"Gallen," Sol moaned hoarsely as she pushed her hands on the stones and hauled her head forward to a seated position, moving Malinar with her.

Malinar pulled in a short breath, her eyes scanning Sol's body for any sign of discomfort or strain, but she looked utterly calm and effortlessly stunning. Gallen hands glided over Sol's shoulders, arms, and stomach as if taking stock of her health.

"You are…unharmed?"

His eyes looked into hers, utterly stunned.

"Yes," she breathed. "I feel…reborn."

Malinar grasped Sol's head in her hands, placing their foreheads together.

"We thought you were…" Malinar looked deeply into Sol's eyes, savoring every fleck and shade of blue, tucking it away in the recesses of her mind for safekeeping.

Sol's warm hand rested on the curve of her waist, the sensation heating Malinar at her core. When Sol's thumb rubbed her side, the sensation intensified, moving swiftly from her core to her face.

"I am with you," Sol whispered, "right. Here,"

Their heads remained together, Malinar convincing herself that if she kept Sol close she would never be in harms way. She held out a hand to Gallen and the moment his hand touched hers, she lowered her lips to graze Sol's waiting smile. The heat lowered between Malinar's legs.

"Then let us make it count." She smirked

Before she could lean in for another kiss, a purposeful cough echoed through the cave. Malinar turned to see Avelia standing with their hands behind their back.

"I have many observations and even greater questions, yet I believe the time for query is not quite upon us." They cleared their throat again, "I am happy to see you well, Flyer Sol. I shall await out of earshot. I believe I spied another opening above. I will see you all when the sun rises once more."

They began pulling Cotton to join when they called over their shoulder, "I am taking this marvelous being along, if all is well with you, Flyer Gallen."

Gallen squeaked awkwardly.

Avelia shrugged. "That should suffice. I also gathered food for my night. Be well, warriors."

Gallen's blush tinged his ears an adorable shade of pink, while Sol pressed her hand against Malinar's back. She heard the gentle sound of hoofs clomping away as Avelia and Cotton left the three alone. Even Kinsle left his post to settle near the cave's entrance.

Rain continued to pour just outside, the moon casting a dim light within. For Malinar, it provided just enough light to see Sol strip off the brown shirt that clung to her body, her heavy breasts falling deliciously on her torso. She watched in awe as Sol's wet hair fell along her shoulders. Gallen's hand stroked the side of Sol's face, his jaw ticking, his golden eyes heavy with desire. He turned to Malinar, taking off his own worn clothing and throwing it to the far side of the cave. She feasted upon the bare blue skin as each inch came into view. The strength in his legs and arms, the softness at his core, and lower, the length of him standing at attention. She fought the impulse to rush forward and take him completely. She bit her bottom lip at the thought. Gallen ran a large hand through his blonde hair, wiping the strands from his face. Malinar expected him to sit near them, to shower them both with kisses and strokes of his tongue. Instead, he turned. The curve of his ass made Malinar nearly moan with desire as she watched him slip back into the pool of water and turn back to the women waiting on the edge.

"Enjoy each other," he said in a husky voice. "I want to watch first. I want to watch the women I love together."

Gallen's hand reach beneath the surface, the water rippling with the slow strokes of his arm. It was a mesmerizing sight. Gallen, hand to the King, pleasuring himself at the thought of them. The women he loved.

Malinar blinked as the word settled.

Love.

Sol reached her hand forward, her nails seizing Malinar's tunic. Their next kiss was wondrous. Sol's taste, her lips, her tongue. Malinar could not get enough of her. After hours of looking at Sol's body in the water, dedicating each precious minute to remembering every enticing inch, Malinar was ready to explore with more than her eyes.

The pool purified the three warriors, cleansing them of the grime and blood and leaving behind a clean smell of linen and jasmine. It gave Malinar the energy to sink her teeth gently into Sol's bottom lip, to slip her hand over Sol's waiting breast, to savor this. To savor her.

This was what Malinar needed. Her entire life she worked to support her family, her town, her name. She constantly weighed the consequences of each action and every success. Yet, as the three took care to attend to each other, as they reached blissful fulfillment in the glow of the cavern pool, as they settled into each other on the cavern floor a new sense of self emerged.

This is what she needed. Not only to love, but to *be* loved.

She leaned back, closing her eyes and emptying her mind. Sol combed her fingers through her hair as Gallen traced swirls along her ankles. The implications of this word, this monumental word that Gallen offered to them, could be addressed tomorrow. But tonight, being loved, that was enough.

24

Gallen

Rolling on the soft pile of blankets found in the shadows of the cave, Gallen eyed the two women sleeping soundly near him. The night was impossibly perfect. Talking. Laughing. Making love. Then making love once more. Gallen could not have asked for more. Well, perhaps a glass of wine and bowl of food. However, the taste of Malinar and Sol was enough to satiate his hunger for now.

He could not deter the momentary worries that stirred within him. Was it wise to remain in enemy lands as Helzaf's dead body lay frozen in the cold? Should they not fly home, or at the very least find refuge with allies nearer by. Yet, the recurring storms, Avelia keeping watch above, his own ability to attack at a moment's notice—it all convinced him to rest. To enjoy the night. To enjoy his partners, alive and accepting and flawless.

The two women were magnificently sprawled before him, naked and still and stunning. In the dim light of the stars, their faces glowed with an immortal beauty. And to him, they were goddesses. Two resilient, wise, and caring goddesses. He would treat them with that respect. The respect he showed Mist herself.

Though his eyes were heavy, tired from a day that began with such frustration and ended with such peace, he could not convince his mind to rest. He was glad Malinar found space to sleep. Gods knew she also suffered many a sleepless night. As she cuddled close to Sol, Gallen pushed a wayward hair behind her ear.

Gallen watched as droplets dripped from the ceiling of this mystical cavern's opening to the floor. Though the rain ceased hours ago, the dripping served as evidence of the former storm. He shifted his weight to his feet, standing slowly so as to not disturb Sol and Malinar.

Drawn to the cold air that whirled just outside, Gallen walked toward the moonlight. His skin, still warm from the blankets and the women within them, soaked in the brisk breeze as flakes of snow landed gently on his arms. The scene was like a painting. The forest leaves just beyond the edge of the cave maintained a deep green color despite the snow. The mossy grass sparkled as the few flakes of ice that managed to sneak past the trees landed like jewels upon the forest floor.

Gallen could see the appeal of such a place. The elegance, the magic.

His mind wandered as he followed various flakes of snow floating slowly along the wind. As a rogue flake landed in a puddle of rainwater, his thoughts went to his home. He hardly considered the lies his mother told them as she sent Sol to her demise. Sol told them of the ruse that forced her to flee, to ride an enchanted chariot to the Ice Realm. She told them all that Helzaf said in their violent encounter.

Despite the years of toil, the many meetings and dinners and long nights of debates, Kattegat was lost to their cause. Would she have sacrificed him as well if it were for the realm? Gallen could not consider this question too seriously, fearing the question's natural conclusion.

Helzaf also mentioned the North's power. Could it be enough to destroy entire oceans? To control entire realms?

Gallen shook his head, turning to the stars for comfort. He wished Alcor could hear the many queries that plagued his mind.

Another gust of wind bit Gallen's naked skin. He hugged himself before shuffling back toward the bundle of blankets.

Contentment in its purest form filled Gallen to the brim as he watched Sol's chest rise and fall. They nearly lost her today. Whatever power lay in these caves, he would be indebted to it for eternity. He drew close to Sol's warmth as he pulled a fur to his chin. The soft snores from Malinar coaxed him to relax which eventually led to a few hours of sleep.

~

"THE SUN IS AWAKE!"

Sol's face shone brightly as Gallen's eyes squinted open. She leaned over him as the sun poured into the space, highlighting the many curves and crevices carved into the stone. In the center of the cave, Sol tended a small fire where both Avelia and Malinar huddled for warmth. Each used a fur blanket to drive away the chill as the reality of Ice Realm temperatures truly set in.

Gallen noticed his clothes crumpled in a wayward pile near the edge of the pool, still glowing a mystically blue color. He looked to Avelia, to the pile, then back.

Malinar pointed. "The blanket," she mouthed.

Gallen nearly rolled his eyes at his own stupidity. With a flourish, he wrapped the nearest blanket around his waist and retrieved his clothes before sliding the trousers around his hips under the protection of the furs. He thrust his hand into the pocket for the familiar metal ring before moving forward.

At the fire, the others giggled, absolutely tickled despite the dire circumstances of their larger quest. Gallen could not fault them as he, too, felt an unnatural sense of jubilation that kept the corners of his mouth permanently upturned.

The illogical emotional bubble the four found themselves was sure to burst. At some point, they would need to leave the confines of this cave. To leave the miraculous power that flooded through these pools, etched into the very fabric of the place.

Then what?

The thought lay dismally on the edge of his mind as he stepped toward the others, the warmth of their small fire growing as he took step after heavy step. Though the negative thought was a mere speck in the overwhelming happiness that flowed through Gallen, he noticed Malinar tilt her head to the side as he approached. She raised her brows ever so slightly, as if signaling her concern.

Damn. She was perceptive.

He sent her a slight nod and an overexaggerated smile, baring his pearly teeth in delight. Malinar rolled her eyes and turned her attention back to Avelia, who also made note of Gallen's approach.

"Flyer Gallen. I am overjoyed to see you encounter a night of true rest. Your body looks rejuvenated."

They smirked a bit as Sol stood to greet Gallen properly, offering a hand to lead him to the fire.

"We were recounting last night's events," Sol said, the glow on her cheeks only magnifying her natural elegance. "'Twas a confounding night, to be certain."

"What have you shared?" he stated meekly, cursing the shade of rouge that crept up his neck.

Avelia's laugh was hearty and loud. The loudest noise Gallen had heard from the warrior since the four set out from the High Realm.

"We need not speak in great detail of what occurred at my departure," they spoke between cackles. "My temporary abode was far too close for my liking, let me assure you. Even with the storm's enduring rain, I heard…much."

They wrapped their arms over their stomach, rolling back and forth as they cackled. Sol set her hand on his knee, but the gleeful recollection of last night was contagious and Gallen himself began chuckling along. He heard Malinar join in, then Sol. Soon the four warriors took a moment of absolute and irrational happiness. It was almost cathartic. The unbridled amusement prepared them to face the world once more. As if they each realized that once the silence resumed, the true work would begin once more.

And so, they continued to laugh, Gallen clapping his hand on Avelia's shoulder. Sol pressing her elbow on Malinar's side. And Malinar giving Gallen that same look from before, her brow lifting slightly while she quieted as if to ask, *Are you well?*

He nodded as his own laughs faded.

He would be well.

He would.

After the group settled, Malinar cleared her throat. "We were conferring with Avelia to see if they knew a mythology explaining Sol's healing. That is…that is what occurred, correct?"

Avelia nodded emphatically, wiping their tears from their cheeks and returning to more important matters. "It is like nothing I have witnessed. Master Zelan told of such enchantment. Yet, in a metaphorical sense rather than literal."

Gallen could imagine Zelan utilizing metaphor to his detriment. Avelia's eyes widened as they continued. "At a distance, it appeared as though the pool responded to a power that lay deep within the cave. Perhaps drawing some from the woods beyond." They waved a hand toward the entrance where the sun cast a dazzling shine on the green pines. "The fairies reside there. Their enchantment could be enough."

"Could be?" Sol questioned.

Gallen knew much of fairy lore. His mother required him to learn their native tongue as a diplomatic measure and he found an interest in their history, their customs. They were resilient, much stronger than many realms realized. Yet, Avelia spoke as if even their enchantment would not be enough to save Sol.

"Sol. You were not merely saved from death. You emerged utterly spotless." Avelia gestured up and down Sol's body in emphasis. "To save a soul takes a great deal of power. But to heal multiple wounds? To leave a body as...complete?"

Avelia shook their head as they considered that type of power. Gallen also considered it.

"Could the pools draw magic from another source?" He posed, scratching the back of his neck as he pondered his own question.

Avelia stared into the fire, as if the explanation lay somewhere amongst the ash and flickering flames. Then, as if the fire truly did confer with them, Avelia's eyes grew wide as their mouth fell agape.

"Malinar, do you have the map?" They muttered beneath their breath, as if stating their hypothesis aloud might detract from its validity.

Malinar spryly rose to her feet, retrieving the pack from its place in the corner before returning to the circle. She pulled papers from the pack, some filled with inked scribbles, others waiting for Sol's observations. Malinar carefully set the stack away from the fire before her hands held the folded cream-colored parchment. The purple flecks in her eyes seemed to waver as she eyed the map, her fingers rubbing against its worn edges.

Sol moved forward, balancing against Gallen's leg as she peered over his lap to Malinar and the map.

"Open it," Sol said, eyes glued to the paper.

Malinar obliged, pulling the map open to fully display its contents. The entirety of Nourels hovered above the page, bustling with movement.

She lifted her eyes to see the others watching her curiously. "This is what I managed to create. I cannot seem to fully encapsulate regions I have not seen or heard of or read about. It is difficult."

Avelia moved from their spot near the fire to kneel by Malinar's side, their palm floating above the illuminated model of their continent.

"I would like to experiment, if you would indulge me," they said.

They placed their other hand on Malinar's shoulder, moving their fingers intently over each region, from the Star Realm to the south and eastward, until they reached the Desert Realm. They moved their fingers closer, as if attempting to peer into the realm itself. And, as they did, the map responded, shifting and zooming, the bright light flickering in various levels of intensity before the picture blurred, no longer showing much of anything at all.

"I have never set foot in this realm," Malinar admitted, disappointment pulling at her throat as she spoke.

Gallen saw the hand on her shoulder squeeze as Avelia encouraged her.

"Put forth your mind to this place. Reach deep into your stomach, deep into the place where your power and resilience resides. Pull from that the answers you seek."

Rather than scoff at Avelia's words, as Gallen likely would, Malinar shut her eyes and scrunched her brows together in concentration. He saw her core tense and her toes curl beneath her feet as she attempted to move the map to her will.

Sol's hand pinched at his knees as she held a breath. Gallen also found himself breathless as he watched.

The blur of illumination began to take form, shifting in fluid-like motions that reminded Gallen of the pool nearby. The colors of the map, too, shifted, moving from its original shade to a deep purple to blue then purple once more.

Then, Gallen saw individual forms emerge. Some toiling, some walking, some standing and observing. But they were alive. He wondered what year this represented; he wondered if Malinar knew. Before he could ask, the image shifted drastically, the figures blurring into new shapes. Malinar cringed, her jaw clenching and brows harshly winding together.

"Should she cease?" He said aloud, though neither Avelia nor Sol appeared to hear him. A gasp from Sol brought his attention back to the map as a phoenix flew into view. The fire from its wings ripped through the air just above the map, followed swiftly by another, then another. Gallen's face grew cold and a deep discomfort pushed against his stomach. Beneath the flying beasts, the Desert Realm came to life. Brick buildings emerged from the sand. Hundreds of people shuffled to and fro as they worked. Nausea threatened his throat as he noted the chains that bound many to specific buildings. He instinctively pressed a hand to his neck as he saw the hundreds of laborers, those enslaved and suffering, dragged by metal collars brandished upon their necks.

Then, he saw them. The sight brought him to his feet, stuttering away from the map and its ugly truths.

"Nests," Sol whispered, placing a horrified hand to her mouth.

And where there were nests, there were tens, dozens, hundreds of eggs.

The map halted on this scene, as if Malinar plucked a moment in time and placed it before them. Only then did she open her eyes and bare witness what they each now knew. The Desert Realm, and all who allied with them, they were breeding an army. And if one young phoenix was impenetrable, how would they defeat them *all*?

Horrified, Malinar dropped the map, the images evaporating from view as the page floated gently to the cold stone floor. She jumped to her feet, away from Avelia and the fire, away from the truth that was now revealed.

She looked to Gallen then down to Sol, still seated on the ground.

"What are we to do?"

KINSLE AND COTTON stood at attention near the forest just outside the cave. Sol and Malinar gathered the few belongings into the turquoise satchel. He smiled at the use the bag truly served on their quest, then scowled at the failure the quest had been.

Avelia approached a third winged beast, a white stallion with dark blue wings. The horse's fur reminded him grimly of the friend they lost, his stomach turning as the scene replayed in his helpless memories. Avelia appeared more receptive to the beast than before yet skittered away as the pegasus pushed their shoulder with his snout.

"You must echo the respect you want to receive," Gallen stated sympathetically, running the back of his hand from the horse's forehead to its nose.

"Tis a simple task for one more accustomed to such things," they stated.

"Will you make the journey with ease? We could join you—" he offered.

They shook their head in response. "It is no worry. Please, you must journey home. We each must share this information posthaste."

Gallen nodded slowly, reminded of the duty they each held.

"Do try to write," he said, petting the horse once more, "to confirm your safety, of course."

He could not manage to meet their eyes, yet he saw Avelia's smirk from the side of his vision.

"Of course." They bowed their head, their brown skin dewy in the last rays of sunlight.

Sol and Malinar approached to say their sincere goodbyes before Avelia swung their trousered leg over the pegasus.

"For King and Sol?" They stated shyly.

Gallen chuckled and Malinar hugged her sides as Sol said, "For King and Sol."

The winged horse rushed into the air and flew southward with an urgency that pulled Gallen back to his own task.

Avelia was correct. They did need to return home. To tell Alcor and the others of the Desert Realm. Of the enslaved. Of the eggs and nests. Of the ways the war would shift.

But he also needed to know what happened to Sol. To the woman he once loved then lost. To the version of this woman he'd grown to love again. Fear grasped his chest tightly as he once again considered the potential consequence of this venture.

Sol's hand gently stroked his forearm as he saw the horse fade into a speck amongst the stars.

"We must depart," she whispered in his ear, rubbing his arm lovingly.

He grasped the hand, the feel of her fingers slightly soothing his worries. Yet, the concern persisted.

"The memories…have they returned?" Gallen sucked in a breath as soon as the words left his lips. Malinar raised her brows, leaning in curiously.

With a trembling hand, Sol replied calmly, "I feel soft differences. The smell of the air. The feel of the cold. The touch of your skin…" She smirked slightly. "Though, they are not concrete, not tangible. Just whispers of past knowledge."

Malinar stepped toward them and wrapped her hands around Gallen's and Sol's.

"My heart has not wavered," she continued, "not one second. Despite the anxieties and unknowns. Despite what transpired and what has yet to be. I truly believe from deep within me, that this," she squeezed the two Flyers, "this is eternal."

The knot that settled in Gallen's stomach subsided as Sol spoke. He pulled a blanket of fur from his shoulders and wrapped it around the women before him.

"Eternal," he whispered, placing a kiss atop each of their heads.

Malinar looked at Gallen, her purple eyes shining. "Eternal, indeed."

They stood huddled together, their shared heat staving off the cold of night. Gallen's heart hummed. Any caution that remained dissipated in their embrace.

Sol cleared her throat. "Shall we return?"

"Together." Malinar smiled.

Gallen gave the two another kiss each, their future cemented in the snowy wilderness.

The two women soon sat on Kinsle's back, waiting for Gallen to move. He looked back to the caves, to the pools of magic still swirling, their reflections painting stunning rainbows along the cave walls. What he would give to remain here with them. To sit by fires. To swim in pools of enchantment.

Though, it was not to be.

They each had their own calling now, their own part to play to end a force far more sinister than they initially believed. Though now, they faced it together.

Gallen knew he would follow Sol and Malinar to whatever end. Into the very depths of the underworld. Into darkness itself. He would face any number of evils if he knew he could be near them for eternity.

It was that thought—eternity—that pushed his foot to move, pushed him to climb onto Cotton's familiar back. To whistle a final command. To fly home.

25

Sol

Three months past, Sol lay bleeding in the snow. Three months past, she wished she could remember a time before this. Three months past, she realized who she truly was.

When she woke upon a soft pallet of blankets in her tent, she reached across the sheets for any sign of Gallen or Malinar, sighing when she found none but rustled silks. Since Malinar gained an advanced post amongst Alcor's strategical Flyers and Gallen took back control of training recruits, Sol often woke to an empty tent. As she rose to her feet, pushing the various fabrics to the side and walking toward her trunk, she hummed to herself in wondrous delight.

Today marked a momentous occasion for the three Flyers: their first night together in a shared abode. Their connection had only grown since their quest, and the move to share a tent was a natural extension of the relationship. In preparation, Sol expanded her home, losing the smallest bit of grass that separated her tent from the others to create more room for her new tentmates. She forged three separate rooms: a sleeping space, a living space, and a bathing space. After their stay in the Valley Realm, Malinar pressed for a tub and Sol gladly obliged.

Freshly dressed, Sol moved into the living space, tempted to sit at her writing desk to jot down a few ideas that emerged before she fell asleep. She should have left the bed before sleep took her, but the warmth of her partners was too lovely to leave. Now leaning over the pages, she scribbled only a few notes on the corner with a fine ink quill. Satisfied, she straightened her spine, pulling the silver coat over her Flyers uniform before exiting through the tent's main flap.

The stars shone bright, and the lanterns that guided the paths in Celestra glowed. Sol looked toward Alcor's tent before following the path in the opposite direction. She would join Malinar soon, but first—

"Sol!"

Gallen's dazzling smile appeared just before her, his cheeks slightly red with effort from a full morning of training, sweat falling from his temples to his bare shoulders. Sol returned his smile.

"I was to meet you there," she whined playfully, rushing to Gallen's side as they began down the path together.

Sol laced her fingers with his, gleefully grasping his arm with her other hand to keep him close.

"I thought you might appreciate the company." He leaned into her. "Anything new this morn?"

Sol looked down before meeting his eyes. "Not yet."

Each day, Sol attempted to remember who she once was before her capture. Just a glimmer of that life. Yet, no such images emerged. Though, as the days wore on, she had less and less desire to know that person. She quite enjoyed her days here as the Keeper of Records. And, despite the visible pity that lined her brother's features each time they discussed their last quest, she felt almost glad that the power beneath the caverns saved only the best parts of her.

Gallen and Sol strolled past tent after tent in the dim blue lights, talking of the most recent recruits from the edges of the realm, of the drink of choice from the Night Streets, and of Sol's last visit to Kinsle and the other pegasi that settled in the fields outside the city.

"He is, the best of them," she beamed with pride.

Gallen scoffed, "Cotton is far more level-headed."

Sol laughed. "Even Cotton followed him in their attempts of abolition. He will certainly be the feature of his own record."

"Of course," Gallen conceded. "Fearless, headstrong, and incredibly foolish."

"He sacrificed his life to free those left behind in the stables of the Ice Realm," she said with pride. "Perhaps it was fate that led him back to me that day."

Despite the absurdity, whether fate, foolishness, or a bit of both, Sol knew she could never leave him alone again. She trusted the animal with her life and now knew that he had a propensity for illogical movements and impassioned justice. Familiar characteristics.

Gallen gripped her hand earnestly. "For that I owe him my life."

Sol blushed, turning to Kinsle's most recent display of righteous anger, "The beautiful beast refused to abate as he noticed the far end of the field receives less hay than those nearest the city. He cannot speak, but he can certainly bite. The poor caretaker of the pegasi nearly jumped from his boots when Kinsle threatened to nip at his collar."

Gallen chuckled heartily. "Could you blame him?"

"Certainly not!" Sol followed, enjoying a brief breeze as they walked on.

She lowered her voice. "How has she been?"

"They believe it is finally nothing of concern. She is a strong, old woman. Stubborn and strong, like other women I know."

Gallen placed his hand over hers, sending a jolt through her arm. She cut her eyes flirtatiously as he continued, "She should recover in a few days or so."

Sol nodded solemnly as Gallen explained, "Piré has been essential to her. The bakery itself may have been lost in her absence. Thank Mist for her."

Sol knew she could say little to console Gallen. A few weeks after their return to Celestra, Mama Ishpa fell ill. She lived alone, and at her age, that made Gallen anxious. He insisted upon staying nearby during the worst of it. Though, Gallen was correct in saying she was strong and stubborn, unwilling to release herself from this mortal world.

During her recovery, Piré ensured the baking tent continued to provide for the people of this city with the briefest of interruptions. Sol knew she woke far before the morning stars and worked through each afternoon.

"There are a few young bakers eager to assist. They begin apprenticeships as soon as Ishpa is well."

Sol nodded. "That is good news, Love."

Gallen's body shuttered excitedly at the mention of the word. Sol was generous with it since returning home. She could never be sure when their last days would come, and she wanted those she cared for to have no doubt of her feelings.

Sol could smell the baking tent long before the two arrived at its entrance. And, as she pulled the thin fabric and stepped inside, she was met with a bustling group of people, rushing through lines and seated at small tables. Piré donned a bright orange apron, her golden curls gathered in a knot at the nape of her neck. Her typically pale complexion was flushed from the mixture of work and heat and jubilation. She truly enjoyed baking and serving, and she was a great talent.

When Piré saw her friends enter the tent, she waved both hands over her head with great enthusiasm, her bright eyes alight as she brushed by a few customers to approach Sol. The embrace of a good friend was far sweeter than any pastry. Though, as Piré released Sol from the hug, Sol's thoughts certainly considered which tasty treat would serve as her morning snack.

"How very wonderful to see you both!"

Piré's natural tone was nearly too soft to hear over the constant cacophony of people talking and laughing and enjoying the day. Gallen pouted as he received his own embrace.

"Now, she certainly does not afford me such a greeting when I arrive on my own." The corners of his mouth turned upward to emphasize the humor in his words.

Piré smacked his chest. "I do show my excitement, Gallen! You are a daily customer, and Sol rarely finds the opportunity to grace this tent. Do not plant such deceit into my dear friend's heart."

She reached out her hand to Sol who took it emphatically. "I would never." Sol assured her.

Gallen rolled his eyes and stalked toward a basket of croissants as the two women giggled to themselves.

He grabbed a pastry from the top of a stack and ate it gingerly before heading back to visit Mama Ishpa. As she waited for him to return, Sol and Piré discussed more recent plans for the future.

"Alcor has presented an opportunity, Sol." Though her tone was hesitant, Piré's eyes glimmered with excitement. "There is a place. A place where youth attend an education. Well, vocational education. A place where I may refine my craft. He believes I should go."

Sol grabbed the young Piré's small hands in her own. It was an exciting time for her to see new places and learn new things.

"He says, this will soon be a kingdom and the kitchens of a kingdom need a tender with experience. Sol! He referred to *me* as such a tender!"

She could hardly mask her glee as she explained the details. And Sol listened intently, the young woman before her surely to take a life-altering journey.

As the conversation continued, Gallen approached, a fruit loaf in his hand and a large grin on his face. Sol loved when Gallen wore such a remarkable smile. When the apples of his cheeks rose and his eyes squinted slightly. He was a reckless beauty, a person who certainly did not know of the extent of his attractiveness. Sol and Malinar attempted to explain such to him with no avail. But perhaps that was better. Gallen continued living in beautiful, blissful ignorance while they enjoyed observing as he went. Sol smirked as he took a bite of the bread.

"Ready?" He chewed the piece slowly, savoring the bite.

She nodded, giving a last hug to her friend and beginning the long walk to Alcor's common tent.

They spoke of everything and nothing on their walk. Of Piré's adventure. Of Ishpa's delectable recipe. Of the light of the stars. Of the smell of the wind.

When they finally approached the common tent, it was ablaze with commotion. Alcor sat with Malinar and three other Flyers as they discussed potential maneuvers over a pile of maps. Malinar who combed her hands through her dark hair, deep in contemplation.

"Could we not halt the flow of resources between the Ice and Desert Realms, to stunt the power of those…enslavers?" Malinar offered to the group.

Alcor shook his head. "We need to consider the implications that arise when dividing our own resources. There are battles in the West. We cannot abandon those fighting in those realms on our behalf. And the power of the flying fires grows ever stronger by the day."

Sol's nightmares often featured the bird from their past, Storm's murderer. Its feathers held death in their wake, its fire able to decimate entire towns, destroy their kingdom before it ever emerged. Then, they assumed a few existed. Now, scouts spotted dozens. The power of their enemies grew, and Alcor was attempting desperately to find any way forward.

The Flyer sitting nearest Malinar, with pink hair and a deep voice, contributed, "should we seek out further research? What have we heard from those in the High Realm?"

"Those in the High Realm work tirelessly for further answers. They wish to know of the truth behind these beasts as desperately as we do. And, from the Ocean Realm, we have heard very little."

Gallen flinched as Alcor explained their plight. Malinar shot a glance toward Sol and Gallen, as if sensing the ache that fell upon Sol's chest at the mention of the Ocean Realm. Since leaving Eckral's bounds, Kattegat and the Twelve refused to intervene, even as Gallen pleaded with his mother to see reason. Sol knew of the toll the subject took on Gallen and wished they could avoid the discussion altogether. Yet, alas, they were intertwined in the inner workings of the realm.

"Do you see anything, Malinar? Anything at all that may imply distress?"

Malinar swept a hand over the various pieces of parchment, closing her eyes and knitting her brows. Though she realized each day, each moment, was paramount, Sol took great pleasure in observing Malinar conduct her work. Her hair sat in shining straight strands that flowed over her collar and down the front of her shoulders. It grazed the top of the table as she leaned close to explore the maps.

Without a sound, she sprang to attention, her eyes wide and filled with a furious mix of emotions. Rather than explain her findings, she took rushed steps toward the far corner of the room, finding blank pages to record her vision.

Alcor patted one of the other Flyers on the shoulder as she worked. "Meeting adjourned for today."

The Flyers filed out of the tent, off to enjoy an unexpectedly free day, and Gallen moved to take their place, ushering Sol along with him. As they approached the main table, Sol's gaze wavered on the golden primrose statue sitting at the center—a memorial to Storm and a reminder of what they fought against. Scrolled along its stem read the words: *For one who has fallen.* Sol whispered a silent prayer to the heavens, as she did whenever she thought of their lost friend.

The two men shared an embrace before Alcor gestured for them to sit at the now empty table.

"Before I join at the head, I wish to present you with something, fine sister."

Sol turned her head with intrigue. She could not possibly guess at the gift Alcor could provide. There truly was so little she actually desired. How could there be when she had so much?

Alcor disappeared in the shadows of the tents, fiddling with the lock of a wicker trunk. When the top of the box clicked open, he fished his hand inside and tucked something within his cape. The sight of Alcor as he walked back to the table warmed Sol's heart. His broad shoulders hunched over his wide frame in an attempt to hide the gift as he shuffled toward Sol, a look of pure bliss in his blue eyes. He lifted both hands, revealing two shining daggers.

"Your original pair was lost to the snow. And these will be yours, more completely yours. More so than the others."

He reached his hands out with palms outstretched. The two blades glimmered as she felt the cool metal against her fingers.

Rather than the pure silver metal of most dueling pairs, these daggers were made of gold, with a swirl of silver set into the blade. The hilts were also unlike anything she'd seen in the realm. Embedded within the stone's carvings were strips of wood that seemed to glow in the right light.

"I traded wood from the fairies' forest with our beloved allies in the Ice Realm. It was their enchantments, their power, that offered you new life."

Sol grasped the handles and held them tight to her chest. She honestly believed she would never own her own set again. Not truly a warrior, she had little need to train as the others did.

"This is an expense far beyond my needs—" she began.

Alcor held up a hand. "There are far too many enemies surrounding us, sister. I will not have you unprotected."

The thoughtfulness brought Sol to tears, and she hugged her brother with the sincerest thanks she could muster. After settling in his seat, he returned to matters of state and warfare.

"Any news, dear friend?" He shot a look to Gallen.

"Mawl states that the armory is a delight, though villagers are wrought with concern over misuse of such weaponry." He relayed, "I also heard from a trusted advisor in the Mountain Realm. She claims the skies grow grey, unnaturally so. Their Seer worries of a growing power that pulls from above and below."

Alcor pursed his lips. "And we are to trust this advisor. To trust the Seer of their realm. You are quite certain, yes?"

Sol offered her own words, "Brother, we must have faith in others if we are to succeed in this long war."

He nodded solemnly. "But how are we ever to know?"

The words left his lips as a whisper. Alcor was certainly transparent in his leadership, but he was no fool. To admit dire concerns could lead to distrust amongst their ranks. Sol looked deep into his eyes, mustering up as much genuine hope she could convey.

"If I know anything at all, it is that Nourels needs a king who is kind and just and good. And I believe that your fate is to be that king." She pressed her hand on his arm gently. "It is your fate, brother."

Gallen nodded in the corner of her eye. Alcor was a king others would sacrifice anything to follow, and Gallen was proof. Mawl and Piré and Luminor and Asha. All sacrificing to support his rise.

Alcor cleared his throat, ready to continue their discussion, yet as he moved to speak, the flap of the tent swept open in a hurried rush that drew the focus of every Flyer present. Asha's slender form rushed into the space, her breath coming in short rasps.

"Hello, all," she stated frankly, an obligatory acknowledgement of her unexpected entrance.

She quickly found a place to sit near Sol, grabbing her arm with a frantic jolt. Sol shifted her full attention to her closest confidante. Concern fiercely seized her throat as Asha spoke to them in low gasps.

"I have received word from my father. He has been the victim of an attack. He requested my presence there at once."

Asha's golden-brown skin was uncharacteristically blotchy, red streaks painted across her shoulders and neck and cheeks. Beads of sweat fell from her temples as she continued, "King Alcor, I must leave."

Sol looked from the desperation of her oldest friend to Alcor, who scratched his freshly cut hair in frustration. While Gallen joined Sol and Malinar on the quest, Asha had become indispensable to their cause. She had grown as a teacher and mentor to the recruits and young Flyers and developed a system of pure genius to better organize and communicate with the Star Realm's growing army. Sol could see Alcor's mind pull in different directions as he considered the consequences of losing Asha at this pivotal point in preparing for a battle that came closer to home with each passing day.

Asha's hand seize Sol's arm, a silent plea for her advocacy. And, while Sol also felt torn, she knew the importance of family and connection and love.

"Brother, Asha must. She must see those she cares for most in this world. If we haven't that, the care for those we love most, then what have we at all?"

As her words settled on Alcor's broad shoulders, she saw his countenance lift slightly, the furrow of his brow soften and jaw slacken.

"Of course, my wise younger sister."

Sol looked at Gallen, whose face reflected her own concern for their friend and her father's position.

"We shall coordinate a path for you to follow; it is much too dangerous to take the skies. Malinar will assist in conjuring a suitable place to ride," Alcor stated. "You may leave in the morning."

Asha lowered her head, tears brimming the edges of the purple kohl along her lower lids. "Many thanks, my king."

Alcor bowed his head in gratitude, then looked at Gallen.

"We shall prepare for Gallen to take lead of the recruits. Asha, you shall provide all information regarding the latest formations tonight."

"Of course," she exclaimed, now brimming with a sense of purpose.

Sol grasped her hand. "For now, let us pack your things to depart."

Asha nodded. The two women stood, Asha offering another bow toward Alcor, before heading into the city.

Asha moved between the four corners of her tent in a flurry of haste. Sol watched as she moved from her trunk to a silver bag to a stack of books and so on. The business of packing for a quest did not typically involve so much maneuvering about, yet Sol could sense the nervous energy from Asha's movements. The two arrived in her dust-colored tent but an hour ago, and Asha still debated whether to include her red scarf or flat shoes in the pile of necessities for the trip.

"But my father adores this scarf," she explained, more to herself than to Sol. "Perhaps it is not necessary, but it *is* necessary, do you not agree?"

Sol sat on the pile of blankets set in the center of the room and grinned sympathetically.

"Yes, of course. You must wear it when you see him."

The warrior still held the scarf in her hands undecidedly.

The golden threads woven into the tent's tan fabric caught the light of Asha's lantern as it flickered.

"I want it all to be alright," she whispered to Sol as she finally set the scarf into the silver pack.

"It shall, my friend. You must trust."

Trust. It was difficult to place how Sol believed so wholeheartedly that trusting was enough to face the many terrors that befell the realms. Yet, she was drawn to the concept. Perhaps it was her mind's way of coping with all they had seen—the enslavement, the betrayal, the torture, the evil. Trust was all she could cling to as even hope wavered.

As Asha continued her packing, Sol reached inside the familiar kelp fold of her teal satchel to reveal the soft leather of a book.

"I believe there is another important object to take," she said with a weary smile. "I am afraid it is a regift. A former gift from a friend."

She placed the book on the blankets before her, and Asha beamed at the worn cover.

"This was to be your gift!" She swooned as she scooped the book into her hands and flipped through the pages. "Did you cry?" she asked sweetly.

"I suppose you will have to read my notes." Sol held her legs in her hands, hugging her knees to her chest as she watched her friend scan the crowded words lining the edges of each page.

Asha closed the book and held it tightly to her chest. "Many thanks, my friend."

"It will be as if I am there with you. Always with you." Sol nodded toward the book with a smirk.

Asha reached to Sol and pulled her into a deep embrace, tears beginning to fall.

"Forever?" she asked.

Sol nodded against Asha's shoulder. "Forever."

Sol heard a slight whistle from the doorway as Malinar poked her head through the flap of fabric. "May I enter?"

Malinar's voice alone sent Sol's heart soaring. It was an amazing experience, loving two people. While Gallen calmed Sol like no one else, Malinar excited her more than anything could. As the Flyer sat beside the two friends, she offered Sol a brief kiss on the cheek before addressing Asha.

"Let us prepare your most befitting path home." she said, pulling a small map from her pack.

"I shall leave you both. Asha, would you enjoy one last drink in the Night Streets tonight? 'Tis tradition, after all." Sol grinned.

Asha shook her head slightly. "Perhaps we could spend my final night enjoying a calming tea with Luminor?"

Sol nodded affectionately, "Of course."

She was certain Luminor would enjoy the company. And Asha was likely correct in seeking some peace before heading out alone toward her endangered father.

Sol stood and left the two to work out a suitable plan for Asha to follow. As she walked out of the tent, she sped toward her own tent to ready for the night.

~

"I worry for him, Luminor. He has grown quite serious and strained."

Sol could hear Zeffra's voice as soon as she entered the common library tent. Stacks of books set upon short tables lined the walls of fabric. Luminor sat with a mug of tea in hand upon one of the many pillows strewn about the room. Zeffra, her blonde hair hastily thrown in a braid and green eyes darting manically from Luminor to the books to the floor, sat beside him.

Sol saw less and less of Alcor's right hand as she traveled for the war effort. Her brown skin was a shade darker than Sol remembered, likely due to her last trip in the Valley Realm. When she was not on a quest, she spent many hours in the temple of the city, praying to the gods for providence. Twirling her finger around a stray strand of hair, Zeffra sighed helplessly.

"It *is* as it will be." Luminor took a long sip of his drink. "The king is merely shifting to meet the demands of his position. It is not anything you have done, nor anyone else for that matter."

Zeffra rubbed her temples with her fingertips. "I know," she whispered.

As Sol stepped toward them, she noticed Zeffra straighten and stand, walking briskly away from Luminor without a word of goodbye. Sol lifted a hand of greeting, yet Zeffra met it with a short nod as she walked out of the space.

"She is adjusting. As we all must," was Luminor's excuse on Zeffra's behalf. "To what do I owe this grandest of pleasures? No last hurrah in the Night Streets?"

Sol shook her head. "Asha requested you by name."

"Aren't I a lucky man," he placed a sarcastic hand over his heart, "that a strong set of women would join me for my nightly tea."

"And men." Gallen's voice emerged from the fabric flap as he, Asha, Malinar, and Tress walked into the library.

A few grumbling elder Flyers gathered their books and tea and marched outside at the sight of the group. Luminor chortled.

"Now you know, young ones, this is a space of serenity. Take that to heart, will you."

Asha plopped onto one of the many pillows near Luminor, the others following close behind. "It is why we are here."

Gallen rummaged through a box of clean teacups to select a few for the group while Tress placed a kettle of water upon a small fire plate.

"We were eager to hear one of your many harrowing stories." Sol fluttered her eyes toward Luminor.

The middle-aged Flyer laughed aloud before clapping a hand over his mouth. Sol noticed a few more Flyers mutter disdainful words as they rushed out.

"Well, I could tell you of my time as a youth in the thralls of love?" He offered, his words intentionally quiet as he glanced around the space.

Asha rolled her eyes. "There is no need to convince us of your…appeal, Luminor."

"I think it is quite romantic," Gallen said sweetly as he handed out cups filled with floral-scented teas.

"Of course you do." Asha grinned. "I did tell you, Sol, did I not? The love story of the ages. Yet, with a twist I did not foresee."

She glanced gleefully toward Malinar who reached for her own cup. Sol followed the glance with a deep, appreciative smile.

"I know," she whispered.

As the group settled in, a rush of wind blew the flap open to reveal Piré holding a basket filled with fresh pastries.

"Apologies for my tardiness!" she exclaimed before the quietness of the space settled upon her. "Oops." She lowered her voice to a whisper. "I was preparing the shop for Ishpa to take over once more."

Gallen's eyes widened as she brought the basket forward, the corners of his mouth turning upward in anticipation. Piré set the basket in the middle of the group.

"She offered these as a parting gift to me. I am honestly happy to sleep past the morning hours."

Asha reached for a pastry marked by long strips of chocolate. "You may have to wake early to see me off."

Piré turned to her, shock reflected in her wide eyes. "When? Why?" Her mousey features scrunched sadly as she sat beside Asha.

"She is to visit her father," Sol said softly. "There was an attack in the Sun Realm."

Piré gasped, pulling at her golden locks anxiously before immediately asking Asha of the details. While the two discussed intently, Malinar placed a hand on Sol's arm, Gallen sitting near them with his hands filled with bread.

"Are you sorrowful? I know how much you appreciate your friend so close," Malinar said.

She slid her hand up and down Sol's arm affectionately. Sol nodded.

"I am happy to have you both to ground me," was all Sol could express. She looked at Luminor, seeking a distraction from the emotions brewing within her. "What of that romance, Luminor?"

The group of Night Flyers laughed and talked and drank and ate for hours. Hours of stories and secrets. Hours of cozying close and playful pushes. Hours of friendship. Hours cherished. Until, one by one, they rose to find comfort in the warm blankets of their own tents.

Sol and Asha were two of the last to leave, prolonging the inevitable. They walked, arm in arm, down the path until they reached their place of parting.

"Until tomorrow," Asha said.

Sol merely nodded, afraid to burst into another round of sobs. She gave her friend a squeeze before they parted ways.

When Sol arrived at her tent, dried tears staining her cheeks, she immediately fell into Malinar's outstretched arms. Malinar's hands combed through her hair as the two sank into the blankets crowding the floor. They sat in silence for a while as Malinar pet Sol's shoulders, her head, her cheeks. Sol relished in the comfort of her partner's touch, her adoration. It was much needed as Asha prepared to depart the safety of this realm.

Gallen walked toward the women from the sleeping section's fabric flap. His hands were closed, a bit of blush heating the tips of his cheeks. Sol sat up, wiping her nose and rubbing her cheeks. Rather than join them on their bedding, he sat cross-legged before them.

"It is our first night together in our new space," he said reverently. "I have worked on a gift for you both, and it feels an auspicious time to give it."

Sol looked curiously as Gallen opened his hands to reveal two necklaces. On each silver chain was set a small emerald stone surrounded by three tiny, pink diamonds. She wrenched her head upward to see Gallen's timid grin.

"I retrieved the ring from the snow the day of your rescue." His smile was effervescent as he spoke. "I was not sure how best to present it to you, Sol. It was yours, *is* yours. Yet, we are all so different now. Different together as two and as three. I thought it was best this way."

He handed the women their necklaces before pulling a matching chain from his tunic.

"The jeweler said the stone was large enough to break into three equal pieces with ease. And the others were simple enough to set together."

Sol lifted the chain to see the emerald more closely. "Gallen, this is magnificent."

He breathed a sigh of relief. "I am so glad to hear you say such."

Malinar nodded her agreement. "It is perfect."

The look of joy on Gallen's face was remarkable. Sol wished she could capture the feeling. Gallen's look, Malinar's hand still resting upon her back, the dim light of their shared tent—it was glorious.

She reached to clip the necklace in place, the stone settling nicely near her mother's locket.

The three spent the night together in each other's arms, blissfully avoiding the world raging outside their realm. For that world —the war and evil and pain—that could wait for tonight.

For now, for this moment, Sol embraced what was known to her. That the Star Realm was her home. That she was safe here. That good would assuredly triumph over all of the evil they had faced.

Within the arms of Gallen and Malinar, it felt as if all the pieces of her life were falling into place. And though she knew challenges lay ahead, hidden on edge of the horizon, she could sleep soundly knowing she had tasted what it meant to be seen, to be understood, and—above all—to be completely and wonderfully loved.

THE SECOND RECORD

A warrior born in the Sun, trained in the skies, and living amongst the Stars must return to her native land and attend to her ailing father. The path is one of peril and uncertainty as the War of Realms rages on. As she journeys, she encounters a people most foreign to her and must rely on her intuition if she is ever to find her way back home.

ACKNOWLEDGMENTS

This has been an insane and beautiful experience.

I have so many people that deserve to be recognized for the many ways they helped shape this story and make me a better writer.

Thanks to Cason, who always supports me no matter how wild my dreams seem. Thanks to Brighton, my ray of sunshine. Thanks to my family who constantly push me to be myself.

Thanks to my forever friends - Ashley, Abby, Morgan, and Sarah - the people who chose me and will never be able to get rid of me. Thanks to my creative soulmates, Sam and Brooke, who constantly build me up and challenge my work in the very best way.

Thanks to the people who helped my worlds come to life - my illustrator, Grace, and editor, Molly. Y'all are the best!

And special thanks to my academic advisor, Linda, who encouraged me to pursue this project alongside my historical research. It is an honor to be your mentee.

And Thank you to those who read *The Nine Realms* and eagerly chose to follow me here. I cannot express how much your support means to me.

Here's to the next adventure!

www.ingramcontent.com/pod-product-compliance
Lightning Source LLC
LaVergne TN
LVHW010308070526
838199LV00065B/5486